A Family Institution

Howard Reiss

DEDICATION

To the women in my life who have made me who I am: my friend Sherri, my grandmothers Sadie and Edie, my mother-in-law Millie, my mother Rose, my daughters Shira and Erin, my granddaughter Lucy, and most of all my wife and best friend Ellen. I have been blessed with a life filled with great women.

Ira's expectations are lower than they once were. He is satisfied with the flimsiest of promises - a train that runs on time, faint praise from a superior, or the passing smile of a pretty woman. When the conversation at parties turns to the old college days or early married life, as compared to middle age in suburbia, as it frequently does, he's the first to volunteer that it's better now.

"It's those little certainties in life that really matter," he'd say to the eyebrows raised in response.

Most of them would profess to disagree citing the thrilling discovery of love and the limitless energy of their innocent youth, but not without nodding unconsciously at the same time, as if some deeper, more honest self recognized it was all a delusion. This was the point where Ira would excuse himself to get more wine counting the little certainties in his head as he did so. It was never very difficult. First, there was the warm bed he shared with his wife, Ellen, who was asleep most work nights long before he found the energy to get up from the den couch, turn off the TV and head to bed. She always felt so warm and welcoming when he slid in beside her.

Second, he would add the animated discussions with Jaime and Scott about school, friends, and the latest gadget that they can't live without, conversations that spring to life like the old pop-up books the moment he walks through the door. Then there are the lazy weekend mornings in bed, breakfasts out, shopping expeditions, Saturday night movies followed by Saturday night embraces, holidays, snowstorms warmed by movie rentals and microwave popcorn, swimming in the town pool, and endless nights of cable filled with action adventures and steamy romances for the late nights. Of course Ira would also have to include their growing savings backed by the full faith and credit of the United States government.

He can't recall when it dawned on him that it was a lot easier moving with a force instead of against it or when he learned that thinking too precisely about things just made them difficult to accept. It was probably after they were married and Jaime was

1

born. It was around that time he realized that he couldn't satisfy everyone all of the time, not even himself; you just had to put the past behind you and move forward. It was obviously a sign of maturity.

Ira was always quick to give Ellen much of the credit. Disappointment and failure was as common as a cold to a third-grade teacher, especially when you were dealing with 28 kids from all different kinds of families, many as nutty as his.

"If you don't move quickly past the failures and disappointments," Ellen always says, "you'll just burn out . . . as quickly as a shooting star."

Shooting stars were pretty and dramatic, but a man needs to last longer than that. Lasting itself was a kind of success. Ellen believed that as well. You can't be disappointed, she said, by a life well lived.

Of course it has all been a little disappointing to his mother, Selma, the high priestess of great expectations, who foretold his name in lights. She expected a Nobel Prize or at least a show at the Metropolitan Museum of Art.

"I'd have settled for a doctor or even a lawyer," Selma said when he told her that he intended to make advertising his career, "or a dentist for crying out loud."

Of course, she didn't really consider what he did, creating coupon campaigns, to be advertising. It certainly wasn't the kind of thing, she said, that real advertising men did, like producing commercials and writing jingles. Selma considered coupons to be at the bottom of the advertising food chain. She said he was like one of those guys in the street handing out circulars, except he did it in the newspaper.

"He could've been a genius Murray," she liked to say to the ceiling fan in the kitchen, where the spirit of Ira's father had revolved since his death fifteen years earlier.

She loved to remind him about her great Uncle Johann, who supposedly invented the thumbtack, and her father's second cousin, who wrote a sonata for the left-handed piano player.

Ellen told him to ignore his mother when she got like that. She called it Selma's ancestral refrain.

When his mother really wanted to put on the finishing touch, she'll repeat his name slowly; I . . . RA . . . I . . . RA, turning her head each time from side to side with a little sigh like she was letting out some gas at the same time.

She knew how much he hated his name. It didn't sound intellectual or athletic, and it didn't slide off the tongue like Charles or Andrew. It was the first-person singular I followed by RA, the ancient Egyptian sun god and the symbol for radium. Unfortunately, he didn't have a heavenly body, and he certainly didn't glow.

Ira was in charge of couponing at American Family Care Products and the father of the tip-in coupon, lightly glued to the page of a magazine so that the consumer could simply rip it off. It's far more expensive than the traditional printed-on-a-page coupon - the kind you cut out - but it has a much higher redemption rate. It is especially good for new products. Ira specialized in over-the-counter drugs and his biggest successes to date have come with colds and hemorrhoids.

"My son provides relief from itching at both ends," was the way Selma liked to describe it to her friends.

Ira liked what he did. He liked coupons. They had a single, clear purpose. He liked dealing with things that had expiration dates. You know what to expect and when to expect it. He took great delight in patrolling the refrigerator, tossing out milk, cottage cheese, or anything else on the exact date stamped on the container. Even though Ellen insisted that the stamped date was only the last sale date and that it remained edible for days afterward, he refused to treat them that lightly.

About eight months ago Ira turned forty. He's always been a little chubby, so the few extra pounds he's put on over the last five years weren't really that noticeable. Although his once fiery reddish-brown hair has faded like the den curtains and the top of his head had begun to rise to the surface like a wild mushroom.

His father, of course, his mother often pointed out, had a full head of dark hair until the day he died. Not a hint of grey, although his mother wasn't around to remind him of all his failings. She had died before he even married Selma.

Ira's eyes were still dark and clear, framed by crow's feet like his mother, which she never said a word about. His nose bent slightly to the left, as if it had grown up in the face of a stiff breeze, perhaps because he always sat to the left of his mother at the dinner table. He had a mustache left over from college and a large mouth, the kind that needed something to keep it busy like a pipe or gum. It dominated his whole face like Jimmy Carter, but without the toothy smile.

Ira considered his life safe, secure, certain, and relatively satisfying, as predictable and episodic as a television sitcom. Unfortunately, it was about to be preempted by, of all things, a tombstone.

It all started on a Monday, always an unwelcome day.

MONDAY

Ira could barely make his tie in the morning. The knot kept coming out too small, leaving the back way too long, like Jaime always made it for him when she insisted on trying. She had his small hands, which made it difficult, although he knew she'd eventually get it since she had Ellen's concentration and determination. She stared so intently at her fingers when she tried that it seemed as if her eyes were controlling them instead of her brain. He could look right into them unobserved, which made him feel like a Peeping Tom, but he liked what he saw . . . she enjoyed the challenge and was unafraid of failure, another one of Ellen's traits. A good teacher needs that.

It took four tries for him to get the knot right, not a good way to start the week, which meant he had to hurry to catch the train. He grabbed his brief case and rushed into Jamie's room. The floor was strewn with outfits and books. Jaime always looked neat, her face washed, her hair combed, her clothes coordinated just like her mother, but everything else around her was always a mess and she always left a mess when she left a room. He liked to call her Pigpen, after the Peanuts character. He bent down to give her a kiss on her forehead. Her lips were slightly parted and fell naturally into a mysterious little grin. She didn't stir as Ira brushed a strand of hair away from her eyes; she never did. Jamie has always been a good sleeper.

Scott is nine and you could perform open-heart surgery on the floor of his room. He won't go to sleep if there's a piece of paper on the floor or anything out of place. Every drawer is shut tight, not a single sock or shirt sticking out. His comic books are neatly stacked on the bookcase, and the pictures on the dresser all arranged in neat rows.

There was always a little tension in Scott's face while he slept, particularly around the eyes. He was troubled by dreams that forced him to make impossible choices between people he loved, choices that always seemed to make the difference between life and death. Ira knew the feeling. His bad dreams didn't disappear until 5 years after he moved out of his house and away from his mother. They didn't really stop until he married Ellen.

Scott was a light sleeper, probably because he was always afraid of missing something, so he didn't get too close. Ira just blew him a kiss and tiptoed out of the room. Even so, Scott lifted his head slightly and looked up at him with a vague sense of recognition before mumbling something about a falling rock. Fortunately, he turned onto his side away from the door and instantly fell back asleep.

Ira went back to their bedroom to say good-bye to Ellen, who looked pale under the bent spotlight thrown by the 75-watt light bulb in the hall. Sleep always deepened the lines in her forehead, making her look more thoughtful. The static lifted a few strands of hair like little hands calling out in school for attention.

Not even sleep could hide that third-grade teacher cuteness. Those big, cheerful eyes filled with kindness when opened and intensely occupied by whatever or whoever was in front of them. A little circular nose and a wide, comfortable mouth that brought her students a great rush of affection with each smile, just as it did with Ira.

Ellen had the petite body of a model from the waist up, but from the waist down it's been the slow escalation of the Vietnam War. The groves in her thighs have grown more committed and intransigent every year. Sometimes she stared at them in the mirror and wondered out loud whether they were actually turning into Jell-o. Then she slapped them together and laughed because it sounded almost as if they were clapping. Ira has always been jealous of her complete lack of self-consciousness.

He bent down to kiss her good-bye, another one of his rituals, and she reflexively covered her mouth to hide her bad breath. He kissed her forehead instead.

By seven-twenty he had his paper and stood waiting for the seven-twenty-eight train. It was the same time every day, give or take a minute or two, and the platform was crowded as always. Everyone was facing north waiting for that first glimpse of the train as it came around the bend. When it did there would be the usual cacophony of folding newspapers, opening and closing attaché cases, and dropped conversations, as well-dressed feet fluttered like birds to the spots on the platform where they'd be close to the opening doors.

The seven-twenty-eight is one of the new trains with state-of-the-art features like a red emergency stop button instead of a cord. The seats don't flip like the older cars, half face one way and half the other, so you either watch where you're going or watch where you've been. Since most people pick the former, on days when Ira's not fast enough he winds up traveling backwards. He doesn't like watching the past recede quickly like that and it makes him a little nauseous.

Today's ride to Grand Central took the usual forty-two minutes. He read *the New York Times*, skimmed it really, and near the end of the ride turned to the business section to check his American Family's stock. It was the only stock he owned, not counting some mutual funds, the contents of which were a mystery to him, and he was glad to see that it was slowly creeping back up after dropping a month ago because of disappointing earnings.

He noticed that the lottery was up to forty million. Ira never played, but he'd been thinking about starting and fantasized about how his life would change if he won. He'd have more time to spend with Jaime and Scott for one thing. He'd be waiting for them when they got home from school with a warm snack. He could meet Ellen for lunch sometimes. Maybe open a small business near home or do absolutely nothing.

He knew that would make his mother proud.

He wasn't much of a get-rich-quick schemer or dreamer, so he attributed his recent thoughts to the lunacy of turning forty. Decades were like lines in the sand that sometimes you crossed with the promise - or threat - of living the rest of life somehow differently. However, like most promises and threats, it never amounted to much, nothing ever changed.

Ira wondered how he could live the rest of his life somehow differently and all he could come up with was going back to art. He had dreamed about being a cartoonist in high school. It was delusional to think of becoming an artist at his age with household expenses so high and Jaime and Scott not all that many years away from college. He used to work on the sets for the plays in high school and do caricatures for the yearbook. He took some art classes in college, but it was clear that he only had a small talent at best. He was good with landscapes, but terrible with people, just like in real life.

He felt worse the more he thought about it, not because he couldn't come up with another viable idea about something different to do, but because he knew there was no chance he'd try even if he had. Maybe he was just overreacting to the widow Selma, who never hid her disappointment.

"Your father," she told him when she handed him his fortieth birthday gift, a book entitled <u>The Ten Best Ways To Stay Motivated</u>, "may he rest in peace, didn't have your advantages. He grew up without a nickel in his pocket, but by the time he was your age he had his own accounting practice. Now that's motivation."

"He worked day and night," he said.

"So I could stay home with you."

Ira remembered that all too well.

"I hate numbers; I like advertising."

Selma rolled her eyes upward like she expected Murray to smack him on the back of his head on his next pass around the ceiling.

Today, Ira had to begin finalizing the coupon campaign for American Family's newest cold medicine, Sinoral. He had planned hundreds of coupon campaigns, the kind that people rip out of Sunday supplements and had devised some great rebate programs that compelled people to soak labels off jars and cut bar codes from almost indestructible containers. Selling over-the-counter drugs in America was very competitive and coupons were a major weapon in every company's arsenal. The distribution of manufacturer's cents-off coupons exceeded one hundred billion dollars last year. A successful coupon campaign had about a two-percent rate of return. Ira has had a half dozen as high as four percent.

For some reason Selma always found that funny.

She wasn't impressed that the first coupon promotion was in 1880 by C.W. Post of Battle Creek. He gave out one-cent coupons to encourage people to try Grape-Nuts. She didn't care that the Nielsen people, the same ones who monitored television ratings, accumulated and published annual figures on coupon redemption. Most of all she didn't care that the last industry-wide innovation, the tip-in coupon, was Ira's creation.

"Try creating something the world can't live without, "she once said, "like the thumbtack."

Ira was at lunch in the cafeteria with Tom and some of the other guys from marketing. They were talking football but Ira wasn't paying much attention in part because he was a one-sport fan. If it wasn't baseball, he wasn't interested. He was wondering instead about what they'd be having for dinner and whether his favorite show on TV tonight would be a rerun. If it was, he might take Scott to buy that skateboard he wanted. Selma would flip out when she heard, because she thought that they were far too dangerous. She wouldn't let Ira have a bicycle when he was growing up, because she was sure that he'd kill himself. Ellen called it the only child syndrome.

He did listen when the conversation switched to Tom's new secretary.

"They defy gravity."

"It's like they're staring up at me."

"I swear that her nipples stood up and saluted the other day when I walked by."

Heads turned in the cafeteria wondering what was so uproariously funny.

As they were just finishing lunch, the super was letting the police into his grandmother's apartment. His aunt had been calling for over two hours. They found her on the floor in the bathroom still in her nightgown. By the time Ira got back to the office, the police had notified his aunt and the required calls were being made.

Ira was in the middle of proofing the final Sinoral coupon design. There are lots of cardinal rules for coupons. Keep them dollar-bill size since odd shapes create problems for consumers and retailers. Make them simple and clear. Don't use the coupon itself to advertise, but show a picture of the product on the coupon. The face value must be in large type in the top corners. The expiration date must be clearly visible and allow for adequate time, since a short expiration angers consumers and they'll simply rip off the date. Retailers don't care because a manufacturer will accept a coupon until the end of time.

Ira was running through his checklist when he got the call. An acid heart attack, quick and to the point. The funeral was the next morning. His mother didn't believe in wasting time.

"Have Tom finish the Sinoral layout," he told his secretary. "And don't forget to tell Paul what happened. I'll be back the day after tomorrow."

He couldn't focus on his book on the way home or even think about the coupon layouts he'd brought home with him. He kept thinking about Grandma Sadie. They lived with her until he was five. His father was just getting established and money was tight. He remembered warm milk at night that knocked him out like a sucker punch and bedtime stories about what happened to little boys who wandered away at the grocery store or didn't do as they were told.

She was an old woman as long as he could remember with a proud posture and regal, gray hair. She buried her parents and two brothers in Russia and her husband, Ira's grandfather, at a very early age. Although she had a tough exterior, she was the kindest person he knew, not manipulative, not judgmental, and easily pleased, at least by him. She was the opposite of his mother who must have inherited her demanding gene from some pagan ancestor.

Grandma Sadie had three children. His mother was the youngest. She had Sadie's deep-set eyes, overhung by thick eyebrows as sharp as a rocky ledge, so like Ira's that it was almost frightening. Obviously not the personality marker one might think.

His Aunt Sarah was the oldest. Ira has always been very close to her. She spent a lot of time at his house while he was growing up, telling Selma to "leave the poor boy alone already." His late Uncle Max, the middle one, lived in the Midwest and looked nothing like his grandmother. He had a small mouth and always wore a salesman's smile. Max had two girls that he hardly knew who grew up in Sheboygan, Wisconsin.

Ira was always his grandmother's favorite. He always thought it was because he lived closer, but the events that were about to unfold proved to him that there was more to it than that.

Ellen and the kids were upset, of course, but they had a very different relationship with his grandmother. She used to visit three or four times a week when he was growing up in the city, but she didn't travel to the suburbs very often. When she did, the kids didn't sit still, or if they did it was in front of the television. They didn't have time to listen to her stories.

Ira had this peculiar funny feeling in his mouth that night, a kind of tingling in his gums, as if they were tired of holding on to his teeth, as if they were about to let go, so he kept pushing in on his teeth, as if to prevent them from popping out.

"What's wrong with your mouth?" Ellen asked him as he climbed into bed.

He ran his tongue along his gums.

"I don't know. They just feel funny."

"Well pushing in on them isn't going to help. Call the dentist."

"Tonight?"

"No, tomorrow after the funeral."

Ira nodded but he wasn't going to call. He'd let it pass and it would go away, funny feelings like that – stress-related probably – generally did. Besides, the Sinoral campaign was going to keep him busy and he couldn't afford to take off any time for the dentist, certainly not for the next two weeks.

That night Ira dreamt that he was in the dentist's chair.

"So you've finally found your teeth," the dentist said, except it wasn't his dentist it was his late Uncle Max.

"What does that mean?"

"People become aware of their teeth when they reach middle age."

Ira pushed in on his teeth and he could feel them move.

"Unfortunately," Max said, "once they do that feeling never goes away."

TUESDAY

His teeth still felt strange in the morning. He had braces when he was ten to straighten out an overbite that was "barely noticeable" according to the orthodontist, because his mother couldn't live with the imperfection. Now it felt as if they were getting even by pushing back out where nature intended them to be.

They left early and had to wait in the car for the funeral home to open. Ira hated being late, which is probably what comes from living life according to a train schedule and growing up with a mother who considered "Thou Shalt Be On Time" to be the eleventh commandment.

A directory out front listed the recently departed like the menu in a drive-in restaurant. Sadie was on top. His mother wouldn't have had it any other way. Her casket was already at the front of the chapel, sealed tight, his aunt having already made the necessary identification. The room itself was meant to suggest a living room with red drapes on the walls and maroon carpet on the floor. But the line of folding chairs and the heavy chandelier made if feel more like a cheap hotel ballroom.

The service started promptly at nine. There were very few old faces, since Sadie had outlived most of her friends. A rabbi no one knew recited some well-turned phrases, but Ira didn't listen. Instead, he heard her insisting that he eat more in that soft yet unyielding voice of hers. He also smelled the onions, butter, and chicken that attached to all her housedresses like lint.

There should be a *Reader's Digest* in there, he thought, opened to "Personal Glimpses."

The rabbi recited the names of the mourners, which he received moments before from Selma, and called him Ida. He said nothing about the pogroms in Russia, the murder of her two brothers by the White Army, the arranged marriage to her second cousin, Ira's grandfather, his early death, or her refusal to eat anything until everyone else had seconds. Of course, there was not a word about her bedtime stories.

Ira's mother sat with her military posture, eyes straight ahead, wearing that hard, enduring look he first noticed as a child. He used to think it was anger and determination; now he saw it more as disbelief and disappointment. Aunt Sarah, on the other hand, looked around and smiled at him. At least until the coffin creaked and everyone jumped, even the Rabbi. Ira half-hoped that the lid would make a loud pop like a newly opened vacuum-sealed jar, and Sadie would sit up to say it was all a big mistake.

The Rabbi went back to his sermon and Ira thought back to that winter when he turned eight and forced his grandmother to sleep with him whenever she came for a visit. It was because of the light fixture in his room, the Methuselah of all light fixtures, with three naked bulbs for eyes and a nose and a decorative braided line below that looked like an angry little mouth. Perhaps it was originally designed to hold candles in one of those dark torture chambers in the castles of matinee movies and was murderously angry because some fool had electrified it.

Sometimes at night he swore he could hear it thinking.

Most nights he slept under the covers barely able to breathe, but when Grandma Sadie was over, he felt safe pressed up against her. She was big and warm and impervious to fear. No evil spirit could penetrate that force field of chicken and mothballs. Her slow, heavy breathing completely drowned out the whispers from above.

"Don't baby him," Selma would say.

"It's just for a few minutes until he falls asleep."

It was never just for a few minutes.

It got so bad that Ira was afraid to go into his room even in daylight. The problem disappeared once his grandmother convinced his father, over his mother's objection, to change the fixture. He never figured out how she knew, because he never said a word to anyone.

The rabbi finished the sermon by talking about Sadie's living memory. He went on and on about how she wasn't really dead, but alive in each of them, seeing the world through the eyes of her children and experiencing the joy of life through her grandchildren.

Seeing the world through the eyes of Selma was not a very comforting thought.

His mother insisted that Ira ride with her and Aunt Sarah in the limousine, which came, Selma pointed out, "as part of the package."

"It'll be strange without her," Sarah said as they pulled away from the curb.

Selma barely nodded. She just stared straight ahead her mouth snapped shut like her purse and her chin out, as if her jaw had been wired shut.

"She's always been there," Sarah said to Ira. "And I've never been far away."

In fact, Sarah lived with her mother until about 20 years ago, when she finally moved out to a similar apartment two blocks away.

"I spoke to her two or three times a day."

Ira tried touching Aunt Sarah lightly on the arm, the way he'd seen Ellen do a thousand times, but it turned out more like a pat. He didn't know what else to do or say so he stared out the window.

"It's unhealthy to call that often," Selma said.

Sarah sighed.

Ira thought about how death polarizes things. Clear becomes ambiguous and uncertain turns into inevitable. Far away seems so close and near much further away. It's life through both ends of the binoculars. Fortunately, this state of confusion and doubt doesn't last very long.

He was second now, he realized, in the natural order of things, right behind his mother. Instead of depressing him, it made him wonder why he bothered spending two and one half hours every day on a train to nowhere. It couldn't go anywhere because the tracks ended at Grand Central Station. Why spend every waking hour making money for nameless, faceless shareholders?

"It's good to have family at times like this."

Sarah took Ira's hand and held it in her lap. All three of them stared at his hand.

"I liked that coupon for the rash cream. What was the name again?"

"Dermacure."

"That's the one. I liked the funny face. Did you draw it?"

"No."

"Like someone tortured by an itch."

"Exactly."

Ira looked over at his mother who was staring out the window now. She looked smaller when she wasn't speaking.

Wouldn't everyone be surprised if he quit and enrolled in art school.

He closed his eyes and took back his hand. He knew better than to make a decision at a time like this, when death has stirred up all the sediment. He wondered what Ellen, Jaime, and Scott were talking about in the car behind. He hoped it wasn't about death. Of course, Ellen didn't believe in avoiding awkward subjects.

"She had a hard life," Sarah said.

"Who doesn't?" Selma said turning her head away from the window.

"Not like hers."

"It's not a contest. You don't measure life by who you bury and how young."

"Or how sorry you feel about yourself," Sarah said.

They rode the rest of the way in silence.

At the graveside, Sarah and his mother stood apart, arms intertwined like promenading partners at a square dance. Aunt Sarah couldn't remain angry for very long, nor would Selma have let her. The two of them stood there whispering one-syllable words that Ira couldn't quite make out, shaking their heads, and occasionally looking in his direction.

Of course, looking back now, he wondered how he could have missed all the signs over the years. Quiet conversations that stopped the moment he entered the room, eyes scrutinizing him behind his back, hands always fixing his collar, brushing down his hair, and picking lint off his sweater, as though looking for that loose thread that might unravel everything.

The wind was cold and Ira huddled with Ellen and the kids. He could smell Ellen's hair. It had a sandy, ocean smell. The same way it smelled when they first met.

The rabbi droned on and on in a language that no one understood, but which sounded familiar. All eyes were on the frozen hole in the ground.

"From dust to dust, we commend her to your care . . ."

The cemetery also reminded him of the beach. Maybe it was the absence of a skyline or the sea of stones under a gray, rolling horizon. Maybe it was the missing noises of commerce and daily life.

". . . to everlasting happiness and repose . . ."

The cold amplified the breathing of the mourners, almost like the sound of the surf through a seashell.

". . .to eternal fulfillment and reward . . ."

His mother moved perilously close to the edge of the grave, the dirt lapping up against her feet like the tide. She was like that, often standing right in your face during a conversation. No one said a word, but everyone thought the worst. What if she fell in? Of course things like that only happened in the movies.

It was overcast and the gray clouds were scalloped like brain matter. They rumbled softly, as if from a distant storm, or perhaps the reflected sound of some truck from a highway in the distance.

". . .and let us say AMEN."

"Amen," everyone said in unison.

The rabbi closed the book, picked up some dirt, and recited a prayer. Three large men leaning on shovels tried to appear solemn, but only succeeded in looking cold and impatient. They shifted their weight back and forth from foot to foot and kicked at their shovels as if to keep them in line.

There must be a dozen other souls waiting to take up residence today on Paradise Lane and Restful Way.

The rabbi dropped his handful of dirt on the coffin and disappeared. Selma was next. She took a fistful and practically threw it at the coffin. It sounded like the crack of a bat against the ball.

Aunt Sarah went next, followed by Ellen, and then the kids. Everyone took a turn throwing dirt on the coffin before returning to the cars.

Ira waited until the end. The gravediggers coiled their hands around their shovels and cleared their throats, but he ignored them. His handful of dirt barely landed on the coffin before they started shoveling. Furiously, almost frantically, as if too much longer and she might climb back out of the grave.

Their dirt hit the coffin like a gunshot at first until the layers reduced the sound to a dull thud. He wanted to wait until she was completely buried, like a spring bulb and backed up past her stone, which was blank on one side and engraved on the other for his grandfather, Issac Portnoy. He died over forty years earlier and gave Ira the "I" for his name.

There were about fifty graves in this small, walled-in area dedicated to members of the Mozur Lodge. Mozur was a small town in Russia that emptied out after the revolution. There didn't appear to be many vacancies.

He drifted farther back until he stood on a patch of grass that must have been meant for Aunt Sarah. His mother waved him to the car, but he pretended not to see her. She raised her arms higher, but he looked away. Perhaps it was bad luck to stand on an empty grave. His mother knew every superstition and honored them all. He moved over to the next grave and looked down at the stone.

"Eva Portnoy, beloved daughter of Issac and Sadie, born December 12, 1918-died December 12, 1968."

His first thought was that the poor woman died on her fiftieth birthday. The he read the stone again. Something was very odd, but he couldn't put his finger on it. He couldn't focus at first. Perhaps it was the gust of frigid air or the sounds of the gravediggers as they filled the hole where she'd spent the rest of eternity. Out of the corner of his eye, he saw Selma whispering to Scott, who started running toward him.

It seemed as if he were in a movie with the camera retreating so that Scott never seemed to get any closer.

He looked down again at Eva's stone and another gust of wind blew some fine particles of dirt into his eyes. It came right off his grandmother's grave, as if she didn't want him to look again, but it was too late, he'd already figured it out.

How could Eva have been his aunt? Sarah was the oldest, born in 1916. Max, dead ten years, was born four years later. His mother was the last, born in 1923. If Eva came between Aunt Sarah and Max, Ira realized, which meant that he was twenty when she died, how is it that he never heard her name? How is it that no one casually mentioned her during those long Sunday afternoons around the kitchen table when Sarah and his mother tried to describe what it was like growing up in the Bronx? How is that possible that she wasn't in a single photograph?

Scott tugged on his jacket.

"Come on Dad it's getting cold. Grandma wants to go. We're blocking cars. Dad?"

He looked down at Scott. He loved the color of his hair, a shade of brown somewhere between sand and earth. Could he hide him? Erase him from human memory?

He gave him a hug and Scott looked up with tears in his eyes.

"I'm cold," he said.

"Let's go."

Ira put his arm around his shoulder and walked him to the car. He didn't look back once.

Everyone returned to his mother's house, which was filled with fruit baskets, jars of nuts, boxes of cookies, and platters of cold cuts. There was a big bouquet of flowers from his office.

"You're supposed to send food to the house and flowers to the funeral home," Selma said when she read the card.

"They're nice flowers," he said.

"Inappropriate," Selma said turning and walking to the door to greet some recent arrivals.

People sat around eating and discussing Florida vacation spots, inexpensive restaurants, World War II battles, and a host of other subjects, like they were trying out for *Jeopardy*. There was almost a party atmosphere.

His mother played the hostess better than the grieving daughter.

"What's the point," she said. "It won't change anything."

The present always came first for her, followed by the future. The past was a distant third.

He sat quietly in the corner of the living room briefly conversing with the mourners as they left the kitchen plates piled high with roast beef and potato salad. It was the perfect spot - not enough room for anyone to sit comfortably beside him and no lengthy conversations possible with so much food close at hand.

"Sorry about your grandmother."

"Thank you."

"We should all make it to eighty-two."

Ira nodded. That was the most popular line.

Then they raised their plates in benediction and promised to find him later.

He wasn't being sociable, but he's never been good at parties. He's uncomfortable with small talk. He has to think about it too much. He never knows how to fill the silences, whether it's a time of celebration, illness, or death. He can handle the nodding and looking interested part well enough, smiling or frowning depending on what's appropriate, but he normally relies on Ellen to carry the conversation forward. She was, however, busy helping in the kitchen.

That's what attracted him to Ellen the very first time they met. He didn't have to think about what to say next. It was as if she were writing the dialogue and all he had to do was read it, like it was hanging up there in a comic strip balloon. Every response felt spontaneous and sounded right. For a lot of people, that's as good a reason as any to fall in love.

Ira was never sure what Ellen saw in him that day at the coffee shop, but he bet it was the home in the suburbs and the two kids. A life without surprises, although she said it was the look in his eyes, like a little kid hoping that the present was for him.

Ira was startled by Aunt Sarah, who squeezed in beside him.

"You're not eating."

"I had something before."

It was a lie, but safer than saying he wasn't hungry. You didn't skip meals in his family, because it could only be an early sign of illness.

"There's cake."

"Maybe later."

Selma insisted that Sarah was very beautiful when she was young, although it's hard to tell from the few black-and-white pictures that remain and impossible to imagine from the way she looked now. Her eyes, which still looked kindly as they fell on him, carried two big bags around with them these days like they were homeless, and they didn't open that wide anymore, swollen as they were by two cataract operations. Sometimes they filled with tears in the normal course of a conversation, as if they had worries and troubles of their own. Her good-natured mouth has also begun to sag as well. Her entire face seemed to be losing its shape, the years erasing the child-like symmetry that had once defined her features. Selma said it was because she retained too much water.

"She turned down a lot of perfectly good marriage proposals," Selma said, "because she waited too long for Mr. Perfect."

Still, Aunt Sarah didn't complain, didn't criticize, and always kept busy. She worked up until a few years ago in the administrative offices of the garment workers union and the day after retiring she joined the senior citizen's center. Unlike his mother, who filled her days thinking about all the things that could go wrong, Sarah attended Broadway shows, traveled to Atlantic City, and did arts and crafts. Ira's house was full of her clay bowls and potholders.

"She was a good mother and grandmother," Sarah said brushing the hair from the front of Ira's face.

"The best," he said.

"Everyone liked her."

Effortlessly, he thought, just like Ellen.

"Did I ever tell you about this Italian woman who worked with her in the garment center?" Sarah said.

"About a thousand times."

"Sadie helped her find a place to live and she named her first daughter after her. Can you imagine, somewhere in the city there's an Italian girl named Sadie."

They both smiled and stared straight ahead at Selma, who moved constantly, keeping to the edge of everyone's conversation like a moth circling the light.

"Aunt Sarah."

"Yes darling?"

"Who was Eva?"

Sarah's whole body contracted in an instant, like it was a single muscle. Her breathing stopped and then resumed with a start, like a car thrown too quickly into gear.

"She was your sister," he said. "I saw her headstone at the cemetery."

Aunt Sarah watched Selma work the room, heading slowly in their direction.

"Eva was two years younger than me. Grandma had to put her in an institution."

"How old was she?"

"Eighteen. She stayed there for the rest of her life."

"What was wrong with her?"

"Behavioral problems."

"They don't put people away for life for behavioral problems."

"Things were different back then."

"What institution?"

"What's the difference?"

"I'm curious. I suddenly discover at the age of forty that my mother had a sister who died when I was twenty who I didn't even know existed. Don't you think that's a little strange?"

"The world didn't have to know everybody's business back then, not like today."

"Well, this is today and I'd like to know."

"You know all you need to know," Sarah said.

"You sound like my mother."

Sarah shuddered.

"I'm sorry," Ira said.

"Just don't ask her about Eva."

"Why?"

"Because your mother was the youngest and Max and I were in school. My mother had to work, so Eva wound up taking care of her. She took care of your mother until the day they took her away."

"How old was she?"

"Who?"

"My mother . . . when they took Eva away?"

"Eleven. She never saw her again."

"She didn't visit?"

"No."

"Why not?"

"It was hard for her."

"Did you visit?"

"In the beginning."

"It was hard for you."

"I was much older."

Selma was getting closer.

"What's the name of the institution?"

"Your mother is coming."

"Tell me . . . or I'll ask her."

Aunt Sarah swayed back and forth as if the upper part of her body were balancing on a spring.

"I want to know."

The desperation in his voice must have surprised her. It certainly surprised him. He wouldn't have asked his mother - not yet anyway - and certainly not now . . . maybe never, he'd have discussed it with Ellen first.

Selma stopped about ten feet away and rested her hand on the shoulder of one of her cousins. She said something to him, but looked right at Sarah and Ira.

"The name?"

"Pilgrim State Hospital."

"Where is that?"

"Not now."

"Where?"

"Long Island."

"So what are you two whispering about?" Selma said.

"You," Sarah said.

"What about me?"

"How well you handle these things."

"I've had practice."

"You don't get better with practice at things like this."

21

"You two were whispering like a couple of criminals planning a robbery. What else have you been talking about?"

"This new course I'm taking at the center," Sarah said.

"What about?"

"Knitting."

"Sweaters?"

"Afghans."

"Sweaters would be more useful," Selma said. She had an opinion about everything.

"I've made enough sweaters to last a lifetime," Sarah said.

"No one ever has enough sweaters."

Sarah didn't argue. She knew better.

"And that's the big conspiracy?"

Sarah nodded.

"I don't believe you for a minute."

Sarah laughed.

"But I don't have time to stand here and find out," his mother said. "Ira, there's so much food in the kitchen, I want you to take some home."

"We don't need anything."

"I've already made up a platter for you. It's in the refrigerator."

"Fine."

"When are you going to learn to make a tie?" Selma said, bending down to straighten the knot. "Go get some dessert in the kitchen. I want to talk to Aunt Sarah."

Ira jumped up.

"And don't forget to tuck the tie into your shirt while you're eating," she said. "The way your father always did. He saved a fortune on dry-cleaning."

Ira ate a big piece of chocolate cake in the kitchen, letting his tie swing dangerously close to the frosting. He was almost elated to learn that his mother's family wasn't perfect and that they weren't an unbroken string of well-adjusted, success stories. There was a big failure carefully hidden away by his mother, lest she become a yardstick to measure his own accomplishments.

They didn't get home until after ten. They were all exhausted. Ellen and the kids went right to bed, but Ira couldn't sleep. He had this urge to do something domestic, so he sat at the kitchen table balancing the checkbook.

He tried not to think about Eva. It was hard enough comparing the amount on each check with the scribble in the checkbook. He also needed to spend a few minutes looking over the budget for the Sinoral campaign. He'd lost a day already and it had to be finalized by Friday. The big question, as always, was how many consecutive Sundays to run it and how far up front in the supplement.

Ellen didn't know about Eva. There hadn't been a quiet moment to tell her since the cemetery. Besides, he wasn't ready to talk. The whole thing still seemed too bizarre and personal. He needed to think about it awhile and work some answers out in his head in terms of what he wanted to do before talking it over with Ellen, especially since he knew what she was likely to say. She'll try to convince him to respect Aunt Sarah's wishes. Every family has a black sheep, she'll say, some skeleton hidden in the closet. What was your grandmother supposed to do, advertise the fact that her daughter had been committed to a mental institution?

Ellen respects the past. She believes in leaving well enough alone. He's always loved that about her. He usually felt the same way, except not tonight, tonight he felt as if Eva needed to be rescued from obscurity. He felt the passion begin to burn and everyone needed a burning passion from time to time. Lord knows, it's been so long since he's had one.

For a long time it used to be his art. In high school, it was the caricatures of the teachers that he drew senior year for the yearbook. In college, it was the sketching courses, fruits, landscapes and nudes. There were some really talented students, both real and representational, and it quickly became clear that he wasn't one of them. He had the technique, but not the vision. He was pretty good with trees and rocks. Once or twice he caught the light just right surprising even himself. His mother has one of those landscapes in her den. He was a passable artist, but not nearly as good as Selma believes. She didn't see all the failures.

"He could've been another Rockwell, drawing pictures instead of coupons," she occasionally told the kitchen fan, when he was near enough to overhear it.

She couldn't possibly understand that a small talent can be a curse, in some ways worse than no talent at all.

Ira finally climbed into bed about three in the morning. He dreamt that he was at some kind of resort that looked more like a college campus. He had to leave, he was late for something, but he couldn't find his way out. He walked in the same direction for hours, however, the campus never ended. He finally stopped to ask someone for help, an attractive girl in her early twenties with long, curly hair and crystal-clear blue eyes, so blue that it was like looking into the reflection of a mountain lake. She had one flaw, a large mouth, which made her smile look a little silly.

"Don't you know where you are?" she said her voice very soft and sweet, almost melodic.

"On vacation? In college?"

He was sure it was one or the other.

"No Ira, you're in a mental institution."

When he looked down he saw that he was in a straight jacket.

"How do you know my name?"

She looked disappointed and kissed him on the forehead.

Then he woke up.

WEDNESDAY

He couldn't get past the headlines on the front page of the newspaper on the train ride to work the next morning. There were too many questions floating around inside his head. What were the circumstances of Eva's institutionalization? He couldn't imagine his grandmother putting away her own daughter unless she had no choice. She had to have done something horrible. And what kind of behavioral problem could have kept her there for the next thirty years? There must have been rules and rights even back then. Maybe she was profoundly retarded and Sarah just didn't want to admit it. But then how could Eva have been trusted to take care of his mother when she was a little girl? And why the universal conspiracy of silence? What if it was all a mistake, Ira wondered? What if Eva was one of those people you read about who waste away in a mental institution before anyone realizes that it was just a hearing problem or dyslexia?

Ira had to review the proofs for the Sinoral coupon first thing in the morning and confirm the print schedule. In four days a coupon would be appearing in Sunday supplements and magazines in every big city and small town in America. There'd be a rush of redemptions, because Americans love to try new things particularly at a discount. Then there'll be another round 60 days later. This time fewer will be clipped and most of those will get stuck in drawers.

At 11 o'clock he took a fifteen-minute break and called Pilgrim State Hospital. The switchboard connected him to the Records Department.

"I'd like to verify the presence of someone at your institution."

"Try admissions."

"She's not currently a patient. It's a woman who was there twenty years ago."

"Ask her."

He didn't like the sound of that.

"She's dead."

"Then the information is confidential."

The voice belonged to an older woman with the practiced and measured tone of a hardened civil servant.

He tapped his pencil slowly against his teeth. It was better than pushing them in with his finger.

"She was my aunt. I need the information for . . . genetic reasons. It has to do with my wife's pregnancy."

"Congratulations, but all files are confidential."

"If you'll just verify the years that she was there it would be a big help."

"Can't do it, it's against the rules."

It was the bureaucratic kiss of death. He could see her finger moving toward the disconnect button.

"How can I get permission?"

"Try the Attorney General's office in Albany."

With that the connection went dead.

Ira called Albany and reached Lisa Hancock, an attorney in the Health and Hospital Administration assigned to the state mental institutions. She was sympathetic, clearly not a professional bureaucrat, but a young lawyer passing through on her way to a more lucrative job in private practice.

"I wish I could help, I really do, but you need the consent in writing of her nearest living relative, in this case your mother or your aunt. You also need a physician to establish medical need. If the Commissioner agrees, the file can be reviewed, but only by the doctor."

"It's my aunt for God's sake. I just want to see the file, not publish it."

"It's not up to me. If it were, I'd be happy to give it to you."

"What about a letter from a genetic counselor?"

Ellen knew a genetic counselor.

"It has to be an MD and only with the consent of one of her sisters."

"What if I can't get their consent?"

"You can always petition the court. The court can order files released regardless of consent where a physician shows compelling need."

"Can I at least confirm the dates of her stay?"

"Not with me, I don't know them."

Any attempt by a government employee to make a joke should be punishable by a fine and imprisonment.

The Sinoral layouts were screaming to be double-checked and the placements needed to be confirmed. American Family had at least one hundred million dollars riding on Sinoral, much more if you factored in all the research. There were hundreds of jobs

26

hanging in the balance. This weekend the eyes of the company would be on Ira as he fired the first shot.

Of course, the world desperately needed another cold capsule, Ira thought with a chuckle, as he punched in Sarah's telephone number. He asked if she would give her consent. He knew that would be harder than finding a doctor to write a letter.

"Of course not."

"I won't say a word."

"Some things are best left forgotten."

"That sounds like something you read in Ann Landers."

"And what if it is, I think she knows one or two things about families and life."

"You're going to force me to ask my mother."

"Go ahead."

`"What choice do I have?"

"Go ahead you'll get the same answer . . . that is if you don't kill her first."

He couldn't imagine an emotion ever getting the better part of Selma.

"Talking about her doesn't seem to be killing you."

"Eva didn't raise me the way she raised your mother."

He could hear Sarah tapping her knitting needle on the table by the chair.

"What did Eva look like?"

"I really don't want to talk about it."

"Does anyone have a picture?"

Sarah didn't respond.

"Did you visit her in the hospital? Do you remember the name of her doctor?"

"What difference would it make to anyone if I answered your questions?"

"It would make a difference to me."

Sarah sighed into the telephone.

"I'm not giving up so easily," Ira said.

"This is so unlike you. I've never known you to be so indifferent to the wishes . . . and feelings of others."

"But it's a lot like my mother, isn't it?"

"Selma doesn't disturb the past."

"Because she can't argue with it or change it."

"Maybe we made a mistake not mentioning Eva, but what's done is done."

27

He hated that phrase. His mother used it all the time. She made it sound like it was one of the laws of nature, as immutable as gravity.

"What's done can be undone, particularly when it's a secret, that's how you learn from your mistakes."

Aunt Sarah excused herself. She said that she had to go to the laundry room to move her clothes to the dryer before someone dumped them onto the table, but Ira didn't believe her for a minute. Sarah was not the type to leave her laundry alone, which is why she always had a book to read with her.

He tried to push Eva out of his mind and do some work. Half the world had a relative or two hidden in the closet. One crazy aunt was no big deal. Still, he couldn't focus. Everything he tried to do seemed so trivial. Did it really matter that the S in Sinoral had to be larger in the center of the coupon and smaller at the corners? Or that AFC would get a better rate if it didn't insist on an odd page or top placement?

He picked up one of the slick ads that would be gracing the Sunday papers all around the country. It had a giant picture of Sinoral's snot green box, and underneath it read, WATCH OUT SNIFFLES, GRIPPES AND FLU – SINORAL WILL GET THE BEST OF YOU.

He can't imagine what the agency charged for that little ditty.

Below that in smaller letters it called Sinoral the most important discovery since chicken soup.

One-half hour later he gave up and took an early train back home. He left as soon as he felt the urge to highlight the "Sin" in Sinoral to see if anyone noticed.

The woman beside him was reading "The Post." Twins separated at birth had been reunited after fifty years. They grew up in the Midwest one hundred miles apart. They looked alike, their wives looked alike, and they were both mailmen.

It was a sign. He had to reunite with his Aunt Eva. He had to drive out to Pilgrim State in the morning. He'd tell work that he had to do something for his grandmother's estate. He'd be back after lunch and no one would be the wiser. He wouldn't even tell Ellen until afterward, otherwise there'd be too much discussion and she'd probably talk him out of it.

Ellen didn't sense anything at dinner or maybe she just thought that Ira was so quiet because he was still thinking about his grandmother. She was cheerful and kept the conversation going on all kinds of school, neighborhood and household subjects. She was a natural at it.

"You should see the illustrations Anthony made today."

"Anthony?"

"That student in my class I was telling you about last week."

"Right, Anthony."

"He's illustrating an Indian legend for his class project. It's almost good enough for a children's book."

"He'll probably wind up sketching copy for an ad agency."

Ellen ignored him and went on to describe the pictures in detail from the wild turkeys in the woods to the teepees by the river.

It's not that Ellen didn't care or wasn't observant, it's just that sometimes she wasn't all that sensitive to Ira's moods, at least to certain of his moods. Sometimes it was intentional because she sensed that ignoring it was the best way to move Ira past it, but at other times it was because she just didn't notice. It wasn't that she was self-centered or insensitive; it was just a deficiency at times, like high pitch hearing loss. Ellen was so overwhelmingly optimistic that she was blinded on occasion by her own light. She had this ability to soothe and raise his spirits with a kind word and a gentle touch, but sometimes she just didn't recognize when it was necessary.

If Ellen had put her hand on his arm and asked Ira if anything was wrong, he'd probably have told her everything. He'd have blurted it all out as fast as he could, like a little boy with a story to tell. She'd have urged him to let Eva rest in peace and he'd have accepted her advice and let it go. Sometimes you just need to hear it from someone else, someone you love and trust, to recognize that it's the only sensible thing to do.

Instead, it was a typical Wednesday evening. Ellen marked papers while they watched television. Jaime did homework without once looking down at her books. She was a natural when it came to tests, confident and calm like Ellen. Scott, on the other hand, took after Ira. He got anxious and tortured himself with every careless mistake.

After the kids went to bed, Ellen and Ira watched a rerun of *Thirty Something*. They were once like that, the lines in their faces still tentative, their days fragmented and each moment filled with rich and exhausting possibilities. Everything seemed so preordained now, like every day was just another step forward along a well-trod path.

Ira never watched much television growing up. His mother wouldn't let him. Now he knows the TV Guide by heart and has about two hours worth of favorite shows on his card most every night. Of course, that doesn't count baseball. He could watch baseball any time, any team, although the Yankees were his favorite. It's a life he'd be the first to admit, which doesn't burn, although it does last, and there's nothing more important than that.

THURSDAY

Ellen opened her eyes and found Ira sitting in the chair by the window across from the bed staring at her like a hospital patient.

"You're late," she said.

"I'm catching the 7:52."

"Isn't that a local?"

"Yeah."

"You hate locals."

"No I don't."

"Didn't you once tell me that they squeezed people in so tight sometimes that their pimples looked like volcanoes?"

"I was joking."

"How come?"

"How come what?"

"How come you're taking a later train?"

A simple enough question, but he hadn't anticipated it and it stumped him.

"No answer?"

"I have a meeting out of the office," he finally said.

Ellen got up, walked over, and reached over to flatten down his cowlick.

"You look tired," she said.

"I'm fine."

She went into the bathroom and came out a few minutes later, make-up brush in one hand and tissue in the other.

"You sure you're not coming down with something, you're eyes look a little glassy?"

"I didn't sleep well."

Ellen gave him the teacher's nod of understanding.

"I'm just waiting a few more minutes," he said. "There's no point in standing outside on the train platform longer than I have to."

"There will be more traffic on the bridge at this hour."

"I know, I'm taking that into account."

Ellen walked over and put the back of her hand to his forehead.

"You're a little warm."

"It's the morning."

"So what does that mean?"

"People are warmer in the morning."

Ellen laughed.

"What's that from, the exercise you get sleeping?"

"From lying under the covers all night."

"Why don't you call in sick and just relax at home today?"

"I can't."

"I will if you do."

Ellen kissed his cheek. The morning breath had been replaced by the minty-fresh taste of Crest. She'd never made an offer like that before; it almost made Ira blurt out his real plans.

"I wish I could, but I have the Sinoral campaign."

"Oh yes the chicken soup of cold remedies."

"You know how they get at AFC when there's a new product on the launching pad."

"Like it's the D-day invasion."

"Everything's got to be finalized by tomorrow."

Ira looked down at his shoes and bent down to retie one of the shoelaces. He didn't want his face to give anything away since Ellen had a teacher's eye for the truth and the self-conscious.

"You keep things bottled up," Ellen said going back into the bathroom, "and one of these days you're going to explode all over the carpet."

"I'll try to do it outside."

Ellen stuck her head out of the bathroom and smiled. "There's nothing wrong with feeling sad, you were close to your grandmother."

"People work when they're sad."

"Now you sound like your mother."

"It's true."

"One day playing hooky won't make you a traitor to the AFC nation."

"You don't know AFC's high command."

Ira walked over to the bathroom door.

"I'm going," he said.

Ellen came out of the bathroom. Her transformation into a third grade teacher was almost complete, cheeks were rosy, eyes wide open and clear. All she needed were the appropriate clothes and she had a closet full of those, high-collared shirts, long skirts, baggy sweaters.

"Just take it easy today," Ellen said touching his forearm.

He loved when she did that.

"I will."

"I'm going to make sure that you *relax* this weekend," she said.

"Really relax," she repeated before disappearing into the closet like the scenery that passes by everyday on the train.

Relax was the code word. Every suburban couple probably had one.

On the way out, Jamie reminded him that she was trying out for the school play. She wanted to be one of the orphans in Annie.

"Break a leg," he said bending down to give her a kiss on the forehead.

"Why are you still here?" Scott said coming out of the bathroom, the sleepiness replaced instantly by concern.

"A late meeting out of the office."

Scott began to breathe again.

"Can we talk about the skateboard tonight?"

"Sure."

With that he blew the house a kiss and walked out the door.

He had to fight the urge to turn off at his usual exit, almost as if his arms knew the risks and didn't want to go. He felt like a truant, although he couldn't be sure what that feeling was really like since he never skipped a single day of school when he was younger. His mother was too vigilant and he was too conscientious.

The traffic moved slowly. He had no idea if it was normal or unusually heavy. He didn't know which lane moved faster or if there might be a good service road he could use as an alternative - things every commuter should know. These were not train commuters, using anything that runs to get to the station. These were road commuters in for the long haul. Driving large, comfortable cars with cups of coffee stuck to the dash and bags filled with rolls and donuts. They got their news from the radio instead of the newspaper and they sat with jackets off, two or more to a car, talking sports and spouses.

Train commuters are a more solitary bunch.

He did feel a little warm and there was a tickle in his throat, as if he really was coming down with something. Ellen was like a witch sometimes that way. She could see things about him before he even realized it.

He stopped for gas and left a message at work that he'd be late. There were things he had to take care of, he said, with respect to his grandmother's death. Not a complete lie, but not the kind of thing they'd imagine like closing a bank account or emptying an apartment. Disposing of that part of her life he'd leave to his mother and aunt.

The traffic was light after the Throgs Neck Bridge. This was the coveted reverse commute. Few people traveled to Long Island this early in the morning, a few haggard and worn night-shift faces, exhausted doctors and New York City policemen staring at the road through slits and squeezing containers of coffee. Of course, there were also the truckers, their faces so devoid of emotion as to appear empty.

He wondered what his mother was like before Eva was institutionalized? Was she fresh and curious like Jaime, her eyes an open window looking out with wonder and excitement? Or was she already a house with its windows boarded up? How much different would she have turned out if Eva had been normal or at least remained home? Watching her sister disappear like that – over some kind of bad behavior – had to have an effect; maybe it turned her cautious and demanding. What about the trickle down effect? How much different would his childhood have been if Eva's story had another ending? If it had happened today little Selma would have been immediately sent for counseling. It would probably help even now, except his mother would sooner pay retail than speak to a psychologist.

The sun jumped quickly above the horizon dangling a curtain of dust in front of him like a toreador's cape. It felt almost like he was heading out on vacation, a carefree, ambition-less twenty year old driving to the shore without a non-biological desire in the world. It was a forgotten muscle that felt good to stretch, but only for an instant. He did have something to do and he had to do it before lunch.

Pilgrim State Hospital is located in Selden, a town that wasn't originally an Indian village or founded two hundred years earlier by Protestant families in search of fishing freedom. It wasn't the site of a famous battle and it didn't have an historic inn or fashionable racetrack. It was a suburban tract community conceived by the intercourse of a major highway and a large, ravenous institution for the mentally ill.

The hospital consisted of about fifty buildings scattered over twenty-five acres that had more character than the entire town. If not for the high fence and lack of upkeep, Pilgrim State Hospital could easily have been Pilgrim State University, a hot bed of physical and spiritual unrest, instead of suspended animation.

Since it was early, Ira looked around for someplace to have breakfast. About two miles north of the hospital was a big billboard with a picture of the Mayflower and four passengers wearing tri-cornered hats, white aprons and shoes with big buckles.

"Let Us Give Thanks For The Pilgrim Diner," they sang out in one big comic balloon.

The diner was packed with people in stiff, white uniforms, mostly nurses and orderlies. The doctors, Ira figured, ate somewhere else, someplace with the word "GOURMET" in the name and "IMPORTED" plastered on the menu.

He was the only one in a suit and tie.

There were no booths available, so he sat down at the far end of the counter next to an attractive nurse with light red hair and high cheekbones. Ellen was cute, petite, with small breasts and a wholesome smile, the kind of girl who gives rise to fantasies of marriage. This woman was an Amazon in comparison. At least five-ten, a good two inches taller than Ira, with breasts that plunged the counter into shadow like a solar eclipse.

Ira stopped staring out of the corner of his eye long enough to look over the breakfast menu. All diner menus were the same. Eggs any style, eggs with bacon, eggs with ham, eggs with sausage, steak and eggs, hash browns, pancakes, French toast and any combination thereof. And what diner didn't have a bottomless cup of coffee. If it were really any good they'd charge by the cup.

He pretended to study the menu while looking at her arms. They were muscular and tan, which meant she was probably one of those workout junkies who wore skin-tight leotards while pumping iron at the club and finished it off with five minutes under the sunlamp. She had wonderful posture, not hunched over like the kids or slumped slightly forward like Ellen from years of carrying a bag full of notebooks to review and grade. She had tight calves and thighs as well, as best he could tell from the parts exposed by her nurse's uniform, which had pulled up somewhat to accommodate the stool.

No creases or folds anywhere he could see.

Ira guessed late twenties, thirty tops. The legs were a dead give away. When you spend enough summers at the town pool, you realize that thighs are the first things to go on a woman. They spread in inverse proportion to a man's hairline. It's part of nature's symmetrical give and take.

He could have wrapped his fingers around her waist. There was room for a spine to pass through perhaps, but not much else. And her bottom was like one of those airy desserts - angel food cake perhaps - because it had a shape and a size, but there was nothing to it. It didn't spill over the seat like most of their friends, but was small and self-contained, like the pictures Scott carefully colored in when he was younger that always stayed within the lines. He was compulsive about that.

"What'll it be?" A shapeless waitress with the hint of a mustache named Irma stood in front of him.

"Coffee with milk, one scrambled egg with a toasted English muffin."

He looked to his right and saw that his Amazon beauty was drinking her coffee black.

"Visiting a patient?" she said smiling and turning her beautiful Caribbean blue eyes on him like a spotlight.

"N . . . not exactly."

"Salesman?"

"No, I'm in advertising . . . coupon promotions."

She went back to her coffee and Ira turned to add some bacon to his order, but Irma had already left.

"I never use coupons," she said putting her lips together to blow on her coffee.

She had redder lips than Ellen ever had, clearly the result of lip gloss.

"Why not, they save you money."

"I always mean to, but I never have the energy to cut them out."

"You're exactly the kind of consumer I'm trying to reach."

She laughed and Ira felt like a schoolboy after his first kiss.

"Are you a nurse at Pilgrim State?"

"That's the only place to be a nurse around here."

The waitress brought the egg and English muffin. The coffee was already there.

"What do you do there?"

"I work with the lifers."

"The lifers?"

"The patients who've always been there and always will be, not the druggies serving time or the homeless checking in and out like it's a motel . . . the ones who have to die to get out."

Ira squeezed tight to his coffee mug. He couldn't think of anything to say in response, except perhaps to ask her for help.

"What's your name?" she said.

"Ira."

She laughed again. It was different from Ellen's laugh, more ambiguous and less responsible, if that's possible. It was a laugh that was open to interpretation. Maybe it was just younger and he'd forgotten the sound.

"I never met an Ira before," she said, "I'm Rhonda."

"Anything else," Irma said putting a check down by the untouched eggs and English muffin.

"No thank you."

Irma was gone before he could finish his answer.

Rhonda put her coffee down and pushed the cup away. He heard this curious thumping as she looked through her bag for some change. It took a moment to realize that it was his heart, a part of his heart that hadn't been getting much exercise lately, certainly not while riding on the train or pulling the garbage cans to the end of the driveway. It was telling him to take a chance since not too many of them came around these days.

"Maybe you could help me?" he said trying to keep his voice from sounding too squeaky.

He felt like a character out of a cheap murder mystery.

"How?" she said.

Her grin was every bit in proportion to the rest of her.

Ira explained about Eva and Rhonda listened with interest. A lot of short, stubby guys must have handed her lines over the past ten years, but this one had to be unique.

"You're talking about someone who was there twenty years ago, that's a bit before my time."

The thumping stopped.

"There must be a file somewhere."

She raised her hands to her hips and nodded. The blood roared through his aged and partially clogged arteries as he tried to bring his sputtering lungs under control.

"Eva Portnoy." Rhonda rolled the name around her poster-like lips.

"I've always had a weakness for mustaches," she said putting down some change. "I've got a friend in the Records Department. I'll try to find out something. Meet me here at 5:30."

With that Rhonda stood up, flashed a killer celluloid smile, and walked out. By the time he realized what she had said she was gone.

He picked up his English muffin. It was cold and hard and painted with something the color of a urine sample, but he took a bite anyway. What could he tell them at work, he wondered? How would he explain it to Ellen when he got home late? Much to Irma's delight, Ira requested some more of that bottomless cup of coffee to which he added enough milk and sugar to kill the taste. Then he sipped it slowly like a condemned man enjoying his last meal. In a little while the diner emptied out. The Pilgrim State workday had apparently begun.

The way Ira saw it he had three choices. First, stick with the original plan and see what he could learn at Pilgrim on his own. Second, go back to work and forget the whole thing; accept the fact that Eva was an embarrassment and hidden away in a mental institution the way people did it fifty years ago. And finally third, wait around for Rhonda and see what she could find out.

Rejecting the first choice was easy, since he had spent twenty years in a large bureaucracy. He had about as much of a chance at Pilgrim State on his own as he had yesterday on the telephone. Inside help was an absolute necessity. If he chose the second option, gave up and went back to work, then this morning would have been a total waste of time, another badge of cowardice to add to his growing collection.

The Sinoral campaign had a life of its own by now and Tom could handle anything that came up today. If he didn't arrive home on time he'd simply attribute it to a meeting running late. Of course, since he'd be telling Ellen everything as soon as he got home anyway so it wouldn't matter.

Ira called his secretary and told her that he had to help empty out his grandmother's apartment.

"The landlord has already rented it out," he said. "You know how they get when a rent control apartment becomes free."

"I'm so sorry," she said.

She was always apologizing for things that weren't her fault.

"Have Tom put the Sinoral coupon to bed. Remind him that it's all front-page or page 3 on the Sunday inserts with a 30/40 price break on the secondary run."

"There's no number," he said in response to her question. "The phone has already been turned off and I don't have my cell with me. I'm calling from a pay phone. Tell Paul . . . and Dan if he comes by . . . that everything's under control. I'll call in again later."

Now the big question was what to do all day in Selden?

He drove around a while until he wound up in the center of town. The business district consisted of a stationery store, a deli, a hardware store, a gas station and a few parking spots. What appeared to be an old movie theater had been converted to a real estate office and a discount drug store. Selden looked like it had been hard hit, like a lot of small downtown areas, by the shopping malls and strip centers.

He spent the first hour in the stationery store looking at magazines and paperbacks. They didn't sell a single book that couldn't be read in one day at the beach or on a flight across the country. He left after the girl behind the cash register got nervous and called someone.

He stopped at a telephone booth to call Aunt Sarah.

"I'm at Pilgrim State."

"As a patient?"

"Very funny."

Ira explained that he wasn't kidding and that he had indeed driven out to Selden to learn more about Eva.

"This isn't like you," Sarah said.

"People change."

"You're acting crazy."

"It appears to run in the family."

"I hope not. I hope they don't decide to keep you there."

He heard Sarah's knitting needles dueling like a couple of swordsmen.

"You can help prevent that."

"How?"

"By telling me what I'm going to find out."

"That's easy, nothing . . . a troubled child hidden away in an institution. It wasn't all that uncommon back then."

"Troubled?"

"I'm simplifying.

"Was she retarded?"

"No."

"Violent?"

"I'm not playing twenty questions."

"Then tell me why she wound up spending her whole life there?"

"Because after a while it was easier for her in there than out here."

"With her mother and sisters?"

"In the real world where my mother worked and we went to school, and she would've been alone most of the time."

"She was institutionalized so she wouldn't be lonely?"

"You know that's not what I meant.

"Who put her there in the first place? I can't imagine grandma agreeing to it. And why didn't anyone ever mention her name? What did you and mom think I would do?"

"It wasn't about you."

"Didn't you think it would be something I'd like to know . . . that I was entitled to know?"

Sarah thought it over a few moments.

"Remember how mad you used to get when your mother made you those big birthday parties?"

"With all the kids in the neighborhood, even the ones who never spoke to me? I think she enjoyed embarrassing me."

"You didn't want anyone to know that you were born on April Fools' Day."

"I was ten years old."

"We didn't want the endless questions, like the ones you're asking now, or the sympathy, or the matching stories about every other family's heartache. It was enough just thinking about it, we didn't want to talk about it as well."

"Even with the family?"

"Especially with the family."

"So everyone kept quiet, the great-aunts and uncles, the older cousins and all the old friends."

"Everyone has something to hide."

Ira stomped his feet to keep warm.

"Excuse me a moment," she said and he listened to Sarah's footsteps as she walked into the kitchen, did something at the stove and returned.

"Did she have curly hair?" Ira asked.

"That's not hard to guess considering almost everyone in the family does."

"Blue eyes?"

"Go home Ira, you're just wasting your time."

"It won't be the first time. Was she pretty?"

"I've got to go."

"More laundry?" he said.

"Soup on the stove."

"Chicken?"

"Split pea."

"With the cut up hot dogs?"

"I haven't done that since you were a teenager, but I'll put some in if you want to stop over on your way home."

"I'll be coming home too late."

"I hope not," Sarah said before hanging up.

As soon as she did, this little voice in Ira's head whispered, "call your mother." She was going to know soon enough. She'd hear something odd in Sarah's voice when they spoke and they spoke every day, and then she'd pry her open like a can of paint.

"I'm not home," his mother blurted into the receiver like she was annoyed that he didn't already know. "Leave a detailed message after the tone, speak slowly and clearly, state the time and date and leave a telephone number where you can be reached."

He toyed with the idea of telling her that he was at Pilgrim State Hospital and that Aunt Eva sent her best. Instead, he just hung up without leaving any message. His mother hated that. She couldn't understand why anyone would spend a dime and then have nothing to say.

Ira found an antique store on one of the side streets that had a big selection of old tools. Ira was not very handy, but he liked tools. He had all kinds at home that he never used. Aside from the usual stuff, like a hammer, screwdriver and pliers, he had a power drill and a set of metric wrenches. He even had a rusty old Stanley eggbeater drill and an alligator wrench left by the prior owner of the house, which he refused to throw out. Both would have fit in nicely in this shop. Ira picked up a lovely old plane from the turn of the century that must have seen a thousand projects.

"A Stanley fifty-five," the proprietor said. He looked a lot older than the plane and had a heavy German accent. He walked over slowly with a definite list to the left, as if one foot was shorter than the other.

"Would you believe that I used to be a mailman," he said when he noticed Ira staring at his leg, "retired about ten years ago. The limp wasn't so bad back then, probably because I kept it loose by walking so much."

They talked tools for over an hour. He showed him his private collection, which included a rare French bow drill that he said "played like a violin," an old copper blow torch, an OVB oil can and a double claw, no-faced hammer.

He ate lunch at Ginny's Eatery, a tuna melt and coffee. Then he looked at the houses for sale in the window of the local realtor. There were quite a few. Apparently not just the patients wanted out of the area. The homes around Pilgrim State were not expensive. Indeed, some of them went for less than one hundred thousand dollars. Of course, they looked more like mobile homes who had lost their wheels.

There weren't vacant lots back home for that price.

At 2:30 Ira wandered into the library to read the local newspaper. There was a four-day old fire smoldering in the landfill. A high school dropout was being tried for killing his mother. He supposedly lost it after she threw away his collection of nude playing cards. There was going to be a public hearing about selling one of the elementary schools to a developer to turn into condominiums.

He couldn't imagine living in his sixth grade classroom.

Ira was a very bad liar, so he called home before Ellen returned from work, knowing that only Jaime would be home.

"Tell Mom that something came up and I had to take the shuttle to Boston for a meeting on one of the Sinoral field studies. I'll be back late."

"How late?"

"I don't know . . . I might even have to stay overnight."

It slipped out without any thought on his part, as if he were being prompted by his subconscious or a part of his body that had been able to bypass his brain.

"I'll call as soon as I know for sure," he said.

As soon as he hung up he realized that he had forgotten to ask about her tryout for the play. He normally never forgot about things like that.

He went back into the library and looked up Pilgrim State Hospital in the card catalogue. He found a book entitled "The History of Pilgrim State Hospital", which was cheaply bound and appeared to be someone's thesis.

"Pilgrim State was founded in 1888 as a private sanitarium. It was a place for the rich to hide their problems."

Of course, that wouldn't include his grandmother.

"It became a state institution after the Depression."

Opening it up, Ira realized, to immigrant families. He turned to the section entitled "Widespread Abuse in the Forties and Fifties."

42

"In the forties and fifties, hospitalization was frequently used to shield the community from a person under the guise of protecting him from himself. People were institutionalized with little or no mental illness, people who shouted obscenities, who ignored community norms, who were too reclusive, or who had a limited ability to compete in modern society. If you found yourself in a public mental institution there was little hope of recovery. Indeed, it was almost certain that whatever strings still connected you to family and community would be cut."

The clock struck five.

"The forties and fifties were a time of experimentation. Between 1948 and 1952, tens of thousands of prefrontal leucotomies, known in the United States as lobotomies, were performed on people from all walks of life. After drilling two or more holes in a patient's skull, an instrument resembling an apple corer or ice pick was inserted into the brain. Surgeons destroyed large areas of the front of the brain without even knowing what they were cutting.

"Even more patients were subject to radical somatic therapies, such as insulin coma, metrazol shock and electroshock. Pilgrim State Hospital welcomed every experimental procedure, since there weren't enough funds to provide each individual with meaningful traditional psychiatric therapy."

Ira figured that Eva was institutionalized in 1936 and enjoyed the full twenty years of abuse.

He looked at the clock. He couldn't risk the chance that Rhonda might not wait, so he returned the book to the shelf and left the library. There was a parking ticket on the windshield of the car. Someone had actually noticed that he was parked longer than the two-hour limit. He put it in his briefcase and drove back to the diner with Rhonda's picture hanging in his brain like some college poster.

In twenty years of marriage he had never come close to another woman. Avoiding compromising situations was easy. He didn't speak to strange women on business trips and he wasn't very sociable at parties. He couldn't make small talk, which eliminated the elevator romance. He didn't worry much about his appearance, not that it would have made much of a difference, and he didn't spend money. In short, he didn't attract attention. His fidelity might be the result of strong moral character, old-fashion honor and steadfast resolve, or it could simply be fear and circumstance.

Whatever the reason, it was easy if you avoided those spontaneous situations that brought quick intimacy to strangers.

Sometimes, however, even cowards find themselves in situations that don't require bravery or intent, where the waters keep rising and the best swimmers tire, situations governed by hormones and involving third parties whose actions are way beyond your control.

At the last moment Ira thought about driving right past the diner to the Long Island Expressway and heading home for dinner. Thursday was his favorite TV night and the story he had to tell to this point would barely have raised an eyebrow. He made up his mind to do just that, but his arms and legs wouldn't listen to his brain, and they slowed the car down and turned into the diner parking lot. It was almost as if he had no choice but to go along for the ride.

Rhonda was sitting on the same stool sipping coffee, except now her hair was in disarray. There were strands in front of her eyes and bunches gathered around her ears. Her uniform had lost most of its crisp whiteness. It was damp and clung in spots like a wet suit. She looked like a cheerleader after a losing game.

"Hi," Ira said sitting down beside her.

He waved to Irma and indicated the same as Rhonda.

"I wasn't sure you'd come."

"Did you find out anything about my aunt?"

"I spoke to my friend in records. There was an Eva Portnoy there from 1936 until 1968."

"Wow, thirty-two years."

"Not the record, but certainly in the top ten. She died there."

"Unbelievable. Until Tuesday I didn't even know that she had existed."

"That's only seems fair since she probably didn't know that you existed."

Rhonda picked up her coffee.

"Did you find out why she was there?"

Irma put down a cup and filled it without spilling a drop. Then before he could say another word she pushed over the milk, as if she remembered him from the morning.

"No. They have a patient's logbook in records with admission and discharge dates. Anything else you'd have to get from her file."

"How can I get to see it?"

"The old files are stored in the basement below records. They're not in any kind of order and Shirley, that's my friend, says they're planning to hire someone to go through them to inventory certain information before they trash them."

Ira's heart started beating in his ears again, so loudly this time that he was surprised everyone didn't turn around to stare.

Apparently, Records needed more room and the long dead were going to be the first to go. Another month, Rhonda said, and any chance of finding out about Eva would be gone forever. Ira gulped down his coffee and burned his tongue, which started him coughing. Rhonda handed him a napkin.

"Shirley says you can have the job, even if it's only for a little while, so you can find out some more about your aunt. She said to come by in the morning if you're interested."

Ira gets this pain in his lower back sometimes when he's under stress. It's worse when he sits, sort of like he's trying to balance himself on the edge of a razor blade, so he stood up behind the stool and bent forward towards Rhonda. She smelled good, even after a tough day at work, or maybe it was just that she smelled different.

"I can't take another job, I've already got one. I have to get home."

"Suit yourself, but she says they're likely to destroy the files in the next couple of weeks."

Ira sneezed three times fast.

"Cold?"

"Nerves."

Rhonda finished her coffee and dabbed at her lips. She didn't wipe them like Ellen. She was perfectly calm, as if they had just been discussing the weather. Of course, this was nothing more than a little diversion for her, an exciting break in the routine, assuming she had one.

He could barely talk because his tongue was so thick and dry. He played a number of different scenarios in his head. The best one was that he got lucky and found Eva's file first thing in the morning. He couldn't stay longer than another day. And where would he stay? What would he tell Ellen? What would he tell them at work?

"You could stay with me," Rhonda said turning so that the full force of her breasts focused on him like a laser beam.

Can every woman read his mind, Ira wondered, sitting back down and letting the coffee burn his tongue again.

Back home Ellen was boiling water for spaghetti.

"Did he say when he'd call?"

"Just later," Jamie said.

Ellen wasn't anxious, but she was surprised. Ira never took unscheduled business trips. He started talking about a trip two weeks in advance. Two days before he laid his clothes out and stuck a typed itinerary on the refrigerator. The two of them casually discussed his return as if it were an absolute certainty.

"We'll eat out when I get back."

"You can pick up the dry cleaning on the way home."

It was the airplane ritual. A little game they played because Ira hated to fly. He wasn't comfortable discussing his fear outright, because acknowledging it would somehow make the risk seem more real. Instead, they talked about the trip as if it were to the supermarket. They made plans to do things with his return taken for granted in everything they discussed.

Actually, Ira hated most any kind of travel. He didn't care if statistics promised that most accidents happened at home, because he knew statistics could lie. They'd say anything you wanted if you treated them right, after all that was his business. So Ira was taking his first business trip in about a year without the airplane ritual and immediately after his grandmother's death. Ellen was trying to ignore and not climb this little staircase of knots that lead from her stomach to her throat.

Another bad omen, Ellen thought, as she added the olive oil, occurred at Ira's mother's house after the funeral. She overheard one of his great-aunts, an eighty-year old woman from Baltimore, remark about Selma's good fortune, referring to how Ira turned out. She made it sound like the odds had been stacked against him.

"Who would have thought, nice boy, level-headed, down to earth and so responsible."

Why did she expect anything else? Ellen wondered, looking at the telephone. Something didn't feel right and her intuition, unlike statistics, rarely lied.

Rhonda insisted that Ira come back to her apartment, at least until he made up his mind.

"It's a better place to decide than a diner." she said peeling herself off the stool.

The static held up her uniform, defying gravity and modesty. Her thighs were obscene. Although encased in white stockings, he could see that they were one hundred percent fat free, un-dimpled, un-blemished and un-wrinkled. Not the thighs he was used to. Thighs creased from sitting in class and red from rubbing together . . . middle age thighs that trembled with each step as if they had worries of their own.

He was unable to resist the combined power of Eva's mysterious past and Rhonda's legs, and he wound up following her old red Chevy Cavalier with its string of dents and broken tail light to this enormous apartment complex about ten minutes from the diner. It was littered with cars and trucks, some of them on blocks waiting for repairs. Every building was the same, a two story semi-attached mock Tudor with a big cement stoop, a little patch of well-trod grass and a sea of blacktop as far as the eye could see.

"How long have you lived here?" Ira said trying not to sound too out of his element.

"A little over a year."

"It looks like a nice little community."

"It's a hole, but it's cheap and it's near the hospital."

It took Rhonda a while to open all the locks. Once inside Ira saw what she meant. Chipped Formica counters in the kitchen, linoleum decorated with cigarette burns, wood floors in the hallway and living room with scratches that looked like two lane highways and boards that groaned with every step. There were indentations in the walls the size of fists and it didn't look as if they'd ever received a second coat of paint. The apartment had none of the wall-to-wall carpeting and window treatments that were standard fare in Ira's suburban habitat.

"It's not so bad."

"I haven't touched a thing since I moved in, because I'm moving out as soon as I can save enough money."

The furnishings were sparse. The kitchen contained a small rectangular white table with enough gouges and burns to be classified 4F by the Salvation Army. There were two chairs that didn't match the table or each other, except for the fact that both had vinyl seats that must have been punching bags in a prior life. Still, the kitchen was clean, except for some crumbs on the counter surrounding an empty bag of rice cakes. Ira hated rice cakes. Ellen bought them sometimes, but he thought they tasted like paper. He didn't snack for health reasons, purely to quiet his stomach, and he required a certain amount of saturated fats for that.

The living room was like a cup of weak, watered-down coffee. There was a sagging beige couch without a single throw pillow, which was unheard of in Ira's world where accents, like pillows, were often the focal point of the entire room and being propped up was considered the only way to unwind. There was a small battered coffee table covered with TV Guides and People magazines and a small portable television on a stand.

"The only thing I had to buy was the TV," Rhonda said turning on the bright overhead light, "everything else was here."

It also had a funny smell, not a human smell like sweat or oily hair, no Murphy's Oil, Lysol or ammonia, not the powdery scent of washed clothes or the blended odors of roast chicken and tomato sauce that often greet him at home. It was more a neighborhood smell, a combination of dust and alcohol, dampness and cigarette smoke, with a slightly salty almost fishy odor that made Rhonda's smell that much sweeter.

Ira couldn't think of anything to say, so he tried to pretend that he was Ellen.

"You could fix this place up, it's got potential, the rooms are large and there's a lot of light."

Of course, he hadn't yet seen the bedroom.

"It would be a dump no matter what I did to it."

He looked around and nodded.

"Still, it's a lot better than some of the places where I grew up," she said.

"Where was that?"

"Milwaukee, Wisconsin. My mother used to move from one run down apartment to another."

"How come?"

"A free month's rent . . . a new boyfriend. After my father left she went through dozens of them."

"I'm sorry."

"Don't be. My father had rotten teeth and breath that could wake the dead. He sent money occasionally, which my mother usually spent on her boyfriends and booze."

"How old were you when he left?"

"Six."

"Any brothers and sisters?"

"Are you kidding? I was a big accident."

"What did your mother do?"

"When she wasn't drinking?"

Ira nodded.

"Also a nurse."

After getting her nursing degree on her own and while she worked three part-time jobs, Rhonda left Wisconsin and came to New York. It was as far away as she could get. She didn't know a soul in New York, but she didn't care. Two years and one half dozen romances later Rhonda was still on her own, she had a few friends at work, but no one very close.

"Shirley in records is probably my best friend. Wait until you meet her. She's three times my age and about four times my size."

Rhonda was currently on the geriatric ward. Patients abandoned by family and physician alike.

"I mean work is all right, although it's not really psychiatric nursing. Mostly we feed, medicate and clean them, almost like they're newborns."

"What about your family?" she said.

"I'm also an only child. My father's dead. My mother's more than a little overwhelming."

He was trying for some common ground. He always did, whether it was the guy behind the deli counter or the AFC President.

"You know the type, has an opinion on everything. Nothing I did was ever good enough for her."

"I didn't have that problem. My mother was too busy having a good time to notice anything I did," Rhonda said as she took off her white shoes and brushed the scuff marks off with her sleeve.

"Obviously married," she said.

"What?"

"You're obviously married."

Ira looked at his ring finger. He wasn't wearing his wedding band. It bothered him when he wrote. The only time he wore it was when he traveled overnight, and when he left this morning that wasn't part of the plan.

"How can you tell?"

"The look of terror on your face back at the diner when I invited you over."

"That was indecision."

"Happily?"

"Happily what?"

"Happily married, you really haven't done anything like this before, have you?"

"Done what?"

"Jesus," Rhonda said bending over to shake out her hair.

"Yes."

"Yes, what?"

"Yes, I'm happily married."

It didn't occur to him to lie, although he supposed most men would have.

"Kids?"

"A boy and a girl."

"How old?"

He couldn't remember at first. He tried to picture Jaime at her last party blowing the candles out on her cake and Scott opening his presents. Jaime had on this frilly white and pink dress with puffy sleeves that he helped her pick out, which his mother hated. She said puffy sleeves were for proms queens, not little girls. Maybe Ellen felt the same way, although she never said a word.

"Nine and twelve."

"Which is which?"

"Boy nine, girl twelve."

He didn't want to give names, somehow that seemed too intimate.

"You were married young."

"Not really, twenty-four."

"I'm not getting married until I turn sixty."

"The selection gets pretty sparse at that age according to my mother."

"I want a man too sick to yell at me and too old to wander. I won't be picky. As long as he's breathing and has a pension."

Rhonda sat down to massage her feet.

"Does your wife work?"

"She's a teacher."

"How did you and . . . what's her name?"

"Ellen."

"How did you and Ellen meet?"

"In a coffee shop."

"Like us," Rhonda said with a chuckle walking into the bedroom. "Keep talking."

"About what?"

"About you."

He really didn't have anything else to say. He wanted to listen instead to Rhonda undress, the soft sounds of her uniform floating down to the floor, her smooth and unhurried breathing. Different from the sounds he was accustomed to at home. Ellen's sighs and groans, ouches from legs that have been bumping into desks for years, and the thud of shoes and clothes crashing to the floor.

"You've never had an affair, have you?" Rhonda said from the bedroom.

"A what?"

"Never cheated on your wife? No girlfriend?"

There was a whirring down below his belt, as if someone had turned on the switch to an old, rusty boiler.

"No, I never had many girlfriends."

"Even in college?"

"I was busy with studying, part-time jobs . . . the anti-war stuff. I met Ellen right after college."

The sounds of undressing stopped.

"Not that I haven't thought about it, I mean what man doesn't. It's just that - I don't know - how do these things happen? Is it by accident? It's not like I've been looking."

"What anti-war stuff?" Rhonda said walking by in her bra and panties on the way to the kitchen.

Her thighs were exactly as advertised, right to the point where they met her buttocks in a seamless transition.

His mouth fell open.

"What anti-war stuff?" she repeated

"The Vietnam War."

"We studied that in high school. It was the first one we ever lost."

Ira watched Rhonda walk back into the bedroom carrying a glass of water. He couldn't remember ever seeing a rear end that firm on a woman, even on Baywatch, which he occasionally came across late at night while roaming the airwaves.

"What did you do?" Rhonda asked.

"About what?"

He heard the sounds of water running in the bathroom.

"With the Vietnam War."

"I wasn't in the war. I had a high draft number."

That was his first taste of those important little certainties in life.

"What did you do against the war?"

He couldn't think of what he did, although it wasn't much. He attended a few teach-ins and rallies, helped print up some leaflets. Maybe he carried a poster once twice. It was a good place to meet coeds, although he didn't have much success. He tried to think of a good answer, but the only thing on his mind was how transparent Rhonda's bra looked and how it might disappear completely in the sunlight.

"Ira?"

He heard Rhonda moving around in the bedroom.

"I attended some protest marches, candlelight vigils, teach-ins, demonstrations against ROTC. Things like that. It wasn't your typical dating scene."

He was talking like a character in the movies, he realized.

"It was a very political time."

"What's ROTC?" Rhonda said.

He figured she was fifteen maybe twenty years younger. How could things have changed that quickly?

"Isn't ROTC still around on campus?"

"Not in nursing school. What is it?"

"It stands for retired . . . no . . . reserve officers training class, something like that. It's to train students to go into the army."

It sounded so sophomoric told twenty years later to a nearly naked nurse and, in particular, to her wonderfully rounded bottom reflected for a brief instant in the mirror on the bedroom closet door.

"We protested once," she said, "when the administration tried to stop students from bringing beer on campus."

He wondered whether the entire anti-war generation was preoccupied with sex and taxes now. The war was ancient history, like a first kiss.

"Anyway," he said trying to get back on track, "last Monday my grandmother died. At the cemetery, I noticed a stone for her daughter, my mother's older sister, who I had never heard of before."

"I already know that."

He knew her eight hours and already he was repeating himself.

"The only thing my Aunt Sarah would tell me was that Eva was at Pilgrim State."

There was no response from the bedroom.

"So here I am," he said.

"And here I am."

Rhonda stepped from the bedroom completely naked, her large perfectly sculptured breasts held at eye level by the invisible forces of youth, her stomach a flat arrow pointing down to the real attraction below.

Every red blood cell rushed up front to gape out of his eyes and he listed forward like a pleasure boat thrown off balance by the weight of its surging passengers. He fell hard against the wall. Rhonda rushed to his rescue, but they both sank like rocks to the floor.

It's no surprise that sex with another woman is different than sex with your wife. There are no fantasies involved since you're actually in one. It also seems more like a spectator sport. Part of him watched the action as if through the lens of a camera. He watched his short, stubby fingers explore unfamiliar terrain, dive in and out of moist crevices and jump from peak to peak. It was as if he were watching himself involuntarily propelled forward by some kind of maddening chemical reaction.

They both reached the finish line close together, something he and Ellen haven't done in a long time. Although, unlike Ellen, Rhonda refused to lie back and enjoy the prosperity. Instead, she jumped up and went into the kitchen to look for something to eat leaving Ira quivering spread eagle on the floor. He moved up onto the couch and the quivering subsided with a shudder. Unfortunately, there was no afghan to cover up with so he curled into a ball. The regrets poured out now in full force, crowding the post-orgasm celebrants into a dark corner.

Had he jeopardized everything for a few moments of passion? Was he changed? Even if no was the answer, he was still in big trouble. He had to be able to wipe this experience out of his mind without any effect whatsoever, despite the fact that he'd recorded every moment like a human VCR. He had to be thorough because Ellen would notice anything different, no matter how slight.

"Try not to feel too guilty," Rhonda said from the kitchen.

"I'm not," Ira said wishing he hadn't seen "Fatal Attraction."

"I mean what's the point. These things happen all the time. It's really just a form of exercise, and you can't get enough of that.

If you think about it, it's not much more than dinner and a movie. There are husbands who consider it a sort of marital duty . . . keeping things fresh . . . take it from me, I know, I've heard all the lines."

He had exercised plenty in his life, Ira thought, and it was nothing like this.

"I have to call Ellen," he said jumping up from the couch.

"You're kidding?"

"I'm not going to say anything, but she's expecting to hear from me. I call every night when I'm away."

"Well you're the exception, not the rule."

Rhonda came out of the kitchen and Ira had to laugh. It felt as if he were in an x-rated movie, the kind he and Ellen sometimes stumbled across late on Saturday nights on HBO or Showtime. Rhonda carried two cheese sandwiches, a couple of beers and two large breasts on a tray.

"Go ahead, I'll be quiet," Rhonda said turning on the television, lowering the sound, and sitting down on the couch to eat.

"Maybe I should go out somewhere to call?"

"Don't be a baby."

Ira started dialing home and then stopped. He didn't want to leave a record of his home number. He couldn't call collect because Rhonda's number would appear on their bill at home, so he charged the call to the company credit card.

That'll be a tough one to explain, he thought.

Ellen picked up on the first ring.

"Ira."

"Hi, I'm stuck in Boston."

"What happened?"

"There was a problem with the final Sinoral market study. You know the one where we swear that randomly selected cold sufferers preferred Sinoral two to one in a blind test. It didn't come out quite right, but it will."

Ira chuckled, Ellen didn't.

"I've got some early morning meetings. I should be home tomorrow at the normal time."

"What are you watching?" Ellen said.

"What do you mean?"

Ira stared at Rhonda's perfect behind as she bent down to change the channel.

"I hear the TV."

"It's on in the background. I'm not really watching anything."

Rhonda turned around and smiled which caused her breasts to jiggle. She had turned on an old MASH rerun.

"Well, I've got numbers to doctor, then I'm going to bed early. The first meeting is at seven. I'll see you tomorrow night."

"Wait a minute, what hotel are you at? What's the phone number?"

Ira held the phone away from his mouth. Could his breathing be any louder?

"It's the Sheraton in Cambridge." He'd stayed at that one once before. "The number on the phone is scratched out, except for the area code . . . 617."

"Well, find out what it is."

"I've got to run to the bathroom. You can get it from information if you need me, but I'll be gone bright and early."

He used bright and early because it was an upbeat Ellen expression, like rise and shine, but all it did was bring the conversation to a screeching halt.

"I'm going to sleep in 5 minutes, as soon as I finish checking these numbers."

"But what if . . . ."

"Don't worry. I'll see you tomorrow."

Rhonda shook her head from side to side.

"OK?"

"OK," Ellen said slowly after a short pause.

"Love you."

They exchanged kisses over the wire; Ira's was a quiet little pucker.

"Not very good at this are you?" Rhonda said without turning away from the television.

"What do you mean? That was fine. This kind of thing happens all the time. I'm always taking last minute trips."

Rhonda shrugged and continued eating.

If he couldn't even lie well to Rhonda, he thought, what could Ellen be thinking?

"What are you going to tell her tomorrow night?"

"What?"

"There's a basement full of old files. You'll never find your aunt's file in one day."

"Well, that's all the time I've got. If I don't find it so be it."

At least he was still good at lying to himself.

Ira sat down next to Rhonda and picked up the cheese sandwich. He was famished. He hadn't eaten a cheese sandwich in years and it tasted great, better than the gourmet concoctions they sold in the sandwich shops that surrounded his office. He couldn't remember ever eating or watching television in the nude. It turned an ordinary act into something extraordinary.

He covered his lap with a napkin.

MASH was on again at eleven, the last rerun of the day. He and Rhonda watched it on the couch since she didn't have a television in the bedroom. Rhonda was wearing a black lace teddy. Ellen would be freezing. He was shivering in Rhonda's terry cloth robe, which barely closed over his stomach.

Back home, Ellen was in bed also watching MASH. She pictured Ira in Boston, not one hundred and twenty-two miles to the northeast on a couch with a nearly naked twenty-something nurse. Ellen wouldn't have believed it. Neither would anyone else.

Rhonda rested a hand on Ira's knee. Ira's muscles tightened right up to the groin. She might as well have stroked the insides of his thigh and reached for her ultimate destination, since it had the same effect. Her robe parted. Having fought most of the night with his stomach, it no longer had the energy to withstand this newest bulge.

Ellen was thinking that she should have called Ira's mother to see how she was feeling, but it had been too hectic. She hoped Ira had called. She thought about calling him in Boston having already gotten the number, but she didn't want to risk waking him knowing how hard it was for him to fall asleep away from home.

Aunt Sarah called in the middle of MASH. She apologized since it was late, but she needed to speak with Ira.

"He's not home," Ellen said. "Is everything all right?"

"Sure."

She had that little Katherine Hepburn tremor in her voice that she always got when something was upsetting her

"I wanted to ask him something."

"What?"

"Nothing important, it can wait. Where is he?"

"On a business trip to Boston . . . are you sure I can't help?"

"No, it can wait. It's just something that popped into my head about my mother. Besides, I'm very tired, I can barely keep my eyes open."

"You want Ira's hotel number in Boston."

"No."

"You're sure nothing's wrong?" Ellen said.

"I'm sure. I'll call him tomorrow."

Ira was in the middle of his second extra-marital experience when Hawkeye yelled "watch out for that bleeder." Ellen was dozing and she woke up with a start. Her chest felt tight, another bad omen. She had this sensation before when her parents were driving to Florida and didn't call from the motel in Georgia where they were supposed to stop to spend the night. It was about the time that they collided with the gasoline truck.

Ellen believed in signs. She and Ira were both superstitious. He knocked wood and she crossed her fingers. When you live long enough to appreciate how precious time is and how easily the day-to-day activities that form the fiber of a relationship can be torn apart, you realize just how important good luck can be.

Hawkeye screamed "we're losing him," and Ellen's eyes snapped open again. She suddenly remembered that Ira didn't ask about the kids, not about Jamie's tryout for the school play or the mail, which was very unlike him.

Ira had another Eva dream. This time he was strapped to a chair and Eva was the doctor. She was in a short, white smock and her legs were every bit as good as Rhonda's.

"This won't hurt a bit," she said holding up a large hypodermic needle.

He believed her. Maybe it was her smile, which didn't appear to hide a thing, or the gentle way she touched his arm when she said it.

"What is it?" he asked barely feeling the injection.

"Truth serum, it'll take away all the doubts and questions."

"What doubts?" he said. "What questions?"

"See what I mean."

FRIDAY

Rhonda could sleep until seven-thirty since she only had a fifteen-minute commute. Ira had been up since six staring at the clock, which moved slower than the bridge traffic on Thanksgiving. He couldn't fall back asleep, because he was accustomed to a bedroom crammed with furniture and pictures, wrapped in wallpaper, slathered with pillows and stuffed with memories. He needed cozy and dark, vacant and dim just didn't do it for him. He must have entered some kind of catatonic state, because one minute he was wondering whether he should get up and get dressed, turning his underwear inside out, and the next minute Rhonda was in the bathroom putting on make-up.

"You getting out of bed?" she said in her best it's-just-another-day tone of voice. "There's no time to stop at the PD."

He knew immediately that PD stood for the Pilgrim Diner, which meant that he was well on his way to becoming a naturalized citizen of the Pilgrim State community.

"What am I supposed to do?"

He pulled Rhonda's bright green comforter up around his neck. It was a color Ellen has banned from the house. She liked the softer beiges and blues. A forest green might be acceptable, but nothing this neon.

"I'll drop you off at personnel and you can apply for the records job. Shirley has arranged everything. You start today. Thank God I'm not on this weekend."

Ira waited for Rhonda to head into the kitchen before getting out of bed. Waking up in the morning, washing and dressing for work seemed more of a betrayal than making love. Casual nakedness and morning rituals are reserved for more meaningful relationships. He dressed quickly, before Rhonda returned. It felt weird putting on the same clothes, almost like college. His throat felt scratchy and his eyes moist. He needed coffee and a roll. He missed the train and the New York Times. Eva was beginning to feel like a chore, the first item on a long list of things to do. She couldn't be ignored and he couldn't procrastinate . . . that wasn't the way he was brought up.

Rhonda walked out of the kitchen.

"There's coffee on the table. It's weak, but that's the way I like it this early."

"Anything to eat?"

"No time."

She had on a short white uniform trimmed in pink. Her body was tight and new again, which made Ira hard as well, although he'd already had his quota for the next month. When does it stop, he wondered? How much more could a man accomplish if he didn't always have sex on the brain.

Rhonda brushed up against him as she passed by erasing that thought from his memory. All he could think about was that he had stepped into a James Bond movie. He'd bed the enemy, won her loyalty, and now he was off to tackle the dangerous role of clerk in the Records Department.

Before going he called American Family. He couldn't be sick because someone might call home, so he left word that he had to fly to Boston to take care of an important matter for his grandmother.

At least now everyone thought he was in Boston.

"I'll follow," Ira said to Rhonda as they stepped outside.

"Why don't you ride with me?"

"I may not stay the whole day."

"They won't let you park without a permit."

"So I'll get another ticket."

"They'll tow you away."

"I'll take my chances."

"Don't be so stubborn."

That was a new label for him, but he liked it.

"If you want to leave early I'll drive you back or else it's a ten dollar cab ride. It'll be cheaper than a ticket or a tow."

"Fine."

The morning was sunny and cold and in the daylight Rhonda's apartment complex looked even more rundown. The paint was peeling everywhere, the windows were dirty, and the concrete stoops were crumbling. There were a few skinny trees out front held up by broomsticks and wire. Old newspapers and soda cans were rolling around the landscape like tumbleweed. It was not the neat, manicured suburban look to which Ira was accustomed.

The ride to Pilgrim State was a miracle mile of franchises from McDonalds to Seven-Eleven. In strip mall after strip mall he saw solitary figures inside stores cranking up the engines of commerce. At a traffic light between Color Tile and The Home Depot, he spotted a pink food wagon offering a full breakfast for $1.89, including coffee. Ira suggested pulling over.

"Not on your life."

"How about Dunkin Donuts, there's one up ahead."

"No time."

Up until five minutes ago none of this existed for him, just like Eva. Now he wondered if he'd ever be able to get any of it out of his mind.

Rhonda took him to Personnel and gave him with a big, wet kiss on the lips. There was a chorus of oohs and aahs and he felt like a turkey on display for Thanksgiving dinner. Fortunately, there wasn't a familiar face in the room.

"I'll drop by during lunch to see how you're doing," she said.

"I'm going to work through lunch."

Rhonda smiled.

"You'll be starving."

"I can afford to miss a few meals."

Rhonda looked down at Ira's stomach.

"I'll stop by anyway."

Every male in personnel watched Rhonda leave with the same thing on their mind, while every female stared at Ira wondering what the attraction could be, since it clearly wasn't looks or money.

Ira expected an application similar to the one on the place mat at Wendy's. Name, address, telephone, social security number, when can you start? Instead, Pilgrim wanted an employment history going back to junior high school. He had to provide the names of family doctors and trace his family tree with respect to mental disorders back to biblical times. Only dental records escaped their interest. He made up most everything, although he was sure that he'd get in as a legatee if he told them he was the nephew of one of an alumnus. Apparently, mental hospitals have to screen applicants a bit more rigorously than fast food restaurants. How much damage could a crazy employee do at Wendy's? Overcook the burgers and drive away the customers? At Pilgrim State, he could keep the customers from ever driving away.

When he brought the completed application to the counter the clerk turned to the last entry, Position Sought: Clerk, Records Department.

"You're the one Shirley mentioned. You didn't have to fill out any of these questions," he said pointing to the answers he made up. "They're only for the jobs working with patients."

So she didn't check for prior convictions, current medications and drug addictions, or mental illness. She didn't ask him to lower his trousers to check the 1971 entry for appendicitis. She didn't even read the short essay on the most influential person in his life. After all, how dangerous could anyone be in records? Instead, she gave him an ID badge and directions.

"Building 808, ground floor, all the way in back, see Shirley, she's in charge."

Shirley was in charge. She took up as much space as a large file cabinet. She was so heavy that the floor creaked beneath her like it was moaning with each breath. The steps were much harder, almost like an earth tremor. Her clothes snapped and popped as she moved as if there were countless microscopic threads giving up the ghost. Buttons lost their grips leaving Shirley like a window without curtains and offering glimpses of skin and hair from all kinds of private places. Her breasts were off the scale. She was no youngster either. She looked like she might predate the oldest paper records at Pilgrim.

Shirley looked up at him and reached into a newly opened box of donuts.

"So your Rhonda's new boyfriend," she said with a chuckle and a jello-like shake of the skin hanging from her neck, "or should I say her married boyfriend."

"Not really."

"Not really married or not really her boyfriend?"

"Not really her boyfriend."

"You're just here looking for your aunt's file?"

"Yes ma'am."

"And having a little fun p-holing along the way."

It took Ira a few seconds to figure out what she meant.

"It was an accident."

"I hope you're insured."

Shirley laughed so hard that everything in the room seemed to wobble.

"Well Ira, it's gonna take a shit-load of work to find her file. Eva, right?"

"Eva Portnoy."

"Here from 1936 to 1968."

"She died here."

"Doesn't everybody."

Shirley sprayed saliva when she talked, a problem no doubt because of excessive secretions aggravated by weight and age. She also smelled like a gym locker. Despite all this, Ira liked her. She had childlike eyes and seemed completely at ease with herself, as if she no longer knew the meaning of self-consciousness.

She couldn't function, he supposed, if she did.

He told her how he learned about Eva.

"Life's full of things you're better off not knowing and if they ain't tellin ya there's usually a pretty good reason for it."

Before he could think of a reply, Shirley stood up. That by itself was something to watch. It was a slow process involving a great deal of muscle stress and tension and a lot of reflexive movements by the furniture and dust in the vicinity.

Her legs made Rhonda's look like a couple of toothpicks.

He followed her down a short flight of stairs to a large, bright fluorescent basement filled with hundreds of boxes.

"Back then doctors were accountable to nobody."

"What does that mean?"

"It means they could do anything they wanted with a patient and write anything they wanted in a file, so most of the stuff in it is useless. I would just toss'em if I had my way, but the big boys want an inventory."

She stretched the last word out into its own sentence.

"Even if you find your aunt's file, it probably won't tell you a damn thing."

"You never know."

Shirley looked at him like a moldy donut.

"Believe me, I know."

"I still want to try."

"It's your life," she said repeating a line his mother used to use when she disagreed with whatever choice he was making when he was younger. Now she'd shake her head and sigh, before looking up at the fan to appeal to his father's spirit for help.

She picked a file out of the nearest box and put it on the counter.

"Everything down her is prior to 1970."

She turned around and opened her arms like it was a benediction. Enough extra skin hung down to make it look like she had wings.

"They're not in any kind of order."

"What do they want you to do with it?" Ira asked.

"Me, nothing, that's why I got to hire a stooge like you. It's what you're supposed to do."

Shirley pulled the stool over slowly, sat down, and opened the file.

"They want a nice little list with the name, patient number, date of admission and date of discharge. Then they want the diagnosis written next to it. That should keep ya plenty busy."

She stared at Ira, like she was examining his face for something, until he nodded back.

"Bugger in your nose," Shirley said.

He took a tissue out of his pocket and wiped his nose.

"I may be getting a little cold," he said.

"Well keep it away from me. You don't want to be around when I sneeze."

He took a step back.

"After you get out the info, the file gets tossed in there," Shirley said pointing to the garbage cans by the stairs. "Just like that, poof, as if they never existed."

Ira wasn't planning to stay around long enough to fill up a garbage can.

"Can I keep my aunt's file when I find it?"

"You ever work for the government before?"

"No."

"Some inspector from Albany with a tie so tight that the blood can't get to his brain is gonna make me sign something swearing that everything was tossed. You can lose a patient, but mess around with the paperwork and they'll string you up by the thumbs."

"But . . . but . . ."

"Don't have a shit fit, I don't give a damn. Take whatever you want. They can't do anything to me. If you can smuggle the sucker out of here without getting caught, it's yours."

Shirley got off the stool.

"It's all right up front, patient name and number."

Ira nodded.

"DOA, that's date of admission, not dead on arrival, although they meant the same thing back then. DOD, I bet you can figure that one out."

Shirley waited for an answer.

"Date of discharge."

"A college graduate," she said showing him a beautiful set of yellow teeth.

"The main diagnosis is on the inside cover. You see this?"

"PS."

"Paranoid-schizophrenic, which means this is a late sixties file. We didn't have that one back in the forties."

Shirley showed him where to write it down.

"Just write down the damn initials, you don't have to know what they mean. I'll be back down in a couple of hours, you'd better have two or three boxes done by then or you're out of here. Don't just go rummaging through the boxes looking for it. I see that and you're out on your can. You can look for your Aunt's file on your own time."

"When's that?"

"Lunch."

Shirley laughed.

"Who knows, maybe you'll get lucky," she said looking Ira up and down from head to toe, "although you don't look much like the lucky type."

Shirley went upstairs rattling the boxes with each step.

"And I'm gonna be peeking down a lot to check on ya, so no hanky panky."

Framed by the small opening at the top of the stairs, Shirley's backside seemed larger than life. The way the moon does on certain summer nights when it appears to fill the sky. Ira sat down on the stool and surveyed his kingdom. He should be at work sipping coffee and planting coupons like seeds in newspapers across the country, not digging through the files of dead, crazy people.

Ellen is at work. She has a two-hour lunch and planning period on Friday, which begins at 11:30. She usually eats first and then marks papers, but today she couldn't do either. She had a sharp pain all morning just below her left breast like some organ has been stretched to its limits and is about to burst. So instead of eating she decided to call the hotel in Boston on the off chance Ira might still be there.

Of course, the hotel didn't have anyone registered by that name.

"When did he check out?"

"We have no record of his checking in."

You would think that a hotel would guard the confidentiality of their guest's records as zealously as a mental institution, after all the embarrassment can be equally as great.

Ellen called the office next. His secretary was out sick and one of the floaters answered.

"He's not here."

"Where is he?"

"I don't know."

"Can you please check with Tom or Paul?"

Ellen resisted the urge to start biting her nails, which she hasn't done since high school.

"He called this morning. He went to Boston to take care of something for his grandmother. She just died."

"I know that."

I'm his goddamned wife, Ellen thought, mumbling "thank you" before hanging up. For a fleeting moment she thought about calling the police, but it didn't take her long to realize that although whatever was happening might be foul, it wasn't foul play.

Ellen felt like her chest was peeling open layer by layer like an onion, her heart beating wildly at the core. She had no idea what Ira was doing, but knew it had to be trouble.

She called Selma next.

"Mom."

"Ellen? What's wrong?"

Ira's mother answered most calls like she was expecting bad news, although Ellen's unusual call during the middle of the school day made her absolutely certain that this time something bad had indeed happened.

"Is it one of the kids?"

"Nothing's wrong Mom. Did Ira go to Boston for something having to do with Grandma Sadie?"

"Are you crazy?"

"Have you spoken to him?"

Selma was speechless, a rarity for Ira's mother, who didn't understand the concept of pausing or punctuation. It wasn't hard for her to put two and two together. She saw Ira talking with Sarah after the funeral and he looked angry, not upset or sad, but angry, and he was standing very close to Eva's stone while he watched the gravediggers fill in her grave.

"I haven't heard from him."

Ellen didn't try to fight back the tears, even though she was at a public phone by the cafeteria with all the teachers and students walking by. She didn't care what they thought. Besides, everyone knew she was an easy crier. She cried when her students did badly on standardized tests or performed well in a school play. She cried at Kodak commercials.

"You have no idea where he is?" Ellen repeated like it was a lesson at the blackboard.

"No."

Teachers are good at spotting the truth, no matter how many layers of self-denial are piled on top of it. They're like little children that way. They also know when to press the attack and when to retreat. They can always sense just how far to push an unwilling student. Ellen realized that Selma must have known more, but she also realized that she wouldn't get anything by pushing her, certainly not right now.

"If you think of something will you call me?"

"Of course dear, call me when you hear from Ira."

"I will."

Ellen didn't have a clue, although she was sure that it wasn't another woman. She knew Ira too long and too well for that. He's too terrified and would be too tongue-tied. Besides, his interest in sex over the years had waned to the point that he stopped making those silly little hints all the time, particularly on the weekends. It suddenly dawned on her that it might have something to do with Aunt Sarah, which might explain why she called so late last night.

Aunt Sarah's line was busy and there was another teacher waiting to use the phone, so Ellen went into the teacher's lounge to grade papers. Fortunately, no one else was around. Grading papers is a lot like watching television. You can do it without thinking. Ellen could put herself on automatic pilot, a red pencil in one hand, and her head in the other. Question by question, check by check, X by X. If you do it long enough eventually you won't feel a thing.

Meanwhile, Ira was making very little progress. He was still on his first box and there were hundreds more to go. He found it hard to rush through them, since each file was filled with so many family secrets. Lost and forgotten lives measured by daily entries on a chart, days of acting out followed by nights of drug-induced silence, hopeful moments of improvement followed by trips and falls down a dark abyss. Two things were clear, the handwriting back then was barely legible and cured was not a word in the Pilgrim State vocabulary. For every step forward, there were two or three steps back. The same entry was repeated over and over again, file after file -- "NO REAL PROGRESS". At this rate, it would take someone--not him--but someone else a couple of months to go through the files. And whoever did it was likely to need his own diagnosis by the time he was finished.

Shirley was probably right that Eva's file wouldn't be much help. What would it tell him that he couldn't figure out? How she died? Did that really matter? That she didn't have many visitors? That she was subject to all kinds of experimental treatment and abuse? He wanted to know what was wrong with her, but he couldn't be sure her file would even tell him that. All the files so far used the same half-dozen diagnoses, as if that's all there were and each patient got to pick theirs out of a hat. He could feel himself slowing down. He wasn't used to missing breakfast and hunger was beginning to crowd out his thoughts about Eva. He was also thirsty and there was nothing at all down in the basement to drink.

He pulled out the next file, which belonged to Edie Steiffel, a resident for twenty-eight years. There was a big C on the inside cover, which he figured stood for catatonic. They had trouble getting her to eat or sleep, but she loved to walk and wander. They lost her once for an entire weekend. How many nieces and nephews were running around, he wondered, unaware that she existed? He could probably open a business and make a good living airing out hidden family skeletons and providing ammunition for grown up children to use if they were lucky enough to have overbearing, demanding parents.

It was almost lunchtime and Shirley hadn't stuck her head down once. Even if he had the energy to tear through every box looking for Eva's file, he wouldn't be able to hide the mess he'd leave in his wake. There was no place to hide anything down here. There was the counter, the stool and a big stuffed chair. Everything else was a garbage can or a box.

He heard Rhonda talking to Shirley upstairs and emptied the files from the second box on to the counter.

"Hi, lover," Rhonda said coming down the stairs.

She came over, leaned against his lap and pressed her lips to his, shooting out her tongue like a snake. She made Ira feel like a high school senior.

"Let's go to the cafeteria, I'm famished."

What would married life be like with her, Ira wondered? How many years would it take for the newness to wear off? Would the age discrepancy make a difference? When would it settle down to Saturday nights only? The front of his shirt was starting to stick to his stomach by the time Shirley started down the stairs.

"Hey be careful," she said, "those files are flammable."

She looked over at what he had completed.

"Not very swift are you?"

Rhonda stood up and took his hand.

"We're going to lunch."

"I'm going to stay," he said.

"All you've had since last night was a cheese sandwich."

"A lot of good you'll be," Shirley said, "you look like you're about to pass out."

He was starving.

"Come on, we can bring it back," Rhonda said pulling him to the stairs.

"Shirl, you want anything?"

"A couple of those big chocolate chip cookies."

Ira's mother called Sarah as soon as she hung up on Ellen. She might be Selma's older sister, but the roles had been reversed long ago. Sarah was unmarried, a child-like state according to Ira's mother, which indicated a need or unconscious desire for supervision. As a result, Selma felt compelled to constantly lecture and advise Sarah.

Sarah had lots of offers when she was younger, not all of them marriage. She had lots of excuses. She lived with her mother for one. She worked in the garment union for another, a union Selma used to complain that was filled with married men.

Sarah always knew the news. Whether it was a scandal in Washington or a family squabble, so Selma knew she'd get an answer.

"Sarah."

"Selma?"

This wasn't Selma's normal calling time. Normally, Sarah would be at the senior citizen's center, but today she was waiting around for Ira's call.

"Ira's not at work. He supposedly went to Boston, something about mom."

"Really."

"Don't give me really, after the funeral you two were talking in the corner of the living room. Don't think I didn't notice how animated he was . . . and how stiff you were. What did Ira see at the cemetery?"

"What do you mean?"

Sarah didn't have a chance.

"You know what I mean. He saw Eva's stone, didn't he? It completely escaped my mind. Ellen just called, she's upset. Where's Ira?"

Selma was zeroing in like one of those smart bombs. She was at her best when there was domestic trouble.

"He saw it, didn't he?"

Sarah sighed into the receiver.

"What did you tell him?"

"Nothing."

"Baloney."

"Nothing really, I told him that Eva was mentally ill and institutionalized. I asked him to leave her alone."

"What did he say?"

"You walked over just at that moment."

Selma held her breath. It helped her think. No one who really knew her would speak to Selma when she was like this.

"What else?"

"Nothing else, the house was full of people."

"Come on Sarah, you must have said something else. Where did he go?"

"Nothing."

Sarah could feel it coming. Selma was going to wear her down. She wouldn't accept anything less than everything Sarah knew. She wasn't going to drop it. She'd bring the subject up again in the next conversation and the conversation after that until she heard everything . . . or exactly what she wanted to hear.

Ira's father was the master. He knew exactly what to do when she got like that - surrender right away and avoid the aggravation.

"I can wait on the phone forever if I have to."

"He was going to ask you," Sarah said," so I told him."

"You shouldn't have done that."

"He's a grown man."

"In some things . . . so he's at Pilgrim State?"

"I guess so."

"You guess so? He's already called you, hasn't he?"

Sarah didn't respond.

"He's an idiot.

69

"I'm sure he's on his way home by now."

"You shouldn't have told him, but what can he find out there now after all these years? Nothing, he's just wasting his time."

"That's what I told him."

"What do I tell Ellen?" Selma said

"I suppose what Ira knows."

"I have to think."

With that Selma hung up the phone. She didn't mean to be rude. She just forgets what she's doing sometimes when she has something else important on her mind. She just put the phone down, like she might put down a book in response to a knock at the front door, then she looked up at the kitchen fan. She couldn't decide whether to tell Ira's father ghost, let alone Ellen.

When they got back from the cafeteria with their lunch, Shirley was sitting at her desk in front of three sandwiches, a big bag of potato chips and two cans of soda. Rhonda added the cookies to the pile.

"Your aunt was admitted in thirty-six," Rhonda said between bites of a ham and cheese sandwich.

Ira nodded.

"Shirl, you started in the thirties, didn't you?"

"Thirty-six."

"The same year," he said.

"Pretty good with the obvious," Shirley said.

That meant Shirley had to be close to eighty.

"After about twenty years it's impossible to leave, whether you're an inmate or a jailer."

"What was it like back then?" Rhonda asked

"I started young," Shirley said, "seventeen. You didn't need a nursing degree back then or a high school diploma. With what they had to pay, they'd hire anyone who didn't act as crazy as the patients."

"Why did you switch to records?" Rhonda said.

"No patients and better yet no doctors."

Shirley started on her next sandwich, but it didn't stop her from talking.

"Besides, I was too old according to the new state guidelines. They don't give a shit about it when it comes to records. I can stay here until I croak."

"Don't you want to retire?" Ira asked.

"With what, to what? I have no family and no money. I suppose I could check in as a patient, but the food sucks."

All the while, Shirley never stopped eating. She could talk clearly out of the side of her mouth and swallow with hardly chewing. She picked up the third sandwich with one hand and took some potato chips with the other.

"I've got the easiest job in the place."

"Did you know Ira's aunt?" Rhonda said clearly a convert to his quest.

"Are you kidding?" Shirley said staring into her last sandwich. "You know how many patients we have here now? Back then we had three times the number. You're talking fifty years and two hundred pounds ago."

"What was it like?" Ira asked.

Ira might be over forty, the father of two children, and the head of a ten million dollar department at a major corporation, but he felt like a schoolboy sitting in the teacher's lunchroom.

Shirley licked the potato chip crumbs off her fingertips, crumbled the bag, and lifted the cookies up to the light.

"They were burnt the other day," she said taking a big bite of one and working her tongue back and forth across her front teeth so as not to miss a single morsel.

"What was it like? It was like another planet. Even the illnesses had different names. There was nervous prostration and cerebral neurosis, no anxiety or schizophrenia. A lot of shell shock."

"From the war?"

"No from peanuts thrown at the circus."

She took another bite of cookie.

"And there were tons of experiments back then. They tried just about everything. We tortured patients with steam and a water hose – they called that hydrotherapy -and when that didn't work we kept'em comatose with drugs for a week at a time. The doctors called that one sleep therapy."

Shirley laughed.

"You're kidding," Rhonda said her mouth full of sandwich.

"We'd bring'em out of it once a day to drink, eat and pee."

Shirley took advantage of a yawn to stuff the rest of the cookie into her mouth.

"There were thyroidectomies, overiectomies and castrations. You name it, they did it. They'd cut out just about anything that sweat. Then they discovered electricity and they zapped'em right in the noggin . . . electrotherapy. Of course, they haven't given up on that one yet. Then there was brain castration. Lobotomies were bigger than me in the late forties and early fifties.

Shirley finished her last cookie.

"If you ask me, the doctors were crazier than the inmates. Still are. I could write a book about it with more sex, violence and drugs than any Joan Collins novel."

Shirley looked around for more food, but there was nothing left.

"One doctor believed that mental illness was caused by lack of oxygen, so he had patients live in tents breathing the pure stuff. Another believed it was too much oxygen, so he'd make up a mix with more carbon dioxide. I remember one jackass who insisted mental illness was caused by white blood cells. Too many or too little, I forget which, so he injected patients with horse blood."

"Horse blood," Rhonda repeated nearly choking on her sandwich.

"And then there was the mummy bag." Shirley laughed. "That was a good name for it, an aluminum foil blanket like a soft refrigerator. Mental illness caused by an overheated brain, a cold body for a healthy mind. What a crock."

Shirley swept the garbage from her lunch into the trashcan under the desk.

"And you expect me to remember one particular patient?"

Ira could see the crystal clear Eva of his dreams wrapped in her portable freezer. There was no turning back. If he gave up now, he'd be haunted by his imagination for the rest of his life.

"Hey I, how about a movie tonight," Rhonda said leaning close and exhaling ham and cheese.

They used to call him "the Big I" in high school. It wasn't meant as a compliment.

"Here for the weekend?" Shirley said.

Rhonda stared at him.

"No."

"What about tonight?"

Ira shrugged and Rhonda went back to her sandwich. He was already thinking about tonight's call to Ellen, Eva's file, his mother's reaction, his job and Rhonda's thighs, although not necessarily in that order.

He raced through ten boxes in the afternoon and still managed to retrieve and enter all the information for the list. A couple of times his heart jumped into his throat, like when he pulled out the file for Ava, who was at Pilgrim for eighteen years, Eve, who stayed for twelve, and Evan, who came for a two-year cup of coffee.

Thanks to Shirley he was beginning to understand the entries. IST was insulin shock therapy, which she called sleep therapy, used in the thirties and forties to induce a coma, which supposedly cured what they now called schizophrenia. MST was metrazol shock therapy, a drug used to induce convulsions. EST was electric shock therapy, still used to fight depression, not your everyday tired-of-commuting and the-bills-never-stop-coming kind of depression, but the kind where you stay in bed on a sunny afternoon with the shades drawn tight eating cookies and watching the food channel on TV.

Apparently they considered any shock to the system beneficial back then. It wasn't surprising that a patient's behavior changed for a while after a week in a coma or an afternoon of violent convulsions. What was surprising was that the doctors considered that a cure. A number of charts showed patients hospitalized for fractures and dislocations of the arm, jaw and shoulder. These were all side effects, according to Shirley, of the violent convulsions. In one file Ira found the patient had a fractured spine. Apparently, they jumped off tables too.

"You know what bones sound like when they snap like that?" Shirley asked and then answered her own question. "Of course not, you're from the scraped knee world. For people like you the ugly can be taken care of with a band-aid. Well, let me describe for you the sound of a bone smashing against a metal table . . . it's like taking a bat to a car bumper."

Shirley popped something into her mouth and chewed with a look of great satisfaction after that particular outburst.

"It was a big problem," Shirley told him, "until they developed Curare to limit muscle response."

"And that reduced the injuries?"

"Reduced yes, eliminated no. There's a nice size graveyard behind the maintenance building, you figure it out."

Late in the afternoon, Shirley came down the stairs with another nurse, a tall, masculine woman about sixty with a speechless irritation about her. The crusted lines on her face made it clear that she hadn't cracked a smile in years.

"This is Nurse Taylor. She's in charge of Building 902."

"THE WOMEN'S WARD," she said.

"One of the women's wards," Shirley said holding one hand against her chest like just standing next to her gave her a bad case of heartburn.

"This is him?"

Nurse Taylor pushed one of the boxes out of the way with her foot.

"A little old to be filing papers."

Ira didn't react he just stood there like he was part of a diorama in the Museum of Natural History – middle age man having gone off the deep end.

"Two of her orderlies are out Monday" Shirley said, "Personnel said she could borrow you."

"But there's a lot to do here," Ira said pointing to the mountain of boxes and feeling a little like Scott in school.

"Old files can wait," Nurse Taylor said sticking her face in his, "live ones can't." A fine mist accompanied the last word.

Shirley made a fish face behind her back.

"Be there six sharp. If you're lucky, it'll only be one day."

With that pronouncement Nurse Taylor marched upstairs. She had one of those long, wiry bodies--hard and dry--like a human washcloth with all the feelings and emotions wrung out.

"This is my first day," he said after she had left.

"So?"

"I'm not qualified."

"So?"

"Can't you just say that you need me?"

Shirley puffed out her cheeks like she was getting ready to throw up.

"What if I refuse?"

"You'll be outta here quicker than you can say paranoia."

What's the big deal, he realized, since he wasn't planning on sticking around next week anyway.

"Then I'll just have to find her file over the weekend."

"No way, doors lock at 5:30 on Friday in Records and we're not open on weekends. That's one of the reasons I took the job."

"You don't have to pay me."

"I don't pay you anyway, it's not my money."

"So what's the problem?"

"The problem is that I need special permission to open after hours. What am I going to tell them? You're only here to find your aunt's file, because you can't get it legally? We'll both be out on our asses," Shirley said patting hers.

"Tell them you'll never finish the project on time if we don't open this weekend."

"There is no on time in this world, this isn't corporate America. Besides, they'd have to pay overtime, which they're not gonna do."

Ira sat back down on the stool.

"That's bureaucracy," Shirley said checking her watch. "Start cleaning up soon cause we're outta here in about 45 minutes."

He would have kicked something if he were the kicking type. Having resolved not to abandon Eva, he had to stay now at least until Tuesday for any chance of finding her file. If he went home for the weekend, he'd never come back, and everything he'd risked to this point would have been in vain.

Ira slumped against his worktable. He had hardly thought about Ellen, Jaime or Scott the entire day. At American Family Care, he sat in meetings picturing Ellen standing at the blackboard, her back to the class. He loved the lines of her shoulders and the back of her neck. Now his head was crowded with strange, unfamiliar faces, places and times. It worried him, although less than he would have expected.

About an hour later he walked out with Shirley. Rhonda didn't get off until six.

"At one time Pilgrim was the largest psychiatric institution in the world with sixteen thousand patients. Today, there are barely twenty-five hundred."

Shirley was warming up to her mentor status. Maybe he was the son she'd always wanted. What a difference from Selma, he realized just being sane would make Shirley proud.

"It's very different now. The big push is discharge . . . what do they call it? Oh yeah, census reduction . . .if they're not considered too dangerous then throw'em out on the street."

Shirley stopped by her car.

"Would they have kept Eva here if she didn't belong?"

She laughed.

"It wasn't a club. People didn't come for a visit. Hardly anyone left back then. If they didn't belong at first they did before too long."

Shirley fumbled with her key. "This was the end of the line, either no one wanted'em back or they had no one. And they needed to keep'em around to fill beds. We got paid from the State by the patient back then."

Shirley drove away in her battered money green Nova and he sat down on the hood of Rhonda's car to imagine all the things that they did to Eva. He imagined her asleep, strapped down to a narrow cot with an army issue wool blanket pulled up to her neck, row after row of comatose strangers lying beside her. Who was around to speak on her behalf? Certainly not his mother, but what about Sarah? How could his grandmother let it happen? Why didn't anyone speak up?

He closed his eyes and watched wave after wave of drug-induced convulsions rip through Eva's body. Her long curly hair began to smoke with each jolt of electricity; her skin grew thinner and thinner until her veins and arteries turned her into a human road map. She'd have had to turn crazy just to endure all that.

His journey down Eva's memory lane was interrupted by an empty telephone booth that stared at him from about forty yards away; screamed at him was more like it.

He called work first. He should have called earlier, but there had been no opportunities since the only phone in Records sat on Shirley's desk. A substitute secretary put him through to Howard before he had a chance to stop her. He was Dan's boss, the head of domestic sales and the wrong man to speak to about the weather, let alone a sudden non-life threatening absence.

"He's been asking for you all afternoon," she said before pressing the transfer button.

There was a joke about Howard at the office that never got stale in the retelling. A heart transplant patient is offered the heart of an Olympic decathlon champion or Howard's heart. Howard's a big blob of a man, about sixty years old, who spends most of the day sitting at his desk trying to stay awake and most of the night thinking up stupid, meaningless duties to add to everyone's job description. He's got lifetime job protection through his wife who is supposedly related to someone in one of the big corner offices in the executive suite.

"I'll take Howard's heart," the patient says without a moment's hesitation, which of course astonishes the doctor.

"But you could have the heart of a superb athlete, why choose Howard's heart?"

"I want a heart that's never been used before."

It always gets a big laugh, although a nervous one, especially from the newcomers, and there are always a lot of new faces in marketing. Supposedly he once overheard someone telling the joke and fired him on the spot. Of course, that was just a rumor. Ira ran through some different excuses in his head, while waiting for him to pick up. It had to be something more than his grandmother's death, perhaps a bad back or problems at home.

"Where the hell have you been?"

An accusation disguised as a question, not a good way to start.

"We've been calling your house all day."

"I'm not home."

"We figured that much out. What's this about Boston?"

"I had something to do for my grandmother's estate."

"It couldn't wait?"

Howard took a moment to yell something at his secretary.

"I need Monday and Tuesday off next week as well."

It slipped out before Ira had a chance to think about it.

"You're kidding, right? Tom's trying to finish up the Sinoral campaign without you. It took him an hour this morning to find the latest run numbers and who knows what problems developed this afternoon. With Tom, the damn coupon could wind up in the middle of the sports page."

"It's all been put to bed," Ira said. "There's really nothing he can do to mess it up."

"Are you kidding, Tom could mess up a hard boiled egg."

Howard was always eating hard boiled eggs. His office reeked of them.

"And there's a new product coming on board with a March 1 release date, a combination stomach acid and headache pill."

"That sounds great," Ira said although he couldn't recall ever getting both at the same time.

"That's not a helluva lot of time."

"We can do March 1 easily."

"What's your problem?"

Ira drew a blank.

"Are you still there?"

"Yes."

"What are you doing that's so god-damn important?"

"I can't talk about it right now."

Good answer. His kids were far better at this than he was. Of course, they've had a lot more practice.

"I can't wait to tell that to Stoddard."

Stoddard was the President of American Family Care.

"Listen, Ira everyone loses a grandparent. It's no big deal. Hell, I've lost both my parents."

He almost sounded proud.

"It's a little more complicated."

"If you're screwing around on company time you'd better get hold of yourself, because AFC isn't playing second fiddle to some afternoon delight."

"Believe me," Ira said, "it's strictly a personal, family matter."

Ira could hear Howard's stomach rumbling over the phone.

"I'll tell you about it when I get back."

"Call Tom every hour on Monday and Tuesday, I don't want him to fuck anything up."

"Definitely, I should be in on Wednesday."

"Should be? That's very considerate of you Ira. I mean only if it's convenient." Howard cleared his throat. "Listen, I want proposals on my desk for this new product by the end of following week, so unless you're in the hospital, you'd better be here Wednesday, no ifs, ands or buts."

Ira wondered if he'd accept a note from Rhonda.

> To whom it may concern:
>
> Please excuse Ira from work.
>
> He has to stay a few more days at
> Pilgrim State Hospital for observation.

Of course, he's the one doing the observing.

"I'll see you then," Ira said.

Howard hung up without bothering to say good-bye.

Ira stared at the phone, but he didn't hear a thing other than the beating of his heart. Was it because he didn't really believe that Howard would do anything more than scream? How could AFC disregard over twenty years of loyal service because of a few unexplainable days? Maybe there was something they pumped into the air at Pilgrim that numbed everyone, because last week he would have fainted dead away after a conversation like that.

Aunt Sarah was next. She answered on the first ring. Usually he had to wait a minute for her to distinguish the telephone from the television and the dozens of other apartment and bodily noises that were distorted as they passed through the wax in her ear. She was obviously sitting in that enormous armchair by the telephone waiting for his call. The overstuffed brown one he used to play in as a kid pretending to be a pilot. He felt badly about putting her through all this. She has been like a second mother to him, sometimes more like the first.

"It's just a matter of time before I find Eva's file."

"No hello?"

"Hello."

"And what do you expect to find?"

She sounded tired.

"The reason why Eva was such a big secret."

"Is that really so hard to figure out?"

"If it's so obvious," Ira said, "why don't you just tell me."

"Your mother knows where you are, I just spoke to her."

That meant he had to tell Ellen before his mother did.

"You lied to Ellen about Boston." Sarah said.

"I was going to tell her tonight."

"But not until you were forced to . . . sound familiar?"

"You can be sure I'll tell her everything."

"Everything?"

Maybe Aunt Sarah sensed something, something different in his voice, some small satisfaction that comes when one fantasy finally gets checked off a long list?

"Little secrets are as essential to life," Sarah said, "as food and water."

"This isn't a little secret."

"It is after all these years. You're just going to reopen a lot of old wounds."

"Spoon feeding me information only makes it worse."

"If I tell you more, will you go home?"

"Yes."

Sarah took a deep breath.

"They did a lot of terrible things to Eva, all kinds of experiments, because we weren't around to stop them."

"What could you have done?"

"I don't know."

"They experimented on everyone."

79

"But we didn't even try. We didn't talk about Eva, because we didn't talk to Eva. My mother was the only one who visited her, she went almost every week, but she never said a word."

"Why didn't Grandma Sadie do something?"

"She was from the old country. She didn't know how to speak up and certainly not to people in authority. Maybe she tried and they didn't listen, I don't know. We didn't ask and she didn't volunteer."

He heard Sarah playing with her knitting needles. Turning her attention to small details was the way she handled her emotions. She retreated, while his mother attacked.

"What did they do to her?"

"I can't remember."

"Can't or won't?"

"Does it make a difference?"

He didn't answer.

"We were young and it was so hard to understand, because Eva was pretty normal until she turned twelve."

"What does pretty normal mean?"

"Like the rest of us."

"How could that be?"

"I don't know. Sometimes people make a wrong turn or something cracks inside them. I suppose it could have been anything. Maybe puberty, too many hormones can make you crazy, you read about that all the time."

Ira thought about Jaime.

"Sometimes it just happens . . . like flipping a switch that turns on a light . . . or turns it off."

"How could she be trusted to take care of my mother?"

"She acted up a lot so they had to pull Eva out of school, but she wasn't like that all the time, and she wasn't dangerous; your mother was fine. She was such a happy little girl."

"My mother?"

"Eva doted on her like she was her own daughter."

"It doesn't make sense."

"Everything doesn't have to have an explanation. Life is not a statistical survey Ira. Some people are born a lot closer to the edge. They're balance is fragile, they easily fall."

Ira didn't respond.

"So are you going home now?" she said.

"I don't know."

"You said you would."

"I didn't say immediately. Besides, that was only if you told me everything."

"If I told you more."

"That meant everything."

"Listen Ira, your promise is to the living not the dead."

"What about my obligation to the truth?"

"That's not an obligation. It's a choice you can't always afford to make."

Last week Ira would have been the first to agree with her.

"I'm sorry," he said, "I can't keep talking. I've got to call Ellen before my mother does."

"Then I'll wish you good luck," she said, "because I think there's more to what your doing out there than what you're telling me, more than you're willing to admit to me or yourself."

She hung up without waiting for a response and he immediately dialed home. Ellen also answered on the first ring.

"Where are you?" she said without waiting for him to speak.

He told her about Eva's stone at the cemetery and the conversation with Aunt Sarah in the living room. He told her about the job at Pilgrim State and Shirley. He even told her about his call to Howard. He told her about everything, everything except Rhonda.

Ellen has been trained to teach socially acceptable behavior, trained to love and admire it. She has a hard time accepting behaviors that deviate from the norm and Ira normally was no different, which is probably one of the reasons that their marriage has been so successful. They both love certainty and hate surprise. Ellen never expected him to let her down, not like this. He was acting like one of her problem students.

"There must be a better way to do this?" she said trying to hide her disappointment like a good teacher.

"I can't turn back now."

"Have you thought it all through? What do you really expect to find?"

"I don't know."

He waited for Ellen to pick up the conversation, but she didn't. He wondered if she could sense Rhonda like a dark cloud on the horizon.

"Maybe if you wrote a few letters," she said.

"I have this feeling that seeing the stone was no accident. That Eva was calling out to me. That there's something I'm supposed to do before they destroy her records."

Ellen couldn't suppress her gasp this time.

"Really Ira, you're talking like some cult member. The wind at the cemetery wasn't a sign. Families have secrets, they all do . . . don't we?"

"What do you mean?"

"You know what I mean."

She meant the miscarriage ten years ago. They never talked about keeping it from anyone, but they did. They never even told his mother.

"It's not the same thing," he said. "It didn't affect anyone."

"It affected us."

"It wasn't something anyone else needed to know."

"So your mother and aunt felt the same way about Eva, is that so strange?"

"It's different. This is a life we're talking about. Eva lived for fifty years, thinking, eating and sleeping, while we all went about our day to day lives as if she didn't exist."

Just saying her name out loud gave him a chill.

"Don't you think we ought to know what kinds of illnesses run in our family?"

Ellen sighed. He had a point. She really couldn't defend what his mother had done, although that didn't excuse how Ira was acting.

"Don't you think she wondered about us?" he said.

"Perhaps, but don't you think there's another way to find out about her without jeopardizing your job?"

Ellen loved to teach with questions.

"Think about it for a moment," she said and then leaned back to wait for an answer.

It was a question for the entire class. The answer should have been very obvious. Ira could feel her eyes over the telephone, the haven't-you-been-listening-to-what-I-just-said look that moved like a laser beam from student to student.

"Ira?"

"Not if I want the whole truth. Besides, I'm not jeopardizing my job."

"What about your call with Howard?"

"He understood."

"I doubt that."

There was a pause while they both listened to each other breathe.

"This isn't like you."

He couldn't deny that.

"It's something I've got to do."

Ellen said a few half-hearted things in support. After all, she had her masters in learning disabilities and knew that you couldn't reach someone without extending a helping hand.

"What time will you be home?"

"Time?"

"As in hour of the day."

"Tuesday."

"What?"

"I can't leave until I find her file. They're about to destroy it."

"This is crazy. What are you going to do there all weekend? Where are you going to stay?"

"I'm going to search for her file and stay at a motel."

"What motel?"

"The same one I stayed at last night."

"What's the name?"

"Who's name?"

"The motel, who did you think I was talking about?"

"I couldn't hear, there's a shift change and the parking lot is filling up with people."

Rhonda walked out the side door toward the car. She pulled down her uniform, which always seemed to cling to her thighs and waved.

"What's the name of the motel?"

"I don't remember."

"You don't remember?"

"It's not a chain. It's some ten-unit job in the middle of nowhere. It's Rest something I forget . . . Rest Haven or Rest Heaven, something like that."

"No one would name a motel Rest Heaven."

"I'll call you later with the name and number."

"I think you should come home tonight and we can talk about it."

"I'll be fine."

Rhonda came closer.

"I have to go, my car's blocking someone."

Ellen started to say something, but he hung up the receiver before she could finish.

"Hi sweetie," Rhonda said giving him a kiss. Her tongue lingered against his lips like a lollipop.

"Calling home?"

"Damn it."

"What?"

"Nothing."

"Come on, spill it."

"I forgot to ask about the kids again."

"I'll remind you next time. Let's go eat."

As they walked to the car, he couldn't shake this feeling that the phone had eyes, Ellen's eyes, and that it was following every step he took with incredulity.

They stopped at the Pilgrim Diner for dinner. Rhonda went right to the counter, even though there were plenty of empty booths. Either it was their place or the place where she met most of her men. Irma was there to greet them.

"I expect an invite to the wedding," she said.

Rhonda laughed.

"What's good tonight?"

"The fish is fresh, try the fisherman's plate. Stay away from the veal it's tougher than I am."

"I'll stick with the chef's salad," Rhonda said.

"How about you?"

Ira flipped through the menu. He never liked eating in diners, except for breakfast. Of course it had every food imaginable from lobster to burritos.

"Any luck finding your aunt?" Irma said tapping her pencil against her order pad.

She ran around the other day slinging omelets and home fries like Frisbees, but she still managed to follow their conversation.

"No."

"Don't look so down in the mouth about it. At least you got a new girlfriend out of the deal."

"I'll take the fried fish platter," he said handing her back the menu.

Ira glanced at his watch. It was six-thirty. He knew exactly what was happening at home. They were in the middle of dinner, probably a roasted chicken that Ellen picked up on the way home from school, baked potatoes and a frozen vegetable warmed in the microwave. It sounded a lot better than the fried fish platter. It wasn't difficult to imagine that he would be the main topic of conversation.

"When will dad be home?" Scott asked.

Scott is always the one who asks the tough questions. He had his mouth full, which helped him get up the nerve.

"Tuesday," Ellen replied without looking up from her plate.

Both Jamie and Scott stopped eating. Gone over the weekend? Ira had never been gone over the weekend. They watched Ellen pick at her food. She didn't want them to see her eyes.

"What's wrong?"

Scott never knows when it's time to remain silent. He takes after his grandmother in that way.

It's hard for Ellen. She believes in always telling children the truth, about illness, about death, about crime, about catastrophe, about everything. Ira, on the other hand, has this irrational need to insulate them from the real world. He's forever changing the channel when bad news comes on, hiding the newspaper after a mass murder, or quieting down any upsetting conversations the moment one of them enters the room.

The kids were five and eight when Ellen's parents died. Ellen explained the life cycle and insisted that they attend the funeral and burial. Of course, she was right. Scott and Jamie handled it all just fine. During the next year, they excitedly pointed out every cemetery they passed like it was a McDonalds or Burger King.

Having raised them with a mixture of Ellen's philosophy and his, they appeared to have turned out at opposite ends of the spectrum. Jamie handled bad news well. Scott generally reacted in terror. Is the murderer in this area? How close? Can there be an earthquake here? Is that tornado in Georgia headed this way?

"It's because of that new cold medicine," Ellen said. "There's a special weekend consumer survey in Boston."

Of course, the truth didn't really matter at this point, since it was a work in progress. Indeed, it was too soon to know the complete truth. Neither Jaime nor Scott believed a word, but they continued eating. If their mother was hiding something, they realized it must be serious.

After they finished eating and went back to their rooms, Ellen sat and stared at the dishes on the table for awhile. For some reason, when she closed her eyes she saw dinners for three and nights alone in bed with no one to press up against for warmth. She didn't talk about it with the same reverence as Ira, but she recognized the importance of routine. The thought of the stillness and uncertainty of the unfamiliar sent a chill up her spine.

After cleaning up the kitchen, Ellen went into the bedroom to lie down. She was normally very intuitive and something told her that there was more to this, more than what Ira was telling her. He seemed in such a big hurry to get off the phone and there was something troubling in his voice, something unsure and evasive, like the words weren't really his. After a while Ellen decided to call a friend. She shut the bedroom door, because there was no noise tonight to mask the conversation. The television was off and the kids' stereos were silent. She could almost hear their shallow breathing.

"God damn him," she muttered after leaning back in bed having realized that Ira didn't ask to speak to the kids. He didn't even ask about them, which made her certain that he still wasn't telling her everything.

The fried fish platter had one of every kind of fish known to man, fried until all that remained was a hard bread crumb shell with white paste inside. It all sat on a bed of hard, sticky rice, the kind he liked to roll into a ball with his fingers until it turned black and he dropped it to the floor when no one was looking.

"Let's go to a movie," Rhonda said.

She liked movies, but refused to go alone. She was between boyfriends and had been for quite a while.

"I'm too tired."

He wanted to disabuse Rhonda of any notion that there was something between them that would survive the next few days.

"Come on, there are some good movies around that I want to see."

"It's been a long week."

"It'll be fun."

Could someone as beautiful as Rhonda want to sleep with him just to have a companion for the movies? Of course, how would he know, he's always had someone to take to the movies.

"You can sleep late tomorrow."

"I'm going to the library early. There's a book there about Pilgrim State I want to read."

Rhonda went back to her salad and he changed the subject. He was good at that part of a relationship.

"I have to work in Building 902 on Monday."

"Shirley told me. She thinks you won't show up."

He was used to challenges like that from his mother.

"I may surprise her."

"Good."

"I have to be there by six."

"Sharp, you have to wake the patients at 6:15."

"If I do, it's just so I can search one more day. If I can't find Eva's file on Tuesday than I'm quitting and the hell with it, I can pretty well figure out what happened to her anyway."

"What?"

"You heard Shirley. She was probably subjected to all kinds of experimental treatment."

"That doesn't explain why your mother kept her a secret."

"Because she could, and everything's always been on a need to know basis with my mother. Besides, I'm sure she didn't want to spoil her image of perfection."

"My mother never worried about that," Rhonda said taking a sip of her coffee. "All she cared about was her booze and her boyfriends. She never liked to be alone, certainly not with me."

Ira nodded slowly and stared straight ahead.

"What's the chance of getting into records over the weekend?" he asked.

"You mean breaking in?"

"I've got an ID."

"You have a key?"

"No."

"That's an administration building. It's shut tighter than a clam on weekends."

"Let's get out of here," Ira said standing up and opening his wallet to pay for both of their dinners. It was the least he could do.

"I'm running low on cash," he said.

"They take credit cards."

Walking out behind Rhonda, watching Rhonda's behind, he wondered whether he'd have the energy for sex. It was not a question he recalled ever asking before.

SATURDAY

Saturday morning Ellen makes pancakes. Sunday's it is scrambled eggs. During the week breakfast is instant oatmeal or cold cereal and a handful of vitamins. She won't let the kids go to school without eating something, but on the weekends it's something warm and it's slow with time to read the newspaper and watch cartoons and just sit there without saying a word.

Rhonda, on the other hand, doesn't cook. She either eats out or eats out of a box. She does boil water, so for breakfast they have instant coffee and puffed rice, which reminded Ira of those little pieces of packing Styrofoam that are impossible to throw away because they stick to everything. He can't imagine that they taste much different. Worse still, he has to eat it dry since there's barely enough milk for the coffee. He can't even make toast because there's no bread.

The breakfast was considerably improved by Rhonda's skin-tight pink body suit, her work out costume. Her nipples stood out like nail pops, which made him feel as if he'd just walked through the looking glass into the Sports Illustrated swimsuit issue. Of course, not five minutes earlier she was in her robe on the floor arranging her stuffed animals, Jake the elephant in the far corner, Steve the one-eyed lion on the other side of the room. Apparently, they weren't getting along. Nick the black dog had to face the window and Jeff the teddy bear lay on his back looking up at the ceiling.

"Unusual names," Ira said since Jaime's stuffed animals were always alliterative--ally alligator, bobby bird and donny dog.

"Old boyfriends," she said.

Perhaps they'll be an Ira the lizard in a few months, he thought, happy to be underfoot anywhere as long as he had a good view of Rhonda. Of course, it could also be Ira the rat.

"I like my coffee hot," he said putting it back into the microwave.

"It doesn't matter to me," Rhonda said going back to her magazine and humming softly as she sipped her weak, cold coffee. It wasn't one of those oh-what-a-beautiful-morning hums, it was more like one of those unconscious background noises people make when they're used to living alone. He'd much rather be listening to Jaime and Scott bickering over the remote and Ellen running through her list of their weekend chores.

"They certainly don't believe in sugar," he said picking up a spoonful of puffed rice.

"No fat or cholesterol either."

He picked up the box and looked at the ingredients, all four of them, rice and three added vitamins.

"This isn't cereal it's filler, like feed for cattle. Cereal needs thirty ingredients, half of which only a chemist can pronounce."

"That's why they're junk. This is good for you."

"It has no taste."

"You'll get used to it."

Fortunately, in a world filled with Corn Pops and Frosted Flakes he didn't have to try.

Some routines transcend relationships. Planning out the day over Saturday breakfast is one. He and Ellen always divide up the chores. She usually does the food shopping, while he takes care of picking up the dry cleaning and chauffeuring the kids around. They'll also discuss dinner plans. Tonight they had dinner plans with the Krigels. He wondered what Ellen would say when she called to cancel. She'd be angry with him for making her lie again.

Of course, he and Rhonda had a similar conversation.

"I'll be at the club till noon," she said, "then I'm going to the mall. I need sneakers and a new bra. Do you need anything?"

"No."

"How about another shirt and some underwear?"

"I'll pick something up."

"How long are you going to be at the library?"

"I don't know."

"Not too late please, because tonight I definitely want to see a movie."

He nodded. There was no point in resisting. He owed her that much.

"Be back by four," she said.

"Fine."

"We might even be able to see two movies."

"Two?"

"You have something better to do?"

He'd never be able stay awake for two movies. He generally had enough trouble getting through one, unless it had a lot of violence and nudity. Of course, Rhonda had to make up for three months of celluloid celibacy.

"I'll buy the local paper," she said, "and check out the times."

"An early show is better."

"I love movie popcorn," Rhonda said sounding a little like Jaime, who discusses the candy she's going to buy long before they get to the theater. "Are you a butter person or plain?"

"Butter," Ira said.

"Too bad, we'll have to get two."

They drove off in opposite directions. Rhonda gave three toots of her horn as she turned left and waved. He watched her in the rearview mirror and felt as if he were starring in his own movie.

"The History of Pilgrim State Hospital" hadn't been touched since he put it back. It was clearly not a popular book. The author was a graduate student named John Eth. It was written in 1959 and looked like his senior thesis. Ira figured that he was probably a sixty-five year old psychiatrist now living somewhere in the Midwest, drowsily listening to women who wanted to be more assertive in their marriage and men who felt unappreciated. Perhaps he was already burned out and owned a string of car washes, where the toughest emotional problem he faced was a customer who took exception to the term "brushless."

Ira turned right to the 1930s and 1940s.

"In the thirties and forties, there was not much hope for the mentally ill in Pilgrim State or public institutions like it. Conditions had advanced little since the late eighteenth century, when Benjamin Rush first advocated humane treatment for the insane. Patients were still beaten, choked and spit on by attendants. They were still underfed and kept in dark, damp cells. They were restrained in straitjackets at night for weeks at a time and hospital conditions remained unsanitary."

Eva would have been better off in prison, he thought. If she had been guilty of some clever fraud or pyramid scheme it might even have given Selma something to brag about.

"Mental hospitals were isolated from the rest of medicine. There was no convincing explanation of the causes of mental illness and no accepted forms of treatment. To move closer to traditional medicine, neurologists began looking for organic reasons. They had high hopes that mental disorders must result from a faulty metabolism, abnormally high or low glandular secretions, dietary or vitamin deficiencies or some other physical cause.

"In their haste to find solutions, all kinds of radical treatments were tried. These treatments were usually intuitive and rarely based on any accepted scientific method of study. Richard von Krafft-Ebing injected fluid obtained from syphilis sores into mental patients and concluded that their illness had a syphilitic base since they had no reaction.

Wagner von Jauregg believed that fever was therapeutic. He inoculated mental patients with vaccines for tuberculosis and typhoid fever and even infected patients with erysipelas. His malarial fever treatment, for which he won the Nobel Price in Medicine and Physiology in 1927, was widely used at Pilgrim State during the early thirties.

"In the late thirties, after it was allegedly proven that it was not the malaria, but the fever that produced some improvement, presumably because the high body temperature killed some invisible virus, hot baths, hot air, radiotherapy, diathermy, infrared light bulbs and electric bags were all used to induce fever."

Eth's thesis made lively reading for someone accustomed to reviewing empirical studies of coupon redemption rates broken down by age, sex and income, especially since he had had so little contact with psychiatrists, psychologists or the mentally ill. They had a neighbor once who took her son to a child psychologist, over her husband's objection, because he was "too fidgety," and a couple they used to go out with who saw a marriage counselor because they argued over everything from the time to the weather. Eventually they divorced and moved away.

Eth deals with a different world. A world of people who have lost the ability to function in society, who live out of supermarket carts, wear heavy overcoats in the middle of the summer, and walk around swatting at invisible rays that emanate from anything electrical; people with problems far more serious than shop-a-holic spouses, whinny children, overbearing parents, claustrophobic jobs and crabgrass.

Ira's head felt heavy, as if it were soaking up Eth's information like a dry sponge. It didn't help that the library was so warm. He put the book down for a moment and shut his eyes.

Eva was such a melodic name, he thought, repeating it silently was almost like counting sheep. It belonged to some cherub-cheeked little girl with simple, trusting eyes or in a nursery rhyme, not a mental institution. With his eyes closed, Ira saw Eva's knowing smile framed by her cascading brown curly hair . . . her eyes shined like a cat . . . glowing green glass embedded in darkness . . . her smooth, red lips . . . un-kissed . . . her skin without a blemish and hands . . . waving at him from what appeared to be a photographer's studio. He was posing in front of a black background, darker than a starless night, all in white like a high school senior at graduation. The loose-fitting gown completely hid her Rhonda-like figure. Suddenly, she passed through the blackness as if it was a door and Ira was pulled in after her as if by an undertow. The other side was filled with light and when his eyes finally adjusted, Ira found himself in a large corridor lined with cots and surrounded by the throbbing, claustrophobic buzz of mental illness.

Every bed was an island of disarray covered with crumpled sheets and blankets that hadn't been washed in months. Every bed had a woman on it tied down by leather straps. There was an overwhelming odor of urine everywhere.

Ira looked around for Eva.

"You," the nurse called out. She was twice as scary as Nurse Taylor with hair so tight that her eyebrows were pulled up in permanent shock.

"Me?"

"No, the idiot tied to the bed next to you."

Ira walked over. He felt this band tightening around his chest and had to fight the urge to flee.

"Start at that end of the hall," she said holding out a picnic basket filled with candy-colored hypodermic needles. "Everyone gets an injection."

"What is it?"

"It's the milk of human kindness. If you needed to know, I'd tell you, but you don't so no questions . . . just do it."

She stuck the basket in his hand. The needles weren't sealed the way they are now. They'd obviously been used before.

"They're dirty," he said.

"Wipe'em on your sleeve if you're so worried."

With that she turned and shared a laugh with a doctor who had materialized behind her. The two of them started walking toward the other end of the hall chatting and giggling like a couple of high school sweethearts.

He could hear every word they said.

"If we keep them all asleep," the doctor said, "we can handle a hundred more patients."

"We can squeeze more in if we use the bathrooms and outside hall," the nurse said.

"That will mean another ten thousand dollars off the top."

"Hawaii here we come."

The doctor opened a door to leave.

"Just try not to lose any more," he said, "or someone's going to start asking questions."

"Lose," Ira called out, "what do you mean by lose."

They couldn't hear him.

Ira still had to do what was expected of him, even in a dream, so he walked to the end of the hall and stopped at the bed by the window. There was no shade and even though it was the middle of the afternoon it was so dim that he could barely see. It was as if the daylight refused to come in. Of course, it was Eva in the cot by the window. She was in a straight jacket with her legs tied down to the bed. Her color was as gray as the sheet on top of her. Her curly hair was matted to the bed, her lips were limp and open, and her empty eyes floated aimlessly up to the ceiling.

"Eva?" he whispered like he'd known her his whole life.

There was no response. He tapped the hypodermic needle with his finger the way the pediatrician did when he gave the kids their vaccinations. He didn't want to give her the shot, but he couldn't help himself. When he brought the needle close to her arm, Eva turned her head and looked right at him her eyes suddenly flooding with consciousness. He expected a look filled with bitterness, but it was sturdy and sweet, like his grandmother's.

"I can untie you," he said.

"No, you'll get in trouble."

"You won't run away."

"So why bother."

The hand holding the needle began to shake.

"What is it?" he asked.

"Insulin," she said, "I've been asleep for years."

She lifted her head to look out the window.

"I used to do that all the time when I was growing up," she said.

"Do what?"

"Stare out the window waiting for father to come home from work. He looked so tiny from the fifth floor, almost like a little bug that someone might squish."

Ira could see the family resemblance. Eva looked a little like his mother and a lot like Sarah, except she was taller and prettier with a soft smile that stood out in this hallway of horrors like a window in an otherwise dark and airless room. Her thick eyebrows and small hands were just like his.

"I also miss the piano," she said.

"You played the piano?"

"I still do. I hear the notes in my head like a story."

"Why don't you just go home?" he said

Eva smiled.

"This is my home."

"This is an institution."

"It's the family institution."

"But it's dirty in here . . . and it smells."

"Not everyone's meant to be happy."

"But there's nothing wrong with you," he said.

"That's not true," she said her eyes glazing over like someone else had just given her the injection. "I'm very bad. I've done some very bad things."

"Like what?"

It was too late. Eva closed her eyes and fell asleep.

Just then the nurse came striding down the hall, a frown on her face so long that it seemed almost as if she were pushing it in front of her.

"Give me that needle."

She raised her hand to stab Ira when he woke up. For a moment he thought that he was home in bed and that the whole thing, Rhonda included, had been a dream, but his watery eyes and stuffed up nose quickly disabused him of that thought. He needed to stretch his legs, so he found a water fountain and practically had to suck on the nozzle to get anything out of it.

He wondered if he should call home. He wondered if Eva was trying to warn him to go home before it was too late. If he didn't believe in ghosts, he didn't see how he could believe in messages from the great beyond. Maybe Ellen was right and he was going a little soft in the head, after all, it did run in the family. He thought about calling his mother to see if she was ready to talk, except he knew that wasn't going to happen. Anything she had to say would be in the form of a lecture and only partially true, and anything he said in response was going to sound stupid, so he walked over to the newspaper rack instead. He hadn't read the Times in three days, which was the longest gap other than during a vacation since college.

A plane had disintegrated in mid-air. Now there were inflation fears. Last week there were recession fears. The Pope flew over a famine-plagued area of Central Africa and gave his blessings from the air. It was either too unsafe to land or he didn't have time. The President was going to meet with the Russian Prime Minister, who was looking for a five billion dollar loan. He could probably live for the rest of his life off the interest on that for one week.

After a little while he drifted back to Eth's book.

"In this therapeutic and theoretical vacuum, therapists were often defensive and frustrated by their own helplessness. They were willing to try almost any treatment provided it had the potential for treating a large numbers of patients with a minimum of trained staff. Few proposals were too radical to be rejected out of hand.

"Attempts to treat mental disorders by the removal of one or more of a patient's endocrine glands were common. It had been known for some time that mental states and moods were influenced by hormonal imbalances. Doctors removed thyroids, ovaries, testis and all or parts of other glands in the thirties.

"Somatic treatments were particularly attractive since they were easy to administer. Sleep therapy or prolonged narcosis became popular at Pilgrim State in the late thirties. The rationale was that sleep would help restore a stressed and exhausted nervous system. By means of barbiturates or opium derivatives, patients were kept comatose for one to two weeks and in some instances for as long as a month. Patients were awakened for brief periods to take nutrition, for bowel and bladder relief, and for routine nursing care. Cures or substantial improvement were reported in seventy to eighty percent of the cases.

"A Swedish psychiatrist's report that the number of white blood cells in schizophrenics was low when their symptoms were most severe and high when they improved led to a treatment originating in North Carolina where horse blood was injected into the cerebro-spinal fluid. This treatment was used very sparingly at Pilgrim because of the difficulty in obtaining the proper kind of blood."

Why a horse, Ira wondered, instead of a dog? Maybe horses didn't get rabies.

"Hypothermia . . . cooling the body with a "mummy bag" was used at Pilgrim State for a brief period in the late thirties and early forties . . . the focal infection theory held that toxins produced by bacteria at infection sites in different parts of the body were carried to the brain . . . . Dr. Emid, a well-known psychologist, believed that psychotics, without exception, had infected teeth. He reported dramatic cures after pulling out all the teeth of his patients."

That must have saved Pilgrim State a ton of money on steak dinners, Ira thought.

"The great breakthrough in the treatment of mental illness seemed to arrive in the early forties with the introduction of three modes of shock treatment, insulin-coma, metrazol-convulsion and electro-convulsive shock therapy, as well as one surgical procedure, commonly known as a prefrontal lobotomy.

"Insulin-coma therapy was discovered by Manfred Joshua Sakel, who claimed to be a direct lineal descendent of Moses Maimonides. Sakel was working at a sanitarium specializing in drug addiction and frequented by theater people. On one occasion, Sakel accidentally induced a mild coma in an actress, a diabetic as well as a drug addict, by giving her an insulin overdose. Her craving for morphine subsided when she regained consciousness. In 1930, Sakel published an article describing insulin therapy as a cure for drug addiction. Subsequently, Sakel induced a deep coma in a patient, again accidentally, by injecting a high dose of insulin. The mental state of the patient, a psychotic and a drug addict, seemed to improve after waking up from the coma."

No one seemed the least bit concerned about Sakel's propensity for accidental overdoses.

"Encouraged by this observation, Sakel initiated animal experiments in his kitchen and established to his satisfaction that comas could be safely induced by insulin and terminated by an infusion of glucose. In 1936, the New York State Commissioner of Mental Health brought Sakel to Pilgrim State to give a course in insulin therapy to twenty-five psychiatrists from different New York State hospitals. Pilgrim State became one of its leading proponents.

"Ladislas von Meduna introduced metrazol-shock therapy after he became convinced from examining the brains of former epileptic and schizophrenic patients that there was a "mutual antagonism" between epilepsy and schizophrenia. In a 1935 paper, Meduna claimed that the convulsions induced by metrozol resulted in complete recovery in ten out of twenty-six patients and good results in three. Metrazol was used in Pilgrim State and around the United States throughout the forties. Eventually, electroshock, which was a more convenient way to induce convulsions, replaced it.

"Electroshock therapy, though first used with schizophrenic patients, was later found to be effective as a treatment for depression. Ugo Cerletti and his colleague Lucio Bini, the developers of electroshock therapy, did not believe that the convulsions produced the improvement, but thought it was due to acro-amines formed in the body in reaction to the stress.

"The press played a major role in promoting the shock therapies. Enthusiastic articles in Reader's Digest, Time and Newsweek greatly exaggerated cures attributed to insulin, metrazol and electroshock. Reporters took little note of the many injuries produced by the convulsions, focusing instead on the short-term changes."

Time and Newsweek, Ira realized, meant that he would have become a believer as well. He didn't have to fall asleep again to see Eva as a guinea pig for every experiment. With no siblings to sustain her, like some lofty ambition or dream, and no mother strong enough to protect her, she would have let them do anything to her provided it had the potential for helping her forget.

He imagined them wheeling her into a walk-in freezer, where men in white coats stared from behind a small window and watched her fingers curl up from the cold.

"Maybe the curling helps the healing," someone suggested and for the rest of the week they splint her fingers around a tennis ball to see what that did.

"On November 12, 1935, in a Lisbon hospital, a neurosurgeon drilled two holes into the skull of a mental patient and injected absolute alcohol directly into the frontal lobes. This operation was performed six more times the following month. In the eighth operation, the procedure was changed. Instead of destroying nerve cells with alcohol, the surgeon inserted a special instrument into the brain and rotated it to cut or crush the nerve fibers in its path. Similar to coring an apple, Egas Moniz, a Portuguese neurologist, called the procedure a "core operation." He later changed the name to "prefrontal leucotomy."

"Moniz asserted that the frontal lobes were the seat of man's psychic activity. He believed that all mental disorders were the result of "fixed thoughts" that interfered with normal mental life.

These "fixed thoughts" resulted from nerve pathways that were stuck in one position like drawbridges unable to open. Effective therapy required the destruction of these abnormal pathways. The areas destroyed would produce emotional changes, he said, but no intellectual impairment."

The library clock struck three. Ira was weak from hunger and he could almost feel his brain swell. He had no doubt there was a head cold in his immediate future. He needed something to relieve the pressure like an extra-strength Excedrin the size of a grapefruit or a double lobotomy. He put Eth's book back on the shelf and left the library.

He stood on the steps for a few minutes to enjoy his return to the present, the cold air outside, and a feeling of relative mental wellness. Feelings which were quickly crowded out by thoughts of Ellen marking papers by the phone while she waited for his call, the kids sitting in their rooms listening to the silence, the gossip beginning at work and Rhonda's body suit. A shudder ran up and down Ira's spine. He wasn't used to such a wide range of emotions.

It should have been a ten-minute drive, but it was getting dark and he got lost. Barely familiar places look very strange at dusk. He didn't recognize the turn off by the small strip mall and drove past it. He was on a flat, barren stretch of road for fifteen minutes before he finally turned around. He couldn't ask for directions, because he didn't even know Rhonda's address. He had to find his way back to Pilgrim State Hospital and start all over again.

As soon as he opened Rhonda's door with the key that she gave him, his eyes began to water. There was a pungent smell that Ira couldn't immediately identify. It was familiar, but there was something missing, like the psychedelic posters, the lava lamp and the parachute covering the ceiling. What was missing was the college dorm, because the marijuana was here.

"I've been waiting," Rhonda said with a big smile, "but I couldn't wait any longer."

She rocked to the music from her cheap little stereo like a metronome. It wasn't like any music he had heard before. It was more like a collection of sounds, someone clapping, water running and a hundred light switches being turned on and off. Rhonda was wearing a long t-shirt that had a picture of two large breasts over her own. They were almost life-like. In fact, they were life-like.

Perhaps she had posed for it at the mall in one of those shops that use computers and video cameras to personalize shirts.

"Tough day at the office dear?" she said undoubtedly noticing his tongue hanging out of his mouth.

He sat down beside her on the couch. He tried pot in college. It was hard to avoid since it was a staple at every party, like potato chips and pretzels. He never got the high everyone raved about. Mostly he got dizzy and hungry. He and Ellen tried some together once at a party just after they were married. She giggled a lot and he sat on the couch eavesdropping on conversations that made absolutely no sense. All anyone did now was drink, fancy drinks that required special high-priced vodkas that never tasted any different to him.

Ira needed something to clear his head.

"I haven't smoked marijuana in twenty years."

"You haven't done much of anything in twenty years," Rhonda said laughing so hard that she slid off the couch.

She handed him the joint.

"This is potent stuff, one of the advantages of working at a hospital, so be careful."

Rhonda took a handful of almonds from a bag she brought back from the store and slid further down on the floor. Her t-shirt slipped up above her thighs. She had nothing on underneath.

"It was called a toke back in college."

"What was?"

"When you took a drag."

"A hit?"

"Yes."

He inhaled and let the smoke out slowly, the way the potheads used to do it in school, except they swaggered about making rings and spirals, as if blowing smoke was a gift from God, like a beautiful singing voice.

He was happy to manage just a modest coughing fit.

"I told you to go slow."

He wondered if he should be doing this. What if some next door neighbor, an out of work trucker, smelled "something queer" and called the police?

"God damn kids," he'd report, "are stinking up the hall with their weed."

He could see the headlines now, AFC executive busted in drug den with lover. Rhonda must qualify for that title by now, sex more than once with the same woman should be all you need, although maybe not if it occurs all in the same week. When it happens that quickly it hardly seems intentional, almost like a car accident. He wondered if he could be considered an accidental cheater.

"Ellen would be shocked."

"What?"

Ira was answering a question Rhonda hadn't asked. Rhonda passed the joint back and he took another hit. This was better than alcohol. Drinking made him sleepy and sometimes gave him a headache. Instead, the headache he had at the library was gone and he felt energized. He started tapping his foot against the floor as if he were playing a tune, while watching every movement Rhonda made as if she were a laboratory rat.

"It used to be everywhere in college," he said following Rhonda to the floor. "I never bought any, although I knew plenty of people who did. I wouldn't know how to get it now. It's probably too expensive anyway, especially when you're saving for a new dining room set."

He wanted to stop talking, but he couldn't.

"There was one guy in college who lived on my floor, Steve, he was a dealer, smoked twenty-four hours a day, seven days a week. Graduated, but I don't know how."

He took another hit.

"The thing was . . ."

He lost the thought.

"What was I saying?"

Rhonda laughed.

"You were talking about Steve."

"Oh yeah, the thing was that you couldn't upset this guy. He was enormous, I think he played football in high school, but he was so quiet that he almost seemed invisible. Always had this little smile on his face, like he had noticed some big green thing stuck between your teeth. I never saw him go to class. He was always sitting on his bed smoking. The dorm could be burning down and he wouldn't have budged."

Ira thought that was hilarious. He thought of Grateful Dead posters going up in smoke all around him while Steven nodded and smiled. Rhonda, however, didn't smile. She wasn't even listening. His legs felt strange. They were so sleepy that he doubted they could support his weight. He tried unsuccessfully to get them to bend, but they were just too relaxed. It didn't concern him because the music changed and he focused on that. It wasn't Barbara Streisand, but it seemed to reach right inside him. He felt the rhythm beating in time with his heart.

"What happened to him?" Rhonda asked.

"Who?"

"Steve."

"He stayed around after we graduated, probably because he was making so much money dealing. I wish I had some of his money now . . . I'd buy that dining room table Ellen's been talking about the last five years. We have this dining room off the kitchen, but it's empty, I mean there's some sort of credenza, I'm not sure what'd you call it, with a vase on top of it, but there's no table, no chairs . . . I'd definitely buy a dining room table."

Ira tried to picture the room in his head with a table.

"There are a bunch of movies I want to see," Rhonda said. "There's one about a bank robbery . . . ."

Now Rhonda was the one talking and Ira wasn't listening. He was wishing instead that she had some good junk food like potato chips, cheese and crackers, or maybe some chocolate chip cookies. There was always something good in the cupboard at home.

"We can do one of the movies tonight," she said, "and the other one tomorrow. We could do a matinee . . . that would be fun."

"Oh god," Ira said.

"What?"

"I forgot to call home."

Rhonda shrugged and took another hit.

The tension descended on Ira like a thick fog. For an instant, he didn't know what he was doing or where he was and he was terrified. He couldn't call Ellen like this. What would he say?

"Snap out of it Sherlock," Rhonda said leaning over to tickle him.

Ira is very ticklish and once Rhonda noticed she came right at him. He almost hyperventilated from laughing so hard. A moment later, he couldn't recall what it was that upset him.

"Don't bogart that joint," he said.

"What?"

"Don't hog it. They used to say bogart in college."

"After Humphrey Bogart?"

"I don't know, maybe."

The music stopped and Rhonda got up to put something else on.

"You like this t-shirt?"

Ira nodded.

"I got it today." Rhonda stuck out her chest. "They're not mine in case you're wondering."

They were the spitting image, but he wasn't going to start comparing them now because the stillness bothered him. The room needed sound, as if they were in some kind of danger without it, more exposed and more likely to be discovered.

"Put something else on," he said choking on his own saliva.

"What was popular twenty years ago?"

"I don't know."

"Come on, name some groups."

"Beatles, Rolling Stones, Herman's Hermits."

"Who?"

"Herman's Hermits."

"You're kidding."

"Mrs. Brown you've got a lovely daughter? I'm Henry the Eighth I am?"

He could see her real breasts jiggling under her t-shirt as she laughed.

"You have any Beatles?

"No, sorry," Rhonda said flashing a very sweet and indulgent smile, "how about the Talking Heads or more of the New Age stuff? Steven Reich is good."

"Anything."

He wanted sound and he wanted it fast.

Rhonda puts on an album that started out sounding like a rope banging against a flagpole.

"What's that?"

"Steven Reich, Music for Eighteen Musicians."

"It sounds more like a bunch of guys with sticks."

They both laughed.

After a while, Ira could make out a string section and some drums. It was repetitious, but reassuring, like the waves at the shore.

"So how was the library?" Rhonda said.

The room was very smoky. He was sitting there with this nearly naked girl layered with breasts thinking that this couldn't really be happening. Maybe he was really at home watching TV.

"Ira, are you still here?"

He wanted to reach out and grab Rhonda's breasts or the picture of Rhonda's breasts, but he couldn't move. He had something to say first. It had to do with Eva and Pilgrim State. It also had to do with Ellen and the kids, his mother, Aunt Sarah, American Family Care, Rhonda, and just about everything and everybody.

"When I was a child," he said very slowly and deliberately, "I couldn't wait to become an adult. I had this feeling that it would happen suddenly like stepping over a line and the rest of life would be somehow different."

He was holding the tiniest piece of the joint. It was about out. He kept thinking roach, but he didn't know why. He had to finish his thought, but it was getting more and more complicated.

"Instead, one day you're an adult and nothing changes. You're still living in the same type of house, following the same routines, moving from paycheck to paycheck, from holiday to holiday, with the same highs and lows that have been set in stone forever."

The blissful look on Rhonda's face made it clear that she wasn't following any of this.

"Then you see all these mentally ill people who become adults . . . like Eva . . . life bursts in on them like a locomotive. It hardly seems fair."

Ira took a deep breath. It seemed like the most profound thought he'd ever had. He wanted to write it down, but he'd already forgotten it. He looked up at Rhonda for confirmation and she stared at him for what seemed like an eternity.

Just then there was a long, slow whistle from a passing train.

"If it bursts through the living room," Rhonda said, "we're in big trouble."

They both lost it, laughing loud and hard until it hurt, until they were rolling on the floor like little children, tears running down their cheeks. He reached the picture of a breast and found the real thing. They keep laughing until they both realized that they were making love at which point the laughter was replaced by sighs, moans and occasional chuckles.

It was the longest and shortest sexual experience that he'd ever had. Every part of him that Rhonda touched stayed touched long after she moved on, sort of the way a pond seems to ripple forever after you throw in a stone. He had an orgasm in what seemed like an instant, but it never really ended. He could still feel traces of it later that night. He couldn't remember whether Rhonda had one. He thought so, but he wasn't sure. It's something that he was always aware of with Ellen.

When it was over, Rhonda drifted off to sleep on the carpet. He wanted to do the same, except there was a small voice in his head, like a drowning boy in the distance, crying out "call home."

Jamie and Scott were in the den watching television. Watching is probably the wrong word. They were facing the screen and the images of high school girls in tight tops flirting with young men in tighter pants were reflected on the surface of their retinas, but nothing was actually registering in their brains. Their inner vision, the one that really mattered, was staring out the back of their heads toward the bedroom where Ellen paced back and forth beside the telephone looking at her watch.

"Almost six," she whispered to herself.

She had stayed home all day, so there would be no chance of missing his call. She hadn't even started dinner yet.

As soon as she left the bedroom to put up water for spaghetti, the phone rang.

"I got it," she screamed picking up the receiver, but pausing before she put it to her ear to straighten her hair. Her hair has always been a kind of tranquilizer for Ellen.

"Hello," she said in a calm practiced voice.

"Has he called?"

"Oh it's you."

"Me?" Ira's mother said accustomed to a warmer greeting.

"He hasn't called."

"I don't understand it."

She really didn't. With all Ira's failings, his lack of great purpose and social invisibility, he'd never been one to act rashly. He learned early and well the sine qua non of life that every act has a corresponding consequence.

"I don't understand why you and Aunt Sarah won't tell him what he wants to know."

"Sarah did."

Ellen looked up at the ceiling and gave the phone a shake as if his mother was actually inside it.

"Eva was different," Selma said. "She couldn't live a normal life so she lived at Pilgrim State. What more is there tell?"

"There's obviously a lot more."

"Like what?"

Selma sounded like one of Ellen's students. The obvious was always the hardest thing for them to admit to or see.

"How was she different? Was she violent? Learning disabled? Mentally challenged?"

"Emotionally disturbed."

"In what way?"

"Everything wasn't so clearly labeled back then," Selma said.

"How did it manifest itself in terms of her behavior?"

"She didn't speak much and used to spend hours staring out the window. She'd wrap her arms around her chest and rock back and forth. Sometimes she'd cry and bang her head against the wall. She was more a danger to herself than anyone else."

"They don't put people away for life for that."

"They did back then."

"I don't believe it."

"People didn't know their rights. Money was tight; everyone was working. You just had to accept some things the way they were and let them go."

"Why keep her secret?"

"Because it was considered an embarrassment back then, some kind of disgrace, as if we were being punishment for having done something wrong."

"What a shame," Ellen said.

"My mother was sure that someone gave her the evil eye when she was pregnant with Eva."

"Now I know where Ira gets all his superstitions."

"It's easier to forget something if you don't talk about it."

"Something . . . not someone."

"That's nonsense," Selma said.

Ellen looked at her watch.

"I should hang up," Ellen said.

"Eva wasn't stupid. I remember my father bought her a second hand piano and she taught herself to play. During the summer you could hear her from the street. She was pretty good considering she never had a lesson."

"She could learn to play the piano," Ellen said, "but not how to live in the real world?"

"It's hard enough when you're normal."

"Where was your father during all this?"

"He kept things in the family. He didn't trust outsiders. He wouldn't let Eva out of the house."

Ellen sat down on the bed and began to twirl her hair. Being a second or third generation American, she thought, is almost like being from another planet.

"She got a lot worse after my father died. He was only 44 when he had the heart attack. They took her away about a year later."

"So no one talked about her because they were embarrassed?"

"What would be the point?"

"Did you visit her?"

"My mother did . . . almost every week."

"You didn't?"

"She wasn't the same person. I was very young when she left. My mother wouldn't let me at first. Don't think I haven't regretted it every minute of my life."

"Listen, Selma, I need to hang up. I want to keep the phone free for Ira."

"Call me as soon as you hear from him."

"I will."

Ellen lay down on the bed and closed her eyes. She didn't understand anyone's behavior at this point – Selma's, Sarah's or Ira's. Eva was treated unfairly and now it was coming back to haunt all of them. She tried shutting out the feelings of vulnerability that were cluttering up her thoughts. She needed a fifteen-minute nap. The divorced and widowed teachers at work swore that all the grieving and coping sessions weren't worth one good night's sleep.

The telephone rang a moment later and Ellen's hand shot out like she was corralling a runaway student. She had the same conversation with Sarah that she just had with Selma, but with a twist.

"Why the special concern for Ira's mother?" Ellen asked. "Why is bringing Eva up any different for you than Selma?"

"What do you mean?"

"Ira said you told him that after the funeral."

Sarah didn't respond right away.

"You told him it would kill her."

Sarah took a moment to think it over.

"Eva was the beauty of the family. She had these long eyebrows and eyelashes and dark, promising eyes. My father used to say she could stop a bird in mid-air. Her hair was so black that it was almost scary, like absolute silence, and she had these big curls that fell against her shoulders. You just wanted to reach out and touch them. And she blossomed early, if you know what I mean. Men turned their heads when she went outside."

"What about Selma?"

"We lived in a small apartment and had to double up on beds. Selma slept with Eva. And she stayed with her when we were all out working or in school."

"Eva didn't go to school?"

"She did in the beginning. When she got older they didn't want her any more. They said she was too disruptive."

"They'd have to take her now," Ellen said.

"They didn't back then. They were together every day until Selma started school, and Eva was the one waiting for her with something to eat when she came home."

"She doesn't sound like someone who ought to be committed for life."

"She suddenly got worse."

"Did something happen?"

"I don't know."

"Did she see a doctor?"

"Not until Pilgrim State. After Eva went away, Selma wouldn't talk about her. She threw away everything that reminded her of Eva. Selma changed after that. I don't know how else to put it. She became hard - hard on herself and hard on everyone else. She wasn't always the way she is now. She used to be happy. She never saw Eva again."

"Did you?"

"A couple of times early on, but it seemed to upset her more than help. My mother kept going until Eva died."

"What did she say about Eva?"

"That she got a lot worse and after a while didn't want to come home, or couldn't have even if she wanted to."

"What else should I know?"

"Nothing."

Ellen shook her head from side to side. Sarah's answer was too quick and too emphatic. She didn't have to be a third grade teacher to know that she was still hiding something. Ellen looked at her watch again.

"I don't want to tie up the telephone in case Ira's trying to call."

"Call me when you hear from him."

"I will."

Ellen's eyes were moist and she went into the bathroom to sit, a place where she knew she'd be left alone.

Of course, when Ira tried to call the line was busy. He was so dizzy and disoriented from the marijuana that he couldn't remember whether a busy signal automatically converted to a regular ring when the other conversation ended, so he sat at the kitchen table with the phone to his ear waiting for Ellen to finish. He must have been listening to the busy signal for a good five minutes before Rhonda came in. She was already dressed.

"We have to get going."

"In a little bit."

"We'll miss the early show if we don't leave now."

"I have to call home."

"Do it later."

He could feel his heart beating to the rhythm of the busy signal.

"You promised."

Those were magic words in Selma-land.

"The movie starts at 6:30. We'll be home way before eleven. You can call Ellen then."

Ira was feeling light-headed and hungry, but hearing Rhonda say Ellen's name like she were casually referring to his ex made him want to hang up and run.

"Come on Ira, hang up."

The phone was still busy, so that's what he did.

Rhonda insisted on driving, probably to make sure he wouldn't run off at the theater. In any event, he didn't resist. He was still feeling weird, like he couldn't make his mind up whether to start giggling, apologizing or crying.

The Cineplex was a 12-theater complex. At this early hour it was filled with big American cars belonging to retired couples who had already eaten and were making an early night of it. There were at least six movies that Ira would have liked to see, but Rhonda dragged him to one he didn't--"Twins."

Danny DeVito played a short, fat city slicker and, believe it or not, a womanizer. Arnold Schwarzenegger played a tall, muscular

Adonis, a virgin from Hawaii with a pure heart and a head filled with innocent thoughts. It turns out that they are brothers, twins no less, the result of a genetic experiment gone awry. A disaster of such magnitude that their mother was told they both died at birth. The movie follows Danny and Arnie as they chase two sisters, not twins, flee from gangsters, hold a secret weapon hostage, search for their mother and strike it rich. Arnie disarms every bad guy with a philosophical phrase and a single punch. There are little subplots like Arnie losing his virginity, albeit a little late, and Danny learning that honesty also pays, although somewhat less.

Rhonda loved it. Medical science got what it deserved when the former head of the genetic project was flattened. An innocent in the big city got educated. The good guys wound up rich and in love. Rhonda laughed at every appropriate moment. Only a test audience composed of legions of Rhondas, Ira realized, could have convinced the studio that they had a winner.

Ira hated it. It was based on the premise that different people don't belong together. They didn't even belong in the same room. Short people should stay with short people and attractive people with attractive people. All you have to do is mix them together to get comedy. The characters were stupid and unbelievable. Ira identified with Danny DeVito, which is no way to enjoy a movie.

Rhonda was in such a great mood afterward that she didn't even suggest a double feature. This one movie was enough to erase the pictures in her mind of old women in various states of undress, whining like children and displaying body parts like jewelry. All she wanted was a quick burger at the drive-through, which was OK with Ira, and she was ready to race into the bedroom as soon as they got back. Ira insisted that he had to call home first. So Rhonda took a shower while he went into the kitchen.

At home the telephone rang and everyone froze. It was almost ten, a little late for an ordinary call. This time Ellen let it ring. After a few rings, Jaime answered from the kitchen.

"Hello."

"Jamie."

"It's Dad," she called out. "Where are you?"

"I'm still in Long Island."

"I thought you were in Boston."

"I was, but now I'm in Long Island."

"When are you coming home," she said her voice falling like it was being pulled down by gravity.

"Soon."

"Soon?"

That was not a good answer, he realized. Jaime needed something more definite.

"In a few days."

"Days?"

That wasn't any better. She wanted something both definite and immediate like tonight or tomorrow morning. Kids loved certainty and routine just as much if not more than adults.

Jamie didn't say another word. She was probably afraid of the next question and answer. He could imagine the moisture gathering at the corners of her eyes, the place where she'll probably develop crow's feet if she takes after his side of the family.

"Put Mom on."

"MOM," Jamie called out, "IT'S DAD."

"Tell him he'll just have to wait a minute, I'm busy."

"She'll pick up in a minute."

"What's she doing?"

"I don't know . . . nothing."

Jaime held the phone away from her ear.

"MOM."

Ellen waited a little longer before picking up and then she waited for Jaime to hang up before speaking.

"I'm listening," she said.

"I worked all day, but no luck, and I spent the evening at the library. I found this thesis on Pilgrim State covering the years that Eva was there. The things that they did to patients back then were unbelievable."

Ellen didn't respond.

"They pulled teeth, induced fevers, and tried to freeze them."

"I've been waiting all day for your call."

"I was stuck in a dingy basement going through files. There wasn't a phone within a hundred yards."

"What about after?"

"I'm sorry I was in a hurry to get to the library before it closed."

"Where were you the rest of the night? No library stays open this late on Saturday."

"They didn't kick me out until eight. I was famished and went to get something to eat. I just lost track of the time."

He realized right away that was a dumb thing to say. He never lost track of the time. His watch never left his arm, not even when he showered, and he could glance at it out of the corner of his eye in the middle of a one on one conversation without the other person realizing it.

"Scott," Ellen said, "please move away from the door."

He could picture Scott lying there listening to every word, imagining the parts of the conversation that he couldn't hear, imagining that they sounded much worse than they actually were.

"There's a shortage of orderlies, so I have to work in a ward on Monday."

"Monday?"

Ellen cleared her throat. Ira doubted that she was buying any of this, but what could she do over the telephone.

"I can't quit now, not after all I've gone through, not until I find Eva's file."

Ellen tapped her foot like she did when the class misbehaved.

"I'm getting close. I must have gone through a thousand old files already . . . half the boxes in the basement. It can't be much longer. Shirley, she's in charge of records, said I can take it with me. I'm on my way home the moment I find it."

"And if it takes a week."

"It won't take that long."

"And what about your real job? What about AFC?"

He didn't answer, because Rhonda slammed the door as she left the bathroom. They could probably hear her in the next building. Maybe when you live alone you need to make more noise when you do things, just to make sure it's not all a dream.

"This is ridiculous," Ellen said.

Rhonda turned on the TV and started humming to a music video.

"What is that?"

"Music."

"I can hear that. Where is it coming from?"

Ira snapped his fingers to get Rhonda's attention and she stopped humming and turned down the TV.

"Some passing car."

"I think you should come home tonight, we can try to find out more together."

"Shirley says they're going to destroy the old files in the next 30 days. It may be too late."

"We don't need the file. Your mother and Selma are beginning to talk. We'll piece it all together."

Rhonda came into the kitchen and took a can of soda from the refrigerator. She smiled and moved closer to him. He put his finger to his lips menacingly, but he couldn't be menacing. He didn't have the eyes or the mouth. He didn't stand up straight enough or stick out his chest the way Arnold Schwarzenegger did. He was too much like Danny DeVito to intimidate anyone.

"Who's there with you?"

He turned his back on Rhonda.

"No one, I'm alone."

"I hear someone."

"The television."

"Then where was the car passing?"

"Outside the motel window."

Rhonda sighed.

"What's going to happen at work?" she asked again.

"Nothing, they gave me the time off."

"That's just until Wednesday."

"I'll find her file by then. A few more days wouldn't matter anyway; the Sinoral campaign is under control."

"That's not what Tom said. He called this afternoon to see if you were all right. He said Howard was pretty annoyed and told him you'd better be back by Wednesday or else."

"Or else what?"

"You figure it out."

Rhonda came up from behind him and started to rub her palm against his crotch. He got angry, but it began to react anyway. It has been subject to schedules and confined to the same places for so long that it appeared to be rising in rebellion, as if it had a mind of its own. Ira was afraid that Ellen would hear Rhonda's heavy breathing as well as his own.

"I'll call again tomorrow."

"Where are you? What's your number?"

"516-359 . . . ." Ira stopped. He couldn't believe that he was about to give her Rhonda's number. "I can't read the rest, it's crossed out. I'll be at Pilgrim State all day tomorrow."

"On Sunday?"

"Mental hospitals never close."

"Not even the record department?"

"I'll call tomorrow, I promise."

"Listen Ira," Ellen said lowering her voice to a whisper, "I don't know what's going on, but it's more than just Eva. If you're not home tomorrow, maybe you shouldn't bother."

With that Ellen slammed down the telephone and went back to the bathroom to throw up, while Ira dropped his to the floor. He has never made love on a kitchen table before. When you're on the bottom looking up like that, it made the bright overhead light feel almost like an interrogation. With the kitchen cabinets and the stove looking on, it could be a new, erotic way of preparing dinner. In any event, it was hard on his back and would have really strained it if it wasn't over so quickly

Rhonda and Ira climbed into bed afterward, but not until she carefully placed her menagerie of ex-boyfriends out of sight under the window facing the wall. Jaime's stuffed animals slept at the foot of the bed where they could watch over her. Rhonda's stuffed animals were apparently on a limited "need to know" basis, like Ira. The two of them lay still for a while, both on their backs, their breathing hardly noticeable in the quiet of these sleepless moments.

"Why do you think my family kept Eva a secret?" Ira said, breaking the spell.

Rhonda let out a loud breath, as if she'd been holding it in.

"Most families do. It's not something you want to advertise. After a while, there are fewer and fewer visits. I think most people prefer to forget."

Ira couldn't argue with that. He'd prefer to forget if he could and it had been barely a week. He didn't know if it was him or the thin walls of Rhonda's apartment, but he was aware of every car that drove by and every person who fumbled with his key at the door. He slept much better to the sound of crickets and the creaking of his suburban home.

"Are you going to stay until you find her file?"

"I can only stay through Tuesday . . . if that's OK with you."

"Whatever," Rhonda said rolling onto her side away from him.

SUNDAY

No luxuriating in bed, no fresh rolls, no big breakfast and no Sunday paper. The only thing that distinguished Sunday morning from Saturday morning was a headache. The result of falling off last night's high. He felt achy, tired, empty and confused. Every time he looked out the window, through the torn white curtains to the hard blacktop outside it was all he could do to keep his eyes from spilling over.

Sunday mornings are for waking up in your own bed with your own family.

"Can you pass me a tissue?" Rhonda said.

Ira handed over the whole box. She took one, tore it into pieces and put the pieces between her toes. They'd been sitting side by side on the couch for the last half-hour without saying a word. It was almost ten and Rhonda, still in her robe, was working on her toenails. First she trimmed and filed them. Now she was preparing them for the polish.

Who saw toes in the middle of the winter? Ira wondered.

He had been dressed since eight and looked through every magazine in the house, including a year's worth of Glamour and People. The names and faces change from issue to issue, but the stories are always the same, some great tragedy or astounding success.

The only thing that they'd talked about since getting out of bed was food, because there wasn't any. There was no cereal, no bread, not even milk for coffee. Just a few containers of yogurt and he refused to make that his Sunday breakfast. Rhonda promised to go to the grocery store after finishing her nails. He thought that would be ten or fifteen minutes, not two hours.

"Food's just never been that important to me," Rhonda said the intensity in her face fully focused on the small brush applicator.

"You always have to brush in the same direction," she said when she noticed him staring. "Doesn't your wife do her nails?"

"She says it's not worth the effort since they'll just get ruined again in school."

"Pilgrim's not much better, that's why I do it every Sunday."

She brought her face down to her feet. He wished he were that flexible.

"I grew up on peanut butter and jelly, macaroni and cheese," she said, "anything quick and easy."

"Each of us is a shattered urn, grass that withers, a flower that fades, a shadow moving on, a cloud passing by, a particle of dust floating on the wind, a dream soon forgotten."

"Cheery guy," Ira said.

"Sssh."

Rhonda leaned toward the screen, not for a closer look, but for a better view of her toenails.

"Damn I'm good."

"But you are the eternal King, the everlasting Lord God."

Living rooms around the cable nation might resound with Hallelujah and Amen, but Ira could hear none coming from any of the other apartments in the building. The choir began to sway and hum behind him.

"You want me to do your finger nails?" Rhonda asked.

"I'll pass."

"Not with color, clear."

"I prefer to chew them the way they are . . . tasteless."

Reverend Dean looked right at him.

"A wise sage once asked his pupils if a man has a thousand dollars and gives three hundred to charity, what does he have left? Seven hundred his students called out looking at each other in utter disbelief that their teacher had given them such an easy question. Wrong, he said, that seven hundred will soon disappear to pay bills and taxes. It may get lost or stolen. What he has left is three hundred dollars, the three hundred dollars he gave to do God's work . . . that gets credited to him on God's ledger for all eternity."

An address appeared on the screen for donations.

"Do you ever send money?" Ira asked.

"Are you kidding?" Rhonda got up and shut off the television. "Let's go to an early movie."

"Now?"

"No, later in the afternoon, I'm going to buy some food now." She picked up his money. "And you can go buy some clothes."

Ira looked down at the Bud sweatshirt he was wearing that Rhonda found in her closet left there by one of her old boyfriends.

"Is there a discount clothing store nearby?"

He would feel too guilty buying something nice.

"There's one about every mile once you hit the main drag. Try Big Bob's."

117

Rhonda removed the tissues from between her toes and went into the bedroom to get dressed.

"It's almost noon. I'll meet you back here at two."

Once again they drove off in different directions.

He hated shopping alone. He always went with Ellen and usually followed her around the store like a puppy. She picked out all his clothes. In fact, she bought most of them without him, just like his mother, except Ellen picked out clothes she thought he'd like, as opposed to what she liked, and she wasn't the least bit insulted if she had to return anything.

He came back quickly with two pair of socks for one dollar, three pair of underwear for four dollars and an irregular Ralph Lauren shirt for $12.99. Pretty good, he thought, for an amateur. Rhonda was in the kitchen putting away groceries.

"I bought you a present," she said, "two actually."

"You didn't have to."

"I know I didn't have to, I wanted to."

He thought about refusing to accept anything. He hated to raise Rhonda's expectations and wished that he had the nerve to tell her she was putting too much effort into this non-relationship. He also wished that he had called Ellen from the store.

"I bought you some tryptophane. It's a vitamin that increases stamina and reduces stress. It's supposed to be good for sex."

"How?"

"It speeds recovery. You know, so you're ready again quicker."

It was not a complaint he ever recalled hearing. Of course, he's never had a request for an instant replay before. Rhonda put a couple on the table with a glass of water and he took them both.

"Give it a few days and see if you notice any difference."

He noticed a difference quicker than that. The next time he went to the bathroom his urine had turned neon yellow.

Then Rhonda made him close his eyes and hold out his hand.

"What is it?"

"It's a crystal."

"A crystal what?"

"Just a crystal."

"Like a rock?"

"Not like a rock, rocks are black and dirty, this is something special. It comes from deep in the earth. You haven't heard about crystals?"

Ira shook his head from side to side.

"Where have you been the last few years?"

"I'm never in on the new fads unless my kids tell me about them."

"This isn't a fad. People have been using crystals for thousands of years."

"Like a rabbit's foot?"

"Not for luck, not like a rabbit's foot, and how can that be lucky? It certainly wasn't lucky for the rabbit that lost its foot."

"It's not really a foot," Ira said. "It's a replica of a foot."

"Crystals have healing powers. It's a power derived from the earth. They help with headaches, stress, even menstrual cramps."

"I haven't had too many of those lately."

"A lot of the nurses carry crystals."

"Even Shirley?"

"You can't measure anything by Shirley."

Rhonda suddenly reminded him of Jamie, trying to convince him why she desperately needed another sixty-dollar Gap sweatshirt. Everyone else had two and without another color she wouldn't be able to show her face in school.

"So what do you think?"

It felt good in his hand, but so do most rocks small enough to throw at a tree or into a pond.

"You have to hold it in your fist and close your eyes. I've got one that's two million years old. I can feel the energy."

"What energy?"

"The energy that went into forming it, it gets locked in. I don't know how to describe it. It's sort of like a jolt of strong caffeine."

"I'd rather have the coffee."

"Be serious. A crystal is a sort of connection."

"A connection to what?"

Rhonda thought about it.

"The cosmos I suppose."

Ira wasn't sure that he really wanted to be connected to the cosmos, he was having enough trouble staying connected lately to his life, but he made a fist and closed his eyes.

"I don't feel a thing."

"Of course not, it has to be turned on."

"What does it need, batteries?"

Rhonda snatched it back.

"You have to cleanse a crystal, free the energy by soaking it overnight in salt water. After that you can't let anyone else touch it, otherwise you'll break the bond."

"I'm bonding with a crystal?"

"Don't be such a jerk. You're bonding with a form of spiritual energy. There's a lot more about life that we don't know than we do."

Rhonda filled a cereal bowl with salt water and put his crystal into it.

It was hard to imagine how the powers of the universe could be liberated in a bowl that until a few days ago held Puffed Rice and milk. It was also hard to believe that a nurse, a woman of science, could buy into any of this, even a nurse in a mental institution.

"You can take it out tomorrow."

What would Ellen think? Teachers are such empirical creatures. They need facts and studies, although Ellen is so open-minded and, unlike him, can believe as easily as she understands.

They went for lunch at the diner.

"The lovebirds are back." Irma said.

"We're going to an early movie," Rhonda said.

"Any recommendations?" Ira said staring at the menu.

"Honey, I haven't seen a movie in ten years except on the tube. Not since my husband went out for cigarettes and kept on going."

What is it about Long Island, Ira wondered? Do the theaters prohibit women without dates?

"I think the last movie I saw was ET."

"I meant recommendations about dinner."

Irma laughed.

"It's Sunday, so most everything's stale by now. You can always get an omelet."

Ira had the meatloaf special instead, a brick of dense chopped meat pot-marked with green and red peppers. It wasn't bad. The mountain of powdered mash potatoes and the dry string beans were. Rhonda stuck with the chef's salad.

"Big snow storm coming this week," Irma said watching every forkful that Ira ate just like his mother.

"When?" Rhonda said

"Mid-week."

"I hate storms," Irma said.

"Because of the driving?" Ira asked.

"No, I don't even own a car. I live down the road. I walk here. It's just that it gets deader around here than Superbowl Sunday, and I wind up spending the day filling up the salt and pepper shakers and the ketchup. You ever try filling up forty ketchup bottles?"

Ira excused himself to go to the bathroom. The pay phone was right where he expected it. He stood in front of it staring at the receiver. He'd promised to call, but what was the point. He wasn't coming home tonight. Ellen already suspected that he wasn't being completely truthful. But he wanted to speak to Jaime and Scott. He hadn't asked about the play, but how could he get past Ellen?

He went to the bathroom instead.

They saw "D.O.A." It was playing at the half-price theater in the neighboring town. The doctors at Pilgrim State all liked it, according to Rhonda. It has been out a long time, but Rhonda didn't have anyone to see it with.

He enjoyed the movie. It was about a professor who had been poisoned. He had twenty-four hours to find his killer since there was no antidote. He also had a twenty-four hour romance with one of his students. Ira couldn't guess until the very end that the killer was his best friend, another professor with writer's block who had murdered a student to steal his manuscript. Since our hero was familiar with the manuscript, he had to be killed before the professor could publish it as his own. Of course, there were a number of subplots involving a rich widow, her chauffeur, a sister who unknowingly dated her half-brother and another murder.

Rhonda didn't like it. She thought it was a typical murder mystery. There was probably not enough sophomoric humor or romance for her taste.

"I don't like who-done-its," she said on the ride home. "I hate waiting until the end to find out why everything was supposed to be so clever. I always guess wrong. Half the time I don't care who did it anyway."

They had vitamin-enriched sex when they got back, but only once since it was too soon for the tryptophane to take effect. Ira had to be at work by 5:45, so they went to sleep early. He was just drifting off when Rhonda asked his birthday.

"April 1st."

Rhonda chuckled.

"April fools."

It always got the same reaction.

"What time?"

"I don't know, five or six in the morning."

"I need to know the exact time."

"Why?"

"Someone at the hospital does astrological charts and past life readings, but you have to know your exact time of birth. A minute can make a big difference."

The Pilgrim State staff was beginning to sound nuttier than the residents.

"If you believe in reincarnation, which a lot of people do, especially in Asia, the fact that we're together now means we were once together in a prior life, as husband and wife or father and daughter. We could've even been sisters."

"I don't think so."

"Anything's possible."

"Unfortunately, I'm beginning to believe that. Let's go to bed," he said like they were an ordinary married couple.

MONDAY

It was black and overcast when Ira woke up. Not a single star was visible through the new age paper-thin shade that covered Rhonda's window, designed to let everything in except prying eyes, and there was no moon. The digital alarm clock, the only source of light, screamed out 5:20 . . . 5:20 . . . 5:20. He wanted to smash it to the floor and go back to sleep, since it was the only part of his subconscious that Eva and Pilgrim State hadn't completely taken over. He couldn't remember a single dream from last night, which he was very happy about.

He reset the alarm to eight, per Rhonda's instructions, and climbed out of bed. The room was cold, but the floor was like an electric shock. The bedroom at home comes with wall-to-wall carpeting thick enough to cushion most early morning anxieties. Here it was cold, hard linoleum.

Rhonda didn't stir. She was barely visible under the green quilt and her breathing was silent and motionless. He stared at her and imagined her as a work of art, some shapely sculpture or performance piece at the Museum of Modern Art entitled "Lost Mornings." He dressed in the dark without showering and left without eating. No matter how early he left at home, Ellen never failed to open a sleepy eye and mumble something about having a good day. Rhonda, however, remained in a deep sleep. Of course, she was used to final departures.

It got darker, not lighter, during the drive to Pilgrim State. The streetlights shut off prematurely, as if someone had flicked the switch without first looking out the window to confirm that the daylight had actually arrived. Heavy clouds were gathering overhead for Irma's storm, a big break for ketchup companies everywhere. He prayed that this one passed to the south, as forecast by one of the radio weathermen. He had never missed a snowstorm with Jaime and Scott and he didn't want to start now. When they were younger he used to pull them around the house on the sled and spend an hour afterward soaking his back in a hot bath. Now they just hung out together at home, Ellen and Jaime making cookies, while he and Scott shoveled.

Who would shovel the driveway and chop the ice off the front walk, he wondered, if he weren't around?

It was the absence of the ordinary that made it seem like his real life, his observed life, was receding deceptively fast, the way the stars supposedly did. He was afraid that the further away it got, the

123

harder it would be to catch up. He had already missed the night after the school auditions. He could be a snowstorm away from putting his old life completely out of reach, leaving him stranded at a job in a mental institution and a life of Shirley, Rhonda and Reverend Dean.

The oncoming headlights were blinding, forcing Ira to concentrate on the road, so he couldn't become too maudlin or too serious about racing home ahead of the storm and giving up on Eva. There was still too much sleep in his eyes and too many cobwebs in his brain, a good enough reason not to make a decision about anything.

Building 902 stood off on its own like the only boy left after the teams were chosen. It was an old four-story brick building with bars on the windows and steam rising from the roof. The pipes rattled and the floors creaked, and it was as hot as his grandmother's old apartment, which had a radiator by every window. It was a woman's dorm. The first floor contained offices, therapy rooms and supplies. There was also a recreation area and a kitchen. The patient wards were upstairs. The second floor was for the mildly disturbed. They looked and acted almost normal. Some were just tired of taking care of families or living alone and needed some help restoring a sense of equilibrium. They had small delusions and little nervous habits that most people walk around with all the time. They just couldn't keep them to themselves.

One patient twirled her hair around her index finger and sucked on her lower lip. Another walked around, one hand on the wall, glancing nervously down at the floor, as if she expected it to open up at any moment. Another, conscious of the eye of the television, carefully maneuvered herself around its imagined peripheral vision. They were all engaged in a symbolic battle against evil, but they appeared to be holding their own.

The third floor was for the more disturbed women. They muttered to themselves and yelled when they caught you looking in their direction. They sought the safety of the room's center to avoid the harmful rays that pierced the outside walls and pounded inside their heads. Clothes looked funny on them. The gowns were either too big or too small. They grasped at necks or hung limp from shoulders, as if they might slip off with a sudden movement.

Few patients sat still here. Their hands were in constant motion shooing away fears like flies. Their eyes jumped back and forth as if life were racing by before them. There was no outside world here, only an inside world. They were engaged in a physical battle against evil, but appeared to be losing.

Ira was assigned to the fourth floor, a kind of way station for those too disturbed for the second floor, but not bad enough yet for the third. For them, it was only a matter of time. There were twenty-four patients in double rooms, a nursing office, four bathrooms, two shower rooms, an eating area with two long tables and a lounging area with a television. The furnishings were obviously dictated by the need to protect patients from themselves. The chairs were dark and heavily padded. The drapes were long and opaque, intended to hide the bars, but they also killed the natural light. No cords on these drapes, which had to be opened by hand. No soft lamps with shades, no pillows, no decorator touches, only a few forgettable pictures screwed to the wall. The bright overhead fluorescent lights created hard shadows like the inside of a refrigerator.

There was nothing movable, throw-able or homey.

There was a strong winter feeling on the floor as the institutional heat poured out. There wasn't a flower or plant around, probably because none could have survived the dry heat. When the nurse opened the drapes, nothing much changed. The fogged windows acted like filters, the morning grays limping in like reluctant visitors. It reminded Ira of a bus depot. There was this overwhelming sense of waiting. Like a late afternoon departure, real life was hours away and subject to delay or cancellation without notice.

Building 902 didn't have the drug abusers or the court ordered criminal types found in many of the other wards at Pilgrim State and only a few patients were restrained to maintain order. Those with violent tendencies were either kept somewhere else or kept on heavy medication. Ira figured that this older, more traditional patient population resembled somewhat Pilgrim State twenty or thirty years ago when Eva was here. She could have sat in this very room staring out the window at the same sad, stubby trees, their gnarled and deformed branches reaching out instead of up and feeling the same simple longings that she had in his dream.

By six, Ira was walking from bed to bed announcing, "time to get up." It echoed through the halls from other parts of the building, causing women of all ages in pink flannel nightgowns to sit up in bed and fumble for their slippers. They got up and shuffled along invisible, private paths to the bathroom, clinging tightly to their institutional towels and soap.

Hospital policy required that each patient shower every day, unless the patient actively resisted it. In that case, the patient was still required to shower at least twice a week. That meant force if necessary. Not by the male staff members, but by big female orderlies with arms like truckers and bloodshot eyes. Just standing next to them gave Ira the willies.

The morning schedule was important, one of the other orderlies explained, because every delay had a domino effect on the rest of the day.

"Yesterday," he told her while they waited outside the shower room, "this one patient, Mary, she's the one with the crazy hair, we call her the witch, refused to shower, but she refused to see the doctor until she did shower."

"Yesterday was Sunday."

He looked at Ira for a moment and slowly exhaled like he was smoking a cigarette.

"Do you think this place ever closes?"

"I'm new."

He just shrugged and went on with his story.

"So she stands there like a statue. Have you seen her legs yet?"

"No."

"They're like those pillars that hold up the overpass on the interstate. I couldn't budge her, not without a large bulldozer."

Somebody screamed in the shower and he wrapped on the door.

"So she goes catatonic, which means her roommate refuses to get dressed. Her roommate looks like Olive Oil and cries over anything."

Ira could sympathize with that since he felt like crying just standing there.

"It spread around the room like a stink bomb. Everyone started crying. No one would dress or eat. So you know what I did?"

"What?"

"I said fuck'em and sat down and read the paper until they cried themselves out. Nurse Taylor wasn't around to go ballistic. Of course every fucking appointment got screwed up. The medics all got pissed and the orderlies got blamed. It's the same shit where ever you work."

He made it sound all very corporate.

Fortunately, there were no major problems this morning and by eight o'clock, the patients were showered, dressed and sitting in the lounge eating a breakfast of juice, milk, a buttered roll and hot cereal. Most of the women ate silently, unwilling or unable to talk to the person in the next chair. One woman refused to eat and crouched by the window like a sentry expecting a surprise attack. Another ate quickly and then took a seat in front of the television waiting for it to go on, although no television was allowed until everyone was finished with breakfast and their rooms straightened up. A small, oriental woman paced back and forth cradling her arm like an infant.

"What about the ones that aren't eating?" Ira asked the nurse circulating from patient to patient sprinkling out pills like seeds.

She looked down at her tray like she was looking for a pill for him.

"They won't starve if they miss a meal."

Another nurse took a piece of chalk and walked up to the blackboard.

"Today is January 25," she said writing it down like she was standing in front of a class full of third graders.

"You're in Building 902 at Pilgrim State Hospital. The weather is cloudy and cold."

Hardly anyone paid attention. In fact, few of them even looked up.

"Does anyone think it will snow?" she asked.

When no one responded, the nurse with the pills said "I hope not since I've got the next three days off."

"Does anyone know what day this is?"

"Another day in this hell-hole," one of the patients volunteered.

"Today is Monday."

"What's the difference?"

The patient who spoke stood up and held her spoon to her nose. She was a big woman with wild curly hair.

"We do different things on different days Mary. Today is occupational therapy day."

Mary put the spoon in her mouth.

"Sit down Mary."

She sat down very slowly like she really wasn't sure she remembered how to do it.

"Now who has a birthday today?"

Almost everyone raised a hand.

"Not all of you do."

Ira sat there thinking about his mother's family. They weren't a talkative bunch when it came to the distant past. He knew almost nothing about his mother's life before she met and married his father at the age of 19. While he knew absolutely nothing about Eva, he didn't know much more about his grandfather. He knew his name – Henry, like the King of England his mother used to say. He knew that he worked long hours during the week making suits and on weekends selling hats. He had a lot of mouths to feed.

He remembered seeing one old photo when he was about 10 that his grandmother pulled out from deep in the hall closet when he asked to see one, and which she put back there as soon as he was done staring at it. It was a faded, black and white photo in which he was wearing a very old-fashion suit and narrow-brimmed hat and had a carefully trimmed pencil-line moustache. His face was large and flat with most of his smallish features crowded into the middle leaving him with a big forehead and chin. He had a small, hard mouth, very different from his own and his mother's, although he did have the same thick eyebrows and deep set eyes. Even as a child he could see that, although he found his dark black eyes scary at the time. He realized later that what he really found scary was the fact that his grandfather was dead and buried deep in the ground somewhere. His grandfather was no more than thirty in the photo, but he already looked to Ira like an old man.

Maybe it's a family tradition, he wondered, because after his father died his mother put away most of his photos, although she kept the wedding photo on the shelf in the den where it has always been. Keeping the dead and the mentally ill out of sight and out of mind must be a genetic trait, although it can't be all that unusual.

He did know from his mother that Grandpa Henry died when she was still very young. It was sudden, an acid heart attack, quick and to the point, leaving the family in serious financial difficulty. His grandmother had to work two jobs to make ends meet and nothing was quite the same after that. Indeed, it appeared that Eva was institutionalized shortly thereafter. Perhaps it was a cost cutting move, Ira thought.

Ira wondered what Grandpa Henry would have thought of couponing. Could he have ever imagined that one of his grandchildren would make a nice living someday not making something with his hands, but placing little rectangular ads in magazines and newspapers?

"Remember," the nurse at the blackboard said, "no television privileges until everyone makes their bed and puts away their night clothes."

Ira looked closely at the patients searching for anything familiar. He saw a little of Eva in everyone. Maybe those that stay long enough begin to look alike. He stepped back against the wall behind him, a partition actually that separated the assembly room from the nurses' station. There was a yellowed set of rules posted in the corner that looked as if it might have pre-dated Eva's stay.

> 1. Patients using sharps, such as razors, scissors, nail files, and knitting needles must be specialed. Whoever gives out a sharp is responsible for its return.
> 2. Cosmetics are to be kept in the patient's individual box. No glass mirrors are to be kept on the ward or used by patients. No exceptions.
> 3. No smoking in rooms unless the patient is specialed. Patients are not to have matches or cigarette lighters.
> 4. No tampax or other internal tampons are to be worn on the floor without a specific order from the doctor or head nurse. Menstrual cycles are to be recorded in patients file.
> 5. All physical contact with patients is to be avoided unless absolutely necessary.

Ira wondered who they had to know to be specialed? Maybe all it took was a 5 spot in the right palm.

After breakfast Ira assisted the nurses in directing patients to their assigned activities, mostly group therapy and vocational training, clerical stuff like filing and typing. A few had nowhere to go and were allowed to watch game shows on television. He was assigned to accompany five women to a therapy class on the first floor.

Edith, in her early sixties, had been at Pilgrim for as long as anyone could remember. She had stringy gray hair and the smooth, clear complexion of a woman half her age, one of the blessings of life without sun and make-up. He asked Edith if she knew Eva, but all she did was point to her shoes which had all the laces removed.

The pill nurse who was watching Ira like a store detective waved him over.

"No talking to the patients, is that clear?"

He nodded. The nurse didn't get any of the aggrieved or embarrassed looks she expected, after all, he'd been down this road too many times before with his mother, which made her even angrier.

"And don't get close either. No touching."

He nodded again.

"Now see if you can take those five patients downstairs without causing any problems."

"Yes Ma'am."

He fought the urge to salute, turning sharply around instead with a military about-face before walking away.

The five women followed him down the stairs in a straight line, like it was a school trip. Myra walked behind Edith. She was in her late fifties and had been at Pilgrim on and off for eight years. She was neatly dressed and looked more like a visitor than a patient. Apparently, she dressed up every day in case her husband came for a visit, which he did, according to the other orderly, twice a year.

The last three women were in their forties. They shuffled down the stairs like members of a chain gang, half-asleep and mumbling to themselves.

"Please come in and take a seat," the psychologist said as soon as they entered the therapy room.

"Just stand by the wall and don't say anything," she whispered to Ira. Obviously, the nurse upstairs had called to warn her.

She had a pretty face, almond eyes, tiny nose and oval mouth. It would be pretty if it weren't so humorless. All the nurses he'd met this morning seemed the same way. It was probably a hazard of the job. They couldn't just smile and make requests, they had to issue orders like drill sergeants.

The three younger women sat staring at the ceiling, while Edith and Myra bounced up and down in their seats eager to begin.

"Who knows what this is?" the psychologist said holding up a tool even he recognized.

Myra raised her hand, but blurted out the answer.

"A screwdriver."

"That's right, Myra. And what's it used for?"

"For opening paint cans."

"And tightening screws," the psychologist said while Myra nodded in agreement.

If this psychologist thought that screwdrivers were essential to life in the outside world, Ira thought, then she was crazy.

"What about this?"

"A hammer," Edith said, "for nails."

"And closing lids," Myra said.

"For nails," Edith repeated giving Myra an angry dose of her double blues.

"Lids," Myra said lowering her chin to her chest.

Were they preparing for a field trip to a hardware store?

"You're both right," the psychologist said.

She was flat-chested like a boy, but sexy still the same in her starched, white uniform. His mind focused differently at this family institution, Ira realized. The nurse could probably feel his stare because she glanced in his direction and motioned him further away from the class. Or maybe she'd heard that he was Rhonda's main squeeze and was trying to figure out the attraction. She held up the next item.

"This is a tough one."

Myra raised her hand.

"Let's give someone else a chance. How about you Karen, do you know what this is?"

Karen lifted up her skinny face like she was disturbed by the interruption and then looked back down.

"Sandi, Donna, how about you? Want to take a guess?"

Neither one looked up. Myra waved her hand from side to side, like a drowning victim.

"Tell us Myra."

"A potato peeler."

"That's right. Who remembers when we took that tour of the kitchen?"

Only Myra and Edith raised their hands.

"We all went, remember?"

Suddenly Sandi looked up and said, "you have to be crazy to be in this place."

"That's absolutely true," the psychologist said picking up her next kitchen utensil.

At 12:30, the patients returned to the ward for lunch and television. Ira was demoted to the ground floor reception desk to check out patients to the thrift shop, to work programs and for family visits. It was someplace where they figured he couldn't do much harm. Of course, he could get into trouble anywhere these days.

An old woman came shuffling down the hall wearing a nightgown unbuttoned down the front. He tried not to look, but she stopped right in front of him.

"Can I help you?"

She didn't respond, but turned like she was about to walk out the door.

"You know your gown's open."

She looked down and screamed. Not your ordinary yelp of surprise, but the physical assault kind. A nurse ran over. Unfortunately, it was Nurse Taylor.

"What's going on here?"

"She just wandered over and started to walk out."

"Who opened her gown?"

"It was open, when I told her that she screamed."

"You're the one from records?

"Yes."

"How do I know you didn't open up her gown?"

"She must be seventy for God's sake."

"That's not an answer."

"It's the only one you're getting."

Her mouth opened as wide as the gown.

"Listen to me, you have any problems, you call for help."

"She was about to walk out the door without a pass."

"I don't care if she's dangling from a noose. You get a nurse. You're not here to use your head."

"Then what am I here for?"

Nurse Taylor put her hands on her hips and stared at him from behind those dry, crusted lines that crossed her face like prison bars. She looked over at the open gown and back at him like she was weighing a possible attempted rape charge against all the paperwork it would entail.

"Maybe it should be for observation," she said coaxing the patient back down the hall without touching her, "but whatever it's for, it won't be for long."

A little while later, a nurse just starting her shift, who hadn't yet been warned about Ira, stopped to chat. When she learned that this was his first day, she started telling him about what it was like when she began thirty years earlier.

"Everything was much easier back then. There weren't all these complicated schedules and forms to fill out. The patients didn't run the institution like they do now. They followed rules. They weren't always coming and going and they wore identical gray uniforms."

"Did you know an Eva Portnoy?"

"When did she work here?"

"She was a patient."

"You're kidding right?"

"She was a relative of mine."

"Half my relatives belong here too, if you ask me."

At 3:30, Ira was sent back to the fourth floor to straighten up the lounge area before leaving for the day. Three women were watching television.

"I don't give a damn how pathetic you are," the woman in the middle said to the one on her left, who was tapping her foot and muttering that everything was a fight.

"I'm trying to watch television."

She got up and walked away and the mumbler followed.

"She follows me around all day. I take a sip of water she takes a sip of water. She makes me sick."

She looked right at Ira when she said it.

The floor supervisor made rounds quickly before the four o'clock shift change.

"We don't need you tomorrow."

She said it like she still needed someone, just someone else, an orderly who didn't approach each patient as if she might be a long lost relative.

In some ways, Ira realized, this place wasn't all that different from American Family Care. It was a big bureaucracy. Nobody wanted to rock the boat. They put in their time and went home. He figured he could learn to fit right in if he had to.

The familiar smells in the car and the little koala bear hanging down from the glove compartment reminded him of something that he hadn't thought about all day--his family. He wondered how he could keep forgetting about them, especially when they were always standing right there, front and center in his mind's eye. All he had to do was close his eyes to see that little scar Ellen had right below her eyebrow where she was hit by the swing as a toddler. He could see Scott's cowlick and smell the cream he used to plaster it down. He could practically count the freckles on Jaime's nose. The guilt and homesickness washed over him like a wave of nausea.

He was tempted to drive straight home and forget about Eva, but it was too late in the day and he was too tired. He's never been able to make a spur of the moment decision like that. He would have had to be thinking about it all afternoon. An extra day wouldn't make a difference at this point. Besides, that was one lesson his mother did drum into him, always finish what you start, whether it's the vegetables on your plate or a boring book.

Finding Rhonda's apartment was getting easy, almost automatic even though it was dark by the time he got there. The moon, silhouetted behind the clouds, was a yellow crescent. He remembered a night like that about eight years ago. He and Jamie were coming back from his mother's house. It was the same moon, except clear and bright. Jamie called it the banana moon and he laughed out loud. He hasn't been able to look at the crescent moon since without thinking of it as the banana moon.

Jaime must be home from school doing homework, he realized. She always did it quickly without agonizing over it the way Scott did. Ellen would be home in a few minutes carrying papers to correct and worrying about dinner. As he parked the car, Ira pictured the warm glow that always greeted him when he turned the corner and the house came into view, every light burning bright. He could be going home to some wonderfully ordinary conversation and a night in front of the television. He could be dozing on the couch, not a troubling family thought in his head other than the normal ones about his mother.

Instead, he entered into a dark apartment, using the key Rhonda had given him, a key that had undoubtedly been held by a number of other men a lot younger and better looking than him. The movie timetable was open on the kitchen table. "Cousins" was circled at 7:30. Ira couldn't bear to see another sophomoric movie. There were also two vitamins on a napkin alongside the paper, a jogging suit hanging over the chair, and a note.

"Take these, don't forget. I found this jogging suit left by an old boyfriend. I'll be home around six."

Ira hated jogging suits, especially green ones. They pressed around his waist and his stomach always hung out making him feel like the Pillsbury doughboy. What's worse, there were never enough pockets. He needed places for his wallet, tissues, antacid, keys, change, pen and pocketknife. This jogging suit had one shallow pocket, like a bathing suit, with barely enough room for a key.

He looked at his watch. It was 5:40, which meant Ellen would be home by now and thoroughly exhausted. She found days filled with uncertainty completely draining, as did he, at least before Eva. He didn't have much time, but he had to call before Rhonda walked through the door. Ellen must have been standing by the phone in the kitchen, because she picked up in the middle of the first ring.

"Hi."

"Oh, it's you."

"Did you work all day on that line?"

"They just called from work."

"About what?"

"They need to speak to you. Something to do with that new cold pill, what's it called again."

"Sinoral."

"A silly name if you ask me."

"I didn't pick it out," Ira said. "What did you say?"

"I said I don't know how to reach you. Did you want me to give them the number for Pilgrim State Hospital?"

The polyester jogging suit was already pressing against his stomach and he hadn't put it on yet.

"But I'd be happy to give them another number. Where are you right now?"

He looked at the number on the telephone, but didn't answer.

"I thought so. You'd better call them at work."

"I'm at a pay phone I will."

He had one second to change the subject.

"I didn't find out anything about Eva today," he said. "I had to help out on a patient ward, but I'm sure I'll learn something tomorrow."

"You might also consider calling your mother and Aunt Sarah, they're both worried."

"I will."

"When are you coming home?"

Ira let out his breath. She'd forgotten about her Sunday ultimatum.

"Tomorrow night . . . Wednesday at the latest, just as soon as I find her file."

"We'd better talk about it first."

"About the file?"

"About the fact that I don't believe you."

He heard a key in the door.

"That's ridiculous, but I can't discuss it now, it's freezing out here. I've got to go."

"Go where?"

"There are other people who want to use the phone. It's the shift change. I'll call tomorrow."

He hung up before Ellen could protest.

"I'm home," Rhonda said.

She was half undressed by the time she reached the kitchen.

"I need a quick shower, then let's eat and see a movie."

She bent down to give him a kiss and headed to the bathroom.

"How was your day?" she called out.

"Depressing."

"Like my every day," Rhonda said sticking her head out of the bathroom. "I want to see Cousins with Ted Danson. Did you see him in Three Men and a Baby?"

"I missed it."

"It was very funny."

Rhonda disappeared into the shower.

Her body gave him a certain strength and resolve. It cleared out his brain like a shot of bourbon. Or maybe it was the change in routine or the sense of danger, not real danger, but danger for Ira. It scared the hell out of him, but at the same time it made him feel alive.

They ate at Wendy's and then saw Cousins. Rhonda loved it and Ira hated it, confirming that they were at opposite ends of the audience spectrum. It was about marriage and infidelity. It was supposed to be comical. Everyone cheated and everyone got even. Unfortunately, it didn't work that way. It shouldn't work that way. He didn't want Ellen getting even.

They had sex before going to bed. For Rhonda it was like going to the movies. She couldn't or wouldn't do it alone, so she had to do it as often as possible when she had the opportunity. For Ira, firm breasts two sizes larger than his hand and muscular thighs were still a new sensation, although some of the thrill was wearing off or else he was just tired, because he kept thinking that it had been a long day and all he really wanted to do was sleep.

This time he did remember his dream. He was at Pilgrim State, but he didn't have to look for Eva, because he was Eva. He looked into the mirror and Eva stared back. They were two consciousnesses in one body, only it was impossible to communicate. The distance between them, even inside the same head, was too great.

He heard two doctors talking.

"She has two sisters who are perfectly normal."

He wasn't sure he agreed, but he wasn't able to talk.

"We're all egg shells. All it takes is one crack in the wrong place."

He hated to think parenting was that dangerous. Of course, these doctors practiced before the gene era.

"They all bury their mistakes here."

"We wouldn't have a job if they didn't."

"I suppose."

"I've scheduled her for the procedure?"

"What procedure?" he tried to say only nothing came out of Eva's mouth. Eva didn't care. She must have been on some kind of tranquilizer, because her body was completely limp and still, damp from the heat, except for her eyes, which were cool and dry. He looked at her hands, which had a sickly bluish tint.

There was something at the core of her being--a memory, a reason, an explanation of some kind, a justification, a key to her recovery--but he couldn't quite make it out. He kept reaching for it, but his perspective was distorted, like trying to pick up something shiny at the bottom of a lake. The harder he reached for it, the further it slipped away.

The next thing Ira knew he was an eight-year old sitting on a stoop in the city on a street filled with comfortable summer afternoon sounds; a panting dog, a knife-sharpener pushing his cart down the center of the street, someone yelling "I cash clothes," big band music drifting down from a radio by an open window, and an old car shaking as it sat in idle, its driver smoking the biggest cigar that he'd ever seen.

It was September 24, 1926; Ira only knew that because someone walked by with a newspaper. The date was framed in black. It announced the end of an era--Gene Tunney had beaten the champ, Jack Dempsey. Only in a dream could the world change so radically without any mystery or pain.

A little girl sat down next to him.

"Hi," she said, "you're new."

She was about the same age and her whole face from her red lips to her round nose to her blue eyes sparkled with excitement. Her eyes were so bright that it was almost like looking at the sun. Her hair was so long and curly that it just about blotted out everything else behind her.

"I am."

"Want to race me to the corner? I'm very fast for a girl."

He'd seen her before, but he couldn't remember where.

"Sure."

She was ahead for most of the race, but slowed up near the end to let him pull even. She made it seem effortless.

"You are fast," he said

"Fastest of all my sisters, only my brother can beat me."

Although he was only eight, he could feel his heart peeling open like onion and he couldn't help telling her how cute she was. Her smile turned a shade uncertain in response. It was probably the wrong thing to say, he realized. He was moving too fast, but he wanted her to love him as much as he knew he was going to love her.

"I didn't mean it like that," he said.

"I hope you did."

"I did, but I didn't mean to say it, I meant to think it."

"I'm glad you did, because I'm also the prettiest of my sisters."

With that she tagged his arm, screamed, "you're it," and ran down the block. This time he couldn't catch her.

"What's your name," he screamed out as she pulled away from him.

He was praying that his parents would never move again, not to the suburbs as they've been threatening, so that she could be his sweetheart in high school. Then they could marry, have a family and laugh about racing down the block the very first time they met. He wanted to protect her and shelter her, but he couldn't do anything until he caught her. She was getting further and further ahead, receding rapidly, almost as if he were standing still.

Then she disappeared and he heard this siren, the kind you'd hear in the old war movies, and he stopped and closed his eyes because he was afraid of what might have happened. When he opened them, he found himself staring at the alarm clock and wondering whether his dream lover was Eva when, as Aunt Sarah put it, she was still "pretty normal."

Pretty and normal would have been a better way to put it.

TUESDAY

Wake up and get ready for work, Rhonda said, without pretense and without romance. He didn't stare at her body like a Playboy centerfold and she didn't try to avoid looking at his. There was very little effort to make conversation. They stumbled about in various states of undress with tired, ugly expressions that new lovers normally hide. How quickly it all turns to routine, he thought. It was as if he was a carrier spreading routine around like a virus.

He tried to hold onto the eight-year old Eva for a little while longer, but without much luck. Dreams are the most short-lived of all human creations, real one minute, gone the next. He wondered what would have happened if he'd caught up to her? Maybe they'd have tumbled to the ground laughing and wrestling until his lips brushed against her cheek. She'd have stopped to stare at him and he'd have stared back looking for the slightest change in her expression. Perhaps she'd have said something that would have given him a clue. Of course it was just a dream, but his subconscious had always been so much smarter and more dependable than his consciousness.

After they were both dressed, they sat in the kitchen to eat some cold cereal and sip weak coffee. Rhonda talked about movies they could see after work like they were errands that had to get done, while he tried to visualize Eva's file in his stubby little hand. He imagined himself running to Ellen and waving it in the air like a note from the doctor.

Please excuse Ira's absence the past few days. He has not been himself. Be advised that his temporary obsession has been completely cured.

He tried to visualize what they were doing at home, combing hair, filling book bags, scanning the local newspaper, munching on pop tarts. It didn't come in all that clearly, which could be a bad sign were it not for the fact that he always left so early that he didn't actually get to see them getting ready for school. He expected that breakfast would be the hardest part for Ellen this morning. Her appetite was the first thing that went when she was upset. She was so honest with everyone and with herself that it would be hard to hide the damaged look in her eyes.

"It's 8:30," Rhonda said.

His eyes, which had been staring inward, looked back out at his watch.

"It's 8:15.

140

"I'm not talking about the time. I'm talking about the movie tonight."

"OK."

He meant that he understood the difference, not that he wanted to see another movie. He hoped to be home tonight.

"Great."

He didn't try to correct her misunderstanding.

Rhonda insisted that they take his car to work, because it was newer and bigger.

"I don't want to be stuck alone if the weather turns nasty."

They hardly spoke during the ride. Maybe it was the dreary, dark winter morning and the feelings of helplessness and failure that were beginning to cling to the relationship like lint. Rhonda was probably wondering how much longer, even though a small part of her hoped, as it always did, that this might be the one. If not, another couple of movies wouldn't be asking too much from a relationship.

"Is something wrong?" she said when Pilgrim State came into view.

"No."

"You were so quiet at breakfast."

"I'm quiet in the mornings," he said.

"What have you been thinking about?"

"Eva's file."

"You're going to be disappointed when you find it."

"I expect so, but I'll be more disappointed if I don't."

They drove through the front gate. The lights from Pilgrim State, brilliant yesterday morning when it was dark, were lost in the daylight.

"It's the little things that give men away," Rhonda said.

"What are you talking about?"

"When they're getting ready to leave . . . they stop looking at you."

"The same thing happens when you've been married a while."

"And they watch a lot of late night TV or get out of bed early. When they can't sleep my mother used to say they'll be gone in a week."

"Let's check the weather," he said.

He reached for the radio, but Rhonda took his hand before he could get to it.

"Cold hands."

Every woman he has ever known has said the same thing about him, beginning with his mother. Ellen refuses to let him touch her at night until he's warmed his hands under the blanket for at least five minutes.

"It doesn't bother me," she said.

"My hands?"

"No, our relationship, everything has an end and every end has a beginning."

"That sounds like Reverend Dean."

"It is. I just want to make sure you give it a fair chance. I've seen the strangest combinations work. You know opposites and all that."

He wondered why Rhonda even cared. She could have lots of men her own age. This relationship couldn't be very exciting, at least not sexually, although it probably had other advantages. There were no lofty expectations, so the silences weren't awkward. You could accept it for what it was and everything didn't have to be perfect. A lot of younger men don't realize that about relationships. Every relationship, like every day, quickly finds its own level. He could spend the next ten years with Rhonda and things wouldn't change all that much. What it is now is about all it would ever be--movies, meals, sex and work. It wasn't a family type relationship, although it did have a comfortable predictability to it.

Ira tried to imagine marrying Rhonda, but he couldn't. Maybe if he was twenty-five, but he didn't want to start all over again now. There was a certain age, which he had already passed, perhaps prematurely, when the thought of change, at least too much of it, was terrifying. The things that bring it about are never good, like being let go from work, a sudden illness, the loss of love, or death. How could he think like that and marry someone still in her twenties?

"You're quiet again," Rhonda said. "What are you thinking about?"

"Eva."

"Think too much about one thing and you'll wind up in here."

"Thanks for the vote of confidence."

"Not just you, anyone."

"I'll be careful."

"I'll come by for lunch"

"I'm working through lunch. I've got to find Eva's file today."

"I'll come by anyway."

They parted with a quick, light suburban-style kiss.

It was early in the morning, but not too early for Selma and Sarah to be sitting at the kitchen table holding tight to steaming cups of coffee and staring into a plate of Danish pastries; neither wanted to be the first to eat, because denying oneself in Ira's family was considered the truest measure of pain.

"What can he find out?" Selma said.

"Nothing."

"That's right."

"I wish Momma were alive," Sarah said.

"I'm glad she's not."

"Glad?"

"I don't mean it like that. I wouldn't want her to go through it all over again."

They both took sips of coffee.

"I should have remembered Eva's stone," Selma said.

"What could you have done?"

"I could have asked them to cover it up."

"That might've made him more curious."

"Not Ira, he was born without curiosity."

"Well, that appears to have changed."

Selma stared into her cup.

"Middle age onset," Sarah said, "it just kicks in late for some people."

"What?"

"Curiosity."

"I could have stayed by his side," Selma said, "and steered him in the opposite direction."

"You can't do anything about it now."

"We should have been more careful."

"We should have been more open," Sarah said.

"No, we shouldn't have."

Sarah took a bite of an apple turnover and a long, slow sip of coffee, which freed Selma to put something on her plate.

"Even Ann Landers agrees that certain things should remain secret," Selma said.

"Not something like this."

"No, you're wrong . . . it's especially something like this. Would you have told anyone if Eva had been executed for murder?"

"Yes."

"No you wouldn't, you're just being obstinate."

Sarah took another bite of the turnover.

"Look at Momma," Selma said. "You're always saying how you want to be like her, that she was so wise and had so much common sense."

Sarah nodded.

"In all the years did she ever speak about Eva? Not once that I recall. How about us, we got along fine and did we ever talk about it?"

"What would've been the point?"

"Precisely, if we didn't talk about it when we knew, what was the point in knowing in the first place? It's a lot easier if you don't."

"It's different now," Sarah said. "All the studies you read about say it's good to talk, healthy to get things out in the open."

"Who does these studies, bureaucrats and academics, what do they know from real life?"

"Well this certainly wouldn't be happening now," Sarah said, "if we had been more open about Eva with Ira."

"Nothing is happening," Selma said. "Ira will come back with his tail between his legs and everything will be back to normal in a day or two."

Sarah watched the coffee swirl in her cup. Selma always had to get in the last word, so she knew there was no point in responding. They both ate and drank for a while in complete silence.

"When did you see her last?" Selma asked.

"Mom?"

"Eva."

"The end of that first year," Sarah said, "never again after that."

"I never saw her after they took her away."

"I know . . . but you were barely 12."

"I once thought that I'd never get over it," Selma said, "but I did, like everything else it just takes time . . . and persistent effort in the beginning. With enough effort you can forget anything."

Selma looked away. She refused to cry in public, she didn't even like people to see her get teary-eyed.

"I got over it precisely because we didn't talk about it."

Sarah nodded, not because she agreed, but because she couldn't figure out a way to change the subject.

"Which is why they say what you don't know won't hurt you."

Selma made it sound like she was teaching a class and giving out the correct answer. The morning light rose above the kitchen table like smoke from a smoldering fire.

Selma poured them both more coffee.

"Well it's out now," Sarah said, "so maybe we should just tell him."

"Tell him what?"

"Everything."

"Absolutely not, he'll find out some harmless information and that'll be it. You know Ira, he can't stand disorder and he can't stand pain. He'll back off soon enough and come running home, mark my words."

Sarah was too tired to do anything other than nod.

When Ira got to Records, Shirley was downstairs in the basement sitting on his stool eating a donut and drinking coffee. Her clothes were disheveled and her hair was a mess. She looked like she'd been up all night. There were open boxes at her feet and a pile of old files on the floor.

"Really Ira, unbuttoning the gowns of old women, Rhonda isn't enough for you?"

"Nurse Taylor's been here."

"I'd take it as a compliment, since she hates men."

Ira dragged over one of the boxes.

"Eva's last name was Portnoy, right?"

"Right."

Shirley stood up and started to climb the stairs.

"Her file's on the counter."

"You're kidding."

"Do I look like someone who plays practical jokes?"

Ira rushed over to look at it.

"I expect you'll be able to leave by the end of the day now," Shirley said, "so the rest of us can get back to our own lives."

For the first time since he met her, Shirley left the room without making a sound.

Eva's file was thicker than the Manhattan Yellow Pages. It was the thickest file he'd seen yet. Portnoy was written in large letters across the front, DOA 2/1/36 in red circled in black. Not dead on arrival, which might have been appropriate, but date of admission. Below that was DOD 12/12/68. Date of discharge or, in Eva's case, death.

Over thirty-two years, he calculated, most murderers get paroled sooner than that.

There were three large letters in the bottom right corner, LOB, and the date 7/15/46. He hadn't come across that one yet, but he knew what it meant. It meant that Eva had a lobotomy before he was born, probably with the family's consent. That might explain why Eva was such a big secret. There really wasn't much of her left to talk about.

Eth said that Egas Moniz originated the lobotomy in Portugal. He believed that the frontal lobes were the center of "psychic activity" and that all mental illness resulted from potholes in the brain. By destroying the abnormal pathways, the delusions would dissipate as quickly as the morning dew and the paranoia blossom into trust, just like magic. Ira pictured Dr. Moniz as the mad scientist in a Frankenstein movie. Instead of discovering how to bring life to inanimate matter, Moniz discovered how to turn life into inanimate objects. Not something that took all that much talent. How many families made the same mistake? How many lobotomized patients were erased from human memory?

Moniz didn't even perform animal experiments before deciding which parts of the brain to destroy and the method to use. His preparations were casual, as if he were preparing to carve the Thanksgiving turkey. He first tried injecting alcohol into the brain. There was a lot in stock, since a colleague had been using it to destroy nerve tissue in a patient with a twitch. It was very clean and easy to work with. Unfortunately, it wasn't enough of a challenge for Dr. Moniz the surgeon, who found alcohol beneath him, at least the non-imbibing type. So he brought up a brain from the morgue and inserted a pen through the cortex several times until he was satisfied with the angle and depth of destruction. Moniz then picked up a potato peeler and put a wire loop at the end. Without any practice, he inserted the instrument through two holes made at the top of the head of a patient and twirled it like a fork on a plate of spaghetti. Brain fibers crack like knuckles. Moniz must have enjoyed the sound since he repeated the

procedure over and over again. How Dr. Moniz must have
regretted not having had the opportunity to heal himself.

Ira hadn't met a lobotomee, but when he closed his eyes he
saw a zombie, terrifying, not because of any deformity, but because
of the total absence of expression. He saw arms and legs that
jerked about with joints that could hardly bend and a white face of
stone severed from the soul. It was Eva with cement shoes,
instead of the eight-year old flying down the street and churning up
dust like a volley of raindrops. An Eva disconnected from herself,
as if someone has pulled a plug, her speaking eyes silenced forever
and her heart unable to love or be loved.

It was not a pretty picture.

Eva's file was divided into three parts, psychological reports,
medical records and visitor logs. The entries were cryptic and
often illegible. He was going to need Shirley's help, but he wanted
to spend some time alone with it first, so he decided to make sure
that everything was in chronological order. Her entire life
condensed into thirty-two years of yellow, institutional records.
Thirty-two years of colds and viruses, broken bones and arthritis,
depression, acting out and tears. Eva may have been removed
from everyday life, but she still enjoyed all of its torments.

All the records were there, except for three months in early
1951. Only three months lost was a miracle. When he was
finished, he turned to the very first entry in her file:

> "Family commitment. Patient admitted in a state of
> acute panic, overcome by confusion, paranoid
> interpretations and feelings of acute helplessness.
> Feels abandoned and as a result has completely
> restricted any expression."

Overcome by "paranoid interpretations" and "acute
helplessness?" Psychologists, Ira realized, would make lousy ad
men. The terms they used were too cold for such hot feelings. Of
course, Eva had "restricted any expression." She must have been
terrified.

He could never have been a psychologist, Ira realized. It's far
too wordy a profession. It hides behind phrases that mean very
little to most people. He needs simple expressions, like "ten cents
off" and "preferred two to one," things people can understand at a
glance.

"Family commitment" must mean voluntary, but he couldn't
imagine his grandmother voluntarily committing one of her

daughters, certainly not for life. He flipped through some more entries. Intelligence tests showed that Eva was above average, so it wasn't a question of retardation. Her big problem seemed to be behavioral. She was unable to relate to any of the other patients or the doctors.

So it's in the genes, he thought, although his mother's case is milder and his own milder still.

"Patient has little social interaction. Cannot even look at people. Trembles and becomes hysterical when approached by male staff members."

The entries grew more and more cryptic. Institutions, like big corporations, quickly lose interest. She wasn't going anywhere. They had her business for life, so why bother.

"Severely withdrawn."

"Depressed."

"Occasional impulsive outbursts of short duration."

"Hysterical features."

"Delusional interpretations."

"Organic syndrome."

Organic syndrome didn't mean anything to him, unless it was some sort of yeast infection. Of course, Ira lived in more modern times, in the psychological era of anxiety, neurosis, psychosis and schizophrenia. Delusions he could understand, and Eva's delusions appeared to be mostly her belief that she was the only patient on the ward. Everyone else was a staff member masquerading as a patient.

She was described as "5 foot 6, 110 pounds, brown hair, hazel eyes, pretty features and well-developed."

Eva had two basic moods. Her usual catatonic state, when she "sits unable to undertake any activity . . . even the simplest things . . . speaks slowly to herself, but never when spoken to . . . feels helpless and discouraged . . . with no obvious bizarre thoughts, hallucinations or delusions." At infrequent intervals, Eva "manifests excitement characterized by over-activity, yelling . . . suicidal preoccupations . . . threats . . . unreasonable demands . . . inappropriate smiling, compulsive misunderstanding and transient delusions." The acting out behavior frequently occurred after "visits by patient's mother." Ira's grandmother was described as a Russian immigrant "unable to accept the severity of patient's illness or to contribute meaningfully to her treatment."

Eva also exhibited eccentric behavior. Sometimes when she talked, she repeated things two or three times. She closed her eyes when people got too close and sometimes nodded very rapidly, "like she wanted you to do whatever you had to do quickly and be gone." She hated to be touched by anyone, particularly males, and occasionally kept her left hand clenched in a fist and raised over her head as if she were trying to ward off an attacker.

"She likes to sit in front of the piano in the recreation room. Although she doesn't play, she supposedly can."

How would Eva have learned to play? There was no natural musical ability anywhere in the family. Neither his mother nor Aunt Sarah could hold a note. They didn't even dance. His singing was barely better than fingernails scratching a blackboard and although Ira once fantasized about playing the guitar when he listened to his roommate in college, he couldn't get past the second page of the beginner's guitar book he'd bought in the school bookstore.

Not surprisingly, Eva was subject to all kinds of treatment. She had the good fortune to be at Pilgrim during the period that Eth called "the era of great and desperate cures." Eva was the perfect guinea pig, not an assertive patient, indifferent to what was going on around her. Her mother, Ira's grandmother, was too intimidated by authority and easily manipulated by the hospital staff. And, of course, she was abandoned by the rest of her family.

In all fairness, anyone in his grandmother's position would have been overmatched. She was taught to obey authority as a young girl in Czarist Russia. She watched the White Russians drown two of her brothers for their leftist leanings, so she knew exactly what authority could do if you disagreed too vociferously. Besides, she had no formal education. How could she challenge men in uniform with degrees on the wall, who never had the slightest doubt about anything that they recommended and who attributed every failure to the patient's unwillingness to cooperate or to prior family mistakes.

In 1939, Eva received insulin shock therapy. She must have been one of the first because the procedure was carefully monitored and described:

> "Shortly after injection patient became quiet as the insulin began to lower blood sugar and deprive the brain of energy. Immediately patient started to perspire and salivate drooling down the chin. By the

end of the first hour, patient had entered into a coma. She tossed and moaned. Her muscles twitched and she had frequent tremors and spasms. Occasionally, patient's left arm shot up uncontrollably and she gasped for air, as if swimming under water. Other primitive movements were evident, including rapid licking of the lips and clenching of the fists. Violent convulsions emerged the second day, which means restraints will be required during future sessions."

As with most of the radical treatments, the initial results were viewed with blind optimism. After two weeks, Eva was "somewhat disoriented, but much more cooperative and less withdrawn." Two months later, all pretenses were dropped and Eva's file returned to that popular old refrain -- "no progress noted."

In 1942, Doctors Walter Freeman and James Watts published Psychosurgery, which legitimized Moniz's operation in America. By 1951, Eth said, over eighteen thousand lobotomies were performed in the United States. 1946, the year of Eva's operation, was the peak. Most of the lobotomies took place in state mental institutions, according to Eth, because they had very little money for traditional, labor-intensive treatment. In other words, they had to go for the quick fix. Being admitted to a state mental hospital in the thirties and forties was equivalent to a life sentence.

Eva's treatment made very little sense, at least from Ira's advertising point of view. There was no plan of action, no defined reachable goal, no interim or short-range objectives. They just struck out blindly in any direction and hoped for a cure. Of course, they couldn't find one and the rosy entries that followed each experiment were quickly replaced by the same negative diagnosis and prognosis repeated month after month and year after year.

It was Eva's turn for a lobotomy thanks to the confident recommendation of "HF."

"Patient has not responded well to other forms of treatment. LOB offers the best chance for patient to return to a more normal life."

The first two months following the operation, HF was enthusiastic about the results, although the notes indicate that Eva's hair had grown back straight and stiff like a porcupine.

Ira had to look away from the file and dry his eyes on his sleeve, which surprised him since he wasn't normally emotional like that when it came to distant and disconnected things, and Eva couldn't be further away in time or place. Certainly she was completely disconnected in terms of any memories.

"Patient manifests no episodes of excitability . . .smiles frequently . . . anxiety and feelings of hopelessness seem to have disappeared."

By the fourth month, HF had lost interest and the entries had lost their sugarcoating. They resumed their hopeless refrain, although Eva's problems were now somewhat different.

"Patient does not recognize her mother or at least refuses to acknowledge her. She often forgets the function of everyday objects, such as a water glass and soap and often cries quietly, although uncontrollably."

The Eva Ira saw, the one in his dream, died the moment HF inserted his little potato peeler into her brain. It was the result of a long, slow illness that probably started at puberty and went unrecognized and untreated until it was too late. Today it would be a different story. HF would be the one institutionalized and Eva would have therapy at home. She'd be on some kind of drug regiment and have a decent, patient and loving husband. Perhaps even a child or two. She'd be home this very minute, having taken her Prozac, picking up a saucepan with her long, beautiful hands, perfect for the piano.

He closed the file, picked it up, and climbed the stairs to Shirley.

"Finished already?"

She was sitting at her desk, the piles of paper vastly outnumbered by crumbs.

"Going home?"

"I can't understand any of this. Eva never seems to get any better. No one visits her except my grandmother. For three months she disappears. There's no accountability."

Spoken like a true corporate executive.

"This isn't a bank and we don't answer to auditors. At least we didn't back then."

"I can't believe this all went on behind my back."

"So you're not the center of the universe," Shirley said without her usual yellow grin. "Welcome to the world outside suburbia.

Now you can go home and forget it ever happened. You'll be better off, I'll be better off, we'll all be better off."

All he did in response was sneeze three times fast.

"I can hire someone to do some real work and Rhonda can start looking for a real boyfriend."

Shirley bit into a candy bar and buried her head in a stack of papers. Beads of sweat dripped from her forehead and her foot bounced up and down on the floor, causing every inanimate object in the room to quiver. Watching her try to ignore him made Ira wonder why Shirley came in so early to look for Eva's file and why she was so eager for him to go, so he opened her file again and looked at the staff entries. The initials SM were all over the first year . . . Shirley Malone.

"You worked with Eva when she first came, didn't you?"

"I worked with thousands of patients."

"But you remember her. You were there at the beginning."

Shirley bent over to pick up something from the floor, which she tossed into the garbage. Then she stood up teetering on her small feet like a giant tree about to fall. He hadn't noticed before just how tiny her feet were in comparison to everything else.

"Your initials are all over the file. She was probably one of the first patients you ever worked with."

Shirley stood so round-shouldered that her neck disappeared from sight. There was a fine line of moisture around her mouth.

"I worked with Eva for almost eight years. From the very first day I started until she had the lobotomy. After that, I didn't see her again until the late fifties. Then she was on my floor for a little while until I switched to records, but she didn't remember me."

Ira waited for Shirley to continue, but all she did was extend her hand out for the file.

"There were tons more patients back then and most of them were family commitments. They couldn't afford anything better . . . or didn't know any better. Not like today, where most everything's court order."

Shirley opened the file and started flipping through it.

"There was no money for any real treatment. We didn't do much more than feed'em and keep'em from hurting themselves. There were hundreds of Eva's."

"But you remember her, why?"

"First kiss, first patient."

"Why was she committed?"

"How would I know? Trouble at home probably. A neighbor called the police. Or maybe they couldn't handle her anymore. It could've been anything."

"What was she like?"

"She didn't talk much, but she was no dope. You can always tell by the way they listen . . . and their eyes. For the smart ones, it's like they're looking at you through a keyhole."

Ira paced back and forth to stop from sinking into his own imagination.

"So why was she in here her whole life?"

"The same reason most of them were here, she was emotionally disturbed."

"How? Why?"

"If I knew why, I'd be running this place, instead of pushing paper around. She had a few more loose wires than the rest of us . . . that's about it."

"How was she disturbed?"

"Don't you watch television?"

"But what did she do? How did she act?"

"She wanted to be left alone, which I suppose means I'm just as crazy."

"What else?"

Shirley must have been looking back at Eva, frozen as if by a camera's eye, because her vacant look seemed a thousand miles away.

"What else?" Ira repeated.

"She didn't like people coming near her. Your grandmother was an exception . . . me sometimes, some of the other nurses when she got used to them. She hated to be touched, particularly by the doctors, who were all male back then."

"What does that mean?"

"What?"

"That she didn't like men?"

"That she had good taste. Do I look like a fucking psychologist? They all did weird things. They talked to themselves. They stared at walls and flapped their arms like birds. You couldn't touch half of them."

Shirley lowered her chin and tilted her head like someone was whispering in her ear.

"Maybe something happened to her."

"No shit Sherlock. Something happened to all of them, whether it was real or imaginary. The difference didn't mean a damn."

"What happened after the lobotomy?"

"She changed. They all did. They were calmer . . . deader is a better word . . . like vegetables."

That part is exactly the way he imagined it.

Shirley sat back down at her desk.

"Why didn't you say something earlier?"

Shirley stared at Eva's file.

"Why?"

"You really think you're better off knowing any of this shit?"

Ira could almost taste the sour sweet smell rising from Shirley, like an infant that had spit up.

"You sound like my mother. She always knows what's best for me too."

"You feel any better now that you know?"

Her face was the shape and color of a red balloon.

"I'd like to forget half of what I've seen and know," Shirley added.

He couldn't be angry with her. Shirley didn't owe him anything going into this, not like his mother and Aunt Sarah.

"Your grandmother was something else. Most families forgot after a few years. The regular visits reduced to holidays once or twice a year. Not your grandmother, she came just about every Sunday rain or shine and she had to take two trains and a bus. It had to be a real bitch."

Ira felt like kicking himself. How could he have been so unobservant? How is it he never questioned why she only came to visit on Saturdays?

"She came to every visit like she half-expected Eva to be dressed and ready to go home. She always expected too much and always went away disappointed."

"It's a family trait."

"Life's a bitch when it's filled with expectations."

"Are there records about the circumstances of a patient's admission?" Ira asked.

"There used to be records in administration, but I don't think they still exist."

"How can I find out?"

"Go ask'em, I'm sure they'd be happy to check." Shirley smiled her head bobbing up and down like a dashboard ornament. "Forget it Ira, it's all over. They don't worry about patients in administration, why would they worry about patient records. How much more do you need to know? She was here for ten years, had a lobotomy and was a vegetable for twenty more."

"I want to know why she was committed, what was wrong with her . . . and why my mother never said a word all these years."

"You're not gonna to find any of those answers here."

"My aunt said she was fine when she was a little girl."

"We're all fine when we're little girls."

Shirley dropped her head down like it had suddenly grown as heavy as the rest of her.

"We're all like little time bombs," she said. "Some of us have shorter fuses than others. If you're lucky you die before yours goes off."

Ira slumped against the wall.

"There are certain ages, early teens, early twenties, late forties, early sixties, when it tends to go off. A little burst of paranoia, some weird obsessive behavior, a wave of schizophrenia. That's the way it is with people like Eva. They call it bad genes now."

"My aunt thought it was puberty."

"Now there's a hot spot."

"For no reason?" he said.

"For no reason or some reason, what does it matter? Most people can shrug things off, some can't. They're like balloons ready to burst. All it takes is a sharp object."

There had to be a sharp object, Ira could feel it. Whatever it was must have been incredible, since he knew that he was born without intuition.

Shirley put a strand of hair into her mouth and went back to the files on her desk. Before he could say another word Rhonda walked in.

"Pretty quiet around here, did I catch you kids talking about me?"

Rhonda gave him a kiss on the cheek. She gave off a sexual scent that momentarily pulled Ira in a totally different direction.

"So what gives?"

"Shirley found Eva's file."

"Oh," Rhonda exclaimed looking down at her nails. She probably sensed another long stretch without movies. It was hard for Ira to understand what Rhonda saw in him. Maybe stability and maturity was irresistible to today's single woman, although he felt anything but stable and mature at the moment.

"It turns out that Shirley knew Eva. I was just begging her for help."

"Let me see the file."

Ira pointed it out and Rhonda picked it up from Shirley's desk. She flipped through it.

"Lobotomy, tough luck . . . HF . . . isn't that old Doc Fulton?"

Shirley nodded.

"Who's Doc Fulton?"

"Herman Fulton," Rhonda said, "even I've heard about him. He was here forever. They called him Dr. Lobotomy. He must be a hundred years old by now, if he's still alive."

"Ninety, I heard he's in a nursing home in Atlantic City."

"I can't believe it."

"Do me a favor Ira," Shirley said, "there's a box of files downstairs in the corner near the wall with a big red check mark on the top, could you bring it up?"

He went downstairs, but couldn't find it. He was about to call up when he overheard Rhonda and Shirley talking.

"Why didn't you say something?" Rhonda asked.

"Because it wasn't just the lobotomy."

"What do you mean?"

"Did you find the box?" Shirley called out.

"Not yet."

"Try behind the far pole."

He didn't move.

"I don't even think her mother knew."

"Knew what?"

"You have to promise not to say a word."

"I promise."

"I mean it," Shirley said.

"I promise."

Shirley must have whispered or pantomimed something, because the next words came from Rhonda.

"That's too bad."

"For a long time," Shirley said.

"How do you know?"

"She once told me. She was no dummy."

"So why don't you tell him," Rhonda said. "Who ever did it must be dead by now."

"Not everyone's dead," Shirley said. "There are plenty of old people around."

Shirley must have said something with a raised eyebrow and a nod, because all Rhonda said in response was "Oh, I see."

Ira lost his balance and banged against the stairs.

"Ira?"

"I can't find it."

"Never mind," Shirley said, "it's not important."

He climbed slowly up the stairs. His head was pounding. He realized that he should go back home. How much more did he really need to know? Eva was abused by someone. Maybe an uncle or a neighbor, some older boy down the hall, who married, raised a family and enjoyed yearly vacations at the beach, while she lost part of her brain. He decided not to say anything, not yet anyway. He'd try to find out more on his own. The one thing Shirley would probably do that his mother wouldn't was at least confirm the truth if he stumbled upon it.

"I can't believe that Doc Fulton's still alive," Rhonda said when he reached the top of the stairs, as if they'd been discussing an old friend.

"Why is it that jerks like that always seem to live forever."

"Let's go to lunch," Ira said taking Rhonda's arm.

"Want to come?" Rhonda asked Shirley.

"Nope, brought my own."

Ira took Eva's file with him. He waited for Shirley to object, but she didn't. He had this irresistible urge to speak with Dr. Lobotomy and Rhonda volunteered to check for an address in administration.

"But you have to put the file away," she said.

"Why?"

"You can't just take it to lunch. If someone sees you with it you'll be fired, the file will be confiscated and probably lost. I'm surprised Shirley let you walk out with it."

"I'll put it in the car."

"Sure, that's not going to attract any attention, walking past the guard into the parking lot carrying a thick file."

"Where do you suggest I put it?"

"In my locker," Rhonda said holding out her hand.

He clutched the file closer to his breast.

"I'm not going to eat it."

He couldn't shake this image of Rhonda holding the file hostage -- page by page -- in exchange for monthly movie visits.

"Hurry up, before some administrator looking for trouble walks by."

"Take care of it."

"It'll have its own shelf in my locker."

Rhonda took the file and walked down the hall to the nurse's locker room.

He realized that he was breaking one of nature's laws. When you finally find something that you've looking for, don't take any chances with it. Of course, this was Ira's second offense in the past week counting Ellen, Scott and Jamie.

Rhonda was back before he had a chance to panic.

"Where did you put it?"

"On the coffee table in the lounge."

"What?"

"It's safe in my locker. No one saw me."

"Can you get it after lunch?"

"There'll be too many people around. I'll sneak it out in my shoulder bag after quitting time."

"I don't want to wait that long."

"How about a thank you, since it's my ass on line. I don't have another job to go to if I get fired."

"Thank you."

Rhonda smiled and put her arm around Ira's shoulder. Her breast almost poked out his eye.

Ellen had twenty minutes left on her lunch hour. She ate fast so she'd have time to make a few calls. What she really wanted was a glass of wine. Her class had been impossible today, completely out of control. She threatened them with all kinds of academic torture, extra homework, even a special test, but nothing worked. They knew her well enough by now to know that she was bluffing. Punishment was not her style. She preferred to reason with the class. She wanted good behavior that was inner directed, not induced by fear. But Ellen wasn't herself today. She just couldn't focus and the class took full advantage.

Selma picked up after the first ring.

"It's me."

"Did you hear anything?" Selma said.

"No what about you?"

"Not a word."

"It's more than Eva," Ellen said.

"What are you talking about?"

"I think he's involved with someone."

"A patient?"

"Another woman."

"Ira? Don't be ridiculous, he's not the type."

"Everyone's the type."

A group of students walked by and giggled. Teachers doing normal, everyday things, like talking on the telephone, always seemed funny to them.

"You're letting your imagination run away with you."

"What's he going to find out about Eva?"

Selma thought about it. She was probably tempted to spill her guts just this once, but Selma could resist any impulse or desire, no matter how strong. She prided herself on it, whether it was chocolate or television. She used to demonstrate that fact almost daily when Ira was growing up. Besides, purging was not in her nature. Certainly not after all those years of silence and denial, notwithstanding the fact that she used to make Ira stick his finger down his throat when he had a stomachache because she believed vomiting was good for him.

"I was the youngest."

"I know."

"My parents worked and everyone else was at school, everyone but Eva."

Selma took a deep breath. Maybe this is it, Ellen thought. She was tired and wanted something to come easy.

"Eva took care of me."

"I know that also."

"It was a small apartment and we shared the same bed."

"How could she be trusted?" Ellen asked.

"She wasn't dumb. She taught herself to play this old piano my father bought her without a book or a lesson. She was quiet most of the time and always nice to me. She didn't get really bad until the last couple of years."

"I never saw a piano," Ellen said.

"My mother got rid of it a long time ago, once it became clear that Eva wasn't coming back."

"What happened?"

"She gave it away."

"What happened to Eva?"

"She got a lot worse after my father died. She was sixteen, I was eight."

"Eight?"

"Eight."

"I heard Eva was pretty normal when she was eight, even went to school for a while."

"Who told you that?" Selma said.

"Sarah."

"I never knew her when she was that normal."

"What was wrong with her?"

"It's hard to describe."

"Try."

"She was afraid to go outside near the end. Cried a lot, sometimes banged her head against the wall, slowly and deliberately like she was punishing herself for doing something wrong. She used to chew on her lower lip until it was raw and bleeding. I'd almost forgotten that."

"We lived on the fifth floor and she'd sit for hours staring out the window at the people below, watching for father mostly. She'd get so excited when he turned the corner that she'd start to shake."

"She was very pretty," Selma added.

Ellen let Selma talk. Selma and Sarah might have been right to try to keep it secret, she thought, if only they had been more successful.

"Staying home wasn't uncommon in those days. The schools never cared. Besides, my father didn't like her to go out."

"How did she wind up at Pilgrim State?"

"She was never the same after he died. She still sat by the window waiting for him to come home. She stopped doing the little things she used to do around the house . . . dusting, washing clothes and cooking. We washed our clothes in the bathtub back then. She'd get upset over every little thing . . . things I couldn't even see. She'd be sitting there quietly one minute and kicking furniture the next."

"My mother had to keep working. They didn't have life insurance in those days, at least we didn't. He was so young when he died. One day, Sarah and I were home alone. We were in the kitchen when Eva broke the bedroom window and climbed onto the fire escape like she was going to jump. She could have opened it for God's sake; I don't know why she had to break it. She kept screaming that she could see my father coming. It was just a man with a similar hat and overcoat. Someone called the police and they took her away. What were Sarah and I going to do? By the time my mother got to the station, Eva was already on her way to Pilgrim State for observation."

"How awful," Ellen said.

It was a parent's worst nightmare. Ellen tried to imagine what it would feel like if they took Jaime away. She'd seen it happen once before at school, when the nurse mistook a bruise for child abuse and the mother came to pick up her little girl only to find a policeman there instead. It took her a month to get her back.

"Eva had never been to a doctor. My father refused to take her. My mother couldn't get to Pilgrim State until the next morning. The doctors told her that Eva was a danger to herself and possibly us, that she needed immediate help and they could help her without charge. A short stay was all it would take."

"They talked her into signing a piece of paper or told her she had to. She wouldn't have resisted. You wouldn't challenge the authorities back then, not the way you do now. She thought it was for a few days, but it gave them the right to decide when Eva was ready to go home. A few days became a few weeks and a few months and then a few years. Eva never came home again."

"I don't understand how they could do that?" Ellen said. "Did your mother try to get her out?"

"At first she tried, but she got nowhere. There were no patient rights advocates back then. Everyone didn't run to a lawyer. Who had the money? Mental hospitals were like prisons. Maybe she didn't really try, I don't know. Maybe she was afraid. She was an immigrant raising a family alone. She avoided government officials. Her two brothers were drowned by the White Russians and she had three children at home to protect. Besides, Sarah said that Eva deteriorated very quickly and after awhile didn't want to come home."

"There's nothing else?"

"Isn't that enough?"

"Why keep her a secret?"

Selma's breathing sounded like static on the radio.

"When it first happened, it was hard to talk about. I was young and it was so difficult to know what to say that we didn't say anything. And Eva didn't want to see anyone. After a while it seemed easier to keep silent about it. It wasn't a conscious decision after a family discussion or anything like that . . . it just sort of grew into a secret."

That made about as much sense as some of the excuses Ellen got for forgotten homework.

"I never saw Eva again. Sarah went a couple of times the first few years. Max moved away. Only my mother kept going and she never talked about her, not a single word. I thought about going, but by the time I was old enough and felt ready too many years had gone by. She wouldn't have wanted to see me by then. My mother discouraged it and she saw her so she knew. Before you know it a dozen years had gone by. My mother always used to say that the days drag on, but the years fly by."

"I remember," Ellen said.

Neither Ellen nor Selma had their minds any longer on the conversation.

"I really wish I had seen her one more time."

Ellen realized that she had to act fast before Selma started to repeat herself.

"But I was so young when it happened. It was probably for the best. She couldn't have lived outside."

"I have to go," Ellen said.

"I don't even have a picture."

"I have to get back to class."

"It wasn't an easy thing to put out of your mind, not as a child. Not talking about it was the first step, a necessary step."

"I'll let you know as soon as I hear from Ira."

"My mother was the only one who went to Eva's funeral. She didn't even tell us until it was over. It would have been dishonest to go at that point anyway."

"I'll call tonight."

Ellen's head hurt and her muscles were knotted like a staircase from her stomach to her neck, a sign that there was something still missing, something still being concealed. Her intuition was rarely wrong.

Shirley managed to stay away from Records the entire afternoon and Eva's file sat in Rhonda's locker. To pass the time Ira actually worked, pulling out the old files one by one and entering all the required information onto the list. He actually enjoyed it. He'd grown accustomed to busy work over the years at American Family Care. Paperwork could be very reassuring sometimes. It took him out of the moment or, better yet, took the moment out of him and dropped it into his subconscious. It gave him time to think without really being aware of it.

At quitting time, he left Shirley a note.

"Tomorrow I want the whole truth . . . that means everything."

That meant another tomorrow at Pilgrim State. Rhonda was waiting at the car.

"Any problem with the file?"

"A little."

"What?"

"My locker was jammed. I couldn't open it."

His mouth moved, but no sound came out.

"Just joking."

"That's not funny."

"I wanted to see if you could get mad."

"I can."

"Good."

"So where's the file."

"In my bag."

He extended his hand.

Rhonda handed him a piece of paper instead with Doc Fulton's address on it. He was in an old age home in Atlantic City.

"Probably lost his mind by now," she said.

"That would be fitting."

Rhonda put her hand on his thigh, leaned over and gave him a long, arousing kiss. He figured that it was either the thrill of the hunt or the break from dealing with lunacy all day that made his brand of suburban sanity so irresistible. She made him feel twenty-five, thin and handsome. He only needed to glance at his reflection in the window to break that spell.

"Can you take tomorrow off?" he suddenly said.

"Why?"

"To go to Atlantic City."

Now he was the one who didn't want to drive alone.

"Only if we go tonight and stay at one of the casinos."

"You think Shirley will mind?"

"Are you kidding? I'll call in sick for both of us. Where should we stay? How about the Trump Plaza, I've heard it's spectacular."

"It doesn't matter to me."

"I'm going to bring a dress."

Rhonda sounded like Jaime. He took Eva's file out of Rhonda's bag. Just holding it made his lap tingle.

"I've never been to Atlantic City," Rhonda said.

"Me neither."

"That's hard to believe."

"Because I'm in my forties?"

"Because I thought it was the in place to go from Westchester."

"I don't live in Westchester. I live on the poor side of the river in Rockland County."

"Never heard of it," Rhonda said looking somewhat disappointed.

"But I know people who go all the time."

"That's what I mean. I don't know anyone from the hospital who's gone. They're too busy drinking after work to drive that far."

They drove a while in silence. Ira was thinking about what this might meant to his marriage and his job. He kept telling himself that everything would be all right and that he hadn't gone too far, not yet. Ira was great believer in the power of rationalization. Think something often enough and with enough conviction and it not only becomes convincing, it also become true.

"This is really exciting," Rhonda said. "I've got a hundred dollars in a drawer at home, but I can get another hundred from the ATM. You think two hundred is enough?"

Rhonda was probably imagining herself in front of a slot machine, pulling the arm, and hitting the jackpot with bells and lights going off and casino security rushing to surround her. Someone will appear to take her photograph, and she'll become a minor celebrity. Maybe her father will notice the photo in USA Today, wherever he is and give her a call.

"I'm sure it is," she said, "because I'm going to be staying at the slots. I wonder if they have quarter slots. How much money do you have with you? Ira, are you listening?"

"What?"

"How much money do you have with you?"

"Not much," he said, "but I don't gamble."

"You're gambling now Hon. You're betting that Doc Fulton has another piece of the puzzle."

He nodded slowly.

"You'd better bring some money, just in case."

He could get some money from an ATM. He's never done it before, although he did have an ATM card. He considered it something to use only in an emergency and this hardly seems to qualify, at least it wouldn't have last week.

Rhonda put her hand on his thigh and smiled at him.

"Listen," Ira said, "I have to be back home by the weekend."

"How about a week this summer at the beach," she said.

"You and me?"

"No, you and Shirley."

Ira heard beach and thought family vacation, boardwalk, bumper cars, movies and budget. It was a conditioned response.

"We could OD on movies. You could sneak away, take another business trip."

"I don't think so."

"Even for a couple of days?"

"Not likely."

"How about for one night?"

"It's a long drive for a movie."

"We could meet somewhere in the middle, maybe in the city."

It was a nice thought, it really was, but how would it fit into his routine. It was too big a risk.

"We'd have a blast," she said. "We could stay at a nice hotel and go to one of those big single screen theaters . . . and then come back for a little late night fun."

It was every middle age man's dream.

"I'll think about it."

"We could watch a dirty movie at the hotel – they always have those movie-on-demand boxes. I know how you guys like that."

Ira hoped that she did hit the jackpot tonight. A rich woman never has trouble finding a date for the movies.

The car ride to Atlantic City took almost five hours. It was a dreary ride along an invisible coast. A four-lane highway under construction everywhere, surrounded by smokestacks and oil refineries with smells that ranged from burning rubber to decaying garbage. The ocean might as well have been a thousand miles away. The road was full of large trucks. The word accident was written all over the double trailers as they swayed from side to side threatening to break away. Ira could see the headline--"American Family Coupon Executive and Mistress Lobotomized by Tandem Trailer."

The cars on this road weren't heading to the local supermarket or even to the movies. They were automobiles on missions, moving fast on serious business, heading to Washington to meet with important people or fleeing from families, driven by great emotional forces like hope, desperation, and tragedy. Ira glanced in every car they passed. He saw middlemen in drug cartels making overnight deliveries, men and women rushing to affairs and ordinary, hard-working fathers, pockets bulging with car payments and food money, looking for a way out. Most of them would be home before dawn and back at work in the morning, as if all they did last night was sit in front of the television.

He almost wished that he were one of them. He knew that he should call Ellen, but it was almost eleven. Nothing he could say now would improve the situation. He should also have called his boss, even at home, since tomorrow was Wednesday, and AFC was expecting him. Hard falls often followed unmet business expectations at AFC, but since he wouldn't be there anyway, why bother. Besides, he was sure that he had enough credit in AFC's bank of reliability to get a pass for a few days more, especially coming on the heels of a death in the family. He wondered what his grandmother would think of all this, if the world's religions were all right and she were able to look down from heaven.

They were about twenty minutes away when Rhonda picked up Eva's file and started flipping through it.

"She was definitely a family commitment."

"How can you tell?"

"Too wordy to be a court order, besides, it always says so up front if it is."

Rhonda read on while he glanced at her face from time to time looking for some sign of surprise or understanding. After a while, he couldn't stand the silence.

"Doesn't reading in the car make you nauseous?" he asked.

"No."

"It makes me nauseous just watching you."

Rhonda put her hand on his knee."

"Tired?"

"Hungry."

"Me too," she said without moving her hand away.

"So what do you see?"

"Probably home manageable by today's standards."

"Then why is she there?"

"You heard Shirley. They got paid by the patient back then."

"I don't know if I believe Shirley," Ira said. "I think she knows more than she's letting on."

"She didn't just work at Pilgrim," Rhonda said nodding slowly.

"She was a patient?"

"I'm not supposed to say anything."

"Tell me."

"She swore me to secrecy."

"I won't tell, I swear."

"She wasn't a patient her mother was, since she was a little girl. She also died at Pilgrim. Shirley started working there right afterward."

"What a life."

"Her father used to beat her and her brother over the head with it. He wouldn't let her visit. He wanted them to hate her, just like he did, but she wouldn't."

"What happened to him?"

"Drank himself to death."

"That's terrible."

"I think she was happy when he finally died."

"And her brother?"

"She was really close to him. Neither of them ever got married. He died in the war."

"Vietnam?"

"Korea. You won't say anything?"

"No."

"It's different today," Rhonda said. "The big thing is census reduction. Get them out on the streets. The administrators keep their job based on turnover."

Rhonda turned back to Eva's file.

"It's likely that Eva was admitted for observation, because of something that happened and wound up staying."

"Could they hold her forever?"

"I don't think so, but the doctors could do a number on your grandmother. Frighten her to death. Make Eva sound dangerous, even suicidal. They still do it today. They probably got her to sign some kind of conditional commitment that took it out of her hands. Your grandmother didn't stand a chance. And with all that experimentation back then, your aunt probably got a lot worse real quick."

Rhonda was a different person when she talked business, more mature and serious. Everyone had a different personality at work. He could make small talk at AFC. The things to talk about were always so obvious, the boss, the bonus and the new products. He didn't need Ellen's social assistance.

"Sure," Rhonda said flipping through the file, "new symptoms appear all the time. Suddenly, she has delusions. You pick them up like colds. After six months, she probably got so bad that the doctors didn't have to do very much to convince your grandmother she belonged."

His grandmother was such a kind and gentle person, never confrontational. She never asked anything for herself. What a burden, Ira realized, to carry silently all those years. While the car hurtled through the dark, polluted night at sixty-five miles per hour, he passed through Eva's wasted lifetime, from a young girl to an old woman in an instant. Skipping rope one moment and pummeled the next, forced to take refuge in the limitless darkness, heroically patient, profoundly sad, and entirely alone.

It was a dark night. There wasn't a star in the sky and it was getting foggy. The cars that passed now were filled with invisible people. It was hard to concentrate. Steam rose from the side of the road as if the land was simmering. The headlights from the oncoming cars reflected off the windshield. He was hungry and tired. It felt like the walls of his stomach were melting. In less than a week he'd screwed up his job and his family. He must have looked like he felt, because after a few moments of silence Rhonda moved closer and ran her hand, already on his knee, up along his thigh.

"It's not your fault," she said.

Rhonda kept reminding him that man was largely animal. Her fingers triggered a hormonal response that drew the curtain on depression and replaced it with a single new thought - how soon could they get to the hotel.

"How long?" he asked.

Rhonda studied the map.

"Another fifteen minutes."

Spontaneous desire was a new feeling for Ira or else it was an old feeling that he'd forgotten. After almost 20 years of marriage, it wasn't desire that motivated lovemaking, it was the day of the week and the time of night. It wasn't influenced by the tides or the stars, but by the energy left after the chores, the state of the children's health and what was on television. Even the family's finances affected it. Weekdays were never good. Work took its toll. Sunday was too much of a family day. So it was Saturday night by default. Ira guessed that between eleven at night and one in the morning the seismograph needles around the country jumped; not from the normal wobble of the earth, but from the programmed lust of millions of husbands and their complying wives.

"Curious," Rhonda said putting the file back in her bag, "about that three month gap in 1951."

"Could she have gone home?"

"No way, they'd have bragged about that all over the file."

"I'm sure it was lost," Ira said. "I'm amazed they didn't lose the whole thing."

"Of course, she could have been transferred for a while, sent somewhere to be studied. They do that sometimes. Put a lobotomy patient on display. Maybe she was in the hospital for something."

"There's Trumps."

The Trump Castle and Casino looked majestically in the distance. It was like the Taj Mahal compared to what they'd been staring at for the last five hours.

"Have you worked with any lobotomy patients?"

"I've come across a couple. There aren't too many around anymore."

"What are they like?"

"It's hard to say, since I don't know what they were like before the operation and it's been so long for most of them. They're like a lot of older patients. They're not too excitable and easy to manage. The thing is, and this might be because they're older, their language skills are weak and they're very forgetful. Unaware or unconscious is probably a better way to put it. There was this one woman who could be eating dinner and would continue to sit there and act like she was eating after the food was long gone. She just kept doing it, like she was reliving a memory."

Rhonda put her head back on the seat and closed her eyes.

"And of course they never have visitors."

They checked into Trump's Castle and Casino. You're supposed to feel like you're back in Ancient Rome surrounded by beautiful girls in togas with push-up bras and columns of imitation stone. The bellhops looked more like Arabian knights than Roman legionaries. Ira felt more like a Christian about to be fed to the lions than a citizen of the ancient empire.

The room wasn't cheap, one hundred and fifty dollars for the night. He almost suggested getting back into the car and finding a Days Inn or Motel Six, but how could he when the bellboys silently whistled at Rhonda and winked at him with a mixture of envy and incredulity. They clearly thought he was someone rich and successful. He had to put the room on his credit card, so Ellen was sure to find out. So even though it was almost midnight, he decided to call home. The best defense, he figured, was to avoid surprise.

"Let go down," Rhonda said.

"I have to wash up and do a few things first."

"Like what?"

"Like go to the bathroom for one. You go down and I'll meet you in about fifteen minutes."

"Look for me at the slots."

After she left Ira sat down on the bed and picked up the phone. He held it for a while, because he couldn't bring himself to dial. Why was he calling? His intentions didn't feel all that honorable. It was as if this crazy and unpredictable gene had been waiting quietly all these years for Eva to turn up and now it was eager to shock everyone, including himself. Calling after midnight from Atlantic City would certainly do that.

The first time he dialed the line was busy. Ellen was probably talking to his mother for the eightieth time today having the same conversation over and over again. So he took out his wallet and counted the cash, one hundred and forty-two dollars. He had his two emergency checks, but he wasn't sure how much was in the checking account, a strange feeling for someone who checked the balance almost every night. He could use his credit card to get money from a cash machine, but he shuddered at the thought of paying interest.

He dialed again and this time it rang.

"Hello."

It wasn't her sleepy voice; it was her tired but troubled voice.

"Ellen."

"Where are you?"

"Atlantic City."

Ellen took a deep breath, like she couldn't decide whether to act deeply disturbed or faintly amused. It didn't take her long to make up her mind.

"What the hell are you doing in Atlantic City?"

"I found Eva's file. She had a lobotomy."

"And you're looking for her brain in Atlantic City?"

"The guy who did it is in a nursing home here. His name is Doctor Fulton. I'm going to see him in the morning."

"And he's going to tell you what her brain looked like?"

"You don't actually see the brain when you do a lobotomy."

"Perhaps you should consider getting one for yourself."

"I'm hoping that he'll remember something about her."

"You're delusional."

Ellen cleared her throat, just the opportunity he needed for a quick subject change.

"How are Jaime and Scott?"

"I'm glad to see you haven't forgotten their names."

He pretended to chuckle.

"How is school? Are they asleep?"

"They're not here."

"Where are they?"

"Not in Atlantic City, that's for sure." Ellen paused. "They're sleeping at friends."

"It's a school night?"

"They had to get out of the house. It's too upsetting here."

"Come on."

"The phone rings constantly and at all hours, thanks to you."

"It can't be that bad, half their friends' parents are split up."

Ellen's gasp could probably be heard down at the gambling tables.

"Are we split up now? Is that what's happened, because if we are I'd hate to be the last to know."

"I didn't mean it like that. I meant that a lot of families have problems . . . not that this is even a problem. It's just a temporary thing. Searching for a missing aunt is more like an adventure."

"An adventure? Ira, I think you're losing your mind."

"It does run in the family."

"Have you thought for one second about what you're doing?"

"Believe me, I've thought about nothing else."

He couldn't remember Ellen ever being this confrontational.

"Your boss called."

"Dan?"

"No, Paul."

Ellen waited for the obvious question. It probably was a mistake to call he realized. It was like playing a verbal game of chicken. Too much longer of a pause and the only thing left to say would be good-bye.

"Did he say why?"

"There was a problem with the new coupon campaign. He sounded pretty annoyed. You'd better call. It didn't sound to me like you're going to have that job for too much longer."

Her spirits seemed to rise on that note. He didn't want to shock her even more by saying that he didn't care. It should have bothered him, last week it would have sent him fleeing to the bathroom, but it hardly registered now. First, she had to be exaggerating. He'd been a loyal employee for too long. Second, it was hard to get upset about a job or anything else, when you were sitting above a casino filled with thousands of tormented souls teetering between riches and ruin, a casino that was screaming out his name, like his mother used to when he was late for dinner.

"I'll call tomorrow, I should know more in the next day or two."

"Then we can discuss whether or not you should come home."

Ellen waited for some kind of response, an apology, or at least an objection. He did want to return home and ask her forgiveness, but not right now. Now he wanted to go downstairs and stretch his legs, see what he'd been missing all these years.

"Are you there with that woman?"

She caught him off guard and he hesitated. Then he started to stutter and Ellen had her answer.

"I thought so."

"There's a nurse helping me. She's the only one who can understand the file and she knew Doc Fulton. Her name's Shirley. She's fat and pushing seventy-five."

"I bet," Ellen said hanging up the phone.

He held the receiver to his ear until the dial tone clicked back on. There was only one thing he could do now to avoid thinking himself senseless, so he picked up his wallet and headed down to the casino. It was an enormous room probably five times the size of a football field, crowded and smoky with a roar that could have deafened a jet engine. Players cheered for the dice, dealers screamed out numbers, slots went off like fire alarms, oohs and aahs beat like an overworked heart, nubile Roman wenches scampered about with trays of drinks. It took him a few moments to recognize the most striking feature about the casino. It had no windows. It could be day or night, rain or shine. There was no way to know. And there were no clocks. Time and space were meaningless here. You were forced to live in the moment and chips were the only measure of existence. Life was the instant bet and alcohol.

It felt like a dream, as well as a firetrap.

He walked around the slots looking for Rhonda, but there were slots scattered throughout the casino. People stood two and three deep and he couldn't remember what Rhonda was wearing. There were groups of old ladies, the kind that sit on park benches during the summer with their stockings rolled down below the knee, pulling slots like they were in heat. They sat side-by-side talking without ever turning their heads, extolling the merits of their machine and recounting the near misses. He didn't hear a single word about grandchildren. It was as if they had checked their families at the door. Unlike their neat apartments back home, the floor beneath their feet was littered with coin wrappers and large plastic cups.

After looking for Rhonda for almost one-half hour, he gave up and walked over to the blackjack tables. It was the only game he really understood, since simple addition was in his genes thanks to his father. Besides, he was feeling a little claustrophobic and it was less crowded in that part of the casino. He stopped behind a ten-dollar table with two empty chairs. The dealer looked up and hesitated a moment before dealing. It was an Atlantic City invitation. When he didn't move, she dealt the cards.

"Dealer shows six."

The first player had thirteen and stuck and the next player "stood pat" with sixteen. Two more players were "good" at nineteen. The last player had eight.

"Hit me," he said like it was a dare.

He drew an unhappy seven, but stuck with fifteen.

The dealer turned over her down card. It was a picture.

"Dealer has sixteen."

"Bust," the players called out.

The dealer drew a ten.

Players bumped shoulders and slapped palms like teammates after a touchdown as the dealer paid off everyone.

He took out his wallet to check again what was in there. When the dealer looked up and hesitated, he put it away. What was he thinking? He didn't gamble. He picked pennies up from the sidewalk. He hated to waste money. He kept his lunches at work under four dollars, eating every meal at AFP's cafeteria. He bought a lottery ticket once a month, but he didn't consider that gambling. It was more like a donation to the state education fund.

There were four men and one woman at the table. They were probably ordinary working people, but in the soft, forgiving casino light, they looked mysterious, like characters out of a James Bond movie, not really playing blackjack, but on a secret mission - people driven by political and private passions that had nothing to do with cards or money. A fat man in a green suit sat down at the far end leaving one opening at the table. He held a cigarette in one hand and a drink in the other. He talked constantly to the dealer and the cards. His bets were never less than twenty-five dollars and he quickly became the big man at the ten-dollar table.

"Dealer shows a ten."

The big man had thirteen.

"Hit me baby . . . nice and little . . . do it for the kiddies."

He didn't look like the father type, at least not the type that anyone would want as a father. The dealer turned over a six and the big man sat back and lit another cigarette like it was the best sex he'd ever had.

"The cards love me tonight," he said with a wink around the table.

"Nineteen," the dealer said without a smile.

She was short and pretty, her breasts pushed up to her chin. Her nametag said Anita, but she looked more like a Sue.

"You think I'm hitting on nineteen doll? Not unless you want to show me another ten under there," the fat man said with a ho-ho-ho.

"You have to signal your intentions, sir."

He passed his palm over the cards like a priest giving a benediction then she turned over the ten. Of course, she didn't know what it was, she never looked. She didn't even care. It wasn't her money.

"Dealer pays twenty-one."

"For Christ's sake, how do you lose with a hard nineteen? You should warn us in advance, honey."

She took the money with her face wiped clean of any expression.

"Push," she said to the next player rapping her knuckles on the table and leaving his money untouched. He also had a twenty.

There were four losses and one tie.

"Where's the girl?" the fat man said moving his head and shrugging his shoulders like Rodney Dangerfield. "I need a drink."

The dealer raised her hand and a few moments later a waitress appeared.

"Dewars straight up," he said making a big deal of tossing her a dollar chip in exchange for a good look at her cleavage.

The dealer, who had been shuffling five decks and putting them back into the shoe, dealt another round. The dealer's face card was a seven. The first player, a well-dressed oriental man, had two five's.

"Double down," he said putting another ten in the betting circle.

"Picture," he commanded pointing at the table with his index finger.

It was a jack of clubs. His neighbor shook his head in wonderment, like it was a feat of remarkable skill.

"I hope there's one left," he said staring at his nine.

He looked like he had just walked in off the street from one of those dilapidated row houses that surrounded the casino like a moat. He was dressed in oil-stained jeans and a black t-shirt. His hands were callused and dirty. He also drew a ten and nodded at the oriental man like they'd just bridged some kind of cultural gap.

"This is our shoe," the fat man said.

He was betting fifty dollars. There was a disorganized pile of chips in front of him, perhaps a thousand dollars worth. He tried to give the impression that he found money meaningless, but he squeezed a one hundred-dollar chip in his hand and kept one eye on his pile like he was worried about stragglers. No one at the table reacted to any of his comments. No one liked him.

An older woman was in the third seat, expensive, low cut, black evening gown and lots of gaudy jewelry, including a ring with a diamond the size of a grape. She smoked cigarette after cigarette, bet ten dollars every hand and looked completely disinterested, as if she were just killing time. She looked behind her frequently, sometimes at Ira.

She started to "split" two queens, but the dealer stopped her.

"Never break up a good hand," Anita said moving on without even waiting for the "standing pat" signal.

The fourth player was a young kid, barely twenty-one. A friend leaned over his shoulder whispering in his ear with every card, while biting his nails at the same time and bouncing up and down on his toes.

The dealer was showing an ace.

"Get insurance," he said loud enough for everyone to hear.

His friend put down five dollars to protect his ten-dollar bet. If the dealer had blackjack, the house would pay double the insurance, so it would be a wash. If not, he'd lose the insurance. She didn't have blackjack, but he drew an ace for twenty-one, validating Ira's mother's philosophy on insurance--you get it but only to make sure nothing bad will happen.

A woman came up next to him, late thirties, a lot of make-up, very pretty in an evening sort of way.

"I like to watch a table before sitting down," she said, "so I can avoid the hot dealers."

Ira nodded. It made some sense. The dealer turned over a four to go with her seven.

"Eleven," she said dealing herself a nine. "Twenty pays twenty-one."

Only the kid won. The moans from everyone else, including the audience, were not feigned.

"Lucky bitch," the fat man whispered into his drink.

"She's hot," the woman said.

She was standing so close that Ira could feel the heat from her arms.

"Are you going to sit down?"

"I don't know."

"Are you here alone?"

"No, I'm here with . . . my wife. She's at the slots."

"That's nice."

She stood next to him for another ten seconds and than moved to another table to stand beside another potential acquisition. Maybe she thought he had money. He'd been fooling a lot of people lately, a talent he never knew he had. Or perhaps at a certain age even a guy like him becomes interesting. You walk around with a certain resigned indifference at forty that many confuse with confidence; the fact that he wasn't on the make or desperate to score at the tables could be another turn on.

Twenty-one is a fast game that involves both luck and skill. He could see that the better players watched all the cards that came out. No just their own, which probably gave them some idea of what remained in the deck and what the dealer might have in the hole. Ira remembered that someone at work had this supposedly foolproof system. You doubled your bet every time you lost until you won, then returned to your original bet. He never lost or so he said, probably because he never played. You'd need a lot of money to stay on a system like that, more than one hundred and forty-two dollars.

He looked around for Rhonda and spotted a bank cash machine. He walked over, but it was out of order. A casino hostess stood next to it ready to pounce. She dragged him to the credit window around the corner. In five minutes, without opening his mouth, Ira had another five hundred dollars. The credit line on the card was ten thousand dollars, so he was welcome to come back anytime day or night, rain or shine. It was much more personal than the offers of credit he got all the time in the mail.

Ira looked at his watch. It was twelve thirty. Normally, he'd be sleeping for an hour by now. Tonight he didn't feel the least bit tired. He wondered if they pumped in a little extra oxygen to keep the energy level so high. He walked back to the table. The dealer stopped again and looked up at him. This time she didn't move until Ira sat down. He put a one hundred-dollar bill down on the table. He couldn't remember the last time he had a one hundred-dollar bill, let alone five. Smaller bills seemed to last longer.

"Check change one hundred," the dealer called out to no one in particular.

She stood at attention with her hands flat on the table, palms up. The crisp new one hundred-dollar bill was in front of her like a religious offering. A sour-faced, heavy set man with a pinkie ring the size of a brass knuckle and "Laura" tattooed on the back of his hand walked by and peered over her shoulder. He wasn't looking down at her breasts.

"Go ahead," he said looking at the bill like road kill.

The hundred dollars disappeared down a slot in the table. For all that money, he got ten blue chips.

"Good luck, sir," Anita said with a tired smile.

He put up a chip and got a king. The dealer showed a nine. He drew another picture card. He didn't pay any attention to the rest of the table. This was his first bet ever and it looked like a winner. He didn't take his eyes off his cards in case they had any idea of getting up and running away. He kept adding them up and they totaled twenty each time. The dealer turned over a ten to a chorus of moans.

"Nineteen, dealer pays twenty."

It was the easiest ten dollars Ira had ever made.

Forgetting in his excitement that bets were only doubled after a loss, Ira left the two ten-dollar chips in the betting circle and drew eighteen. The dealer showed a picture and turned over a four. She busted with a ten. Ira stared at his thirty dollars in winnings and wondered why he hadn't tried this before. Maybe he was born with the touch; wouldn't his mother be proud.

He drew back his profits and went back to betting ten dollars. His next hand was twelve. The dealer showed a nine. He took a hit and went over. The dealer took his money although she had fifteen and also went over. That didn't seem fair. He doubled the bet, no big deal, since he was still playing with their money. He lost again. Now he put up four chips, doubling his bet according to a theory that made perfect sense to him. Eventually he had to win and that would bring him back to where he started. Still, he found it hard to believe that he had forty dollars riding on a deck of cards. He thought about quitting, after all he was even. Suddenly he felt very tired. He was about to pull back his bet, when Anita dealt his first card so it was too late.

He breathed a sigh of relief, nineteen, his luck held after all. He planned to leave after this one win, which looked like a slam-dunk with Anita showing a six. Unfortunately, she had a four underneath and pulled a ten for twenty and he lost again. He had six chips left. He needed eight to double the bet, but he went with six. Win here, he realized, and he walked away a winner. The odds had to be in his favor after what just happened. Of course, he would never bet sixty dollars if it were real money. The chips made it easy. They were like subway tokens, either you used them or you lost them. The money had already been spent.

Ira had twenty and the dealer had fifteen. He saw the bed waiting for him and he blessed the system. Maybe Rhonda was already up there, her nude body like one of those Spanish paintings in the Metropolitan Museum of Art. However, Anita pulled a six and a cry went up that stopped the heart of every gambler at the blackjack tables throughout the entire casino. They all knew what it meant. Anita looked up sheepishly at him, like she really felt bad about it. Maybe she did, but not nearly as bad as Ira did.

"Did you ever see such luck?" the fat man said.

"I had twenty," Ira said thinking that that fat man only had seventeen and couldn't possible know how he felt.

"You're killing us," the fat man said to Anita giving her another lame Rodney Dangerfield impression complete with the shoulder jerk and head roll. While Anita "shuffled up", the fat man choked on the combination of smoke and free booze.

Ira was now down one hundred dollars, an enormous sum for someone who spent five minutes going through his pockets looking for a missing dime. The next bet was supposed to be one hundred and sixty dollars. That would put him up sixty. She was due to lose. He didn't have to be an expert on game theory and statistics to figure that out. One more hand, one more win, he said to himself, and he would be out of here.

"Check change two hundred," Anita said.

Mr. Pinkie Ring looked Ira over this time instead of the money.

"Go ahead."

He bet one hundred and sixty.

"Hundred sixty up."

"Go ahead."

The Pinkie Man nodded in his direction, clearly a sign of respect. Then he extended his lower lip over his upper as if he were reverting back to his gorilla ancestors. He stayed to watch, looking up from time to time at the mirrored ceiling. On the other side the eyes gathered to watch the new fish on the hook.

He drew lousy cards, a ten and a four. The dealer showed an eight. Suddenly, there was a hand on his collar, like he'd been caught.

"The ten dollar table," Rhonda said, "have you been holding out on me?"

"This is the last hand."

"How are you doing?"

She looked down at his bet.

"Holy shit, how much are you betting?"

"I'm down a hundred. I was up thirty a minute ago. If I win this one I'm up sixty and I quit."

"You're crazy."

She was the second woman to call him that tonight.

"I mean it, I'm quitting if I win."

He meant forever. He looked back at Rhonda and suddenly couldn't wait to go up to the room. But first he had to make the right decision. Anita looked down at him. She wanted him to make up his mind. Her feet hurt. It was near the end of her shift.

"Hit sir."

She didn't realize how important this decision really was. He wasn't like the others, he was an accidental gamble, it was involuntary, more boredom than anything else. It was a one-time thing, he'd had his taste and now he wanted out. It had all been a big mistake. Just let him win this one hand and be gone.

"Hit?" she repeated.

Maybe she was trying to give him a hint. Why didn't she use the word stick? What if the fat man's right and she knew what she had underneath. But how could she? He needed to think. Ira didn't like to rush a decision. What if she had a seven or eight underneath? Her eyes gave nothing away. Of course, it was just another day at the office for her.

"What would you like to do?"

"Hit it," Rhonda said sounding very certain about it.

He needed an empirical study, some reliable statistics and perhaps a written recommendation.

"You can't stick with fourteen pal," the fat man said. "She's probably sitting with a ten in the hole."

"What will it be?" Anita said.

The crowd around the table anxiously awaited his decision.

"Hit me."

It was a five, nineteen. The crowd murmured its approval.

He leaned back on his chair and Rhonda gave him a pat on the back. He could imagine the hero's welcome he'd get when they got back to the room.

"I told you so," the fat man said.

He had sixteen and it was obvious that he should stick. The entire table knew it. All the spectators knew it, as did Mr. Pinky and the people above the ceiling. The next card had to be a big one. It was the law of averages. He started to pass his palm over his cards, but then stopped and tapped the table with his index finger.

"Hit me."

The idiot probably had a feeling, an itch in his throat that he'd been relying on his whole gluttonous life. Anita turned over a ten before anyone could stop him.

"Over," she said making it sound much more final than it really was. The fat man shrugged and fingered his chips. Twenty-five dollars meant nothing to him.

Anita turned over a seven.

"Dealer has fifteen."

Damn that fat man, Ira thought, if he hadn't taken a hit she'd be over and he'd be on his way upstairs.

"Well I blew that one didn't I?" the fat man said sucking down half a cigarette.

Ira hoped it would kill him. Of course, there were still plenty of high cards in the deck. There could always be two in row, the hell with probability. Anita drew a card. It slipped from her grasp before she got a chance to turn it over, but Ira was sure that he saw the serious face of a one-eyed jack. She had a little trouble picking it back up. She didn't want to bend the card and her hands were dry. She turned over a five.

"Dealer has twenty, pays twenty-one."

Pinkyman walked away with a big grin. Ira pulled the trigger on the fat man with a look that was intended to shoot him straight between the eyes. He didn't even notice. He screamed "asshole" in his head loud enough to hurt his own ears. Rhonda punched his shoulder.

"Hot as a pistol," the kid on the other side said getting up.

"Save my place," the fat man said, "I have to find the john."

The dealer put a slug on his spot.

How appropriate, Ira thought.

The bet was now three twenty. He was down two sixty, one month's payment on Ellen's car, three telephone bills, or one heating bill during the winter. He has four chips, two hundred left from the five hundred he borrowed, and another one hundred and forty two of his own. It was his turn to win, he was sure of it.

"Bets up," Anita said.

He gave her the two eighty to change and bet three twenty.

"Wow," Rhonda whispered into his ear, like it was the beginning of foreplay.

"It's a system."

"Three twenty up," Anita called out.

"Go ahead," Pinkyman answered without bothering to look over this time. He knew who was trying to wiggle off the hook.

"Do you have thirty to lend me?" Rhonda said. "All I could find were the dollar slots."

He handed Rhonda the money, hoping she'd leave. Maybe she was the one who brought him bad luck last game, her and the fat man.

"Go ahead and play," he said.

"Not on your life."

Anita dealt him two pictures, but she had an ace showing.

"Insurance?"

Ira knew that he should, because of the size of his bet, but it would have cost $160 and he didn't have it. Besides, the odds weren't good with all the pictures showing on the table. No one took insurance, so they played the hand and everyone at the table had eighteen or better. Unfortunately, Anita turned over a queen of hearts.

"Blackjack."

In twenty minutes, he had lost five hundred and eighty dollars. It felt almost as if he'd lost a limb. He got up from the table reluctantly. The next hand or the one after that was bound to be his. He knew that as surely as he knew that Pilgrim State Hospital didn't cure one single person back in the thirties and forties. But he'd have to bet six hundred and forty and even if he had the nerve there wasn't enough time to get it.

He thought about asking Anita to wait, but someone quickly took his seat, someone who had been watching and knew that the bad luck was leaving with him. He put down ten dollars and the dealer busted. His imaginary winnings pounded like a hammer between his eyes. He needed an aspirin, more than one, probably half a bottle.

"It's all because the fat man took a hit when he shouldn't have," he said to Rhonda.

"That's why I'd never play cards," Rhonda said pulling him over to the roulette table.

She played two rows at a time, six numbers. In fifteen minutes, she'd turned his small loan into one hundred and fifty dollars. While she did, he drifted off and signed for another five hundred. It was very easy. He was an important customer. Yes sir, thank you sir, would you like a thousand sir? They were there all night if he needed any more. He returned to the table and Pinkyman gave him two coupons, comps for free meals anywhere in the hotel. It turned out that they were in the same business.

It was after two in the morning. Instead of emptying out, the casino got more crowded. He couldn't believe that this went on day and night, seven days a week, while he worked and slept. He couldn't believe that all this noise and nervous energy surged through Atlantic City without keeping the rest of the East Coast awake. He was afraid that it would disturb his sleep from now on.

Ira lost the second five hundred faster than the first. He was dizzy and sweating so profusely that even his eyelids were wet. Rhonda took him upstairs and ordered room service. They sat in front of the television eating turkey sandwiches and drinking beer. He was one win away from beating the casino he knew that, he just didn't have the guts, let alone the money.

"What time is it?" he asked.

"A quarter to three."

"I'm going down to watch for a while, you coming?"

"No," Rhonda said, "I'm too tired."

He was back in forty-five minutes, another thousand dollars poorer. He'd lost over two thousand dollars . . . summer camp, sixty percent of the dining room table Ellen had her eye on and almost a year of commuting expenses.

"Did you play again?" Rhonda said half asleep.

"No."

When did he get so good at lying, Ira wondered?

He wanted to leave Atlantic City this very minute, but Rhonda fell back into a deep sleep, no doubt returning to some wonderful dream. He lay on his back with hands under his head. He couldn't keep his eyes open, but he couldn't sleep. He kept thinking about his money imprisoned under the blackjack table. He wanted it back. It belonged to him and to his family, maybe if he asked and explained the situation. What if he told the casino manager that he just discovered that mental illness ran in the family. He could plead temporary insanity.

Maybe if he walked around the casino, he'd find a few hundred dollar chips on the floor, dropped by that damn sixteen-hitting fat man, who couldn't find them because he couldn't see below his stomach. Maybe one pull of the dollar slot would do it. He still had a dollar. Unfortunately, he knew that he was through and that he would always be one hand away from winning his money back. He had taken a vow on the last elevator ride up. A lot of people might follow a night like this with another and another until they've lost everything and had to turn to Gambler's Anonymous. He was going with total abstinence, which certainly was a much healthier approach in the long run.

Rhonda rubbed against him in her sleep, but there was no reaction from down below. He wondered if there ever would be again, certainly not while the only thing on his mind was the things he could do to the fat man if he ever got him alone.

Ellen also had trouble sleeping. Part of her wanted Ira to lose his job. She wanted him to be punished for all this. So what if Eva had a lobotomy. So what if she was institutionalized by mistake and his grandmother didn't know how to free her. So what if no one but his grandmother ever visited Eva. So what if the family tried to keep everything a secret. There was nothing Ira or anybody else could do about that now.

Nothing seemed certain anymore. It was as if she were drowning in a river of lies. Ira was lying to her. His mother was lying to her. Aunt Sarah was lying to her. She was lying to the kids. Occasionally, a piece of truth drifted by, but it was much too small to grab hold of.

WEDNESDAY

Ira's eyes snapped open at dawn. During the night the hotel room was either too hot or too cold. He had to get up three times to adjust the thermostat. Then there were the voices in the hall laughing at their good fortune. He slept lightly most of the night aware of the constant rumblings from the casino, the tumbling of dice, the falling of cards and the clanging of chips. It sounded sometimes almost like distant thunder. The lost money lay on his stomach like a greasy meal. If he slept much, it didn't do him any good.

The dawn's light was harsh. The way it often is in a hotel room. It squirmed through the seams of the heavy curtains and exploded into the room, particles of dust churning about like part of some primordial stew. He felt like some two-dimensional character in a celluloid newsreel.

Rhonda was asleep beside him. Her breath whispered of beer and turkey. He gently lifted the cover. She was nude, her body a geometric paradise of circles and curves. Like many mornings, Ira awoke semi-erect. Semi changed quickly to complete and his hands started to sculpt Rhonda's body. She slept or pretended to sleep. Eventually, Rhonda reacted and they made love, randomly and mechanically, like they were pulling levers on a slot machine or spinning the roulette wheel.

He suspected that everything in Atlantic City kept to the same rhythm.

By the time they were done, the harsh early morning light had been replaced by a dark, overcast sky.

"What are you doing?" Rhonda said as they dressed.

"What do you mean?"

"Rapping on the table like that."

"Nothing."

He was lying again. He knocked on wood when he was worried. Ellen knew that, but he couldn't bring himself to explain it to Rhonda. It was an old German superstition. Knocking on a tree freed the good spirits. He watched his grandmother do it often enough. He needed luck this morning with Doc Fulton, something good to erase the bad taste from last night. Since he didn't bring the crystal, he had to depend on an old reliable. He waited until Rhonda went to the bathroom before knocking on the dresser one final time. He just hoped that it worked on laminated and pressed veneer.

After checking out, another two hundred dollars, they used the comps for a free breakfast. Actually, Ira figured that it was more like a $2200 breakfast.

"That was a nice way to wake up," Rhonda said with a mouth full of egg. "You're different from a lot of the other men I've been with."

"How?

"Gentler . . . more considerate . . . slower."

"I'll take that as a compliment."

"That's how I meant it."

He was not used to talking about sex, let alone being praised for his performance. At home, it sometimes seemed like a race to the orgasm. Ellen wanted to get his over with so she could go to sleep. He wanted to get there so he could turn on the TV.

"I guess because you're, you know, more mature . . . and more experienced."

He wasn't sure about the more experienced part. He wasn't even sure lately about the more mature part. He smiled at her and she smiled back. Rhonda was very cute this morning, like a little girl on vacation with her father. That's probably what the people around them were thinking.

"I've got directions to the home," he said. "We should get going. I want to get back."

"Get back where?" Rhonda said, a little anxiety creeping back into her voice.

Ira shrugged.

"Maybe old Doc Fulton will help me out and remember something," he said.

"You're dreaming. You'd have a better shot with Shirley."

"Did she say something to you? Is there something she's not telling me?"

"When would she have had a second to tell me anything?"

Rhonda hid behind her mug of coffee.

"I'll have to drive you back home whatever I decide."

Rhonda nodded.

"All I meant was that Shirley knows a lot about what went on back then. You never know what memories will come back to her."

She kept her word about Shirley's secret; Ira liked that.

Atlantic City was bi-polar. The shore was lined with elegant casinos well lit by neon signs and patrolled by uniformed guards.

There were directions to each one of them the size of billboards. The rest of Atlantic City, however, was worn and discouraged, without any sense of direction or purpose and with very few street signs. The nursing home was, of course, in the latter world.

"How the hell can you find anything," Ira said, "when the street signs are all torn down?"

"So you do get mad."

"Frustrated."

"Close enough."

Rhonda finally rolled down her window while they were stopped at a light and asked for directions. It was the old, four-story brick building that they had passed twice already. Once it probably sat on a few acres of land, the small estate of a prosperous sea captain. It looked like the property has been sold off piece-meal over the years leaving it surrounded by a variety of buildings at all different angles. Sort of the way the world might look if designed through a prism. It was not a place to send anyone you cared about, not if you had a choice.

"We're here to see Doctor Herman Fulton."

Another thing he hated was talking through a glass partition. He couldn't figure out why they bothered with that little circle of perforations, since it didn't make it any easier to hear.

"There's no Doctor Fulton on staff here."

The receptionist appeared to be in her early eighties. Her eyes had sunk deep enough into her head to resemble a couple of potholes and her skin had worn so thin that it was almost transparent. A pulse beat against her temple, like a prisoner trying to get out. She reminded him of the skull that sat in his dentist's office. His first patient, he always joked. Ira figured that she was working off her room and board.

"He's a patient."

"A patient," she said giggling like it was the funniest thing she'd heard in years, which it may very well have been. She checked through her box of index cards chuckling the whole time.

"Fallon, Fellman, Fick, Flaustein, Fortman, Frank . . . we have a lot of F's. They must live longer," she said laughing at her own joke.

"Oh yes, Fulton, Herman. He's a doctor?"

"Was."

She shuffled slowly back to the window.

"Are you a relative?"

"No, I'm not."

Ira scribbled his name illegibly in the visitor's book.

"You need the doctor's permission if you're not a relative."

"He's not, I am," Rhonda said. "I'm his great-grandniece. Ira and I were just passing through Atlantic City. We got married yesterday."

The receptionist's look of suspicion melted away in the glare of Rhonda's smile. She wrote Herman Fulton's name very slowly on two pieces of yellow paper stamped "VISITOR." Her handwriting was firm, unlike her voice. Maybe she was younger than she looked.

"Take the elevator to the third floor and follow the arrows to the nurse's station."

"How do you like the way I married us?" Rhonda said in the elevator.

"It'll never work out."

"Why not?"

"I'm too old."

"No you're not."

"And set in my ways."

"How would you know unless you try?"

"Once is enough."

"You're behind the times. All the men your age take trophy wives."

"I never won a trophy in my life," Ira said thinking to himself that he wasn't going to start now."

Rhonda shrugged and stepped off the elevator.

"This place makes Pilgrim State look like a four star hotel," Rhonda said.

"Just follow the arrows."

It took them to the nurse's station where the only nurse on duty, a heavy set, middle age woman, sat reading Star magazine. She looked up long enough to look over the passes.

"Old Doc Fulton, I can't believe it. I've been here eleven years and you're his first visitors. I didn't think he had any relatives, none alive anyway."

Rhonda smiled. "He's my father's second cousin."

"You're not from New Jersey, are you?"

"No, from Shaboygan, Wisconsin, just outside Milwaukee."

"I was in Milwaukee once with my father when I was a child," the nurse said.

"Bet you took a beer factory tour."

"Schlitz."

"The beer that made Milwaukee famous."

They both laughed.

"What's so funny?" he said.

"You have to come from a family of beer drinkers to appreciate it," Rhonda said.

"They're out of business," the nurse said. "I used to like that beer. Remember Reingold?"

Ronda nodded.

"What are you two doing way out here?"

"Honeymooning."

"Congratulations."

"Ira likes to gamble."

"Everyone around here likes to gamble. You look like a craps man."

"Twenty-one," Rhonda says. "He lost a bundle last night."

"Well, you know what they say, unlucky in cards lucky in love."

"I hope so."

Rhonda had the gift of gab, just like Ellen.

"Well, follow me."

They walked down a long corridor.

"Won't he be surprised."

She clearly didn't mean pleasantly.

Fulton had a private room at the end of the hall, a small room with a window overlooking the A & P. The pictures in the room were hospital issue, buildings that looked like churches in frames that came from the five and ten. No books, no magazines, no clothes and no plants, just a bare room with a television.

"Hey, Doc, you've got visitors."

"I don't want any visitors."

"Well you've got them anyway."

She handed Ira back the passes.

"I'll leave you three alone. Good luck."

Rhonda sat down in the chair by the bed and Ira stood behind her. Fulton looked them over like a couple of would be muggers.

"What do you want? Who are you?"

"I'm a nurse at Pilgrim State. I don't suppose you remember working there?"

Rhonda leaned close to him and smiled.

"Hell I don't, I practically built the place."

Doc Fulton no longer had full control of his arms. They jerked about as if they were off on their own swatting at flies. He also had trouble controlling his eyelids. They quivered when they were shut and rolled up with a snap like window shades. Saliva ran down the left corner of his mouth, which he couldn't quite close. Ira could almost see Fulton's body shriveling before his eyes, as if it was being rapidly consumed by the invisible fire of time. Only his head, propped up on a pillow, remained life size, white with large dark spots and glowing eyes. The hair swarmed around it like a fistful of worms. A visible pulse beat under his left eye. The effect was almost supernatural.

Too bad he wasn't a balloon, Ira thought, because he'd pop him with his pocketknife and enjoy the terror on his face as the air ran out.

Doc Fulton looked Rhonda over carefully, paying no attention to him.

"I don't remember you. How could I," he growled, "you're eighteen years old."

"I didn't work there when you were around, but I've heard a lot about you."

He lay there taking it all in, like Rhonda had just validated all the years of neglect. After all, turning people to vegetables had to be tough work.

"What do you want?"

"This is Ira."

Ira smiled and gave a compact little wave. Fulton frowned. He wished that he could lobotomize him with his eyes.

"He's writing a book about Pilgrim State. After all, it was one of the leading psychiatric institutions in the state."

"In the country."

"In the country, and you were a big part of it for so long. Ira wants to find out about what it was like in the thirties and forties."

Fulton closed his eyes and appeared to drift off to sleep. Ira cleared his throat, but Rhonda put her finger to her lips. They were full red lips, redder than usual, like her cheeks. Perhaps it was the heat.

In here, she ran the show. He couldn't help thinking that they were already like a married couple playing to their strengths and weaknesses.

Fulton opened his eyes a minute later.

"I started at Pilgrim in the twenties. Things were different. The state just wanted a caretaker. It didn't provide money for anything but babysitting."

He closed his eyes again. He needed time to clear seventy years of cobwebs from his unused brain. He opened his mouth wide to breath. His tongue was scaly and white.

"They didn't give a damn what the doctors did so long as it was easy and cheap."

Fulton strained to look at Ira, his eyes bulging out, as if they were reaching for his neck.

"You think a god-damn bureaucrat knows anything about insanity, not a damn thing, most of them are crazy themselves."

The old lobotomizer stared at Ira when he said that. He could almost feel Doc Fulton boring into his brain with his mental potato peeler. Fulton motioned Rhonda closer.

"I don't trust him."

"He's OK."

"Looks like a patient."

He stuck his tongue out in Rhonda's direction, like he was hoping to reach those ruby red lips of hers.

"Look at his mouth."

Fulton's hands pointed at Ira and then brushed against Rhonda's breasts, which took a superhuman effort on his part.

"Damn bureaucrat," he said as Rhonda took his hands and clutched them to her chest.

"You think I would bring him here if he couldn't be trusted. You can trust him every bit as much as you can trust me."

He looked at his hand resting on Rhonda's breast and then at Ira.

"Just keep him quiet."

Rhonda let go of Fulton's hand and it shook back and forth, clutching an imaginary breast. Ira wished that he was hooked up to a few tubes, because then he could have pulled one out. Justifiable homicide, he thought, although fifty years too late.

"Patients were running around without clothes, shitting on the floor and stabbing themselves with mirrors. They had to let us take over."

Fulton tried for a weak smile, but it couldn't escape all the deep crevices. Ira could hear his face crack from the effort.

"Water," he whispered.

Rhonda picked up the glass while Ira fought the urge to knock it to the floor.

"Pathways in the brain get stuck. Thoughts and feelings get backed up. Cut away the bottleneck, reroute the impulses, and the problems disappear."

Fulton closed his eyes and took a long, deep breath. He expelled the air with a hum like a room air conditioner. Rhonda looked down at Ira's foot, which was tapping an impatient tune.

"I remember this Italian woman, walked around all day screaming that her clothes were another person trying to take over her body. Two weeks after the operation she was quiet as a mouse."

"What happened to her?" he asked.

"How the hell should I know?"

Fulton motioned Rhonda closer again. She took his hand and he gazed longingly at her breasts. Interest in the female anatomy should disappear when you're too old to do anything about it. With so little time and energy left, why waste any of it. When he reached Fulton's age, and he certainly wanted to, Ira hoped that breasts would be about as fascinating as tax returns.

"I helped more people in two years than they did in twenty."

Fulton looked up at the ceiling and forgot about Rhonda for a moment, like he was answering a question from someone else in the audience. Ira hoped it was the Devil telling him that it was time to go. More likely the brain bandit was hatching a plan to cop one last feel.

"They made me stop, because they didn't want them cured, not really. They wanted to keep them inside. The families didn't want them around to embarrass anyone."

They observed a moment of silence serenaded by Fulton's wheezing. This trip was shaping up to be a big, expensive waste of time.

"That's all very helpful," Ira said, "but can you tell us how many lobotomies you did? And how you decided who to do them on?"

"How come he doesn't take notes?"

The brain beautician addressed his remarks to Rhonda. Ira did not exist for Doc Fulton. He did not deal with the family of lobotomees.

"He has one of those photographic memories," Rhonda said with a wink.

"A little short for you, isn't he? And too damn old."

Rhonda laughed.

"I know that face." Fulton squinted at him. "It's got insanity written all over it."

Ira wondered whether he could shock Fulton into cardiac arrest by jumping on his bed and screaming BOO. Rhonda would never have squealed.

"More than they know," Fulton said answering his earlier question. "Hundreds and not just on nobodies . . . politicians . . . athletes; I'd give you names . . . if I could remember any of them. Almost everyone can benefit from a lobotomy."

Fulton rolled his eyes in Ira's direction. Ira looked at Rhonda and raised his eyebrows. Ellen knew the signal well, it meant it was time to leave, but Rhonda was clueless.

"That example with the Italian woman is just the type of information Ira needs for the book. We pulled one of your old files and brought it with us."

Fulton didn't react. His mouth was wide open and he was gasping for air. Rhonda didn't seem in the least bit concerned. She took the file from Ira and opened it.

"Eva Portnoy. Does that name ring a bell?"

"Let me see that."

Rhonda held the file up for Fulton to see.

"Hold it higher. Does it look like I'm sitting up?"

His eyes were reduced to little slits. What was left of his life was clearly seeping out.

"It's too damn small to see."

He looked over at Ira and glared at him like he was to blame.

"But I can still hear. I can hear those damned nurse's talking about me all day long. They think they're so smart."

"Let me read it to you," Rhonda said.

"They're waiting for me to die, but I won't give them the satisfaction. I'll outlive them all."

"Eva Portnoy was admitted in the mid-thirties."

Doc Fulton turned his focus back on Rhonda's breasts.

"You gave her a lobotomy in 1946."

"That was a big year, right after the war. Full or partial?"

"I can't tell."

"Probably full, didn't do too many partials. It just wasn't enough for most of them."

Fulton sighed and closed his eyes. Rhonda waited.

"Go home?"

"What?"

"Did she go home?" Fulton said pounding his fist against the air. "What do you think I mean?"

"She never left the hospital, died at Pilgrim in 1968."

Rhonda flipped through the file looking for something that might refresh his recollection.

"The brain has the consistency of pudding," he said moistening his lips. "People eat it in some countries. Monkeys mostly. I tasted one once, it was sour, like a grapefruit, not like pudding."

Fulton's hands jumped at Rhonda's chest, but fell short.

"She never went home?" he asked.

"No."

"She might have been hospitalized a few years later for three months in 1951. Could it have been related to the lobotomy?"

"I never lost a single patient. They all got a little better. What was her name again?"

"Eva Portnoy."

"Some went home and came back. You've got to expect that. Brains have tendencies, like people. Cut one area and the problem moves to another. They needed regular lobotomies, but they wouldn't let me do more than one."

Fulton looked around and motioned Rhonda closer.

"But I did some anyway."

He licked unsuccessfully at her lips.

"She never went home?"

"No."

"Did she have a family?"

"Yes."

"Probably didn't want her."

Ira gave Rhonda the universally understood signal to get going by pointing his thumb at the door. Fulton looked like he was sleeping anyway. Just then another nurse walked in.

"Mr. Fulton has to go for an x-ray. He'll be back in about an hour if you want to wait."

"No, thank you," Ira said, "we've got to get going."

"Good-bye doctor." Rhonda patted Fulton's hand.

"Good riddance," he said.

From the hall they could hear Fulton screaming at the nurse. "A few of them got knocked up. Most of them were like whores anyway."

Ira and Rhonda froze for an instant and then continued walking down the hall. They got into the car and Ira drove off like it was a race. He wanted to get back to Shirley.

"That might explain the gap." Rhonda said.

"Three months?"

"That's long, but there could have been complications . . . or . . . ."

"Or what?"

"Or they found out too late to abort."

"How's that possible?"

"We keep close track of periods now, but in those days who knows. Maybe she didn't show. Besides, we're just guessing that she got pregnant."

"I think we jarred Fulton's memory."

"You heard him, he did hundreds of lobotomies and I'm sure more than one of them got knocked up. He could mean anybody."

Concentrate on the road, Ira reminded himself. His mother taught him to drive like his life was always on the line. He had to put his imagination in check for a while and rely on Rhonda.

"It could be . . . ."

"Could be what?" he said looking back and forth between Rhonda and the road.

"I've heard stories back then. Sometimes they found out too late to abort and sometimes they didn't even try."

"What would they do?"

"Sell the babies or give them up for adoption."

"Look where you're going," Rhonda said as he nearly climbed up the back of the car ahead of them.

"Maybe I have a cousin somewhere?"

"Or maybe the baby didn't survive. Or maybe there was no pregnancy. Or maybe she broke her leg or had pneumonia, or maybe they just lost three months of her file, that's the most likely explanation."

"But it might explain why it was all such a big secret," Ira said.

"No it wouldn't, because they'd hide something like that from the family as well, so they'd never know."

"Unless they had a patient whose mother visited almost every week?"

"They could have sent her somewhere or put her in the hospital, and told your grandmother she wasn't allowed visitors for a while. So she would have called for three months."

"Maybe, but you didn't know my grandmother. She couldn't be put off that easily. Maybe she didn't know how to get Eva out, but she certainly would have laid her life on the line to see her. Hell, all her kids were grown up by then, what did she care. What more could they do to her?"

They drove a while in silence.

"I suppose they wouldn't tell people that the baby was from a mental institution," Rhonda said.

"How can we find out?"

"You think they kept records about things like that?"

Another cousin would be nice, Ira thought. For all practical purposes he's never had one. His father was an only child and although his mother's brother had two kids, they grew up in the Midwest. If he saw them once every five years it was a lot. He imagined meeting his new cousin for the first time. She'd look more like Eva than his mother or Aunt Sarah, meaning she'd be taller and thinner with dark, curly hair. The resemblance would be around the mouth, large and overpowering like his. Of course, the baby could have had the same problems as Eva. She might be a patient at Pilgrim today, part of the special early admissions program for children of alumni.

"I bet Shirley knows something," Ira said.

Rhonda nodded slowly.

Something more than what he overheard.

Ira pushed the car passed the speed limit, but Shirley was gone by the time they got back to Pilgrim State. Rhonda suggested that they pick up a couple of pizzas and some beer and drop in on her at home.

"She's always home and she's always hungry."

Shirley lived near Pilgrim. The pizza place was out of the way. They ordered one with sausage and one with pepperoni.

"Shirley likes toppings."

Rhonda, the big winner, paid.

"Oh, God," he said while they sat there waiting.

"What?"

"I never called the office. I didn't even call home."

It was instant stomach cramps.

"Too late to do anything about it now."

Rhonda patted his hand, just like she did with Doc Fulton.

Shirley lived in a tiny bungalow at the end of a dirt road. There were three other houses on the road equally old and run down. Across the highway was a large, new development of suburban tract homes, splits, colonials and contemporary ranches. Down the road a new strip mall was going up, the future home of Stop and Shop, Rite Aide, Baskin Robbins, Good Wok and Kleen Dry Cleaners. A small professional office building was also going up next to it, soon to be filled with lawyers, dentists, doctors, chiropractors and accountants. They were like parasites that attached themselves to shopping centers everywhere. Ira couldn't figure out how they all survived. He didn't have to be a fortune teller to know that the four tired little houses on Shirley's block would be gone in a year or two, replaced by a Seven-Eleven or gas station. All memory of human habitation obliterated forever, Shirley's existence, like Eva's, confirmed only by her file at Pilgrim State.

Shirley answered the door in a blue housecoat. The kind the patients wore. It had a torn pocket and was crusted over with dried food. Fresh donut crumbs clung for their life. Shirley looked the two of them over like a couple of encyclopedia salesmen. Then her eyes softened with recognition and she examined him for signs of anything unusual, much the way his grandmother used to when he came for a Sunday visit.

"Two pies, one with pepperoni and one with sausage," Rhonda said walking into the kitchen, "and two six packs."

"No luck at the tables and no luck with old man Fulton that's my guess," Shirley said seeing Eva's file sticking out between the pies.

Ellen turned off the engine and sat in the car. She didn't want to go into Ira's mother's house, but she had to. Sarah had begged her to come. They needed to talk to her, she said. It felt more like a job interview. She never gave a second thought to visiting before, now her stomach was in knots.

The kids were home alone. Ellen's belief in the absolute truth, no matter how ugly or painful, had finally won out and she had told them everything, everything that she knew for certain, which didn't include anything about another woman. She told them about Eva and about how things between them were strained. She added that Ira had been calling frequently to ask about them, either at school or after they were asleep. The latter she would have admitted was a little white lie, but it was a charitable gesture that was necessary for the children's sake. The kids reacted exactly as she would have expected. Scott ran into his room and slammed the door. He cried and blamed Ira for ruining his life. Jamie went right to the phone and called her friends. There were a few others with strained marriages and absent fathers. The house was quiet when Ellen left. It cried out for the sound of the television.

Sarah and Selma had dark shadows under their eyes. In the last week, Selma's crow's feet had spread like an oil spill. Ellen sat with them at the kitchen table in front of the ever-present coffee and cake. No one spoke. No one ate. Selma broke the stalemate.

"I was the youngest," she said. "My mother had to work. Sarah and Max went to school. Eva stayed home and took care of me."

Ellen nodded. She'd heard all of that before.

"She went to school for a while," Sarah said, "but it didn't work out."

"It wasn't that Eva was dumb," Selma said, "because she wasn't. She was generally all right if you left her alone. Her problem was dealing with people. She would shake and cry . . . especially with strange men."

"Father was the only one who could handle her. She got much worse after he died."

Sarah watched Selma closely.

"Did I tell you that she played the piano?" Selma said.

"Yes."

"Taught herself after father bought her a used one. She was really the apple of his eye."

Sarah wiped her eyes.

Ellen realized that it would be very different now. They wouldn't let Eva skip school. They have all kinds of medication and special classes. Her whole life would have changed.

"You know, my mother and father were second cousins," Sarah said.

"Third," Selma said.

"Whatever, they didn't know any better back then."

Ellen continued to nod. Still nothing she didn't already know.

Sarah and Selma stared at each other, as if they were arguing telepathically.

"Eva could sit perfectly still for hours," Selma said. "She'd rock back and forth while she stared down at the street. Then suddenly she'd start screaming and crying as if she just saw something horrible. And she'd bang her head against the window like she was trying to shake something loose."

"One day she really lost it. Broke the bedroom window and climbed out onto the fire escape screaming. Sarah and I were home alone. Before we could get her back in someone called the police. They took her to the hospital for observation. What could we do? We were just kids."

"You told me all this," Ellen said

Selma took a sip of coffee.

"She never came back."

"You were eleven," Ellen said.

"Yes."

"My mother was frightened of authority," Sarah said, "she never made trouble. She went to Pilgrim the next day, but the doctors wouldn't let Eva go. They said she was a danger to herself. They talked my mother into signing something. It was supposed to be for a few days. They were going to help her."

Ellen wondered what she signed.

"My mother never doubted the word of a doctor, at least not back then. By the time she did, it was too late. She couldn't get Eva out. Maybe legally she could have, but she didn't know how or maybe she didn't want to try."

Sarah blew her nose and wiped her eyes. She had prepared for tonight by not wearing make-up, unlike Selma who never appeared without it.

"My mother stopped speaking about her," Selma continued. "After a while, I'm sure Eva didn't want to leave . . . or didn't care."

"We don't know that," Sarah said.

Tears were running down Sarah's cheeks. Selma's stopped at the rim.

"It isn't hard to figure out," Selma said. "Eva felt betrayed."

Sarah nodded. "I stopped visiting after that first year. It was too hard . . . and my mother discouraged it."

"She wouldn't take me," Selma said, "because I was too young."

They both stopped talking. The only sound was the dishwasher entering the rinse cycle.

"Mom kept visiting, week after week and year after year. Up until she died. Eva hardly spoke to her, but she went anyway."

Ellen wanted to feel sympathy. She was normally very good at it. Her natural instinct would have been to take Selma's hand and tell her that everything would be all right and that she understood, but she couldn't do it. She didn't believe that everything would be all right and she was angry. Their problem had become her problem because of their secrecy. If it had been out in the open, it would have been resolved long ago. More importantly, Ellen still hadn't heard anything she really didn't know or suspect. She felt sure that she still wasn't getting the whole story.

"Over time, we just stopped talking about Eva," Sarah said. "Mom stopped telling us about her and no one asked."

Sarah hesitated, stared at Selma.

Maybe this was it, Ellen thought, the big secret was finally coming out.

Sarah nodded her head at Selma, who just stared back.

"Eva had a lobotomy."

Selma looked up at Ellen after she said it, looking for the shock and surprise, but there was none. Instead, all she saw was Ellen's disappointment.

"I knew that."

"You did?"

"Ira told me."

Selma looked at Sarah.

"How did Ira find out?" Selma said.

"He found her file and visited the doctor who did it."

"He's still alive?"

"In Atlantic City."

Selma took a big gulp of coffee spilling some of it on the table.

"Eva didn't remember anyone after the operation," Sarah said.

"That's what you wanted to tell me?" Ellen said.

Selma shook her head yes, while Sarah shook her head no.

The kitchen was a mess. There was a crumbled bag of potato chips on the counter with crumbs fanning out to the sink, followed by an open can of soda and a candy wrapper. The trash overflowed the yellow plastic pail, a cornucopia of cookie boxes and canned soup. The sink was full of dishes. The cupboards were all open. Their timing appeared to be perfect. Shirley must have been rummaging around in search of a snack. Shirley went looking for some clean plates. The vibrations set off by her stride sent a cheese and salami wrapper crashing to the floor like lovers in a suicide leap.

It was a dramatic comparison. At Ira's house dishes went right into the dishwasher and food was immediately put away. The cupboards were continuously restocked and the dust buster patrolled the kitchen like a night watchman. Still, there was something very reassuring about sitting in Shirley's kitchen. It made his life, even under the present circumstances, seem tidy and secure in comparison.

Rhonda opened the pizzas. They were all starved. Driving made him hungry and thinking did the same for Rhonda. The eating and drinking was fast and furious. There was no conversation, just the chewing of cheese, the crunching of crust, and the gulping of beer. One pie just about vaporized. Ira was done after three slices and sat back to wait for Shirley to finish. As soon as she started picking her teeth with a toothpick, he pulled out Eva's file.

"Fulton wasn't much help," he said.

Shirley picked off pieces of sausage from one of the uneaten slices. His kids knew better than to do that since it left the rest of the slice inedible.

"But he said something interesting."

Now she grabbed the cheese. It was going to be a slow dismemberment.

"He said that maybe Eva got pregnant."

"He didn't say that," Rhonda said, "what he really said was that some of the lobotomized patients were taken advantage of and may have gotten pregnant."

"I'd be surprised if it was just some," Shirley said.

"Which might explain the missing three months," Ira said.

Shirley ripped off the burnt bubble at the edge of the crust. After she finished licking her fingers, she reached for the file.

Rhonda gazed at him over the crumbs and spent napkins. She still had that hungry look. Actually, now that Ira thought about it, she usually did.

"Did Eva get pregnant?"

Shirley finished her beer and pushed the empty pizza box onto the floor. It made Ira wince.

"I was twenty-two when I started at Pilgrim. It was a bad time, post-depression, pre-war. There wasn't a dime to spare."

Shirley opened another beer. Ira did also to keep up and to keep her talking.

"We had less than fifteen cents a day to feed, cloth and care for every patient. Successful psychiatry care was preventing them from pissing on the floor and putting their heads through the wall. So no one really cared if the doctors used Pilgrim State as a laboratory experimenting with patients instead of mice.

"Eva was a bit of a head banger and she kept to herself, a lot of them did, but she knew what was what. You could see it in her eyes. But she didn't care what they did to her, as long as she didn't have to watch. I suppose she figured that if no one else cared, why should she."

Ira remembered how Scott used to bang his head against the wall when he was younger. He thought that was just a kid thing, but what if it was something that ran in the family? Fortunately, he hasn't done anything like that in a long time, although he did get easily frustrated.

"Another beer?" Shirley asked.

Ira guzzled down what was left in the one he was holding and Shirley handed him another one.

"She hated the male orderlies . . . but so did I."

Rhonda got up and started to straighten out the kitchen like she already knew what was coming.

"She was so young. She couldn't have been more than nineteen or twenty."

"Where is this going?" Ira said taking another gulp of beer. For the first time in his life it was beginning to taste good.

"Don't rush me or I'll go inside and find something to watch on the tube."

"Sorry."

"She cried before and after every one of your grandmother's visits, at least when I was around. But she never spoke to her. I'm sure your grandmother thought Eva was a lot worse than she really was. Most of the families did. It took Eva a day or two to get back to normal."

What a funny word, Ira thought, to use to describe someone committed like that for life.

"Eva would've been better off at home, but your grandmother couldn't have known that and the doctors weren't going to tell her. Did I tell you that they got paid by the patient back then?"

Ira nodded.

Shirley flipped through the file.

"Fulton was doing lobotomies like he was handing out business cards. What did your grandmother know? He wasn't much different than a salesman on commission if you ask me."

Shirley took a long drink and wiped her mouth with her sleeve.

"He wanted to be a real doctor on Park Avenue with a fancy office and paying patients, but he had the bedside manner of a Nazi storm trooper and wound up at Pilgrim State performing volume surgery."

Ira took a sip and held tight to the beer bottle.

"Fulton could recommend a lobotomy after a five minute consultation."

Shirley scanned the box for more sausage and settled for some pieces of left over crust.

"She wasn't the same after the lobotomy. They all turned out different. I guess it depended on how deep the butcher cut. Eva didn't do much banging afterwards. She didn't get upset when your grandmother came to visit. She didn't get upset much at all, she sort of just rattled around like a hollow, dried up gourd. Had trouble remembering what do with things. Cried, but at all different times, it wasn't just men any more."

"What happened in 1951? Where was she for three months?"

Shirley looked at Rhonda, then at Ira and back to Rhonda. Suddenly, Rhonda's sleepy eyes opened wide. She reached over and grabbed a beer of her own.

"She got pregnant. It happened, could have been anyone, another patient, an orderly, even one of the doctors. They never got caught and if they did the worst that happened was that they'd get transferred to another building or fired. No one got punished for abusing a patient. Why should they since the doctors did it too. Most of the families didn't know or didn't care."

A soft, slow whine outside grew louder like an approaching airplane. There was a rapping on the window.

"What's that?" Ira said.

"You ever hear of the wind?" Shirley said.

The house groaned.

"Sounds like a blizzard," he said.

"There's no fooling you."

"It's really coming down," Rhonda said walking over to the window.

"Where have you guys been? The radio's been talking about this blizzard all day."

"We weren't listening," Rhonda said.

The radio was off the whole way back. Normally, Ira is a news and weather fanatic, especially in the winter. He'll spend hours in the evening in front of the Weather Channel empathizing with forecasts around the country. Shivering with the cold Canadian air masses and moving to the edge of his seat when they collide with the warm, moisture-laden, low pressure centers from the Gulf.

"You'll never get out of here now," Shirley said.

Rhonda smiled, like a little girl waking up to a surprise school holiday.

"I need a sit down," Shirley said getting up slowly and walking to the bathroom.

"I knew Shirley was holding out on me, but why?"

"Her mother," Rhonda suggested.

"That's bullshit."

"Does it really matter?"

"I bet she knows where my cousin is."

For an only child, a first cousin is better than a big tax refund. Rhonda shook her head from side to side.

"Just because she got pregnant doesn't mean she had the kid."

"You don't need three months for an abortion."

"Don't you think you grandmother would've found out if Eva had a baby?"

"Maybe they moved her like you said or wouldn't allow visitors."

"Maybe you should just assume," Rhonda said in the cold, clinical way of the medical profession, "that she lost the baby."

Ira rolled his head around his shoulders in a slow circle. It was stiff from the sleepless night at the casino, the long drive and a week of unfamiliar beds and awkward positions.

"The time for making assumptions is over," he said.

"I was just trying to help."

Rhonda went over to the window and watched the storm.

"Now is the time for answers."

Rhonda turned slowly from the window. Her eyes were liquid and her lips were drawn in hiding their fullness.

"Maybe it's time for you to go home."

Ira was too blinded by his own thoughts to see the concern and disappointment in her eyes. The wind rattled the window in the kitchen and they both stopped to stare, as if it might barge right in.

"If it wasn't snowing," I said, "I would."

Spoken like a true ten-year old, he realized. The wind filled the silence that followed.

"I'm going to check on Shirley," Rhonda finally said walking out of the kitchen without looking in Ira's direction.

"That's not all," Sarah said. "Go ahead Selma, tell her the rest."

Selma's breathing was almost loud enough to drown out the wind.

"Tell her so she can get home before the storm gets much worse."

Selma just sat there. Ellen noticed a slight tremor, something she had never seen before, as if Selma's head had suddenly grown too heavy for her neck.

"I'll tell her if you won't," Sarah said.

"No, I'll do it."

Selma took a sip of coffee.

"A few years after the lobotomy, Eva got . . . pregnant."

"Oh, my," Ellen said with just the right mixture of surprise and compassion. Just the inflection you'd expect from the educator of small children. That didn't mean to suggest that her reaction was phony, because it wasn't. It was appropriate, perfectly appropriate, a talent you have to be born with.

"How?" Ellen asked.

Sarah and Selma both shrugged.

"Did they abort?"

"She had the baby," Selma said.

"A boy," Sarah added.

"What happened to him?"

Ira looked out the window. It was snowing hard. The wind was blowing steadily so that it almost came down sideways. It was a real blizzard, the kind he loved to watch from his own den window with the fire roaring and the popcorn popping. Perhaps a little wine after the kids fell asleep, particularly if it looked like the roads would be impassable in the morning, and they could stay up late for a little unscheduled fun.

"Ira, we're in here," Rhonda called out.

"Where?"

"In the bedroom."

Rhonda and Shirley were sitting on the bed. Shirley's bathrobe was loose and Ira could see the taffy-like rolls of fat that kept her breasts from hitting the floor. Shirley's hair was undone. She had a small bald spot that he'd never noticed before. Not the first thing you want to look at after eating three slices of greasy pizza and drinking an equal number of beers.

"Did Eva have the baby? Did my grandmother know? Why did she have to stay in the hospital for three months?"

The wind delayed Shirley's answer.

"They were afraid she'd hurt herself . . . and the baby."

He could feel Rhonda's eyes on him, but he refused to look at her. Instead, he kept his eyes locked on Shirley.

"It was too late to abort by the time they found out. No one bothered to check periods back then and you can't always tell. Some of them really didn't show until they were pretty far along."

Shirley stood up. Her legs disappeared, but the robe opened to the waist like a low cut dress. It was like looking down a wishing well. Her gargantuan thighs had given up any pretense of individuality.

"Most families never knew. They'd have the baby and the hospital would get rid of it. There were plenty of places. Adoption was much less formal back then. They couldn't do that because your grandmother was always around, always asking questions. I give her a lot of credit."

Ira backed up against the frigid wall. He could almost feel the snow on his back, like he was falling out into it, the driving flakes obscuring his vision.

"So Eva had the baby," he said over the wind.

"Yes."

"What was it?"

"A boy."

"What happened to him?"

"He was adopted."

"By who?"

Shirley smiled weakly.

"Don't you know?"

"Who?"

He needed to hear it.

"Eva's youngest sister . . . your mother."

He didn't see it coming, not until the very last minute. Either he was incredibly dense or incredibly agile. He dodged every bullet. He sensed something as soon as Shirley said his grandmother knew. She would never have let one of her own go to a stranger.

The storm blew the words around the room.

"Eva's younger sister . . . your mother."

Not his mother anymore is what Ira would have said if his tongue wasn't stuck to the roof of his mouth.

"Welcome to the family," Shirley said, "my mother was also a lifer."

"I'm my own cousin," he mumbled sitting down beside Rhonda on the bed. "I can't believe it."

Rhonda rested her hand on his thigh.

"Roe," Shirley said, "there's some whiskey in the kitchen below the sink. I think Ira could use a shot."

He felt like he was unraveling, coming apart at the seams. He knew now why his grandmother, his ex-mother and his still aunt used to stare at him all the time. They were staring at a constant reminder of Eva's wasted life. They were looking for cracks to see if he was headed in the same direction.

Rhonda handed him a glass and poured him some bourbon. He drank it down like water. It burned at first, but then felt pleasantly warm. He took the bottle from her and poured himself another.

"We adopted him," Selma said suddenly very calm.

"Ira is Eva's son," Sarah said to make sure that Ellen got it.

Ellen didn't say anything at first. She felt as if someone had put a rope around her heart and jerked it up into her throat.

"I can't believe it."

She had to fight to prevent her sympathy and concern from changing into anger. Her philosophy had been vindicated once again. If Selma had been truthful and told Ira as soon as he was old enough to understand, then he wouldn't be making such a mess of everything now.

"You've got to tell him," Ellen said.

"I will, as soon as he calls. How do you think he'll react?"

"It can't be any crazier than he's acting now."

Ellen immediately regretted using the word crazy in light of the circumstances.

Ira sat by himself for awhile at the kitchen table, just him and the bottle of bourbon. There was about a foot of snow on the ground and he couldn't see two feet out the window. The wind was screaming like a wounded dog as it whipped across the road and the forecast was for another eight to ten inches. Rhonda came in to tell him that she had made up a bed for them in the living room on the foldout couch.

"I'm wiped," she said.

"I'm angry."

"I understand; it'll wear off."

"No it won't."

"Everything does over time, take it from me, I know."

"I won't let it."

"You're drunk."

"My whole life has been a lie."

"No, just the beginning. Anyway you're not alone. Most parents aren't what they're cracked up to be."

"How could they?"

"I could've done without my father, believe me, and all my mother's boyfriends."

"I have no father, who knows who he might be . . . and now I have no mother."

"The one you got turned out a helluva lot better than mine."

"So now Shirley and I have a lot in common."

"You're not your mother," Rhonda said, "any more than I'm mine."

"Drink?"

"I'm going to sleep," Rhonda said as Ira poured himself another shot.

"Come to bed soon."

That's what Ellen always said to him, but usually when he was half-asleep on the couch, not shivering in some dilapidated, old house in the middle of nowhere.

"Sure."

Up until his grandmother's funeral, he considered himself a moderate, level headed, feet-on-the-ground, family sort of guy. Predictable, not inclined to take chances and easy to please. Not someone prone to extravagant demands or unreasonable desires. A few dreams that he never seriously expected to come true, but certainly none that he was obsessed with and certainly no desire for change, at least none that he was aware of.

Now he had a girlfriend, a new mother and a mysterious father; the first not much older than his daughter, the second certifiably insane, and the third a felon. He wasn't sure whether he had a job or a marriage. He hadn't spoken to his kids in a week. He'd lost a fortune at the casino and his naive familial quest, which was supposed to provide some mildly interesting cocktail party conversation, had become a nightmare. If he could erase the entire week like a VHS tape he would. Otherwise, he was afraid that he was doomed to live the rest of his life somehow differently. He just had no idea how differently.

Ira always trusted his heart more than his head in situations like this, so he sat in the kitchen looking for some sign in the rumblings of undigested sausage and the alcohol induced numbness in his chest. Should he leave tomorrow morning or stay? Was there anything more to find out? What about his real father? Should he let him get away with it? He listened intently, but his body offered no clues. The stomach rumblings were gas and the numbness was the emptiness that follows an emotional shock. The storm was the only sign that said stay.

What frightened Ira the most was how easy it had been to put Ellen, the kids and the job out of his mind. He couldn't be bothered with responsibility. The gods of routine had abandoned him and the only thing fueling the fire now was Eva and his father, the rapist. Perhaps he was a rich doctor. Another patient was more likely. He could be the son of two lobotomized and institutionalized lunatics.

He was still drinking whiskey about an hour later. When the wind paused, he swore that he could hear Rhonda's slow breathing from the living room. He got up to go to the bathroom. It wasn't easy. The hallway seemed to sway in the storm and he wound up bouncing from one wall to the other. He had never drunk this much before. He could hardly walk and his bladder felt like it was reaching out way beyond Shirley's stomach. He wanted to throw up, but he couldn't.

If this was drunk, he thought, why would anyone ever want to do it a second time?

He couldn't find the light switch and his zipper had become as complex as the office computer. It gave way just seconds before he was about to rip it open. He didn't have to lift the seat because in an instant he was sitting on it with his head over the sink. He was feeling pressure from both ends, but he was in the perfect position, he could pee in the toilet and throw up in the sink at the same time.

"Hey Shirley," he called out.

"Go to bed."

"Did my mother ever see me?"

"How do I know, they knocked everyone out those days."

"That sucks."

He wondered if his father came for a visit.

He sat there for a long time listening to the pizza bubble through his intestines. After a while he stuck his finger down his throat, the way his mother . . . his aunt . . . used to tell him as a kid, but it didn't work. It kept popping out just short of vomiting. Probably because he didn't have the willpower, he never did.

He finally got up and stumbled into the hall. The wind was blowing right through the house and the cool draft felt good. Shirley was asleep in the bedroom and Rhonda was asleep in the living room. There was a small but inviting place for him right next to Rhonda, but he had to take care of something in the kitchen first.

It was two in the morning when he dialed his mother, his adoptive mother. She picked up after one ring and he hung up. Then he dialed again.

"Ira, I know it's you."

"So Eva is my real mother . . . that's the big secret."

"It's Ira," she said to Sarah who must have rushed in after the first ring.

"So Ellen told you."

"Does everyone know but me? No, Ellen didn't tell me, I found out from one of the nurses."

"So now you know. Maybe it was a mistake not to tell you, but what can you do about it now. You can't throw your life away over it?"

"It's my life, not yours, that's for sure." Ira started to laugh. "It's certainly not yours."

"Are you drunk?"

"Did Eva ever hold me? Did she ever see me?"

"I don't know. I wasn't there."

He suddenly felt very tired. He wanted to put his arms around Ellen's warm body and sleep forever, but he'd settle for Rhonda. He could barely hold his head up.

"I'm going to bed."

"Wait, Ira don't . . . ."

He hung up the phone and took off his clothes somewhere between the kitchen and the bedroom. The bed was very warm and soft with a deep valley that pulled him right up against her. He started to get aroused thinking with some disappointment that Rhonda's behind wasn't anywhere near as firm as he remembered it. It must have been all that pizza. It felt doughy, as if he could push his hand into it up to the elbow. It seemed to go on forever, one cheek a mile apart from the other. Still, it was warm and soft.

Ira reached around for her breasts, but his arms were way too short. Besides, Rhonda's breasts had moved. They had fallen down below her waist. It was a real effort to keep hard and as he rubbed against her he vaguely wondered whether her ponderous mammary glands wouldn't be more at home on Shirley. She began to move slowly in her sleep. He felt as if he were trying to pull her up from a great distance, not a distance measured by space alone, but by time as well. It would require an enormous amount of energy on his part, which he didn't have. It had been a long day and he had neither the strength nor the desire, and he finally gave up and fell asleep.

It would have been nice to dream about Eva. Tell her that he knew and understood. Tell her about her perfectly normal grandchildren. Ask her who did it. He had a lot of other questions. She would understand him. Who would know human weaknesses better than she would? How different would it have been with Eva as his mother? How much lower the expectations? She wouldn't have been as hard on him as Selma that's for sure. All she would have care about was that he stayed on the road within the acceptable limits of consistency and contentment. She wouldn't have cared if he couldn't always color between the lines.

But you can't expect dreams when you fall asleep the victim of blind exhaustion, and shock. The sleep that comes is dark and soundless, almost like lying down in a coffin. After a sleep like that, you have to be grateful just to wake up again.

THURSDAY

Ira panicked when he saw that the time was 9:15. He hadn't overslept in years. His body always woke him up a few minutes before the alarm went off. Now he had missed the train and the first of the Sinoral post-mortems. He hated being late for anything. He wondered why Ellen didn't wake him. His head was pounding so he could be sick, which might explain why he was reluctant to open his eyes. Bright light had a way of boring right into his brain when he was under the weather. Or maybe he forgot and it was actually Saturday, that had happened on occasion. Then Ira felt the cover and it was different, harder, not like it had been laundered a thousand times. And the bed sagged in the middle like it was fifty years old and the room smelled like it hadn't tasted fresh air since Neil Armstrong walked on the moon. When he opened his eyes the room was not even vaguely familiar, although the light from the hall did burn his retina like a laser beam.

Then it all came back to him. He was snowbound in a bungalow with two women of diametrically opposed ages and figures. He had a new mother, no father, a girlfriend and a hangover that clamped onto him like a vice. The only escape was to fall back asleep, but he couldn't. His mouth was dry and his throat felt like the inside of a vacuum cleaner. Besides, the sound from the kitchen of Shirley clearing her throat sounded like a jet coming in for a landing.

If he were home, Ellen would be coming in about now with a warm cup of coffee and a snow holiday grin from ear to ear. She loved an unexpected day off, provided the impassable roads applied to his commute as well. Instead, he got up and put on pants that felt like skin shed from some primordial creature and looked out the window at the white, burning silence. It was like staring into a 1000-watt light bulb. There were a dozen bad thoughts rattling around in his brain with no way of escape and every breath he took was accompanied by a sharp jab in his chest. He had a case of anxiety that he could feel on his face like acne.

He tried slow breathing with a focal point, in this case an enormous pair of Shirley's underwear hanging down from the dresser, but it didn't work. The half-empty bag of cheese doodles on top of it worked no better. The package said real cheese, but Ira couldn't recall seeing cheese that neon shade of orange before. Nothing helped because this anxiety was different. It was not the kind he carried around the morning of an important meeting or after the completion of a coupon campaign that always passed. This was the kind you might take to bed after being dumped by the love of your life. Actually, this was even worse. This anxiety was a lifetime sentence like a diagnosis of cancer.

"I suppose I should be jealous," Rhonda said when Ira walked into the kitchen ready to kill for a cup of coffee.

"Nothing happened I swear," Shirley said.

"What are you two talking about?"

"You know who you slept with last night?"

The answer went off in his head like a flashbulb illuminating breasts the size of giant water balloons and folds of flesh as malleable as Play-Dough. He had this sudden urge to take an all day shower.

"Oh, God."

He looked at Shirley to get him off the hook.

"I thought it was going to be our little secret."

"Nothing happened," he said although he was unsure.

Rhonda and Shirley laughed.

"Because you're not man enough," Shirley said. "It would have taken an army."

Rhonda had to hold on to her chair to keep from falling off.

"I need coffee."

Shirley poured him a cup strong enough to dissolve a nail.

"No work today," Shirley said, "no way to get outta here."

"The radio said the day shift didn't have to report," Rhonda said, "except for essential personnel."

"And that ain't us," Shirley said to him. "Besides, they probably won't get around to plowing this road until the early spring."

"Who cares," Rhonda said.

"More coffee?"

Ira growled in response and Rhonda poured him another cup. He looked around, but didn't see the bottle of bourbon anywhere. Maybe he'd finished it. They sat around most of the morning eating stale crackers and watching soap operas. Around noon, Shirley took a shower.

"So what are you going to do now?" Rhonda said.

"Stay here today."

"No kidding."

"The week is shot. I might as well stay through Friday. Maybe I can find out something about my father."

"Oh yeah, that'll be a piece of cake."

"You never know, I'm on a role. With my luck he'll turn out to be Doc Fulton."

"Who ever it is won't admit it."

"Maybe I'm his only child?"

"All he'll want is money."

"He won't get it from me."

"You'll be surprised sometimes how hard it is to say no," Rhonda said. "My mother still calls when she's low."

"And you send her money?"

Rhonda nodded slowly.

"Anyway, my guess is that he's in jail," she said. "You don't do something like that once."

"That's reassuring," Ira said. "That way I'll have a convicted felon to drag out alongside my insane mother the next time my mother . . . Selma . . . gives me that forever disappointing look."

"You can have my father if you want," Rhonda said.

"Maybe there's someone at Pilgrim who remembers Eva."

"And can identify the rapist?"

"It's possible."

"Why don't you just put an ad in the Pilgrim newspaper?"

"Is there one?"

"The Pilgrim Pride, it comes out once a month. You can put it in the classified, right alongside cars for sale."

"I'll try to be more discrete."

"What if it wasn't someone from Pilgrim, but a visitor with an hour to kill?"

"I'd still like to know."

"Suit yourself," Rhonda said switching the channel to a different soap opera.

In five seconds he knew the whole plot. A young woman was pregnant and desperate for an abortion. Her boyfriend wanted the child and was willing to pay cash for it, except it wasn't really his child. If someone had noticed early enough, Ira realized, he would've been an abortion. His birth was the fortuitous combination of a criminal act and someone's negligence.

Rhonda leaned against him on the couch engrossed by the unfolding television drama while he tried to ignore the list of things he should be doing like calling work, calling Ellen and speaking to the kids. He wondered if he could use his new parentage as a kind of get out of jail free card. Ellen was bound to accept it at least the first time. He also wondered what his father was doing this very moment, provided he wasn't already roasting in hell. Perhaps he was tackling some tough job around the house like replacing the toilet bowl or painting the den. Or maybe he was sitting by the fire with a good mystery. It was more likely that he was trying to raise bail.

"Wouldn't it be something if I could find him?"

"Wouldn't it be something," Rhonda said with all the enthusiasm of someone hooked up to a breathing tube.

The woman in the soap decided to have the baby and marry the boyfriend, but she didn't tell him he was not the real father. She left that for a later episode.

"They'll be lousy parents," Rhonda said.

"How do you know?"

"Christ, he wanted to buy the baby and she thought about selling it. What does that say?"

"That they're part of the consumer economy?"

"That they're more in love with themselves than each other," Rhonda said. "They're going to find that child a big pain in the ass."

In the afternoon they watched a Godzilla movie while a parade of ants marched across the floor behind the television, residents of the outside wall fleeing the storm.

"They don't bother me," Shirley said when Ira pointed them out. "They keep me company."

Ellen would have gone nuts. One spring, about four years ago, she found a few near the pantry, big ants with enormous antennae. She emptied the entire closet, threw out anything that was opened and littered the floor with ant traps. Her body counts were probably no more accurate than the government's during the Vietnam War.

"Shirley," Ira said as thousands of Japanese fled Godzilla's path.

"What?"

"Any ideas about who my father was?"

Shirley pried her eyes off the tube and her lips off a pretzel rod.

"Yeah, a real sonofabitch."

"Was it someone who worked there or do you think it was a patient?"

"He could have been anybody."

"Who would you guess?"

"I don't guess."

"I bet it was someone who worked there," he said.

"Afraid of being a native son?"

"It makes more sense."

"Well that narrows the field down to about five hundred men."

They broke to a commercial just as Godzilla approached the power lines.

"How about your mother?" Ira asked.

"What about her?" Shirley responded giving Rhonda a dirty look.

"You mentioned it last night," Rhonda said.

"I was just curious."

"She died before I started working here."

"Not all the crazy mothers wind up in the asylum," Rhonda said to herself more than to anyone else.

"Yeah," Shirley said, "only the mothers driven crazy by their men are the ones who wound up at Pilgrim. I kept away from men and look where I wound up."

"On the other side of the partition," Rhonda said.

"Not much of a difference if you ask me."

Ira wondered if someone or something drove Eva crazy, as the electricity fried Godzilla to a golden crisp. He'd seen him die so often that he now rooted for him to win. Maybe one day Godzilla would learn to duck.

"The best thing my mother had going for her," Shirley said, "was that she looked like me, so they left her alone."

"For you and me," Ira said, "Pilgrim State is the family institution."

Rhonda laughed.

"My father was a shitty drunk," Shirley said staring out into space. "And he didn't wait for the dark. He used to slap her around with the back of his hand, like he was shooing away a fly. My brother and I got the front, so we didn't get the ring marks."

"What do you think made Eva crazy?"

A beautiful young girl holding a bottle of mouthwash behind her back kissed a handsome boy. The camera slowly pulled away until the product name came into focus. It was a thirty-second story with a happy ending. It was one of Ira's products that he introduced with an expensive tip-in coupon campaign about a year ago.

"Some people are like egg shells," Shirley said, "so it doesn't take much."

There was a special news bulletin about the storm damage. There were the usual deaths due to shoveling heroics.

"Pass me the TV guide."

Shirley turned to Thursday afternoon.

"I wonder if he was a doctor."

"Don't get your hopes up Ira. The diplomas usually kept to the nurses. It didn't take much, just a few empty promises."

"You said Eva was pretty."

Shirley nodded.

"Who ever it was doesn't deserve it," Shirley said.

"Deserve what?"

"He doesn't deserve to know."

"The hell with him, I want to know."

"No you don't."

"Yes I do."

"If I could've wiped my father out of my life, maybe I wouldn't have wound up sleeping with my first man at 75."

With that Shirley got up, walked into the bedroom and slammed the door shut.

"Is that true?"

"There's a difference," Rhonda said, "between having sex and sleeping with a man."

She brushed a few lonely strands of hair away from her face. "I wish I could have wiped my father out of my life too."

He could really like Rhonda, Ira thought, if he was single and twenty years younger.

"You care if I put on a game show?" she said.

"No."

He closed his eyes and lay back on the couch.

He'd been putting off calling Ellen and American Family Care all day. This would be the perfect time to do it, except he wasn't finished enjoying his completely useless morning in front of the television filling up on junk food. Everyone should do it at least once a year, if only to confirm that the things you rush to do every day, which always seem so important, rarely are.

Back home Ellen made chicken soup and shoveled the front walk. She liked to make soup from scratch on snowy days with a whole chicken, carrots, celery and lots of onions. It restored the circulation to hands and feet numb from shoveling and making snowmen. For years, he and Ellen shoveled the driveway with the kids. It took about two hours. Longer if the snow was heavy and wet. He didn't mind doing it. But after reading each winter about all the men in their thirties and forties who dropped dead shovel in hand, Ellen finally convinced him a few years ago to have it plowed for three hundred and fifty dollars a season, whether it snowed once or one hundred times. So far the snowplow driver was way ahead.

Now they just did the front walk and around to the back door, which wasn't easy, particularly since the front faced north and always iced up. It required quite a bit of chopping and scrapping. Sometimes he had to do it two or three times during a storm, because otherwise the ice got too thick. He even swept it with a broom. It was important to keep the walk clean, since it had a slight incline and could become very slippery. No one had taken a bad fall yet, but if someone did, he didn't want it to be his fault.

Today, there was no fire because Ira wasn't there to light it. The front walk did ice up but Ellen wasn't going out there to clean it for a second time. Instead, she took a bath and read her magazines. Selma called every few hours. With the truth out, she expected everything to return to normal like the skies after a storm. She expected the truth to settle comfortably to the bottom of everyone's mind until it disappeared from view under layers of time, the way it did before.

She might be right. Certain truths are like the sun, too hard to look at for very long. They eventually have to be buried and denied or, at the very least, forgotten.

Ellen spoke to Ira's boss. The storm had bought him a little time, but he was very annoyed that Ira hadn't been calling.

"He's always been very reliable," Paul said.

Ellen didn't disagree. Reliable was the word that belonged on his tombstone; at least it did until last week.

Paul told Ellen that if he didn't show up for work on Monday, he'd have to start looking for a replacement. Clearly, Ira's ladder to the top of American Family Care was now missing a few rungs. If he managed to keep his job, he'd probably be stuck in couponing for the rest of his life, although knowing Ira as she did she was sure he would prefer it that way.

From where Ira sat on Shirley's moldy couch, a lifetime in coupons didn't seem all that bad. To redeem himself - to use a couponer's favorite word - would require a superhuman effort. Late nights and some weekend work, which he hadn't done in a number of years, but he would do whatever it takes. Once you begin to let go, Ira realized, there's a domino effect. If you don't call home, it becomes easier not to call work. If you don't call work, it becomes easier to sit around and watch television. If you sit around and watch television, it becomes easier not to shave or dress. It's a gradual spiral that's hardly noticeable as you ride it down.

He wondered if this middle age, suburban death wish was his mother's legacy, a kind of genetic time bomb that had been ticking all these years waiting to go off. He could start a club for children of lobotomees. They could compare notes. There might be an age when they all begin to self-destruct. Of course, it's possible that he might be the only member.

"I'm glad the secret's out," Sarah said as soon as Ellen picked up the telephone.

"Aunt Sarah?"

"I'm still Ira's aunt, that hasn't changed."

"I realize that."

"I wanted to be the one to raise Ira," she said, "but I wasn't married. If I had, I would've told him the truth."

"Did they ever find the man who did it?"

"I don't think anyone tried. Who needs a father like that?"

"He deserved to go to prison."

"I called to say . . . ." Sarah took a deep breath. "Don't be too hard on Ira. This was all handled very badly from every prospective."

"Yes it was," Ellen said using her serious teacher's voice.

"We didn't give him much of a choice."

Ellen weighed her words carefully, much more now than she did the week before.

"He hasn't given me much of a choice."

"You'll see, a year from now we'll all be laughing about it."

"I don't think so."

"At least it won't be on our minds like it is now."

That much Ellen agreed with. She promised to call Sarah as soon as she heard from Ira.

The next call was from one of Ellen's divorced teacher friends who gave her the name of a good therapist.

"Joan's wonderful," Gail said, "and very compassionate, she specializes in family problems and only treats women."

Ellen had never been to a therapist before, but she was considering it, especially since Ira hated them so. He called therapists overpaid listeners. He believed that spouses provided the same service for free.

"He's such an asshole," Gail kept repeating, as if it were another way of saying I told you so.

Ellen didn't disagree.

Ira never cared much for Gail. She always called during dinner or woke him up early on Saturday mornings when he was hoping to sleep a little late. He thought she did it purposely because she hated men. Ellen said her sense of timing was out of whack, like body odor, and she couldn't help it. Gail offered to come for a visit, but Ellen said she had schoolwork to correct. She'd been using that same excuse for years. Late in the afternoon, with the kids out at friends, Ellen opened some red wine, an expensive bottle that Ira had been saving for a special occasion, and tried to enjoy the solitude.

Shirley was in the bedroom for about two hours. Her snoring sounded like last night's storm. When she came out, she went right into the kitchen and opened up three cans of Chef-Boy-R-Dee ravioli. It had a new label with a high tech look, no doubt the result of product testing and design engineering, but the raviolis were just the way Ira remembered them--tiny, hard, tasteless pieces of pasta and meat in a thick, sugary tomato sauce.

They were absolutely delicious.

Ira wondered if they had Chef-Boy-R-Dee for the aging generation, low in salt with half the sugar.

They finished off the remaining beers while watching an old Jerry Lewis movie. He was a clumsy, shy professor part of the time and a confident, outgoing Don Juan the rest. In the end, the two personalities collided on a nightclub stage. The shy Jerry got the girl and both Jerrys reconciled. Sort of a slapstick "Three Faces of Eve."

Rhonda took a shower and Shirley and Ira moved on to some stale cookies.

"I don't understand it," Shirley said looking over the TV Guide.

"Don't understand what?"

"Why Rhonda keeps getting involved in these dead-end relationships."

"She hasn't talked to me about any of the others."

"Most of the guys were real shits and they never last more than a couple of months."

Shirley listened to the sound of the shower.

"She can't help herself," she added. "She can't say no."

"That's too bad," Ira said.

"If I tell you something, you have to promise not to say a word. If you do, I'll fall on top of you and crush you like a bag of chips."

"I promise."

"Her father was more than a sonofabitch. He wasn't around much, but when he was he was a pretty big shit, and not with the back of his hand if you know what I mean."

Eva, Shirley and now Rhonda, Ira thought, was it all that common or just common at psychiatric institutions?

"I guess she doesn't expect anything better," Shirley said. "You're the first married man, but I can see'em coming."

"What about Eva?"

"What about her."

"You think she was abused also."

"Rhonda told you."

"No, I overheard you talking the other day."

"It wasn't so much what she said at first, it was more in her eyes. I'm sure that's why she was so afraid of the male orderlies."

"Did she ever mention who?"

"Nope, I'm sure it was one of the usual suspects, some relative or neighbor."

The shower stopped and Shirley leaned close to him.

"Try not to act like an asshole when you leave."

He nodded.

"And make it soon, so she can get on with her life. Make it a clean break. Don't come back for seconds the next time you want to go pee-holing. You know what I'm saying?"

He nodded again.

Rhonda came back wrapped in a towel.

He tried unsuccessfully to watch television and ignore her breasts as they strained against the fold. His head was turned toward the television, but his eyes followed them like the words of a sing-a-long. Filing her nails caused them to bounce, as if she were working a jackhammer. Shirley, however, was engrossed in a game show. The Price is Right. She shouted encouragement and called out prices. She was never even close.

"Never go shopping," she said, "except for food."

The snowplow came in the late afternoon. Before they left Rhonda straightened up the living room while he sat with Shirley in the kitchen.

"What a wasted life Eva had," he said.

Shirley cracked her knuckles one at a time. It sounded as if she were trying to break them.

"A lot of wasted lives around here."

"Did she ever talk about her family?"

"Nope."

"Did she ever ask about me?"

"Are you kidding, she probably thought you were the mother of all stomach aches."

"Thanks."

"She didn't remember much of anything after the lobotomy. It's not always that way. Maybe Fulton had a bad night's sleep and cut a little deeper that day or gave his potato peeler a extra little twirl."

"I'd like to find out who did it."

"Are you going to question everyone over sixty-five or just the short, stocky ones with small hands?"

"The road's clear," Rhonda said, "I'll get our coats."

"I might as well finish out the week."

"Sort of like a vacation at the ancestral home," Shirley said.

"Is there anyone else at Pilgrim who might remember Eva?" Ira asked.

Shirley stood up.

"I'll see you tomorrow."

"Maybe there are records in administration."

Shirley walked to the door.

"Did any of the lobotomies work?"

"Not really, not unless you count the suicidal patients who no longer knew they had wrists to slit."

On the way home, Rhonda and Ira stopped for dinner. Not at the diner this time, but at a real steak house. Ira insisted. The kind that check coats and serve big bloody marys, lots of warm bread, giant bowls of salad and thick, juicy steaks. He needed meat. His body craved it. Rhonda ordered fish; she didn't eat red meat. She got most of the protein she needed, she said, from a powder she bought at the gym.

"Shirley never talked much about her father before," Rhonda said.

"Do you really think I'm the first man she slept with?"

"No, but I bet you're the first one that spent the night . . . and didn't turn her stomach."

They drove back to Rhonda's apartment in relative silence, Eva's file burning a hole in his lap. Back at the apartment, Ira steeled himself to call home. What a strange feeling it was. He had spoken to Ellen every day for at least twenty years, sharing every thought and fear that entered his head no matter how stupid and irrational. The conversations were always unconscious; he never thought about what to say or worried about how to say it.

He missed the 5:15 call from the office to tell her that he was leaving to catch the train home. He missed those wonderful midday calls when Ellen was on school holiday just to say hello. He even missed those absent-minded conversations at work about sports and movies, although he couldn't remember any of them. The ordinary and everyday seemed so out of reach now.

He avoided the telephone for a while by sitting with Rhonda and watching "Cheers." Cliff was trying to change his personality with electric shock. Neither of them found it funny. But for Eva, he would be home with Ellen laughing until his sides ached. Maybe they were both too tired. Maybe Rhonda was staring at a long stretch without movies and wondering about the next guy who would come up to her at the diner to ask for help because she suggested going to sleep and it was clearly not for anything else. Maybe Shirley had spoken to her.

"Go ahead," Ira said, "I have to make a few calls first."

"Isn't it a little late?"

"If it were noon it would be a little late."

"Don't be long," she said, exactly the way Ellen had said it to him a thousand times before.

He waited until Rhonda arranged her stuffed animals and climbed into bed.

The first call was to Paul. They generally got along well. Paul left Ira alone when it came to coupons and he provided him a nice little closing binder at the end of each campaign filled with statistics and color charts.

"Paul."

"Yes."

"It's Ira."

"We can't get in touch with you at work, but you call me late at night at home. Are you going off the deep end or what?"

"I need another day. I should be back Monday."

"I don't like the sound of the word *should*, I never did."

"I will be back Monday."

"You're not the first guy to break up with his wife."

"We haven't broken up. I'm just not home. This really does have to do with my grandmother."

"If it's not Monday Ira, you just may find your things in a box."

That was the way they did it at American Family. One day you came to work and everything from your desk was in a box, except for company manuals, memos, pads and pens. Then you and your box were escorted to the Director of Personnel for an exit interview that lasted about one minute for every year of service. The guard then carried your box to the lobby. After that you needed a pass to get in like everybody else.

"I understand."

"I don't know what else to tell you."

"I'll see you then," Ira said trying to sound upbeat.

"By the way, there was a slight problem with the Sinoral campaign," Paul said.

"What was it?"

"Instead of fifty cents off some of the coupons said five hundred cents off."

That was about a fifty million dollar error, but only if they were all redeemed, which they never were, although redemption rates did increase dramatically as the dollar value rose.

"How many went out like that?"

"None, we caught it in time, but we had to scramble to double check them everywhere. I don't know how a mistake like that could have gotten that far along."

"I'll look into it on Monday."

"You do that."

He didn't know which of them hung up faster.

The line at home was busy so he called Selma. He couldn't think of what else to call her. Aunt sounded too comical.

"Selma."

"Ira, is that you?"

"Yes."

"Are you home?"

"I'm still at Pilgrim State. There's one more thing I need to find out."

"There's nothing more, you know everything."

"Who is my real father?"

"No one knows and that's the truth."

"What a relief to know that you're out of secrets."

"Where are you staying?"

"Nowhere."

"No one stays no where. Are you at a motel . . . someone's house?"

"Someone's house."

Selma was probably wondering just how far she could push him in her new role. Eventually, she'll decide that there's no difference and resume her Selma-ways, but for now she's being relatively cautious.

"Ellen thinks you're with another woman."

He didn't respond.

"Are you?"

"Not right now, no."

Selma continued talking rapidly and emotionally, but Ira wasn't listening. Instead, he was picturing life at Pilgrim State Hospital in the late forties. Eva in a sundress on the front lawn, lobotomized and serene, being courted by his father, a distinguished psychiatrist. It didn't have to be rape. What if it was a secret tryst on his leather couch? Two star-crossed lovers separated by an insurmountable mental divide?

It had been a long, hard winter and Eva's color was a stubborn, immovable white. Her piercing blue eyes were uncertain, but not scared. She had no crow's feet or worry lines like Selma and Ira. She remained beautiful, despite the fragile way her hair had grown back after the procedure, almost brittle to the touch. Her delicate features were still doll-like. Her sad and serious mouth, frozen in a kind of permanent pout, was impossible to turn away from.

Her beauty eliminated any need for words.

When the doctor took her hand, he couldn't help noticing her long fingers. They were the hands of a concert pianist.

"You've got to go back home," Selma said. "They need you. Are you listening to me? Ira?"

He didn't draw a breath for fear of disturbing this lovely picture.

"This woman you're staying with?"

"What?"

One word and the grounds melted away, replaced by Rhonda's cold and bleak kitchen.

"Who is this woman you're staying with?"

"I didn't say I was staying with a woman."

"Ellen did."

"She's a nurse, a harmless nurse."

"Nurses are dangerous."

"How are nurses dangerous?"

"They're notorious home wreckers."

"You've been watching too many soap operas."

Selma took a deep breath. She didn't know what else to say or maybe she just didn't want to know any more.

"Why didn't you visit my mother?" he asked.

"I was too young."

"She was there for thirty years for Christ's sake."

"I know that, you don't have to curse."

"Sorry."

"By the time I turned eighteen, too many years had passed. Eva didn't want to see anyone, not even my mother. Then she had that brain operation. I don't think she would have remembered me at that point."

"There was one sure-fire way to find out."

"Don't think for one minute that I didn't think about it."

"Listen, ma . . . Selma . . . I've got to call Ellen."

"Will you be home in the morning?"

"No."

"The weekend?"

"I don't know."

With that Ira hung up and dialed home. After the first ring, he realized that he'd forgotten to charge his office and that his home number would now appear on Rhonda's bill. Scott answered before he had a chance to hang up.

"Dad?"

"Hi Scotty. What are you doing up so late?"

"When are you coming home?"

It was a plea, not a demand.

"Soon."

The silence was sickening.

"Probably this weekend, there are a few things I have to do here first."

"Here?"

"Who is it?"

Ira heard Ellen calling out in the background. She was probably coming out of the bathroom.

"It's Dad."

Ellen picked up the telephone. He heard the bedroom door slam. Scott stayed on the line for a moment, probably hoping to hear something reassuring. Neither of them spoke until he hung up.

"Bye Scotty," he said but it was too late.

"That was the first time you've said two words to him in a week."

"How's Jamie?"

"Doing better than Scott, she has some friends in class with the same problem."

"What problem?"

"Parents separating."

"We're not separating."

"No, we're separated."

"For another day or two."

"Is that what you call it? Is that when you'll be finished screwing around with another woman and working at another job?"

Ellen paused to catch her breath, like a boxer between rounds.

"I want to try to find out something about my father before I go."

"There isn't anything more to find out Ira. You're just avoiding the issue. Maybe subconsciously you really don't want to come home."

He didn't respond, not because there was any truth to it, but because he wasn't sure how to say what he wanted to say. He never had to say anything like it before. He really did want to come home; he just wasn't ready. When he was, he wanted to erase the entire week, forget about Eva and return to whatever little certainties still remained. He doubted Ellen would have believed a word of it. He was afraid that whatever he said would come out wrong. He looked around for some wood to knock on and settled for the wall. Surely there was a beam back there somewhere.

He knew what Ellen must have been thinking. You spend half your life with a man and think you know him, think he's devoted to a relationship that's so intimate it needs no witness. A relationship filled with soft words and endearments, desire and release, subtlety and patience, almost like a religious ceremony, but the very first time an opportunity presents itself he rushes into someone else's arms and undermines everything.

The silence on the other end sent a chill down Ellen's spine. She felt this pressure welling up inside her, like she was being pumped up with air. Pressure that would eventually force out a torrent of tears, but certainly not until she hung up.

"I hate you," she whispered to herself putting her hand to her mouth and squeezing the lines around her eyes.

"What?"

"Nothing."

Just like that Ellen set the feeling free. She never liked making an issue of doubt or acting in anger. She tells that to all her students. Don't let emotions get the better of you. Let them go and you'll perform better. She has always been good at it. She had that in common with Rhonda.

"I think you should face up to the possibility that this girl may be better for you," Ellen said calmly and rationally, as if Ira was trying to decide between two ties, although she said "girl" like she was referring to an adolescent or a prostitute. For some reason, it made Ira aware of how Rhonda's smell was everywhere, even on his clothes and hands.

"That's nonsense."

"Maybe it'll be better, more exciting, this time around."

"I'll be home this weekend, whether or not I find anything out about my father."

Ellen took a deep breath. No doubt she was weighing the pro and cons of taking a stand. They were both from the Vietnam War generation and appreciated the risks of escalation. He had to have more than enough credit in the marital bank, he thought, to pay for this one mistake, even though it was a big one.

"I spoke to Paul. Everything's going to be fine at work. They're expecting me on Monday."

"Oh, Ira," Ellen cried out. The emotion surged up again and she had to swallow hard. "What a mess you've made of things, all over something that was best left forgotten."

"I'm sorry," he said although he was really thinking that she was wrong because she had missed the step in between. It had to be known first before it could be forgotten. Now that he knew, he was almost ready to forget.

Neither of them could think of anything else to say. If Ellen couldn't keep the conversation going then it was way beyond his ability to do so.

"How old is she?" Ellen finally said.

"Who?"

"Who do you think? Your girlfriend."

"She's not my girlfriend."

"Your private nurse."

"Late-twenties."

"Big breasts I bet."

She was always right about things like that. He wondered how she knew.

"She really has been helping me with Eva."

"So now you've had two women, Ira. I'm very proud of you."

With that Ellen hung up the telephone. Instead of calling her back, he looked in the cupboards for something sweet. Chocolate was as good as valium at a time like this. He found a box of Oreo cookies hidden behind the canned vegetables. He ate half a dozen while sitting there listening for some life outside. It was very quiet. Few people were driving so soon after the storm and the snow muffled the sounds of those who did. It was also quiet inside as well, except for the reassuring sound of the heat pouring out from the radiators.

After forcing himself to stop eating, he climbed quietly into bed. He would have loved to watch some television. It would have made it easier to fall asleep, even with the sound turned off. Instead, he lifted up the blanket and studied Rhonda's body like a cartographer. He wanted to remember every detail. He didn't intend to, he didn't even want to, but he got aroused anyway. Maybe it was all that sugar. Rhonda didn't push him away or complain that it was too late. Of course, Shirley would say that was because she couldn't say no. They made love without a word

and without breaking a sweat. It was their first ordinary experience
. . . nice, but hardly worth leaving home for.

After it was over, Rhonda quickly fell back asleep. His heart,
however, continued to race and Ira felt as if he couldn't unclench
his teeth. The snow blowing against the wall sounded like
someone scratching to get inside. He tried playing a game of
baseball in his head, but it didn't work. He had to identify this
tightness in his chest, which felt like a fist squeezing around his
heart. There was an element of sadness to it, but it was more than
sadness. It would be a mistake to call it fear. It was part surprise
and part confusion; frustration perhaps, but it was probably closer
to anger than anything else.

He tried to list the things he was angry about, but it didn't
help because he was angry at everything. At fate and coincidence,
at secrecy and truth, at time and place, he was angry in a dozen
different directions. Angry enough to break something or slam the
door shut, if he had a room of his own. A half-hour later, he was
still tense and wide-awake. He desperately needed to sleep, so he
narrowed his angry list to people only. Rhonda was on the list, so
was his real father. Ellen was there, as was Eva, Shirley, Selma,
Paul and Dan. He was angry at Rhonda for wanting him and
making it so easy. If she had laughed at the short, chubby middle-
age coupon peddler that first day at the diner and gave him the
brush off, things would have turned out very differently. He'd
have learned nothing at Pilgrim State on his own, returned home
and accepted Selma's explanation. Instead, Rhonda added a new
and dangerous dimension to his self-image.

Of course, his real father was number one on the hit list.
Angry was too mild a word; homicidal would be more appropriate.
Ira fantasized about cracking his head open with a hammer, but
not before they talked and had a reasonable opportunity to
reconcile. He'd give him a hug before he did it. After all, he
wouldn't be here if he had any kind of self-control. He had no
right to be angry at Ellen, but he was, just a little. Her innocence
made him guiltier in comparison. If the roles were reversed and
she was staring into the grave of her missing aunt, she would have
asked a few discreet questions and let her rest in peace. She would
have respected everyone's wishes and their family life wouldn't
have missed a beat.

Selma was second on the list for the obvious reasons, for
hiding the truth and hounding him his entire life. For making him

feel that nothing he ever did was good enough. Out of fear no doubt that if she didn't, he might sink slowly into insanity. He was angry at Shirley. She also hid the truth, doling it out in small portions. She should have told him everything right away. He wondered what more Shirley was keeping to herself? Maybe she knew the identity of his father? Maybe she was also one of his victims.

He could feel himself starting to drift off to sleep.

He was also a little mad at Aunt Sarah. She could have been his mother if she had been more forceful. She would have told him everything. She would have been kinder and more accepting, because that was her nature, and she didn't fear the future that way his mother did. And, of course, he was angry at Paul and Dan, because all those years of loyalty didn't appear to mean that much. American Family Care was not really a family that cared. It was a bottom line machine with a very short memory.

Ellen was also having trouble falling asleep. She went to bed determined to make Ira pay, but now she didn't feel the least bit angry, just sad, lonely and small. The trust, once so unconscious, would never be the same. Still, she realized that she was better off trying to fix what was broken than starting all over again. After a while, Ellen sat up and looked at the things on Ira's side of dresser. Everything was just as he left it, as if he never really left. It was as if time in their bedroom was both moving and standing still at the same time, as if the past would never completely leave, no matter how hard the present and future tried to push it out.

Ellen clenched her teeth. Something else was bothering her. She couldn't quite put her finger on it, but she couldn't take her eyes off the dresser. Her eyelids started growing heavy, but she fought against it. Then she noticed the wedding ring. Ira never wore it at work, since it bothered him when he wrote, but he always wore it when he was going on an overnight trip. Ira was far too superstitious to vary that routine.

The fact that it was still on the dresser meant he was planning to return the same day and that this whole thing really was unplanned. It just happened, something he was unable to resist. At first, Ellen felt reassured, but then she felt worse. The fact that Ira couldn't stick to his plan and let himself get carried away could be evidence of a major character flaw, something that didn't appear until late in life, like a double chin or chronic hemorrhoids. Unlike the mistakes Ellen saw at school, this one might not be correctible.

Ira's teeth finally unclenched once he realized that he was most angry at himself. He got into this without a plan in place to get out. He rushed in without thinking it through, like he does with a coupon campaign. He went too far too fast until there was no turning back. He committed to early. He wanted a second chance, a replay, a do-over, so he could try again from the beginning. Perhaps this time he would turn away from Eva's stone with a shrug and know in his bones that there had to be some terrible reason to keep her life a secret and that he had to respect that. And if he had to ask, perhaps this time he'd accept Sarah's explanation and admonition.

Eva would have understood. After a couple of years, she didn't want to see her sisters. After all, what kind of relationship could she have had from inside a mental institution? She must have realized, just as Selma did, that the best thing for everyone was to forget. She would have wanted him to do no less. She would have expected Ira to go on with his life, no matter how much he wanted to get even, and he did want to get even. Of course, up until recently he didn't appreciate how knowing the right thing to do wasn't always enough when it came to the need for truth.

That was the last thought Ira recalled having before the alarm brought him back from a state, which because he awoke exhausted, he was reluctant to call sleep.

FRIDAY

Ira drove to Pilgrim because Rhonda was too tired.

"This is my weekend to work," she said, "what are you going to do?"

"I don't know."

She probably hoped that he would be sitting in her apartment circling movie listings, although she must have known it was more likely he'd be out conducting a house to house search for his father or on his way home to Ellen.

"Remember the party tonight."

"I haven't forgotten," Ira said although he had.

It was a promise he had made sometime during the night, after the sex and before the alarm that he barely remembered. The last thing he wanted to do was attend a Pilgrim State get together. If he went home tonight, he could leave a note and wouldn't have to face her ever again. She'd be better off since she could start interviewing for her next movie buddy at the party. Of course, a promise is a promise. Selma drilled that into him during those young, formative years when it was easy for her to get him to promise anything.

"I didn't sleep that well last night," she said. "Someone woke me out of a deep sleep." Rhonda smiled unsnapped her seatbelt and leaned up against Ira. He held the wheel tightly with both hands.

"You're getting to know your way around here pretty good."

Ira shrugged.

"He's probably a tough old bird by now," he said referring to his father.

"Probably a jail bird."

Ira pictured a cross between Ernest Hemingway and Arnold Schwarzenegger. Very different from the father he grew up with, who finally found the nerve to stand up to Selma by dying.

"You don't have to be a tough guy to do something like that," Rhonda added, "cowards do it all the time."

"I guess so."

"It's not a guess. Fathers, brothers, husbands, friends, neighbors, men you trust, kindly, older men who speak softly and flash big, warm smiles."

He nodded. Clearly this was way beyond his experience.

"Priests, teachers, tall men, short men."

"I get the picture."

"With wives and children, men who do volunteer work, go to church and live otherwise perfectly normal lives, and I'm not exaggerating."

"I didn't say you were."

"Most of it goes unreported."

Thankfully, Ira thought, those genes from his father were recessive.

"They stare out the window or at the floor while they're doing it or watch you out of the corner of their eye, as if that makes it OK. I suppose it's a lot easier if they don't have to see inside you while their doing it. A silent, nameless patient in a mental institution is perfect."

Rhonda shut her eyes the way Ellen did sometimes and moved back to her side of the seat. The headlights coming at him cut through his thoughts like a knife.

"You have to stay away from men like that," he said.

"They don't come with labels."

He slowed down and moved to the right lane behind a line of cars turning into Pilgrim State.

"Could there be a picture of Eva somewhere at the hospital?"

"Like a pig book? Head shots of this year's entering class?"

"Pictures that might help identify patients if they ran away or show changes maybe, you know, after some kind of experimental procedure."

"I once heard that Doc Fulton took before and after pictures."

Ira parked and locked the car. Rhonda smoothed down her skirt. She wasn't radiating much sexual energy this morning.

"Ask Shirley, she might know."

"Is there anyone else who's been at Pilgrim as long as Shirley?"

"Patients?"

"Employees."

"A few," Rhonda said. "They're almost like patients, after a certain amount of time they can't leave. That's why I'm not staying much longer if I can help it."

"Where would you go?"

"Private practice, I can take care of shut-ins at home and sit around all day watching television and eating chocolate."

"That sounds pretty boring."

"Boring's not so bad."

Rhonda was beginning to sound more and more like him, Ira thought.

"I can't come by for lunch today," she said. "I've got lunch duty."

They parted at the entrance with an air kiss.

"Don't forget the party tonight."

"I won't."

Shirley was sitting on the stool downstairs drinking coffee. Her mouth was encircled by powdered sugar like a clown in the middle of putting on her make-up.

"It occurred to me last night," she said, "that you'll probably be the last man I sleep with."

"Maybe not," Ira said.

"It will be if I have anything to say about."

Shirley wiped her forehead. She always seemed to be sweating.

"So what are ya gonna do on your last day Ira, how about some real work for a change?"

She pointed to the mountain of boxes behind her.

"I thought I'd look for someone else who might have known Eva."

Shirley chewed on something, perhaps her tongue, and folded her arms across her chest. It was almost like they were resting on a shelf. That seemed to be her favorite thinking position.

"I'd also like to find a photograph of Eva."

"We didn't take class portraits," Shirley said with a powdered grin.

"Rhonda says Doc Fulton took before and after pictures of the lobotomy patients."

"Shit, I forgot about that." Shirley looked at her index finger for a moment before trying to even out the nail with her teeth. "I haven't seen those in a 100 years."

"Maybe they're in one of the boxes."

"Maybe."

"Help me look?"

"I guess that's the least I can do after the other night," Shirley said pushing herself up from the chair, "but only if you promise to go home if we find'em."

"Even if we don't find them."

"Now you're talkin some sense."

They started opening boxes. All Shirley had to do was glance inside and she knew instantly what was there.

"Who else could I speak to about Eva?"

"Your two aunts?"

"At Pilgrim."

"No one."

"Rhonda says there are others like you."

"Old and fat?"

"Who have been here forever."

"Now that would be my definition of hell."

"A long time."

"Counting the inmates?"

"The staff."

"You're wasting your time."

"I've suddenly discovered I have a real talent for that."

"You're also good at wasting my time."

"That's two things I'm good at."

Shirley moved to the back of the basement.

"There's Rose, manager of food services, she started here about the same time as I did, used to be on the wards. Francis, director of nursing, is another, but she won't talk to you or anybody for that matter. She's one of those dogs that bark and bite. If you ask me, she's been constipated since the early fifties."

"Anyone else?"

"Not who might have worked with patients."

"How about patients?"

"No fucking way," Shirley said.

"No as in none?"

"No as in you can't go around messing with patients."

He turned to the next box.

"Go ahead speak to Rose if you want. I'll keep looking."

"I appreciate that."

"Got to get you home to the little woman and kiddies, so Ro can start looking for a man who has more than one thing on his mind . . . if that's possible."

"It is . . . at least after you hit forty."

"It's a lot older than that if you ask me, I don't think it happens until after they're dead for a few days," Shirley said as Ira ran up the stairs.

He found Rose in her office by the cafeteria. She was a small woman in a small room with a bright overhead light that illuminated her yellow skin and sunken features, like she was a figure in a wax museum.

She remembered Eva, but that was about it.

"Pretty girl, had a lobotomy."

It was the short form version of her biography.

"Anything else?"

Rose shook her head slowly from side to side.

"Shirley says she got pregnant and had a baby."

Rose looked up at him like he'd just uttered a four-letter word.

"I wouldn't know anything about that."

"Did Eva have any boyfriends?"

"Are you kidding, boyfriends in here? You haven't spent much time in a mental institution, have you?"

Born here, Ira thought about telling her, but he didn't. Rose promised to call Shirley if anything else came to mind. As he got up to leave, Rose recalled that Eva had a regular visitor.

"Pretty much every weekend, I'm sure it was her mother, short, stocky, gray-hair, dark eyes."

"My grandmother."

"Tough woman."

Not tough enough, he thought.

"Do you think Francis might be able to help?"

"You're not supposed to talk about patients to non-medical personnel. She'll throw you out on your ear."

Ira dragged himself back to records. Maybe it was time to go home, apologize to Ellen and start the healing and forgetting. It would give him the whole weekend just to start mending the fences. But he still had this feeling, almost like heartburn, that there was something more, a stone nearby with the answers underneath it just waiting to be turned over. Besides, he did promise Rhonda that he'd go to the party.

When he got back, Shirley was upstairs arguing with a hospital administrator about some filing problem. He walked downstairs and took a seat on the stool. Eva's file was on the counter. He'd smuggled it in under his jacket and the guard out front couldn't have been less interested. He could have walked in with a copy machine.

He opened it and flipped through the entries.

He was born on April 1, 1951, which meant that the rape had to take place the prior June or July. On July 1st, there's a "visit by mother," followed by a notation that "patient refused to eat dinner." There was nothing unusual until July 5 when someone noticed some "bruises on patient's elbow and upper arm" during the morning shower. This meant he was probably conceived on July 4th - which might explain his childhood fear of fireworks - during a rape in a backroom somewhere at Pilgrim State Hospital.

Not much to be sentimental about.

It wasn't until the middle of December that anyone noticed her period was late. A month later they figured out that she was in the family way. They certainly were careful not to jump to conclusions. Of course, the records for February, March and April were missing.

Going back to July 4th, Ira tried to make out the initials of the orderly on duty. It looked like someone had deliberately obliterated it, probably his father - obviously, a confession of guilt. Clearly he wasn't too bright, because the same four initials appeared throughout June, July and August--HR, DB, NL and FM. If Ira eliminated the doctors and stray patients, the temporary replacements and wandering administrators, than one of these four was likely to be his father. There were two sets of initials in the nurse's column for July 4--KE and SW . . . Shirley.

Bingo. If his father were still alive, he would probably be in his late-sixties or early seventies. Ira hoped he was rich, repentant and without an heir. If not, hopefully he died a poor, broken, lonely old man. Ira glanced at his reflection in the steel file cabinet against the wall. His mouth still dominated his face, but it looked hard and mean now, like a man capable of just about anything. He had never noticed that before.

Back home, Ellen called in sick. She wasn't actually sick, but she coughed into the receiver while requesting a substitute. She hated pretending to be ill. Anyone the least bit superstitious knows that's not a good thing to do. She just couldn't keep her mind on teaching. It wasn't fair to the class. She left good plans and the sub she asked for was a retired teacher. Ellen just wanted to stay home for a day. She planned to straighten up the house, make some dinners to freeze for next week and do the laundry. She also had a box of photos she'd been meaning to put into an album. Of course, that would be hard to do since Ira was in so many of them.

"It's the same crap, whether it's nursing or files," Shirley said walking slowly down the stairs. Shirley sank into the old armchair in the corner. She was half swallowed by it. The artificial light in the basement soaked into her skin giving her an eerie yellow glow. She looked tired, a lifetime kind of tired - the kind that was not curable by a three-day weekend. Ira turned his stool around and sat there waiting for Shirley to open her eyes.

"Something on your mind?" she said staring back at him like his head was made of glass.

"Occasionally."

"Don't be such a wise-ass. What happened with Rose?"

"Nothing."

"I could have told you that. Well, it's been nice knowing you."

"Not yet."

He sat there with a thin smile, like he was holding a full house.

"Out with it Ira, I'll die of old age before you finally open your trap."

Selma always said that he wore his emotions on his sleeve.

"I was looking through Eva's file. She had to get pregnant sometime in early July. They found bruises on her arm on July 5th, which might mean the rape occurred on July 4th."

"They should have named you Sam."

"The initials of the nurses on duty are KE and SW."

"Let me see."

He handed her the page.

"You should've been a detective, instead of a coupon clipper."

With a tremendous effort, Shirley lifted one leg off the ground. She held her breath until it crossed over and landed hard on top of the other.

"That's me on the night shift, but I never saw anything happen to Eva that night or any other night. If I had, I would have castrated the sucker."

"Could it have happened during the day?"

"Too many people around."

"You were there all night, wouldn't you have seen anyone if they came to the floor?"

"Being the night nurse didn't mean a whole lot back then. The orderlies took care of most everything. The only thing I had to do was giv'em their drugs. Half the time I'd be in the nurse's office sleeping."

"Who was the orderly on duty?"

Shirley turned over the page.

"Bastard crossed out his name."

"It's got to be one of the four initials that appear in June and July."

"Unless there was a sub that night,' Shirley said, "which happened all the time, particularly on holiday weekends."

Shirley looked through the subsequent entries.

"Can you beat that?" she said.

"What?"

"End of September someone writes down that Eva had her period."

"How could that be?"

"Couldn't, they made it up. It was easier than checking or dealing with the hassles."

"It had to be one of the orderlies," Ira said, "why else remove the initials."

"No shit, so what?"

"So what were their names?"

"That was over forty years ago. Who do you think I am Einstein?"

Shirley stared at the file her mouth open wide enough to swallow a good size drumstick.

"You had an opportunity to hate your father, I want mine."

"I earned it," Shirley said.

"So did Eva."

"You don't need a face to hate him. You're better off without one. It'll be easier to sleep."

"That's up to me."

"Why give him the satisfaction."

"What satisfaction?"

"Nothing is gonna happen to him now."

"So."

"So this way he gets a new son without any of the hassles. I know the type, it'll all be let bygones be bygones."

"Not if I have anything to say about it."

"You're a wimp Ira," Shirley said, "that's not gonna change."

Even a wimp can have his moments, Ira thought to himself.

"Maybe Francis can help," he said.

"Miss Constipation, I don't think so. She'll use her foot to help you out the door, probably me along with you."

"You'll get your social security."

"I could eat that in a week."

"You'll watch Richard Simmons."

"That little twerp makes me puke. Give me the page."

He handed her the sheets with the June and July entries.

"Try to remember," he pleaded.

"You know, you're turning into a real prick, probably just like your father."

"I can't help it," Ira said, "if it's in the genes."

Shirley looked over the file.

"Take your time."

"I'll tell you what, while I try to remember your past why don't you run to the cafeteria and buy me some cookies."

"What kind?"

"Anything with chocolate."

He was back in a flash with two packages of chocolate chip cookies.

"How's the memory."

"Unfortunately, I still remember more than I want to."

"So who did you come up with?"

"HR was definitely Henry Raymond. DB was Denny Block, NL, I'm not sure, but it was probably this guy named Nick Lourie, wasn't here too long, a bit of a head case."

"Rapist?"

"I doubt it."

"How about FM?"

"There was a Frank something who was an orderly for a while, could've been that far back. Only F I can think of, but if it's the guy I'm thinking of it couldn't've been him."

"How do you know?"

"He was tall, thin and good-looking."

"That's not funny."

"And black."

"What happened to the other three?"

"What do you mean what happened to them? Nothing happened to them. No one saw anything. They didn't even realize Eva was pregnant for six months. They were so dumb back then that half the staff probably thought it might've been immaculate conception."

"I meant where did they go? Where are they now?"

"Do I look like the alumni office? How would I know?"

"Well, the hell with it," Ira said using one of his rare expletives, "I might as well waltz right into personnel and see what I can find out."

"Sit down," Shirley said, "but this is it, the last shot, then you go home."

He nodded.

"If I see you back on Monday, I'm going to personally call Ellen and have security throw your ass outta here."

"So what do you know?" he asked.

"Not a whole lot. I remember that Henry opened a gas station."

"Where? What kind?"

"Slow down for Christ's sake."

Ira picked up a pencil and one of the index cards and Shirley made sure to keep him waiting.

"Down the road from the courthouse in Mineola. He's the man who wears the star, at least he was the last I heard. I remember someone said they bought a car from Dennis Block at Manly Chevrolet in Happauge. He could be retired in Florida by now for all I know."

"How about Nick Lourie?"

"Died about forty years ago."

"How?"

"Car crash, drunk driver."

"That's too bad."

"He was the drunk driver. Why don't we just call it a day and say it was him."

"Why?"

"Because it'll make everything a lot easier, he had no family, so you can fantasize all you want."

"Why are you so sure it wasn't him?"

"Because he played for the other team."

"Gay?"

"Don't be so surprised they were around forty years ago too."

"What about FM?"

"Still drawing a blank. Just give me your number at home and I'll leave a message with Ellen if I can remember."

Ira stood up to leave.

"Is this good-bye?"

"I promised Rhonda I'd go to this party tonight, so I'll probably stay until Saturday. I'm going to check out Henry Raymond and Dennis Block. Can you give Rhonda a ride home?"

"I hope you don't expect to get paid for today."

"I'll drop by your house to let you know what I find out."

"Bring a chaperone."

There are no two people Ira hates more than mechanics and car salesmen. Talking to a mechanic is like standing on 48th and Madison and suddenly realizing that you forgot your pants. He'll look under the hood and shake his head slowly, as if he's just diagnosed a near-fatal illness. He'll rub the stubble on his chin with one hand, while squeezing a greasy rag with the other for a good five minutes before he starts talking gibberish. About the only thing Ira can ever understand is the cost, which usually means a bank loan, and the fact that he's guilty of auto-abuse.

Of course, he's always been too intimidated to say no.

New car salesmen are not much better. They're genetically bred to know everything. The answer to every question is the best damn one on the market. They always drive whatever car he's looking at or their mothers do and they have a cousin who had a life-threatening problem with the competitor's car. They make you feel cheap and stupid if you don't purchase every option, including the boat trailer hitch, whether or not you ever go near water. You feel as if you should put them in your will, because of the effort they make to get you free mats.

Raymond's Texaco was right across from the courthouse, a mile south of St. John's University. It wasn't one of those gleaming four-bay, six island, convenience store businesses. It was a small run down two-pump job filled with old cars scattered all over the lots who drove in with little hope of ever getting out. Sort of like an automotive Pilgrim State. Ira sat across the road for twenty minutes, debating whether or not to go in. What if he found his father and actually liked him? What if his father hated him in return? What if he couldn't be sure? He wasn't likely to admit it. At least he needed gas, he thought, pulling up to the pump.

"Filler up?"

The question came from a man standing in front of the garage putting air into a tire.

"Yes, please."

He was in his mid-thirties, about Ira's height, although not as heavy. It could be his half-brother. So what if he had straight blond hair, he had a different mother.

"Are you Henry Raymond's son?" Ira said.

"Nah, Henry's got no sons, just daughters. You know Henry?"

"Not really. A friend of mine at work does. She asked me to say hello."

"That's him under the car."

"Thanks."

He walked into the garage. It was freezing. No father of his could bear to work in such cold conditions, not if he had his short, stubby fingers.

"Check your oil?" the guy called out from the pump.

"No, it's fine."

He lifted the hood anyway.

"Hello," Ira said to two knees and a pair of work boots. The only response he heard was his heart beating and the clanging of a wrench.

"Damn."

"Hello."

"Someone out there?"

"Mr. Raymond."

"Yeah."

He didn't move out from under the car, but wiggled his feet in a kind of mechanic's greeting.

"You don't know me."

"You see the wrench by the front tire?"

"Yes."

"Slide it under for me, will ya?"

"Sure."

He pushed the wrench toward his outstretched fingers. For an instant, just an instant, Ira thought about stomping down hard on his hand, but what if it wasn't the hand that squeezed Eva's arm.

"I work at Pilgrim State with this woman named Shirley. She used to work with you."

"Fat Shirley, sure, I remember her. Did she leave me something in her will?"

"I had an aunt who was a patient when you were there--Eva Portnoy."

"What?"

"Eva Portnoy."

"Never heard of her."

Something fell again.

"Damn."

"She was a patient."

"Hold on a minute."

Henry Raymond slipped out from under the car. It took him quite a while to get out, because he was endless, way over six feet, and as thin as a Popsicle stick. He had the long arms of a baboon and enormous hands that reached below his knees. He had straight, gray hair and a compact, featureless face with a mouth that looked barely large enough to take in a hot dog. In short, they didn't have a single feature in common.

"What were you saying about Shirley?" he said wiping his hands on a dirty rag and walking over to the toolbox.

"She says hello."

"Still fat?"

Ira nodded.

"Worked on her car about 15 years ago."

"Do you remember a patient named Eva Portnoy?"

"Are you kidding?"

Henry got down on his back again ready to slide back under the car.

"I can't even remember my kid's names. Why, did she leave me any money?"

"Just curious, she was a relative of mine."

"Say hello to Shirley."

"That'll be one five," the attendant said walking over from the pump.

Ira could see the trail of gas running down the side of the car, where he squeezed in an extra twenty cents. He hated when they did that.

"Gonna need oil soon."

"Thanks."

He couldn't give him directions to Manly Chevrolet, but he did know the way to Happague.

"Are his daughters as tall as him?" he said before pulling away.

"Amazons."

It was almost three by the time he found Manly Chevrolet. Two employees were cleaning snow off cars. They had about a hundred more to do, at least half of them vans. Manly Chevrolet was a big, modern dealership with a sign large enough to be visible from outer space. Inside, it was bright, warm and empty. Who shopped for a new car the day after a blizzard?

Ira planned out his approach. He didn't like to leave these things up to chance. He had to be forceful and up-front, no beating around the bush this time. He'd try to model himself after Shirley. He'd ruled out Henry Raymond, genes that big don't shrink that fast. Besides, there was nothing familiar about him. Ira was sure that his body would go off like a Geiger counter the moment he came close to his real father. If he eliminated the black and gay orderly and assumed it wasn't a visiting dignitary, then that left Dennis Block. He'd better at least own the dealership, Ira thought before walking in.

Across the showroom six men were huddled around a copy of the New York Post. He could eliminate four right away as under age, leaving two possible suspects. At least he should be sales manager by now. Ira stopped by the Chevy Lumina, his first mistake.

"The best car on the floor," a voice behind him boomed.

Ira turned around.

"The name's Wild Bill Clasen."

A man in a shiny, tight suit stepped out from the shadow of a Chevy truck and shook his hand making Ira feel like a part of the automotive food chain.

"And that's not just my opinion. We can't keep these babies in stock."

Wild Bill was in his early-twenties, a salesman in training. The other six watched with amusement. This was more interesting than the Post, even with its winter picture of a bikini-clad beauty from Australia.

"Working man with a family I bet."

He nodded.

"I can always tell; it's a sixth sense."

"Love reliability, am I right?"

He nodded again.

Car salesmen, like lawyers, are trained to ask questions that only allow for one-syllable answers.

"The Lumina's the best family car around. And it's more than just reliable, if you know what I mean, it's got plenty of kick. And look at those sporty lines," he said stroking the car like a racehorse.

"Handles like a sports car. Hugs the corner and gets real good gas mileage. You like to have fun when you drive, don't you?"

"Uh huh."

"Don't be put off by the sticker price, because I can deal. It's a blizzard bargain day and if you really want to save big bucks, I've got a great demo, clean as a whistle, how about a test drive?"

It's always the same. After two minutes with a car salesman, Ira wanted to run out the door and keep his old car for the rest of his life.

"I'm here to see Dennis Block."

Wild Bill turned red enough to melt butter.

"Dennis, he's yours."

Wild Bill slunk back into the shadow of the truck to wait for his next prey. Dennis stood up and the others returned to the Post. He was in the hands of a professional now. He wasn't much taller than Ira and he was heavy, which was a good sign. He had big features, not naturally big, more overripe with age, as if the blood has been gathering in stagnant pools in his ears and nose for the last ten years, instead of circulating around his face, the sign of a drinker. He was round shouldered, dressed in polyester and looked like a character out of "American Graffiti."

"Come into my office," he said after squeezing the blood from Ira's hand.

His office meant a four by four windowless room with a plate glass view of the showroom floor. The walls were covered with twenty years of Chevy appreciation awards. Twelve years ago he was salesman of the year for Long Island, but his fifteen minutes of fame and fortune had long since past. At least he was a couple of rungs up from Wild Bill. Dennis took out a form and calculator from the drawer and a pencil from his pocket.

"Ira, what's your last name."

"Portnoy."

No reaction, he was hoping the pencil would fall to the floor.

"Address?"

When he told him that he put the pencil down.

"Isn't that upstate by Albany?"

"Not that far," Ira said.

"Come a long way to buy a car."

"I didn't come to buy a car, I came to see you."

Now Dennis was nervous. He was probably thinking IRS.

"I work at Pilgrim State."

The air rushed out of Dennis like a popped balloon. He was clearly relieved.

"Am I being committed," he said with a smile.

Ira didn't smile back.

"You used to work at Pilgrim State."

"For a few minutes about forty years ago."

"My mother was there. Her name was Eva Portnoy?"

He shook his head.

"Where did she work?"

"She was a patient, had a lobotomy."

"Sorry."

"The file indicates that you were one of the orderlies who worked with her."

"Could be, I worked with a lot of patients, I just don't remember any of them."

"She was raped. That's how I got here."

No reaction, no red face, no biting of the lips, no blinking of the eyes, no clearing of the throat, no looking away, just the salesman's confused stare.

"Sorry about that too."

"I'm looking for my father."

Dennis thought about it a moment than broke into a huge grin.

"I'm flattered, but it isn't me. I wish it were. I could use someone to take care of me in my old age."

Ira believed him. People can only lie so often. Car salesmen exceed their quota selling cars. There's very little left for real life. Besides, the needle on the body meter was flat, no cramps or chest pains. It wasn't him.

"I just saw Henry Raymond."

"I remember Hank the Giant. He bought a gas station. Struck out there too?"

Ira nodded.

"Do you remember Nick Lourie?" he asked.

"Died in a car crash," he said.

"Gay?"

"I heard that, although he never tried anything with me."

"You remember anyone else?"

"Shirley, the big, ball busting nurse," Dennis said.

"How about an orderly named Frank?"

"No."

"A black orderly?"

"No way, there were no blacks back then, mostly ex-GIs trying to make some money for a house and a business. It was a different world back then if you know what I mean."

He stood up to leave and Dennis gave him his card.

"Listen, give me a call when you're in the market for a new car. I may not be your father, but I'll still give you the family discount."

"Thanks."

As he walked out, Wild Bill cast his hook out one final time.

"Remember, we'll beat any price."

It was too late to go back to Pilgrim State since the day shift would soon be getting out, so he headed back to Rhonda's apartment.

Shirley had her timing all screwed up, which was understandable. Frank was probably an orderly in the 1960s, after the civil rights movement made some headway, which meant that FM must be someone else. The choice was down to him and a dead drunk who was probably gay.

Rhonda was sitting on the couch watching a "Happy Days" rerun by the time he got there. The Fonz snapped his fingers and a bevy of beauties came running. If his father were anything like the Fonz, he wouldn't have had to use force.

"Any luck?"

"No."

He told her about Henry and Dennis.

"I could use a new car," she said. "Maybe he'd include me in the family discount."

"Shirley was wrong about the black orderly."

"We're kind of like a family," Rhonda said.

"She clearly mixed him up with someone else."

"Do you have any pets at home?"

"What?"

"Do you have a pet?" Rhonda asked.

"No, I'm allergic."

"I think a dog would be fun, you, me and a dog . . . that's a family."

"Or Dennis could be wrong. He's no scholar. I think FM is the missing link."

"I could find a job in Rockland County," Rhonda said.

"It wasn't either of them, I'm sure of that."

"You could come by once a week. Say you're working late. We should give it a try."

"What?"

"Us."

"Us what?" Ira said.

"Never mind."

Richie Cunningham oozed cuteness, like a teddy bear, and had very little trouble attracting the giggling, bright-eyed, malt shop sweet-sixteeners.

"I suppose it's hopeless," Rhonda said.

Ira didn't even bother asking what she meant this time.

Ralphie struck out, but he was so funny and eager to please that it was only a matter of time before the girls came without a fuss. It was never easy for him, although he never felt all that frustrated about it, not nearly enough to ever think about following in his father's footsteps.

"What about the drunk?" Rhonda asked.

"Nick."

"It could've been him," Rhonda said. "I suppose a lot of gay guys went both ways back then."

"Rapes her, then gets drunk and kills himself in a car accident? "Maybe out of guilt."

"I don't think so. Justice is never that swift. Besides, gay is gay, even Dennis had heard that."

"Everyone needs a change of pace once in a while," Rhonda said. "Look at you."

Rhonda walked up to him and grabbed his butt. Ira jumped back.

"Don't get nervous, I'm going to the gym."

Rhonda's muscles were restless. She invited him to pump some iron and climb the Stairmaster.

"No thanks."

"I've got a guest pass."

He shook his head from side to side. He didn't believe in health clubs. He never had a body worth working on or exposing. No amount of pumping or climbing was going to change that. He didn't mind a physical challenge, an occasional Sunday walk around the lake or a short burst of speed to catch the train. His heart did enough racing at work.

"It'll do you good," she said.

"Next time."

"I like the sound of that."

In a strange way, so did he. An occasional visit wouldn't be so bad, as long as Rhonda could accept the limits. With her expectations that shouldn't be too hard, but what kind of life would that be for her? Not one he'd ever want for his daughter, so how could he do it to someone else's child?

Who was he trying to kid, Ira realized, he could never handle it.

"I'll be back around seven, the party's at eight," Rhonda said closing the door.

He thought about sneaking out while she was at the gym and driving home. It was either that or continuing with this futile quest to solve a forty-year old unreported crime. He couldn't make a decision by dwelling on it. He needed a diversion for the ingredients to cook in his subconscious.

He tried an "F-Troop" rerun. It was one of his favorite shows as a kid. He had a crush on Trapper Jane, the frontier trader. Mr. Ed was next, but there were plenty of cable choices. He could watch the news, "The Brady Bunch," tax tips, a Ronald Reagan western, pro wrestling, a special on polar bears or a discussion on computer chips and import quotas.

Cable television is like a drug. He could flip the visual images so quickly with the remote that it was almost a form of self-hypnosis. So he ran a marathon around a track of channels, forgetting everything else, and entering into a state of televised unawareness. He came to about an hour later, turned the television off and sat quietly in the living room listening to the sounds of cars idling in the dark and people yelling. On the other side of the wall a mother refused to let her daughter leave.

"How can I trust you after the other night?"

"I'll see him at school," she screamed.

There was a lot of crying and a door slammed.

"We'll see about that. And stay off the phone."

After it quieted down, he decided to check out Rhonda's bedroom. Her drawers were, to quote his former mother, "a pig sty." Nothing was folded. Everything was tossed in there like a chef's salad. There was little if any organization. Sweaters were in the same drawer as underwear. Socks were mixed in with blouses.

Ellen keeps everything neatly folded, socks and underwear together in one drawer, t-shirts and shorts in another, the oldest things to the bottom. All her sweaters and turtlenecks were on a shelf in the closet. It seemed to Ira like basic common sense. Living alone, he realized, probably made order and organization seem less important.

He opened a draw with some of Rhonda's bras. They made Ellen look like a teenager entering puberty. Rhonda also had some erotic lingerie that he had only seen in pictures, teddies with holes for the nipples, black leather G-strings, lace panties about two sizes too small, even edible chocolate ones. He and Rhonda hadn't reached that course yet on the sexual menu. Apparently, they were still stuck on the appetizers.

There were some joints hidden under her gym shorts, a pipe and some nude Polaroid shots of Rhonda, fairly straightforward back and front shots. The kind probably found in a lot of suburban homes. He once suggested it to Ellen. Something to look at when they got older and to show to their grandchildren, but Ellen didn't want to remember what her body looked like and she didn't want Ira to remember it either. He of all people could understand that.

He put one of Rhonda's pictures in his wallet. He was sure she'd understand.

There were copies of Playgirl magazine in the closet. The top one had an article entitled "Fat Can Be Beautiful." It was not the centerfold, but it was still a major pictorial review. A couple of the guys made him look thin. It was hard to imagine himself as a sex object, except to the very near-sighted.

There was a jewelry box on the dresser, which contained at least a hundred pairs of earrings. Alongside it were four big bottles of perfume strong enough to announce their presence even while closed. There were harlequin romances under the bed and the contents of Rhonda's childhood seemed to have been reduced to the contents of a shoebox. There were a dozen high school pins confirming Rhonda's popularity with the athletes, a four foot long chain of bubble gum wrappers, a report card with decent grades, although none that would have been acceptable to Selma, and a birthday card signed "Your Father" with no salutation and no closing.

There was also a picture of Rhonda's mother. She had the same great body, but her long, teased hair dominated the picture. She clearly believed that was her best feature. The funny part was that it wasn't like looking at someone's mother. She wasn't much older than him and he could just as easily been sleeping with her as with her daughter. Just the thought made him shiver. How could he be that depraved? It was a legacy no doubt from his father's side of the family.

At the bottom of the box, there was a picture of an older man, probably Rhonda's father. His features were hard and sharp and his mouth looked like it had worn the same tired, unhappy expression his entire life, as if he had been cheated out of something since birth. He was short and stocky, hence the attraction. What a disappointment to realize that it was Rhonda's subconscious desire for her father more than anything else.

That brought up Ira's father, his real father, who had been pumping iron for the last two hours in his subconscious. Should he stay another day or return home and forget him? He ran through the options looking for some tightness in his chest or some queasiness in his stomach to help make up his mind. He imagined a weekend at home with Ellen and the kids. The bills taken care of, the house filled with groceries and some quiet time to prepare for the week ahead. However he felt nauseated at the thought of unknowingly passing his father at the mall. What if he had brothers and sisters?

He felt this hollow in his chest where the well of emotions was running dry.

He thought about tossing a coin?

Just then the telephone rang. He wanted to let it ring, but after the fifth ring he couldn't stand it any longer. What if Shirley was calling to come clean?

"Hello."

"Ira?"

"Ellen? How did you . . . ."

"Know where to call?"

He nodded.

"I called personnel and said I was your mother."

Another pretender to the throne, he thought.

"They knew your girlfriend's name."

"She's not my girlfriend."

"Long legs, big breasts, probably everything you've ever dreamed of."

There was no loud breathing this time, just cool, calm anger.

"I told you, she's been helping me find out about Eva . . . and my father."

"I've talked it over with some friends."

"Which friends?"

"Never mind, you've got forty-eight hours. If you don't return by Sunday, don't bother. I mean it, because otherwise I'm going to keep this appointment I made with an attorney Tuesday after school."

What more could he say, Ellen had made the decision for him. He'd stay until Sunday.

"I'll be home."

"I won't change my mind. I won't take you back after Sunday, regardless of what you find out, even if your father turns out to be Donald Trump or Jimmy Carter. Not even when body beautiful gets bored with you."

"I understand."

He felt like a kid whose curfew had been extended for an extra hour.

"I mean it," she said.

"So do I, I'll see you Sunday."

His mind was no longer on the conversation. He was imagining dinner at his father's house. An antique oak dining room table with one of those big crystal chandeliers you see in the old movies hanging above it. He was listening to his footsteps upstairs, waiting for him to come down, sitting perfectly straight, silent and still, unemotional, like an executioner waiting for his next victim.

"This isn't school," Ellen said. "You don't automatically get a second chance."

"You've been speaking to Gail."

"So what if I have?"

"She's got a one way mind that's always going in the wrong direction."

"What is that supposed to mean?"

"This was all about Eva . . . and my mother and father."

"I wish I could believe that."

So did Ira.

"How are the kids?"

"Fine."

"Put them on."

"They're not home."

Ellen waited for a long moment to pass before continuing.

"What's happening to your job?"

He let out a breath that he hadn't even realized he was holding. Thankfully, Ellen couldn't remain angry for very long. It was the teacher's instinct again.

"It'll be all right."

"Did you call today?"

"No, I called yesterday."

"Maybe you should call again."

Suddenly there was a loud crash from next door.

"Wait till you need money," the mother yelled, "or want clothes."

Ira bet that the girl had thrown some clothes in a bag and was running out of the house. He could hear a car idling outside in need of a new muffler.

"Did you hear what I said?"

"Yes, call Dan at home."

The apartment looked so different while he was talking with Ellen. It seemed almost warm and livable a minute ago. Now it was cold and bare. It looked like the scene of a crime, as if he were looking at it through Ellen's eyes. There was evidence everywhere and it all pointed to him. He wondered how he could have spent a week here.

"I have to try and find my father," he said.

"Why, do you think he ever tried to find you . . . or even wanted to?"

"I want to see what he's like, make sure he's not . . . ."

"Not what?"

"Not a criminal . . . not anymore."

That was not asking much from a parent.

"You commit a crime, you're a criminal."

"Maybe it was just a one time thing," Ira said. "An invitation . . . or an opportunity he just couldn't pass up."

"An invitation, what's wrong with you."

"I didn't mean it like that."

"You do it once and you're a rapist the rest of your life," Ellen said.

"Can you understand how this all feels?"

"I can, Ira, I really can. It's a tremendous shock."

"Exactly," he said.

"Suddenly there's a big void and a lot of uncertainty. I can understand all that, but you're a grown man . . . with a family and a good job. I can understand what you're feeling. I just can't understand what you're doing."

"That makes two of us," he said.

"That's not very reassuring."

"I don't know what else to say."

"Nor do I," Ellen said before hanging up.

"Sunday," Ira repeated to a dead phone line.

Since he was sitting by the telephone he called his aunt, the one who used to be his mother. He'd have to leave Rhonda some money for all these calls.

"Selma."

It took her a moment to identify his voice, probably because she wasn't used to hearing him call her by her first name.

"So I'm not mom anymore."

"You never really were."

"That depends on your definition of Mom. Giving birth is the easy part."

"I thought telling the truth was supposed to be the easy part too."

"We had plenty of reasons not to tell you."

"I don't doubt you believe that."

"Your father and I discussed it for a long time," Selma said. "It wasn't something you really needed to know."

"Maybe that made some sense when I was really young," Ira said, "but certainly not when I was old enough to understand."

"We had good reasons."

"You already said that, I'm waiting to hear one."

"Her illness for one."

"My mother had a name."

"Eva's illness, we didn't want you to worry about it or be afraid it might happen to you."

"That's ridiculous."

"If you grow up knowing that one of your parents is an alcoholic, isn't it more likely that you'll become one?"

"Just by knowing, who told you that?"

"You don't have to be a psychiatrist to figure it out," she said.

"So just by knowing about Eva and my father, I'd have a greater risk of what, going crazy or becoming a rapist?"

"There are certain things I'd have been better off not knowing."

"But you did know them and you had the opportunity to decide what you wanted to do with what you knew. Don't you think that helped you in the long run?"

"You miss my point."

"What is your point?" Ira said.

Selma was clearly put off by his tone of voice, because it took her a while to answer.

"It's much easier never knowing than it is trying to forget."

"You sound like Shirley."

"Who?"

"Your twin sister at Pilgrim."

"Well, she's right. Your father and I thought about it for a long time. It wasn't a decision we made lightly. Just think about it, if it hadn't been for the stone at the cemetery you would never have found out and life would have continued on its merry little way."

"Maybe I would have found out some other way and it would have turned out worse."

"I doubt that."

"What about the commandment to honor your mother and father . . . or at least my mother, shouldn't I have the opportunity to do that? And what about learning from the past, so we don't repeat the same mistakes? Would you suggest keeping the holocaust a secret?"

"It's not the same thing."

"It is. Hiding the truth is no different than living a lie."

"It was for your own good, you'll see that when this is all over. Look how you are with your own kids, always changing the channel when anything bad comes on the news."

"That will stop once they're old enough to understand and put it in perspective."

"Some things you can never understand whatever the age, which is why they say that what you don't know, can't hurt you."

"It can . . . and it has."

"Only because you found out and you let it take over your life, because you ignored your common sense and let it happen."

Even in better times, it's important to change the subject with Selma. Otherwise, she starts repeating things over and over again. Ira has never known her to budge when it came to her opinion, nothing was ever grey in her world - everything was always black or white. Ira couldn't ever remember her changing her mind.

"I'm going to try to find my real father."

Selma groaned.

"This is suicide . . . murder."

Selma always needed to cover all the bases.

"Who gets murdered?"

"Are you planning to visit on the holidays or just invite him to Jamie's wedding?"

"Why not?"

Selma gasped. Of course, he'd never do that.

"Believe me he won't have any interest in you. He'll just want money. I know the type."

Shirley again.

"When are you coming home?"

"I'm not sure."

He shouldn't be getting any pleasure out of this, but he was. It felt almost like getting even.

"You're throwing your life away over nothing. Murray was your real father and I'm your real mother. We were the ones who sat up with you when you were sick."

"Eva didn't have a chance?"

"She didn't want to. She didn't want you. She didn't want any of us."

"Do you blame her?"

"What do you know," Selma said stopping the conversation short like hitting the brakes on a car. Of course, she couldn't bring herself to say what she was really thinking, not if it might reveal the slightest flaw or a weakness. Before she could start repeating herself for the third time, Ira promised to call again and hung up.

By the time Rhonda returned he was on his second beer. The second time in his life that he'd had more than one. Rhonda casually kissed him and went into the bedroom to put away her gym bag and take off her sweats. She walked back into the living room in her workout shorts and a damp t-shirt. Every detail of her anatomy was highlighted in sweat. She sat down beside him and took a sip of his beer.

"Are you staying the weekend to look for daddy?"

"Until Sunday."

"That's a start."

"That's the finish."

Rhonda frowned and stood up to get ready for the party.

"Stick around," Ira said pulling at her shorts and pulling them down slightly. Rhonda easily slipped from his grasp and walked away.

"Later Casanova."

He jumped up and stumbled after her like a puppy at the dinner table begging for sexual crumbs. He sat outside the bathroom door while Rhonda showered pretending that they were married and that this was a typical Friday evening. It was a good marriage, young nurse and senior hospital administrator. Their salaries were not enormous, but when added together they were more than enough for a good life, especially when their only dependent was a small Yorkie named Sam with hair instead of fur to save Ira from watery, itchy eyes. The fridge was full of snacks and beer. The apartment was a mess, but neither of them cared. They had few plans and fewer ambitions beyond the moment, except for a summer place they hoped to have one day by the beach and a long vacation they were saving for in Hawaii.

It was a rotten fantasy. Ira had passed that stage of life a long time ago. Of course, he missed out on most of it, but he couldn't go back now. At this stage in his life he needed plans and schedules. He had to fill his head with easy, achievable day-to-day and week-to-week expectations, however small.

He closed his eyes and had this picture in his mind of his parents. The rapist, an old man set in his ways, and Eva, his young wife with both feet off the ground. His father looked at his life and nodded with approval. Eva shook her head with disappointment, too ordinary, she thought, it needed a touch of madness.

Rhonda came out of the shower. She moved slowly. Probably sore from lifting weights. She dropped the towel and said something he couldn't make out. He was too busy trying to commit her body to memory like the multiplication tables.

"Did you hear me?"

"What?"

"I said if the party's a bust, maybe we can go to a movie."

She mentioned one of those violent good guy defeats an army of bad guy movies, which Ellen refused to see, but which every red-blooded American male loves. Ira nodded, although he had no desire to see another movie. They dressed slowly. The room seemed to be shrinking.

"Excuse me," she said bumping into him on the way to the closet. "Could you move over a little so I can see in the mirror?"

"Sorry."

"Not there, I need to get at my make-up."

"Sorry."

She tried on a black jump suit, unbuttoning it down too low, buttoning it up too high, and then took it off.

"That looked nice," Ira said.

"No, it didn't."

She put on a low cut brown dress made of a crepe-like material that clung to her body like cellophane.

"I like that."

It wasn't like she was his wife, what did he care what hung out.

"I don't," she said turning around to stare at her back in the mirror.

Rhonda took much longer getting dressed than Ellen ever did. You'd think that being young and beautiful would be enough. Rhonda didn't need make-up and the clothes hardly mattered, yet she tried on four different outfits and spent twenty minutes putting a red glow on her cheeks that looked more like a rash.

Ellen always knew in advance what she wanted to wear. She glanced briefly in the mirror to make sure that there were no obvious rips or stains, no glaring errors in the color combination or unsightly sags and bulges. Then she took a minute to dab on a bit of make-up. At our age, Ira realized, it didn't much matter. You might still think of yourself as being in your early twenties, but nothing you wore or put on would ever convince anyone else of that fact. You had to try to project a deeper image from the heart, like a hologram, something bright enough to obscure reality. You couldn't fool the camera and what the camera actually saw didn't much matter anyway, not anymore.

They rode in silence to the party. The loudest thing in the car was Rhonda's perfume. Nothing felt right probably because everything begins to change once you put a deadline on romance. The dance of withdrawal had begun. Ira wasn't sure how it was done since he'd never really done it before, but like everything else in life it involved a substantial amount of rationalization and second-guessing.

The night was dark. Small mountains of dirt, once pure white snow, lined the side of the road. There was no moon and no stars, just the invisible shadow of a very large asteroid passing ten million miles out in space, a "near miss" according to the news.

"You're quiet," Rhonda said.

"I don't have anything to say."

"So what are you thinking?"

He has never liked that question. If he wanted someone to know what he was thinking, he wouldn't be thinking it, he'd be saying it.

"Nothing," he said.

"Come on, I deserve a little honesty, don't you think?"

What he was thinking was how nice it was to go to a party with someone who knew you well . . . like Ellen. He didn't have to explain anything or pretend or marshal whatever patience was left at the end of a long week. Ellen knew what to expect and how to react. She knew enough to wait for his thoughts to distill themselves into words without trying to drag them out. She knew that he hated parties and usually fell into a moody silence on the way. She knew enough to help out with the small talk and to make sure he didn't get stuck with someone he couldn't bear. Most of all, she knew that he'd want to leave early. Kids are a great excuse for that.

"Just wondering about my father."

"Let it go for a little while," Rhonda said, "it's Friday night. Try to enjoy yourself."

"I've never been very good at that."

Perhaps another legacy of his two mothers, he thought, part nature and part nurture. Ira stopped at a red light and looked at Rhonda who raised her shoulders to her ears in an exaggerated shrug. The smoke rising from the tailpipe on the car ahead of them gave off an eerie glow, as if the air were alive or possessed. Maybe it was just the reflection from their headlights, but it almost felt as if they were entering into another dimension, one where unusual things happened as a matter of course.

An old car pulled up next to them. Some young boy, hair slicked back and wearing an earring, had his arm around a gum chewing young girl, her hair blasted with color as if the spray paint had gone wild. They must have had the radio blasting, because they were jumping around like they were undergoing electric shock treatment, although with the windows rolled up he couldn't hear a thing.

"I think the four of them should share the guilt," Rhonda said.

"Who?"

"The four orderlies, this way you're part salesman, part mechanic, part gay and part mystery."

"Like a mutt."

"A real son of the institution."

The light turned green.

"Go left here," she said, "in front of the Seven-Eleven."

Ira was driving, but it felt like he was having one of Shirley MacLaine's out of body experiences, like he was seeing the road from a distance through the wrong end of the binoculars. Even Rhonda sounded far away.

"Too bad your grandfather didn't die younger."

"Why?"

"Because it might have turned out differently for Eva if he had."

"No one knows what happened to her . . . if anything, and if it did how do you know it was him," Ira said. "It could have been anyone, a relative, a friend, even a neighbor."

"To be that bad it had to be someone in the family," Rhonda said, "and it's usually the father."

Apparently, Rhonda knew from experience who tended to be the abusers. Which meant it was on both sides of his family . . . his mother's father and his own. How did he get so lucky? Is it the type of thing that skips a generation? What about Scott? Does it ever die out?

"I wonder if your grandmother ever suspected anything."

"No way," Ira said shaking his head strongly from side to side.

"You knew her as an old woman; a lot of them, they put on blinders when they're young, they're still afraid. Maybe the same thing happened to her. It almost seems normal."

Ira wanted to rise to his grandmother's defense, but the words died in his throat. It was another trap door. Nothing about his past could surprise him anymore. He saw Rhonda's lips continue to move out of the corner of his eye, but he didn't hear a word she was saying. He couldn't take it any further. He had reached his limit. He was not going back to his grandfather and great-grandfather. A new mother and a new father were more than enough. So he erased the word abuse from his Eva vocabulary, returned to his place behind the wheel and took control of the conversation.

"Do you think I should hate my father?"

"You don't know him. Why waste the energy over something that happened forty years ago. Of course, if it wasn't for him you wouldn't be here . . . that was my father's line."

"How about for refusing to ever acknowledge my existence," Ira said.

"They can do that even when they come around from time to time."

"You'd think he'd be a little curious."

"On your right," Rhonda said, "it's the house with all the cars. I hope you're not going to sulk all night or act like a prude."

"Have I so far?"

"No comment."

Ellen was having coffee with Gail, her divorced friend from school.

"He's a real SOB attorney, but that's the kind you need. The first thing he told me was to protect myself. When they go off the deep end, you never know what they'll do. He could be spending a fortune on this bimbo."

"Not Ira."

"I was also too stupid to listen and he emptied our savings account. You should put all the money in your own name, cancel the credit cards, and change the locks."

"I'm not worried."

"I don't want to be the one to say I told you so."

"It's not Ira."

"Men are all the same."

Ellen sipped her coffee.

"Anyway, he charges five hundred for the initial consultation and a five thousand retainer if he takes the case."

"That's pretty expensive."

"He's a barracuda."

"I'd rather buy the dining room table."

"I'll tell you what else you should do. Show him that you mean business. Clean out his drawers. Empty the closet. Pack his things away. Let him get nervous if he does come back. Otherwise, the same thing could happen again. Once they get a taste of it, it gets a lot easier the second time around."

Ellen poured Gail some more coffee.

"I don't think there are any more family secrets left to uncover."

Gail laughed. "Men can get very creative when it comes to their penises."

Ellen turned away to look at the sink. She was probably thinking that it was a mistake to have invited Gail over.

"At least go out and buy something extravagant for yourself like a diamond bracelet."

"Now that's something I'd consider," Ellen said. "Nothing bothers Ira more than an unnecessary expenditure."

Ira parked the car about fifty yards from the house. The street was filled with Novas and Malibus. Chevy was king at Pilgrim State, probably because no one made very much money, not even the doctors.

"These parties are mostly nurses and staff," Rhonda said, "dates and friends of friends."

He locked the car and checked the door. Rhonda watched him as if it was another strange middle age, suburban tribal ritual up there with knocking on wood.

"They get pretty wild sometimes . . . . because of all the drugs. I'm not into that, except for grass. I prefer beer, but there are always plenty of pills. That's the one advantage of working in a mental hospital."

Ira was not excited at the thought of a wild party. For the past twenty years, parties have been quiet affairs with the emphasis on food and drink. They were small and intimate and ended early with an occasional costume or come as you were in high school party. Conversations were confined to real estate, interest rates, homes, landscaping, kids, clothes, other people's illnesses, restaurants, vacations and work. Everyone was "doing fine," work was always "OK" and except for some off color jokes or subtle references to sex there was rarely anything risqué.

The house looked like a converted summer bungalow with music, light and conversation leaking out like natural gas. Rhonda threw back her hair and straightened her shoulders. Her breasts literally knocked at the front door, which opened slowly as if by an unseen hand. Rhonda quickly disappeared into a small, dark room smelling of beer and marijuana, pounded by drums and a bass that he could feel in his kidneys, and haunted by the glowing eyes of a dozen burning cigarettes.

Ira was sucked in after her and as soon as he came to rest in an empty spot in front of the bay window in the living room he instinctively looked around for a familiar, friendly face. He found no one, because he was looking for faces his own age. However, through the smoky haze he did recognize people from his past. Ed, his first college roommate, sat on the floor taking a long, slow hit on a joint. His hair was still blond and curly, only now he had a beard to match. His eyes were as restless as ever darting back and forth between two young nurses, licking his lips like they were sweets in a candy shop. When he turned on his smile, it was like a ray of sunlight. Ira was always jealous of that talent.

Ed looked at him for a moment and Ira could almost hear the accusations. What happened to their college promises never to wear a tie and to live life somehow differently? They swore not to wind up like their fathers, but what did they really know back then? Apparently Ed hadn't yet learned that an ordinary life was one of the toughest to find and even tougher to hold on to. Wait until he married and had children. Let him find out that his mother was not his mother, that his father was a criminal, and that Pilgrim State was more than just a workplace, it was his birthplace.

It was strange how many people from Ira's past seemed to be reincarnated in this room filled with twenty-five year olds. The swaggering leer of Les, the starting quarterback in high school, was pasted on this tall guy leaning against the bookcase in the corner. He had the same deep blue eyes that used to trip up every girl that walked by, like a pothole in the road. There was a young woman on the couch nervously twisting and turning her head like Sandy, a very shy girl from high school, who married a man arrested for exposing himself to children. A short guy with enormous shoulders shuffled over to the chips with the same, jerky stride as Andy Brophy, the biggest, most uncoordinated kid in high school. Ira had to restrain himself from calling out his name. They all looked exactly the way he remembered them. The same way he saw himself sometimes when he wasn't looking in a mirror.

It wasn't a bad party as parties go. There was no pressure to socialize or make small talk. Everyone just stood around holding onto their beer or cigarette trying to send out the same signal . . . look at me . . . I'm different and complicated--part athlete, part artist, part scholar, part musician, part explorer, part social worker and part lover. Don't be deceived by appearances. It was a message Ira never managed to get across. Maybe he should warn them that over the next ten years they'll give up those dream roles one by one until all that remains is a middle age man or woman looking for security, comfort and regularity.

In the far corner of the room sat Robin, a girl he had a crush on in high school. She had the same long, straight sandy-brown hair. The same cute little pushed up nose and a body so thin that he'd have had trouble finding her hips with his hands. It was a one-sided relationship twenty some odd years ago, just as it was now. He used to watch Robin eat with her friends in the cafeteria. He'd stare at her in the gym out of the corner of his eye, deathly afraid that someone would notice. If anyone did, he was always prepared with some inane comment about those stupid gym outfits. He didn't say more than ten words to her in four years. He had an intense desire to start up a conversation now with this new Robin, but just like old times the thought of it tightened this invisible noose around his vocal cords.

A guy who was the spitting image of someone he shared an office with during his first year at American Family Care came up beside him with a large can of beer, the sixteen-ounce variety. Jim loved a good party. He always made fun of Ira for getting married right out of college and missing all the "desperate women." This Jim had black bags under his eyes, only it was from the night shift, not partying, and anyone could see that there was a big beer belly in his future. He bet the real Jim had one by now. While Ira made a career at American Family, Jim moved to California after a year to try to make it in pictures. He never heard from him again.

"YoufromPil?" the new Jim said.

"What?"

"You work at Pilgrim?"

"No . . . I mean yes. How about you?"

"Nah, I'm with the highway department."

They stood side by side surveying the room.

"You married?" Ira said to break the ice. It was a stupid question, but he felt this compulsion to ask about kids, spouses, lawns, houses and vacation plans.

"No way man, I'm here with my girlfriend. She's a nurse."

Jim looked him over like a museum exhibit.

"I need another beer," he said walking away.

The loud music made it easy to stand-alone. He didn't have to pretend that he was listening to someone else's conversation or worry about saying something witty. He just tapped his foot and swayed slightly like he was into the beat. Hard rock, harder than any rock he remembered from college, filled with a lot of angry and unintelligible words that tugged uncomfortably at his prostate. He looked around for Rhonda. Maybe she'd leave if he dangled a movie in front of her nose, but she was nowhere in sight. Ellen knew better than to disappear from view for very long. He moved past his old girlfriend into the kitchen. Instead of Rhonda he found a girl sitting on the counter by herself smoking a joint.

"Hi."

"Hi."

"I'm Beth.

She leaned close to him and almost lost her balance. Ira had to extend his hand to keep her from falling off the counter.

"Haven't seen you around before," she said.

She made the word "you" sound like a dessert.

"I came with Rhonda."

"Ohhh."

"Did you see her?"

Beth started giggling.

"I don't know. What she look like? Want a hit?"

He shook his head from side to side.

"Come on, I won't bite." She put the joint to his lips and rested her hand on his shoulder for balance. She had long fingers and even longer fingernails painted the bright yellow color of the summer sun.

He inhaled slowly and with confidence, the way a forty-something year old man should in front of a twenty-something year old girl. His throat burned and he immediately started coughing. Tears ran down the crow's feet that were beginning to squeeze the corners of his eyes like a vice.

Beth laughed hysterically.

"I should've warned you. This is potent weed."

She put the joint to her lips and inhaled so slowly that it appeared to move away from him, like it was some kind magic trick. He took another hit, this time taking it in gradually and not as deeply, exhaling without a single cough.

"Got a name?"

"Ira."

"Three letters, that's cool."

Beth was about Rhonda's age, perhaps a little younger. She was pretty, but in a different way. Her face was softer and her features were smaller, almost doll-like. Her cheeks were bright red like she'd just come in from the cold and her brown eyes were glassy revealing little more than Ira's own reflection. She was sort of androgynous, her body straight and flat, petite with little mounds where Rhonda had hills. She radiated something, although Ira wasn't sure what. Perhaps it was just her membership in the local tanning salon.

Beth handed him back the joint with a grin.

"Go ahead finish it. I'm already on . . . "

He couldn't hear what she said, her words drowned out by the music vibrating through the thin wall.

"Hold it longer in your lungs," she said. She said something else, but he raised his hands in frustration. Someone had turned the music up even louder.

"Follow me," she said taking his hand and leading him downstairs to the basement. She held it so tightly that he couldn't pull away. He half-thought she was taking him to anther room where he might find Rhonda. They wound up in an empty, unfinished basement.

"Take it in deeper and hold it longer," she said. "That's the secret."

"To what?"

"To the monster high," Beth said as she laughed. "You're funny."

Ira took another hit, inhaling deeply and this time it didn't burn in the least, in fact it actually felt good, as if something hard inside him that had been there for quite some time was finally beginning to soften and break up. The tightness in his shoulders and neck that he'd felt all week also began to disappear. Still, there was a little tickle in his throat. That cold he was fighting just wouldn't go away, no matter how many vitamins Rhonda gave him. He cleared his throat and Beth handed him a sip of beer that went down with more of a burn than the smoke.

It was quieter down here, he liked that, and he liked the fact that Beth didn't seem to find him the least bit tiresome. She lit up at whatever he had to say, which came out without him having to think about it, and the big smile that covered her small face looked to Ira like an invitation. Not with strangers, he reminded himself in response to a certain improper thought that drift into his eyes with the smoke. He couldn't cheat on Rhonda while he cheated on Ellen. That would be a step over the edge and down into an abyss where the sunlight didn't reach. And what about AIDS, he thought to himself. In a community for the insane, what were the chances? Besides, being careful had to be second nature to a nurse, even one as giggly as Beth.

They passed the joint back and forth, the easy conversation accompanied by some knowing looks. It got really small and when she put it to her lips, holding it so daintily between her thumb and index finger it could have been a china tea cup, she closed her eyes and he couldn't help noticing her tight sweater and tighter jeans. He suddenly realized what Beth radiated. It was desire, pure, pretense-free desire. She radiated it even more than she attracted it. He didn't want to do this, Ira thought to himself. It was wrong, but it felt as if he was being carried away by a strong current. Either he moved closer to Beth or she moved closer to him, he couldn't be sure, but they were much closer than socially acceptable at any of the parties he attended with Ellen. She leaned against him for support or perhaps he leaned against her. He felt a little unsteady and light, very light, as if he could be carried aloft by the breeze, and he felt ethereal, ethereal enough to pass right through her. Suddenly it felt as if he needed something or someone not only to hold him up, but to hold him down.

Ira was used to staring at beautiful women in shoots for coupon advertisements and at parties, in Playboy magazine and on the streets of New York City, particularly during the summer. It's part of the culture. Beautiful people are worth watching. They somehow do things better, they're more photogenic and more newsworthy. But he wasn't used to being this close to it. He could handle the frustration of repressed desire much easier than he could handle the intoxication that accompanied opportunity. He needed routines and restrictions, his wife by his side, the physical limits imposed by a magazine photograph and the rules of social engagement. Married men look, but they don't touch. He was in trouble in an unfamiliar environment without the walls and rules, a sign, no doubt, of his potential to go off the deep end and to wind up like his mother . . . or, even worse, like his father.

They started swaying together to the music. Ira felt like a lit fuse. Beth made a soothing sound like a hum and reached behind him like she was going to pick his pocket. Instead she slipped her hands down the back of his pants and his body exploded. He couldn't touch her fast enough or hard enough. There weren't enough places for his lips. He was careening down a steep sexual hill, out of control, trembling, uncertain what to do or what would happen next. There was no little voice whispering stop, no thoughts of Ellen or the kids. Not even of Rhonda. He was a celestial body in orbit around Beth, who changed like the seasons from a little girl to a mature woman. He couldn't remember what he was thinking or feeling from one moment to the next. He finished in what seemed like an instant. There wasn't even time to take off all of their clothes.

After it was over, they both lay on an old carpet surrounded by boxes. Ira was drenched in sweat.

"That was nice," Beth said generously giving him a passing grade.

She popped up, lowered her sweater, and pulled up her jeans. He was too tired to move or speak. He felt like he was descending slowly down some long, psychological spiral.

"How old are you?" Beth said.

"Forty."

"Wow, you're the oldest man I've ever been with. My father's only forty-eight. Wait until I tell the gang at the office."

"Aren't you a nurse?"

"No, I'm a secretary at Verity Auto Parts."

Beth bound up the stairs like she had just come home from the mall, completely unaffected by the experience, as if they had just shared a seat on the bus.

"Nice meeting you," she called back as if she suddenly remembered something her mother had taught her.

Ira felt terrible. He knew what she really thought. He devoured her small breasts like a starving man, pushed inside her like he needed a place to hide, and came quickly like he was afraid of the dark. He panicked, running around in circles like a squirrel in the late fall, desperately trying to store sensations for the endless winter ahead.

"A secretary," he said out loud pushing the thought of AIDS out of his mind and straightening out his clothes.

He wondered if Rhonda was looking for him by now.

It occurred to Ira as he slowly climbed the steps that in a way he was just like his father, although a harmless, modern day version. He took a girl under the influence of drugs and didn't care if he never saw her again. In fact, he preferred it that way. What if she wasn't on birth control? What if he'd just created his own bastard son? Does history repeat itself like that? Perhaps twenty-four years from now some kid fresh out of college will come up to him with a chip on his shoulder.

Fortunately, the music went dead just as he got to the kitchen and stunned by the sudden silence he forgot whatever it was that was bothering him, forgot it completely, thanks to the magic of marijuana. He smoothed down his hair and returned to the party. His throat was parched and he felt a little dizzy. He wished he were home in the den watching television with Ellen, the kids in their rooms, the shopping done, the bills paid and the house locked up for the night. They could be snacking on some chips about now, which sounded fantastic. Ira felt like a stranger envying himself.

There were some older people at the party now, although his record with Beth would certainly remain intact at least for this evening. Everyone's attention was focused on the coffee table around which an animated group were sucking on beer cans and talking about Pilgrim State. Ira sat down on a folding chair in the corner next to Robin within whiffing distance of her freshly shampooed straight brown hair. Only a small snack table stood between them, but his heart skipped a beat when he saw what was on it. He started shoveling chips and dip into his mouth without even bothering to chew. He was starving. It felt as if he hadn't eaten in a week.

"This happened my second day on the job," someone sitting at the table said. "You know the rule, only a doctor can declare a patient dead."

There was a wave of experienced nods around the room.

"Well, I'm working the night shift. It's about three in the morning, so you know where the on-duty MD is."

"Hiding somewhere fast asleep," someone said and everyone in the room laughed.

"I'm walking down the hall and it's very quiet. I'm supposed to check on this woman patient. She's been acting up in the middle of the night for the entire week, trouble sleeping. I'm supposed to medicate her if she needs it, but tonight she's quiet. Of course, when I look closely I can she that she's dead as a doornail."

Ira listened with half an ear, because he was too focused on eating. The chips were big and crunchy. He'd never tasted dip this good, onion with a slight kiss of garlic. It had a wonderful texture, smooth and creamy, with slivers of crisp onion. He looked into the half-empty bowl with disappointment.

"I'm not allowed to write dead and I'm not going to wake up his highness, so I write stable, no acting out. The next morning the orderly brings her breakfast."

There were chuckles and groans.

"He actually propped her up to eat."

Now it was laughter and moans.

"Tell them your story Frank."

Frank puffed out his chest. You could see right away that this was a man with opinions, a professional man used to giving orders, but not a successful one judging by his dazed and artificial look.

"It was just after med school. I'm walking by some ward and come across this patient lying dead on the floor. I immediately start CPR. A few staff people stop to watch and then walk on. No one says a word. No one stops to help. I figure that it's not only the patients who are crazy at Pilgrim, but I continue CPR waiting for some help to arrive. Of course no tells me that this woman's been dead for over an hour and that they're just waiting for the wagon to come for the body. When someone finally said something and I stopped and walked away, the entire floor staff started applauding."

There were a few courtesy chuckles and most everyone turned away to start talking to their neighbor, but Frank didn't care. He just turned his attention to his drink.

Ira had a small chip overloaded with dip on its way. His white shrouded tongue hung out ready to catch every drop. Just then his old girlfriend turned to him and smiled.

"Hi," she said with a filly-like shake of her long, beautiful mane, "I'm Sue."

His tongue was just starting to stroke the excess dip from around the edge of the chip. His head was maneuvering under it like a dump truck ready to receive its load. Sue's greeting hit him like a rear end collision. His head snapped to the left and his hand jerked forward missing his mouth and depositing most of the dip onto his cheek. Instead of getting up, running out of the room, and rushing home to painfully relive the chip calamity for the remainder of his life, Ira just laughed. So did Sue.

"What a waste of good dip," she said handing him a napkin. "It's on your pants too."

She pointed between his legs to a white glob on his crotch. They both laughed again. Without thinking he wiped it off with his finger and stuck it in his mouth.

"You are one hungry guy," she said.

"Is there any more dip around?"

"There's never much to eat at these things," she said with a wink and a smile.

It sounded to Ira like another invitation. All he had to do was ask her if she wanted to join him at the diner. Where were all these women twenty years ago, he wondered?

"Are there any patients you'd sleep with?" one of the nurses at the table said.

"For that matter are there any doctors."

"I can't think of a doctor, but there are a few patients."

The nurses all laughed.

Ira wondered if his father took part in a similar conversation forty years earlier. Maybe he volunteered that there was one patient in particular that he had his eye on.

"What's your name?" Sue asked.

"Ira."

"Pilgrim?"

"AFP."

"What that?"

"I'm sorry I'm a little out of it . . . Pilgrim. I'm in Records."

"It rubs off on all of us."

Sue was not that attractive close up. She had mousy features. Her eyes were too small and close together. Her lips were too thin. She could have been a squirrel except for her flat cheeks. Her face had not been served well by her teenage acne. Still, her hair compensated for a lot. It was straight and shiny. Even from here it smelled like the beach on a warm, sunny day. Ira couldn't help thinking that it would make a wonderful shampoo and conditioner advertisement. He looked out of the corner of his eye for Rhonda. He wondered if he should get up and look for her, but he decided against it. He had no obligations in this fantasy world. Who knows, maybe he'd have more women tonight than he'd had his entire life.

At the parties back home, sooner or later the men wind up standing around together talking about sports, money and work, while the women sit around talking about kids, clothes and husbands. They're beyond flirting and have no concerns about first impressions. They know each other too well and come with vacant expectations, leaving any hopes and dreams back home. This, however, was an alien culture. Older men were sparse here.

Outcomes were not predetermined. Everyone started fresh. He could be a doctor, someone with a real sense of humor or a wild and crazy guy. Sue had no idea and she seemed open to finding out.

"What do you do, Sue?" he said with a voice that came out more high-pitched than he intended. He was going for manly and confident, but it came out almost squeaky.

Sue smiled and leaned into him.

"Just about anything."

It sounded like a line from a movie, he thought. If not, it should be.

"Seriously," she said, "I'm in the Pilgrim pharmacy."

"You must be a popular person."

"Ira . . . Ira."

The booming voice came from behind him and was followed immediately by a hand on his shoulder. The hiss he heard was the deflation of the moment. He half-expected the voice to belong to Ellen. He wouldn't have been surprised to hear that the baby-sitter called and one of the kids was running a fever, sort of the way he was beginning to feel. Instead, Rhonda kneeled down beside him.

"I've been looking for you. I've got a splitting headache. Let's go home."

Sue had already turned to the man on her right.

"Census reduction," someone said from the center of the room, "if I hear those two words again I'll scream."

"Census reduction," the crowd roared.

She screamed and everyone laughed.

"Get'em out on the streets . . . that's all that matters."

"I had more trouble last year at my annual inspection trying to convince them to let me keep my car on the road."

Ira's legs felt heavy as they walked back to the car. The cold air was draining the power from his battery.

"Where were you?" Rhonda said climbing into the passenger seat.

"Hanging out in the kitchen, I was looking for you, where did you go?"

"No where, saw a few people I knew."

He and Ellen were never this dishonest. A few white lies maybe, but they could never hide anything truly significant. Certainly Ellen would spot it on his face in an instant. He'd like to think he would as well on hers. Of course, they've never had very much to hide.

Neither he nor Rhonda had anything else to say on the ride home.

SATURDAY

Ira woke up with the worst morning breath. He smelled like an overripe salad bar. Or maybe it was Rhonda's breath. Two people on a twin bed, it was hard to tell, although Rhonda smelled less like food and more like smoke, as if she had spent the evening in front of a fireplace. Rhonda showered and dressed for work while Ira stayed in bed fighting this craving to take garbage cans to the curb and to pick up dry cleaning. Somewhere there was a pile of bills waiting for his attention, but not here.

"You staying in bed all day?"

"I'm getting up in a minute and going to Pilgrim. Shirley is working today."

"Saturday?"

"That's what she said."

"Why."

"She said she's behind because I've screwed up her schedule."

"I don't doubt that."

Rhonda stood at the bedroom door in her tight white uniform. With all that was on his mind, it still started to swell raising the cover like a little tent. This might be his last opportunity for quite some time Ira remembered thinking as he bent his knees to hide the evidence, since Ellen was sure to banish him to her sexual desert.

"Strip the bed when you get up."

The word took on a whole new meaning when Rhonda said it.

"I will."

She walked over.

"You look flushed."

The tent began to deflate and he straightened his knees. Now that she mentioned it, he could feel a drip in his throat.

"I think I may be coming down with something."

Rhonda put her hand to his forehead.

"You feel a little warm."

"My chest feels a little congested."

A remark like that would normally send Ellen rushing to the store for some decongestant and soup stock. Rhonda just frowned.

"Could be the beginning of a cold."

His eyes began to water as if on cue.

"Take some of the vitamin C on top of the fridge. I'd like to see a movie tonight."

Rhonda had no idea how bad his colds got, particularly in the beginning. They came on like the flu, his head a soaked sponge, his nose an open faucet, and his joints rusted stiff, like the Tin Man in The Wizard of Oz. He's been known to sweat so profusely and shake so violently with chills and fever that Ellen would drug him into unconsciousness to get some sleep, so she wouldn't be a zombie in class the next morning.

"Figure 7:30."

"For what?"

"A movie."

Ellen would have the thermometer out by now. Rhonda just left with a wave.

Ira drifted in and out of sleep, awakened from time to time by these voices whispering around him like disembodied spirits at a bedside vigil. They didn't sound anything like Ellen, Jaime or Scott. They were probably coming from next door, but they sounded old and odd, and he couldn't understand a word they said. He dreamt that one of the voices, one that he could understand, was urging him to buy a dining room table before it was too late.

When Ira finally woke up for good his nose was bleeding and he had to feel his way to the bathroom with his head tilted back. Someone at work told him once to pinch his nose and hold it between his knees, but it didn't make sense. The head back and swallow technique was his mother's remedy and eventually it always worked. While he was doing that the bulb in the lamp by the bed went out with a pop leaving the room dark and depressing. At home, neither cold nor bloody nose would have stopped Ira from replacing it, especially since there was always a replacement waiting in the closet. He doubted Rhonda kept any spares around.

He forced himself to get dressed and go into the kitchen to make tea. He was hoping for an old-faithful like Lipton or Tetley. He'd even take a sociable herbal tea provided it wasn't green or minty, he could drink green if he had no choice, but he hated minty. Unfortunately, the only tea he could find was the kind that came with Chinese take out, which tasted like dishwater. He made it anyway and sat in front of the TV while he drank it.

His eyes were really watering now as if the germs had set up their own sprinkler system. The worst was coming; the question was how soon. Rhonda's apartment was not high on his list of places to be sick. It was just above Pilgrim State and a few rungs below the office. When he looked around, it felt like he was sitting in a bus depot. Back home, every piece of furniture had a place on the family tree, either before Jamie or after Scott. Like the children, each piece was conceived after a long and passionate debate. The delivery one rainy day by two burly men was almost as nerve racking. Ira thought of the furniture as part of the family, a witness to scenes of affection and disappointment, comforting and undemanding, each with their own memories and expectations.

He felt a little better after finishing the tea, but he knew his body. It would put up some initial resistance, but eventually it would give in. This was just the calm before the storm. Still, he forced himself to drive to Pilgrim to see what he could find out about FM, the supposedly black orderly, and Nick, the supposedly gay one. He had paternity down to the flip of a coin.

Ellen sat in the kitchen drinking coffee. She woke up at first light, instead of the eight-thirty luxury she usually allowed herself on Saturday mornings. She had picked up the telephone a half-dozen times already to call Ira and slammed it back down each time. She hadn't gotten beyond the area code. The house was a mess. Normally she'd clean and straighten up on Saturdays, except today she had to do Ira's chores. She did the food shopping, picked up the laundry and chopped the ice off the front walk. She didn't have the energy to clean.

Jaime and Scott were at friends and Ellen wasn't used to Saturdays alone. The neighborhood was full of unfamiliar sounds, sinister sounds like car doors slamming, engines racing, and voices calling out names that she did not recognize. The heat clicked on with a loud pop, almost like a gunshot, and the hot water muttered through the pipes. The natural light from the windows swung back and forth, harsh at times and then softer, almost tender when the clouds thickened. The house either looked stark and empty or warm and full. There was no in between.

Indecisiveness like that always disturbed Ellen.

She tried to take her mind off Ira by looking at a catalogue, but it didn't work. She was thinking that she ought to do something more than making threats. That wasn't the way to reach problem kids at school and it wasn't the way to reach a wandering, lost husband. The personal one on one approach always worked best.

Shirley was downstairs working with the old files when Ira got there.

"This Saturday's thanks to you," she said.

The smell of eggs and bacon was overpowering. Used ketchup packets were scattered around like confetti.

"You better believe this will be the last Saturday I'm ever working."

"Sorry."

Ira came closer.

"I don't need a kiss good-bye."

"I'm not going yet."

Shirley groaned.

"Looking a little red around the gills."

"I'm fighting a head cold."

"Well fight it away from me."

He backed up to the other end of the table.

"I met Henry and Dennis yesterday."

"I heard all about it from Rhonda."

"It's not either of them."

"I could've told you that."

"Dennis said there were no black orderlies at Pilgrim back then."

"The guy had a brain like a sieve."

"You're absolutely sure FM was Frank?"

"I'm not absolutely sure about anything," Shirley said. "That's the last thing you learn in life . . . it oughta be the first."

"He said Frank, the black orderly, worked in the sixties."

"He's probably right."

"Then who could FM be?" Ira said slumping back against the table.

"I'm drawin a blank."

"Try again, but don't focus on it," Ira said. "Think of something else and let it sneak up on you."

"What am I trying to do, surprise myself?"

"Just try it."

Shirley closed her eyes.

"It's like a fuzzy black and white movie in here."

She opened her eyes and pulled a donut out from behind her back like it was a magic trick.

"Maybe it'll come to me while I work." Shirley opened up a file. "Cause this stuff gotta get done. You wanna help?"

Shirley looked up at him, her eyes bugging out like those glasses with the eyeballs on springs.

"Is he dead?"

"Who?"

"FM."

"If I can't remember who he is, how would I know?"

Before he could say another word, Rhonda came bouncing down the stairs.

"I'm on break," she said, "anything interesting happen?"

"Shirley's brain is turning into a black and white movie."

"What?"

"She refuses to name names."

"What are you talking about?"

"She can't remember who FM was . . . or won't."

"I do, it's a radio station," Shirley said. "There's FM and AM, twin brothers."

"You two are both nuts," Rhonda said.

"It must run in the family," Shirley said.

"Isn't there someone else who might remember?" Ira asked.

"What about Sonny," Rhonda said raising her hand and her eyebrow.

"Who's Sonny?" Ira asked.

"Sonny doesn't talk," Shirley said chewing on something, "she's like Eva."

"She's been a patient here for over 50 years," Rhonda said.

"Maybe Sonny knew Eva?"

"You can't mess around with patients."

"What's the harm," Rhonda said, "she's not going any where. She's got no relatives. No one ever visits."

"I'll be subtle."

"You'll get kicked out on your ass."

"That's the best thing that could happen," Ira said. "Where is she?"

"Building 104," Rhonda said, "second floor day room. She's always sitting in a wheelchair by the window."

"You get her upset and I'll kick your ass," Shirley said.

"I'll be back," Ira said running up the stairs.

Back home, Ellen picked up the telephone and put it back down for the hundredth time. Then she had an idea and called Pilgrim State for directions. It was either going to turn into a knock down drag out battle or a tearful reconciliation, but at least there'd be a resolution. She planned to be back before the kids even knew she was gone.

Ellen wasn't convinced it was a good idea. In fact, she was pretty sure that it was a stupid idea, but she just couldn't continue to sit at home and wait for events to take place that would shape her future. She wanted to influence the outcome and this was the only way she could think of. Ira certainly hadn't left her with too many options.

Ira was out of breath by the time he got to Building 104. He was holding back the cold now by force of will. Sonny sat in a wheelchair by the window just where Rhonda said she would be. She was illuminated like in a biblical painting by a ray of dusty sunlight. Bones stuck out through her nightgown like the frame of a house. Her hair was brittle and sparse and her lips as white as her hair. Her skin was an ashen grey, which matched the color of her eyes, which looked like they were once blue. If they hadn't moved to follow some birds in flight, he'd have doubted that they still worked.

No one questioned him as he pulled up a chair next to her.

"Good morning."

Sonny didn't react. She didn't even blink.

"Some snowstorm the other day," he said.

Sonny turned her head slowly. She looked through him for a second, didn't appear interested in what she saw, and turned back to the window.

"You're Sonny, aren't you?"

He was probably no more than the buzz of a mosquito in her ear.

He needed an idea, something to break the ice, so he looked around the room. Two old women sat at a table trying to make potholders with their gnarled fingers. It was a struggle to get the thin bands of colored cloth hooked onto the ends of the metal squares. He'd have thrown it to the floor a long time ago, but they just kept trying, as if the only thing they had left at this stage of their lives was patience.

An incredibly thin old woman swayed in the corner as if she was at a dance. Another paced back and forth, nodding her head as she walked and gesturing wildly with her hands. This was a room of silence. No one spoke. All conversations were internal, so Ira sat quietly beside Sonny and stared out the window.

The world outside was alive with movement, contrasting with Sonny, who sat as rigid as a corpse. Trees bent toward the sun, some still holding onto wilted, brown leaves that fluttered in the wind like the wings of a wounded bird. The parking lot wasn't visible from Sonny's window. Neither were any of the other buildings or roads. She looked out on a large snow covered field encircled by trees. In Ira's mind it cried out for some human footprints, children running and pulling their sleds behind them. He wondered what was on the other side of the woods, probably a highway. He'd rather imagine a simple eighteenth century village, a place that never changed, a town without distractions, no newspapers, no cars and no phones; someplace completely off the map, a place where families always stay together, a place far too small for secrets.

"It's like looking back in time," he said.

Without turning her head, Sonny nodded very slowly. He waited for her to stop nodding. When she didn't, he continued talking.

"My name's Ira. I don't really work here. I came to find out about Eva Portnoy. I'm her son. I just learned that the other day."

Sonny's mouth moved slightly, but nothing came out, almost as if she had forgotten how to work it. She leaned a tiny bit in his direction and a few strands of gray hair brushed against his cheek.

"Shirley in records said that you might remember Eva. I'm trying to find out what happened. I was wondering about the circumstances of my birth."

"You mean your father," Sonny whispered without turning her head. She sounded far away and her words died quickly.

"Yes, my father."

Ira remained very still. The sunlight was warm, very different from the artificial heat pouring out of the radiator, healing as opposed to feverish. Sonny's chest moved up and down. He could hear a sucking and hissing sound, like she was breathing through a pair of bellows.

"I was there."

"Where?"

"Didn't say a word, never did."

Sonny never stopped staring out the window.

"He came out fixing his pants. I helped her clean up."

Sonny turned her head and examined his face.

"The same hard, mean mouth."

"As who?"

"Him."

"What's his name?"

"They wanted me to have one of those operations, but my father wouldn't let them. That's why I'm still here."

"Who was it?"

"Who was it?" Sonny said repeating his question without any of his urgency.

"Who did that to Eva?"

"The janitor."

"What was his name?" Ira said.

Sonny didn't reply.

"What happened to him?"

Her face grew stiff again, as if something had taken control of it. He stood up.

"Thank you Sonny. Thank you very much."

He had to tell himself to calm down about a dozen times on the way back to Shirley. The nice thing about doing that in a mental institution is that you can talk to yourself without attracting attention. Shirley was still working downstairs with the old files when he got back. She looked up when he came in, but didn't say a word.

"I saw Sonny."

"So."

"So she spoke to me."

"Bullshit."

"She did."

"What about, World War II?"

"Sonny witnessed the rape."

Shirley stuck out her lower lip and curled it down. Her head bobbed up and down, like it was coming loose.

"How about that," she said, "we could've nailed the bastard if only she'd talked." Shirley stared out into space and narrowed her eyes. "So who was it?"

"The janitor," Ira answered.

Shirley's effort at remembering made her face look younger.

"What was his name?"

"Who the hell can remember that long ago?" Shirley said.

"We ought to be able to look it up."

"Just hold your horses a minute.

Shirley took a deep breath and looked down at her stomach. After a few moments she looked up, her eyes wide open, and brought her hand to her mouth.

"Holy shit," she said.

"You remember his name," Ira said forgetting about his cold and moving close to Shirley.

"I should've fuckin known."

"Who, who is he?"

Shirley looked at his mouth and shook her head slowly from side to side.

"I can see the resemblance around the mouth."

"Who?"

Shirley moved her hand away from her mouth and slapped the table.

"She didn't mean the janitor back then, she meant the janitor now."

"What are you talking about?"

"Fred fucking McCaw, the Head of Custodial Services . . . FM . . . I forgot that asshole used to fill in as an orderly when he first started."

Ira's stomach collapsed like a black star. He was staring straight ahead at a calendar on the wall, but he didn't see it. Instead, he was looking inside his head at a picture of his parents. They were sitting side by side for a family portrait, except they had no faces. Fred was holding a bucket and a mop and Eva was wearing a straight jacket.

Now that his father was so close, Ira realized that he would probably have been better off if he was dead or at least retired in Florida.

"I should have known . . . that fucking guy was always in heat. He talked to your tits half the time like you didn't have eyes. If I had thought about checking the file back then I could have figured it out."

"It's not your fault," Ira said.

"I was a scared pup back then, afraid of my own shadow, afraid to rock the boat. I wasn't always like this. I can afford to be fearless now. What can anyone do to me?"

"I'm going to find him."

"The bastard doesn't deserve it."

"Deserve what?"

"Closure."

Ira hated that word.

"He chased everything in skirts back then, every fucking nurse."

"You?"

"He didn't give me the time of day. Still doesn't. Because he knew I could see right through him. He pretended that he was some big time war hero, but I knew what he really did. He went in after a battle and picked up bodies. He was a janitor back then too."

At least, Ira thought, he sounded like someone who might have stood up to Selma.

"Who knows how many other patients he raped?" Shirley said.

"I can't believe it."

"I wonder if they knew," Shirley said.

"Who?"

"I wonder if the fucking administrators suspected something. I bet they did, which is why he stopped filling in on the wards on the weekends and holidays."

"He'd still have contact with patients."

"Not at night. That was the prime time for pee-holing. And he got married right after that to some chubby little girl off the boat from Ireland and got too busy spittin out kids of his own."

The angrier Shirley got, the more interested Ira became. Now he had siblings.

"He doesn't deserve to have it all turn out OK."

"OK?"

"Yeah, another son to forgive him," Shirley said, "and you know that's what you're going to do."

"I am not."

"And more grandchildren to send him cards on Father's Day."

"No one's sending him any cards."

"Give it a few years. Wait till your kids want to meet him."

"I won't tell them."

"What happen to your big truth kick?"

"Not right away."

"I say let him keep wondering and looking over his shoulder," Shirley said.

"At what?"

"I don't know what . . . at judgment day."

Ira walked over to the other side of the room and sat down on a box. Finding out about Fred was not going to add much to his family life or his self-image.

"Where's Fred's office?"

"In the back of the Administration Building."

He felt as heavy as Shirley climbing up the stairs.

"He thinks he's some fucking family man," Shirley called out. "He probably can't even get it up any more."

Ira heard the word family echoing in his head as he walked out the door.

"I'm his family," he said to himself.

Meanwhile, Ellen was leaving the Administration building. They had given her a visitor's badge and directions to Records. She and Ira passed on opposite sides of the building like lost lovers in a movie. Shirley was upstairs looking through Eva's file when Ellen walked in.

"Excuse me, I'm looking for Ira."

Shirley smiled, because she knew instantly who she was. Everyone loves a real life soap opera. Shirley took a moment to compare Rhonda to Ellen. Ellen was a lot shorter. Middle age gravity was beginning to cause the skin below her chin and her upper arms to hang and sway like little hammocks. She had broader hips, the result no doubt of multiple births, and much smaller breasts. For some reason, Shirley remembered reading that multiple pregnancies can cause feet to grow and breasts to shrink. Maybe that's nature's way of making sure that you're more grounded as a mother and have better balance. She was slender from the waist up, but heavy from the waist down. Not heavy like Shirley, thin compared to Shirley.

Ellen had a more wholesome look with an ankle length brown skirt and high-collared white blouse. She had a nice face, straight features, smaller, kinder and, of course, older than Rhonda with lots more lines. Black circles around her eyes. Last week had taken its toll. She was clearly more likable than Ira. Shirley could tell that in an instant.

"He's not here. You must be Ellen."

"How did you know?"

"Ira hasn't stopped talking about you since he got here."

Ellen knew that was a lie. Ira never talked about his family, just like he never bragged about good fortune. He considered it bad luck. His mother taught him about the evil eye and warned about the jealousy of strangers and friends. Still, it was a nice gesture.

"Where is he?"

"On his way to meet his father."

"*His father?*"

"The head custodian."

"Oh, God, is it as bad as it sounds?"

Shirley nodded and both of them stood there looking away from each other like kids at a high school dance. Shirley finally broke the silence by telling Ellen what Ira had just learned about Fred. She even showed her Eva's file. At least Shirley and the file must have seemed reassuring. It hadn't all been a complete lie. Shirley was just the way Ira described her, not in the least bit threatening.

"I don't know how he's going to handle all this," Ellen said, "especially after the past week."

His wife worrying, Shirley thought, was a good sign. She seemed the perfect type for Ira, too stable to fly off the handle, and too cautious to get in over her head. Not like Rhonda. Some people need a relationship that burns; some need one that lasts. They rarely did both.

"Stick around, you'll find out soon enough when he gets back. Knowing Fred, he won't be long."

"You think so?"

"He's gonna hate Fred and Fred's gonna hate him."

"Why?"

"Because he's got a brain, like a sieve and he's a son of a bitch. There may be a resemblance, but that's about it. They're from different planets up here," Shirley said tapping her forehead.

"You don't know Ira," Ellen said, "he wants to like everyone . . . and he wants everyone to like him. He'd vote for both parties if they'd let him."

"He won't have a chance with Fred, even his kids hate him."

Ellen flashed one of her appropriate teacher half-smiles.

"I doubt Ira will have the nerve to knock on Fred's door," Ellen said, "at least not right away. He usually needs a day or two for anything new to simmer in his head before he can make a decision."

"He is a bit of a wimp."

Ellen let go with one of her genuine, 18-carat smiles.

"Actually, that was one of the things I liked about him when we met."

"Me too," Shirley said. "Wait'll he finds out that he has a half-dozen brothers and sisters?"

"Really, six?"

"Three girls and three boys, apparently that jerk doesn't shoot blanks. God has got one rotten sense of humor if you ask me." Ellen looked down at Eva's file.

"One of his sons works in the hospital," Shirley said.

"What's he like?"

"Dumber than his father, if that's possible, without any of the sex appeal. It's reverse evolution in the McCaw family."

Ellen thought over her next move while Shirley answered the telephone. There was something else she needed to know. You couldn't keep Ellen off track for long. As a teacher, she comes with plans imprinted on her brain like a genetic code.

"What about this girl," Ellen said with the emphasis on the word girl, "that Ira's been staying with."

"A nurse," Shirley said trying to render Rhonda harmlessly medicinal, "her name's Rhonda."

"What's she like?"

"Like a playboy bunny with some brains, but little common sense."

That didn't help.

The Head Custodian's office was a small room on the backside of the Administration Building far away from the other offices. The sign on front read "Fred McCaw, Supervisor." It hung on the door courtesy of duct tape. Ira wasn't sure that he'd be around on a Saturday, but that's often when they do the major waxing and moping, at least at American Family Care.

When he heard some noise from inside his knees went weak and his mouth dried up. His head said turn and walk away, he needed more time to think about it, to make sure it made sense, but he couldn't make his legs move. What if he was a male version of Selma, judgmental and permanently exasperated, strutting around like he was the one who invented the orgasm, expectations tattooed on his brain? Of course, they'd be different kinds of expectations; no dreams of a Nobel Prize or a successful practice in Plastic Surgery. His expectations were likely to be more physical, focusing on the number of female notches on his belt and the quantity of beers he could drink; expectations based on the moment, not ambitious, and indifferent to Ira's small successes, except perhaps for Rhonda. Rhonda could make him a real chip off the old block.

While Ira debated with himself, his hand in an almost involuntary reflex knocked weakly at the door. There was no answer and before he could turn around his hand knocked again harder this time.

"Come in."

He couldn't move.

"COME IN."

He opened the door with a jerk and almost fell forward on his face.

"What can I do ya for?"

The voice was gravely and deep, sinister because of the total absence of interest or emotion. When he finally looked up, Ira discovered that Father Christmas spent his off-season at a desk in a mental institution and went by the name Fred. Here was a chubby, old man with a bright red nose, fat cheeks and a white beard. All that was missing was the red hat. He had the same hairline as Ira, which was to say two large widow's peaks. He looked wise and grandfatherly, kind and reassuring, at least until he opened his mouth. The mirror shattered when he opened his mouth.

"Ya deaf or what?"

Fred was wearing a short sleeve shirt that barely managed to make it around his arm, which was as thick and hard as a tree limb. Moping up must be like lifting weights, Ira thought. His eyes were clear, round marbles, so far forward on his face that they could have popped out of his head with one good slap on the back. His mouth, despite mellowing over the years and hiding behind the beard, still had traces of meanness. It was an older and smaller version of his mouth.

"Huh?" was all Ira managed to say.

Fred must have been wondering whether he was one of the inmates, instead of one of the jailers.

"Forget to take ya meds this morning, did ya?"

"I'm . . . ."

"Spit it out boy."

"Looking for Fred . . . Fred McCaw."

"No fooling you, what gave it away, the sign on the fuckin door?"

Fred stood up and rested both hands flat on the desk. They weren't big hands, but they were thick hands almost like knotted rope. Ira extended his hand and Fred stared at it like a new kind of lunchmeat. Then he reluctantly lifted one hand and grabbed it, like he was squeezing the life out of a gnat. It wasn't Ira's hand or grip. His was thin and delicate, the kind that comes from a lifetime pushing pencils.

It must come from Eva, he thought.

They were about the same height with the same stocky build. Fred just had a few more years to inflate. Did he notice anything? Don't animals instinctively recognize their offspring?

"What d'ya want? I don't got all day."

"I'm from Records."

"Fat Shirley, she's been here longer than me."

Ira stood in awkward silence.

"Biggest thing in the place," he said with a chuckle. "Always been, we used to call her the hungry hippo . . . biggest nut in the nut house if you ask me."

Fred's gut, which rested on the desk like a trophy, was nothing to brag about.

"So what d'ya want?"

He wanted to accuse him of raping his mother. He wanted to hug him and call him dad. He wanted to scream and pick up the janitor's drum paperweight on his desk and smash it in his face, except he'd probably be able to kill him with a single punch before Ira got close enough.

"Well?"

Clearly Dad had a very limited vocabulary.

He wanted to see pictures of his brothers and sisters and he wanted to tell him all about his own family. He wanted to make him suffer, but the lump in his throat was far too large to breathe let alone talk. His vocal cords were searching frantically for a one-syllable word.

"Broom."

"What?"

"Broom. Shirley . . . needs . . . a broom."

Ira's heart was beating in his fingertips. Why couldn't he figure it out on his own? How could he be so blind?

"Broom," he repeated.

"Take it easy. Geez, they'll hire anyone in this fuckin place."

Fred walked over to the closet.

"What a moron," he mumbled.

He took out a broom and dustpan and handed them over.

"Better not tell Fat Shirley what I said or she's liable to roll over here and sit on me." He cut a big ho-ho-ho with that one as he shut the closet. "And she would have liked to, let me tell ya. Forty years ago she used to look at me like a box of chocolate chip cookies, but I was never that desperate."

Fred went back around the desk and sat down.

"I don't wanna be around when that one explodes."

Fred laughed again and then dismissed him with a nod. He nodded back, but it was too late, Fred was already thumbing through a cleaning supply catalogue, studying the latest technological advancements in disinfectants. Ira didn't move. He couldn't. Fred looked up again and dismissed him this time with the back of his hand. He didn't look amused. It would be a fist to his solar plexus next. Ira turned slowly around and walked out the door. He no longer hated his father, at least not as much as he hated himself.

He needed to time to refocus his thoughts, but where should he go? Home or back to Shirley? What about Rhonda? Should he call Ellen? If he stuck around would he have the nerve to confront Fred the next time? Was it worth it? He knew all he needed to know just from asking for the broom. Anyway, as an employee of Pilgrim State Hospital, Ira had the hopefully once in a lifetime opportunity to wander aimlessly through one of the largest mental institutions in the free world, carrying a broom and a dustpan, one mess in search of another.

Ellen glanced down at her watch. She had to get going. The kids would be home coming home for dinner in a couple of hours and she had to get back to get it ready. She couldn't let them come home to an empty house, not with what had been going on over the past week. Besides, she and Shirley had run out of things to talk about. Just standing there gave her the willies, as if this was the very place where all her teaching failures were destined to wind up. She could see twenty years of misbehaved faces on the other side of the wall. She wanted to run out, but a good teacher didn't do anything in a hurry.

"He shoulda been back by now," Shirley said.

"If he's coming back," Ellen said. "If I know Ira, he lost his nerve and needs some time alone to kick himself."

"That sounds about right," Shirley said after she finished laughing.

Ellen started pacing slowly back and forth in front of the counter.

"Can you call him?"

"Who, Fred?"

"Yes."

"Yeah sure."

Shirley looked up the extension and then dialed the number. Fred picked up on the first ring and Shirley asked about Ira.

"That jerk left about fifteen minutes ago," he said, "a real drink of water if you ask me."

"What did you two talk about?"

Fred laughed.

"What did we talk about? You, who else? What the hell is goin on? For Christ's sake, I knew somethin was wrong with that guy. I could tell just looking at him. He's one of the inmates workin off his room and board, ain't he? Or is he another one of your pet projects? Maybe he's one of those April December things?'

"You're an idiot," Shirley said before hanging up.

"What is it?" Ellen said.

"He chickened out."

Ellen nodded.

"Stick around I'm sure he'll be back soon."

Ellen wasn't listening. Her thoughts were rattling back and forth as she shook her head. Then she looked at her watch. She had to leave at once to make it back in time.

"Tell him I was here," she said. "Ask him to call me if he can find the time."

"I'm sure it'll be the first thing he does."

Ellen put on her coat and gloves slowly and deliberately as if she were leaving the home of a good friend. She never let anything rush her. A measured pace was crucial to a teacher. Of course, because of the extra time she took she was still there when Rhonda walked in.

"Where's Ira?" Rhonda asked with a possessive, sexual tone no ordinary co-worker would ever use.

Shirley rolled her eyes in Ellen's direction, a clear signal to proceed with caution, but Rhonda was not good with subtleties.

"Ira," she called out again like they were late for something.

"Hello," Ellen said turning towards her so that their profiles hung side by side like a pair of swinging saloon doors. Rhonda's breasts made a mockery of the small bulges under Ellen's winter coat. Ellen struggled to maintain an even rhythm to her breathing. Rhonda was oblivious to everything.

"Hello," Rhonda said like one of those bouncy, sex-teasing characters in a situation comedy.

Ellen just stared like she's trying to focus in the dark.

"Do I know you?" Rhonda asked.

Ellen probably looked familiar. The enemy always does, at least in the movies. The music always changes and the light dims whenever the perpetrator is near, giving the detective this funny feeling sort of like gas.

"I'm Ira's wife."

Rhonda didn't move. Her smile changed to a look of bewilderment and she clenched her fist. This could be the part in the movie where the wife reaches into her bag and pulls out a gun.

"You must be the nurse Ira's been sleeping with."

Shirley reached for her emergency stash under the counter and pulled out a jumbo candy bar.

"Just once," Rhonda said still frozen in place.

"I doubt that. He's been dying for big breasts since he was thirteen."

Rhonda looked down at her chest as if she hadn't noticed them before.

"They didn't have anything to do with it."

"Right, I suppose it was your mind he couldn't keep his hands off." When Rhonda didn't respond Ellen turned to Shirley. "What kind of woman sleeps with a married man?"

Shirley chewed vigorously.

Rhonda looked for Shirley to throw her a life preserver.

"Maybe she didn't know he was married," Shirley said.

"He's got married written all over his face," Ellen said.

"She's not like that," Shirley said, "really."

"That may be, but I bet it gets a whole lot easier after the first one."

"I didn't hold a gun to his head," Rhonda said.

Ellen's lips disappeared.

"He wasn't thinking straight," Shirley said. "It's not everyday a man finds out his mother is nuts."

Ellen didn't respond. She couldn't help thinking that she was partially at fault. She's been falling asleep earlier and earlier every night, worn out by schoolwork and chores, even on Saturdays. Sex hasn't been easy to squeeze in now that the kids were bigger. Life required as much planning these days as her lessons.

Ellen looked up at Rhonda. She looked like one of her students waiting anxiously for her grade. One of the students she was sometimes tempted to rap across the knuckles with a ruler, because they never perform up to their potential. Ellen shook her head. The bottom line was that searching for Eva and Fred was no excuse for Rhonda. The thing was that under different circumstances Ellen would probably have liked Rhonda. She was like one of those new, young teachers that Ellen befriends at the beginning of every school year. They have the good stuff inside they just need some advice and a guiding hand to help it come out.

"I suppose it could be worse," Ellen said. "He could have found someone with more than a few tumbles in the sack to offer. You can't lead them by the penis for very long . . . not at his age."

"There you go," Shirley said like the riddle had been solved.

"I can do a lot of things," Rhonda said.

"I don't doubt it dear, I'm sure you've had a lot of practice." With that Ellen turned to Shirley. "Tell Ira that if he's not home by Sunday he can move in with hooters over here, because I won't take him back. And believe me in a couple of weeks she won't want him and he won't want her."

Shirley nodded and finished her candy bar.

"When he does," Ellen said pointing her teacher's finger at Rhonda's face, "stay away from him, because if I ever see you around I swear to God I'll pop them with a pin."

"You think they're fake?"

"I think they're monstrosities."

With that Ellen walked out the door. She replayed the final scene the whole ride home disappointed each time at the way she behaved. She wound up driving too fast and got her first speeding ticket.

Ira wasn't allowed to wander through the maximum-security wards at Pilgrim, so he stuck to the open areas. They had a more traditional patient population, nonviolent and older. After a number of years most of the patients seemed very similar, as if all their illnesses have blended together.

There were patients who gestured furiously as he went by or stood like statues, their faces frozen in accusation. There were patients who talked in endless streams of gibberish about lines on the floor and messages from outer space, and patients who flipped through magazines and smoked imaginary cigarettes as if they were sitting around waiting to be called for an appointment. They all had one thing in common, their reason had fled and the void had been filled with emotion. A light bulb that blew was reason enough to break into a sweat. A ball of dust that rolled across the room brought on hysterics. Feelings live intensely in the insane. There's no such thing as happiness, only euphoria, no plain sadness, only deep depression. Anger is rage and dislike is disgust. Fortunately, no feelings last very long on that kind of emotional merry-ground.

So Ira wandered from building to building, hearing as much as seeing insanity. The sounds often being more powerful than the pictures - slow, loud breathing that filled the room with tension and cries that poisoned the air like smoke. Unnatural sounds that he hadn't heard before, except perhaps in a childhood nightmare. Still, as the child of a lifelong patient and employee he felt right at home.

"A classy lady," Shirley said after Ellen left.

"I didn't say she wasn't. She's just not all that attractive."

"You mean she's not all that young."

"Whatever. And she's wrong about men," Rhonda said. "They can be led around by the penis at any age."

"I wouldn't know," Shirley said.

"Where is Ira?"

"He went to visit his father."

"His father?"

"Yeah, but he appears to have chickened out."

"He's here?"

"Yep."

"Oh shit, who is he?"

"Fred, the head custodian."

"He gives some of the nurses the creeps, but I think he's all talk."

"He wasn't always."

"At least he's not always trying to look down my blouse like some of the others."

"Because you're too tall, he wouldn't make it if he stood on his toes. You can't tell by the way he is now, but he used to be the scum of the earth."

"What a bummer for Ira. He'd be been better off if his father was dead."

"At least this way he gets the truth he's always so hot about instead of another fantasy."

"I've got to get back to the floor. Tell Ira I'll see him back at the apartment. We're supposed to go to a movie."

Shirley picked up a few crumbs with her fingers while shaking her head slowly from side to side.

"And she's wrong about something else," Rhonda said.

"What?"

"Ira could be happy with me."

With that Rhonda left.

"The lunacy in this place rubs off on everyone," Shirley said to herself before turning around to walk back down the stairs.

People stopped talking when Ira passed by. Both patients and staff watched him closely, the stranger with a broom, all of them undoubtedly hoping that the mess he was looking for was someplace else. He passed by one of the high security wards and looked inside. Most of the patients were young, eighteen to thirty-five. About forty percent of them were MICAs, Mentally Ill Chemical Abusers. It looked like a prison and from what Rhonda said they were just as dangerous. There were inmate gangs that set secret rules and regulations. Ira figured that rape was probably an institutional activity now, like ping-pong and television.

All Pilgrim wanted to do was find some kind of drug-induced normalcy so it could get them out on the street or at least keep the lid closed until they turned forty. Something happened at forty, Rhonda told him even the worst cases became more manageable at that point. If they stayed until forty, they usually got transferred to the open wards, to the world of potholders and afternoon passes. It was amazing what he picked up after one week at a mental institution, even in Records. Ira realized that he was getting a particularly negative point of view from Shirley and Rhonda, and was probably being overly critical, but he was entitled. After all, he was talking about his extended family. Ira wasn't looking where he was going and as he turned the corner he bumped into a large trashcan pushed by a short, fat man. He couldn't be more than 35, yet he was already balding.

"Hey asshole, watch where ya going."

"Sorry."

His nametag read Roy McCaw. He looked Ira over to make sure he wasn't medical staff or administration.

"Try openin ya eyes next time."

"Are you Fred McCaw's son?"

"What's it to ya?"

"I just saw him."

He held up the broom and dustpan.

"Well aren't you a lucky sonofabitch."

"I'm in Records."

Roy wasn't the least bit interested and appeared to have even less of a facility at small talk than Ira. He just looked down and started pushing his garbage can past him. He was shorter than Ira, so Roy was short by anyone's standards. He was also fatter. His clothes could barely contain him. Flesh spilled from his belt like water over the top of a tub. His skin was the texture of a lemon rind, yellowed and spotted, like it needed a good scrub. The little hair he has left was a light brown color that probably always looked greasy and dirty. They had little in common except for the same hard, mean McCaw mouth.

"What's he like?" Ira said.

"What's who like?"

"Your father."

"He's a fuckin saint, the saint of all ball-busters."

That got a big chuckle from Roy.

"How many of you are there at Pilgrim?"

Roy stopped.

"How many what? What'dya think I am a god-damn patient?"

"I meant how many work here beside you and your father."

"Two in this shit hole's enough."

Roy did have one talent. He could talk without moving his lips. The trashcan jerked forward like it was pulling him away.

"I just started in Records this week with Shirley."

Roy kept moving.

"Big family?" he called out.

Roy stopped and turned around staring at him like a piece of garbage too big for the can.

"What the fuck is your problem?"

Would it be too much too soon, Ira wondered, to walk over and give him a big hug explaining why he also had it in for his father . . . their father.

"Just curious."

"Do I look like I got nothin to do?"

Roy squinted at him like he was taking aim, then he revved up the can.

"There's a McCaw in my family. You never know, we could be related."

Roy stopped again. His mouth was a thin scar above his chin, razor sharp. He either looked like a mental patient or looked at Ira like one.

"Fuck off," he said throwing his weight behind the can for a fast start, "go back to the ward where ya came from."

"Let's have lunch," Ira said.

The only reply came from the jingle of Roy's keys as the can gained momentum and turned the next corner. He could hear him spit into the garbage. It must be wonderful, Ira thought, not to be cursed in the slightest with self-consciousness. When he got back to Records, Ira could hear grunts and groans from downstairs and the unmistakable whine of a heavy cardboard box scrapping against floor. He leaned the broom and dustpan against the counter and walked down the stairs.

"What are you doing," he said rushing over to help Shirley pull out a box from way in the back.

"I found . . . the . . . pictures."

Shirley stumbled across the room and fell into the armchair like she had just run a marathon. She tried to put her head down between her knees, but she couldn't get close.

Ira finished pulling the box over to the counter.

"The lobotomy photos?"

Shirley nodded.

He pulled one out. There were two pictures stuck together, a before and after photo. Just like an advertisement for a weight loss program. The names were at the bottom along with the date. Louis Auchin, March 13, 1936. His before picture was angry, eyes pulled back, lurking in the shadows, and his mouth pressed flat as if it had been pounded by a skillet. The after picture was wiped clean of emotion, his face lightened by a blank, white stare and his open mouth a vast, empty tunnel to nowhere.

Ira pulled out a handful of pictures, not a smile among them, not before or after. He almost expected a testimonial on the bottom of the after-picture. The weight of the world was once on my shoulders, now, thanks to Doc Fulton, all my worries are gone forever. Underneath that, in bold print, would be written Doc Fulton, Family Lobotomist, his address and telephone number and perhaps a guarantee -- instant and painless, money back, if not completely satisfied. He could probably do a coupon campaign with a record high rate of retention. Ten percent off would do it.

He passed a few of the pictures over to Shirley.

"Your wife . . . was here," Shirley said still trying to catch her breath.

"Very funny."

"She was."

"Rhonda?"

"No, Ellen."

"I don't believe you."

"About five two . . . cute little nose . . . flat chest, big hips, dressed like a teacher."

Ira put down the photos and looked around as if Ellen was about to pop up from behind one of the boxes. If she did, he would have fallen to his knees and begged her forgiveness. He'd have followed her home and the hell with Fred. Fred could remain forever behind his desk thumbing through cleaning supply catalogues and handing out brooms. It's funny how timing can make so many of life's important decisions for you. Ten minutes earlier and it would have all been over.

"Where is she?"

"Gone home."

Ira slumped beside the box.

"She waited around, heard that you chickened out with Fred, and left."

"How did she know?"

"I called him."

"Did he say anything about me?"

"Nerd, twerp, I forgot the word he used."

He stared into the box.

"How did she seem?"

"Like a parent coming to take her misbehaved child home from school."

"That's good."

"Except she got to meet Rhonda instead."

"That's bad."

"You're a lucky man Ira. She still wants you back. Why, I don't know, but she said to tell you that you had until Sunday."

He would have given himself a lobotomy on the spot if he could have. There's something to be said for living the rest of life unaware and without a care.

Shirley took a long, deep breath and let it out slowly.

"It was a nice contrast in figures," she said.

Lobotomies had to be easier than suicide.

"What else happened?"

"It wasn't much of a cat fight, if that's what you're wondering. She circled around Rhonda for a while, but didn't throw a punch."

It felt like there was a lawnmower blade spinning round and round in his stomach. He was going to be sick unless he did something quick, so he stuck his hand in the box of photos. Of course, the next one he pulled out was Eva's. She looked about thirty in the photo. She had a big, kind mouth, not a trace of meanness, and a small, perfectly symmetrical nose. Her cheeks were high, unlike his, and she had that long curly hair from his dream that cascaded down to her shoulders. Women these days spend hours in the beauty parlor trying to chemically induce that look. Her eyes were hidden behind the shadow of her eyebrows. They were dark and mysterious, but not fearful, accepting perhaps or just thick skinned.

In black and white Eva looked like an early suffragette. He could see her smoking in a restaurant and drawing stares as she sat down in her black trousers. She was the only person in the family that could ever bring to mind the words intriguing and exotic. The picture was grainy and Ira strained to find some hint of understanding and forgiveness in her eyes . . . a message to future generations, especially to her son, but there was none. The eyes were off somewhere, not present in the photograph.

"She was pretty," he said showing it to Shirley.

"A curse in this place," Shirley said flipping to the other side. "Unfortunately, that's the way I mostly remember her."

In the after picture, Eva looked like a lifetime member of Club Insanity. Her hair was short and had grown back stiff and straight, almost like a porcupine. Her eyes were dim and smaller, if that was possible. Her lower lip hung loose like Doc Fulton had mistakenly cut the muscle that held it up, a sort of two for one deal. Her expression had been wiped clean. It made you want to knock on the top of her head to see if anyone was home.

"She wasn't much of a person after the operation. Some came out worse than others. I guess it depended on how deep he twirled his little apple peeler. And he wasn't above experimenting when he could . . . when there was no one looking over his shoulder."

Ira wiped his eyes, took the picture back and put it in his wallet along with Rhonda's nude shot. Eva would understand.

"Why rape someone like that?" he asked.

"Why not? Is it any worse than dicing up her brain? Or keeping her here forever? If they got caught worst that happened was they got fired. Big fucking deal. Jobs were a dime a dozen back then."

Ira took out the photo again and studied the before side. Eva's mouth was kind and accepting, somewhat childlike, even in the face of this unspeakable horror. It certainly wasn't his mouth. He did have the same vein that scratched the surface below her left eye, like a stray pencil mark. He also shared her thick eyebrows, although his eyes were not nearly as dark and expressive. It could have been a very sociable face, he thought, given a chance. It certainly wasn't the survival of the best features in his case. It was more a dumbing down thanks to the Neanderthal who contributed the sperm.

"Where the hell is everybody?" a voice boomed from upstairs.

Fred stuck his big head downstairs. He must have been shedding because a shower of dust followed after him.

"So that's where ya hiding, strappin on the old feedbag again? What's it, fourth lunch of the day?"

He came down the stairs carrying the broom and dustpan.

"Leave'em up there alone and they're gonna walk out like one of the loonies. Ya just can't trust them nurses."

Fred flashed his crooked, yellow teeth and sat down on the stool. He leaned the broom and dustpan carefully against the counter.

"Looking for trouble?" Shirley said.

"Not with you. I only pick on people my own size."

"Be tough to find anyone if you're talking about your pea brain."

"I'm not."

Fred winked at Ira.

He could take care of that eye problem, Ira thought if he had a sharp pencil.

"What'dya got there?" Fred said leaning over the box of photographs and stirring them around like a pot of soup. "Looks like the Pilgrim family album." Fred looked up at Shirley. "You in here?"

"In your box of old girlfriends, not on your life."

Fred looked at Ira with a greasy little smirk, like they were sharing some male secret.

"Let me take a look," Fred said pulling Eva's photo from Ira's hand.

He had no reaction to the before-picture. Maybe he was puzzled, because he turned it over and stared at the after-picture. Then he rubbed his forehead with his big, meaty paw and squinted down at his feet. Something was on his mind, trying to fight its way into his conscious thought, but there were too many obstacles in the way. If it wasn't food or drink, it probably didn't stand a chance he would recognize it.

Fred looked up and found both Shirley and Ira staring at him.

"What are ya two dumbbells starin at?"

"Looks sorta familiar, doesn't she?" Shirley said.

"How would I know?"

"She was here for forty years."

"How the hell would I remember? They all look the same if ya ask me."

"This one was special."

"What for?"

"You took care of this one once," Shirley said, "back in the days when you were a weekend orderly."

"So."

"Really took care of her." Shirley said.

"What the fuck are you talkin about?"

"Eva."

"Never heard of her."

"Think, I know it doesn't come easy," Shirley said. "You two were an item."

"An item?"

"An item," Ira said his voice breaking like a little boy.

Fred turned his mean mouth on Ira like a spotlight.

"I heard what she said, so but the fuck out. That was before you were born."

That's for sure Ira wanted to say, but he couldn't. If he uttered one more word or took another deep breath, he was sure that his heart would explode in his chest.

"Ira is Eva's son," Shirley said with an equally mean expression.

"I'm happy for him."

"And yours."

Fred didn't respond. Now he was really trying to think, something he obviously didn't have to do too often which, for some reason, made him grab his crotch. Maybe he was afraid it would pop out and confess on its own.

"Sonny saw you pull Eva into the closet."

Ira looked back and forth between Shirley and Fred like a spectator at a tennis match. He's been a spectator most of his life and he couldn't change that even now. With a break in the action Shirley chewed on her thumbnail while Fred twirled at his beard.

A lefty, Ira noticed . . . another confirmation of fatherhood.

"Did it skip your mind?" Shirley said. "Too many rapes to remember them all?"

Fred looked at Ira and then back at Shirley.

"I guess there's no use denyin it, but there's nothing ya can do about it now."

"Nothing?"

A fine spray accompanied Ira's contribution to the conversation.

"I watch TV. I know about the statue of limitations."

"Statute," Ira said, "not statue."

"What ya gonna do, have me arrested . . . your own father? I'd just say it was her idea, that she wanted it. Who's gonna say otherwise?"

All Ira could do was spit back his own words, "wanted it?"

"With you," Shirley said, "no one's that crazy."

Fred looked at Ira and took a deep breath puffing himself up like a frog.

"Shit, that musta been forty years ago."

"Forty-one to be exact."

If he beat him senseless, Ira wondered, could he plead temporary insanity? He was in the right place for it and it did run in the family.

"Well isn't this a ball-buster," Fred said walking over and extended his hand.

Ira stared at it wishing he had enough saliva for a good spit, but he couldn't overcome his Selma years and wound up taking it. The two of them stood there holding hands while Shirley turned green, neither wanted to be the first to let go. Ira looked for the disappointment in Fred's eyes as he applied the wimp-meter to his handshake, but all he saw was indifference. He finally pulled his hand away and Fred sat down on the stool.

"Did you even know she got pregnant?" Shirley said.

"I heard."

"And you didn't do shit about it."

"I thought once about gettin a look at you in the hospital."

"Once?" Ira said.

"Is he supposed to thank you for your interest and concern?" Shirley asked.

"Ya know the way things are."

"No," Shirley said, "tell us the way things are."

Fred looked at Shirley like she was one word away from a roundhouse right.

"I was busy at work."

"Big mess in the cafeteria I bet."

"Before I knew it you were gone."

"And forgotten."

"Can't cry over spilled milk," Fred said picking up the broom like he'd had enough. "Funny that ya wind up working here."

"Yeah, funny," Shirley said.

Ira looked at Fred. Fred looked at Shirley. Shirley looked at Ira. She was waiting for him to explain, but he couldn't say more than one or two words at a time. His tongue felt like it had swollen to twice its normal size.

"Ira doesn't work here, you idiot, he's a big shot at some giant corporation . . . makes more money in a month than you do in a year."

Fred smiled. Ira could see the borrower's gleam in his eye.

"He came here to find out about Eva, who he thought was his aunt, and just figured out she was his mother, which means his mother is now his aunt."

"It's like somethin on TV," Fred said looking down at Ira's left leg, which was bouncing up and down like a basketball. He turned to the side to retrieve the dustpan. In profile, Fred's mouth diminished in importance and his nose took over. It was large and red with small craters, a real drinker's nose.

Fortunately, he had Eva's nose.

Fred turned back to Ira. Despite the news, he still had the unconcerned expression of an older man no longer afraid of failure or tormented by sexual frustration.

"Ira . . . funny name for a son of mine."

Shirley slammed her fist down on the arm of the chair and sent a couple of files tumbling to the floor.

"That makes seven," Fred said, "four boys and two girls and now you."

"Shit," is all Ira could say.

"Five more like Roy," Shirley said, "God help us."

"Nah, he's the worsta the lot."

If they're anything like Roy, Ira thought, they're going to take to him like curdled milk.

"How bout you," Fred asked, "got any kids?"

"Two."

Fred slapped his thigh.

"Damn, that makes ten grandkids. I knew I'd hit double figures. The McCaws don't shoot blanks."

"Only up here," Shirley said tapping her forehead.

Fred was feeling too good now to let Shirley bother him or else he was on his best behavior for his new son.

"What are they?"

Ira could see Shirley coming to a boil out of the corner of his eye.

"A boy and a girl."

"How old?"

"Eight and twelve."

"Which one's eight?"

"The boy."

"Names?"

"Scott and Jaime."

"Both boy's names?"

"Jaime's also a girl's name," Ira said.

"Like a boy named Sue," Fred said with a laugh.

"I wouldn't be setting places for them at Thanksgiving dinner," Shirley said.

"There's a shit load of lot of cousins for them. Let's see . . . Roy's the oldest."

"I am," Ira said.

Fred stopped dead in his tracks, he didn't like to be corrected or interrupted, especially by his children. That felt good, but not nearly enough, although Ira realized that he couldn't let his great ambitions of torture and murder overshadow the small successes.

"Oldest that wasn't a damn mistake," Fred said flashing his teeth, which were just about the shade of urine.

"Roy doesn't have any kids, which is the good news. I'd hate to see what they'd be like. Phil's next, has two boys, Nick and Joe, nine and seven. Mike has one boy, Chris eight. Fred Jr. don't have any either, but he just got married so they'll be coming soon enough. Mary has three, Gary, ten, Frank, also eight, and Jane, six. The little one's a pisser, already has her mother's dirty mouth. Alice has two girls, Suzie and Doreen, seven and eleven. Like craps."

Fred smiled at Shirley, clearly intending to get her angry, which it clearly did. It made her chew harder on her thumbnail.

"Won't they be surprised," Fred said.

"You're going to tell them?" Ira said.

"Why the hell not, shit, Alice's got two and she's never been married."

"Why did you do it?" Ira blurted out, not very subtle, but effective. There was a moment of silence, about as long as they used to spend in elementary school when they started the day with silent meditation.

"Son, I guess I can call ya that, I don't know. I was young and stupid. Let my glands take control of my brain."

"When did that ever change?" Shirley said.

Fred shot her a dirty look and walked over to the box of photographs. He still hadn't let go of the broom and dustpan.

"It got to where ya didn't think of the lobos as real people. They were like zombies. I didn't think anything could happen."

"That they couldn't feel pain?" Shirley said.

"That they could get pregnant."

"Don't nod like an idiot," Shirley said to Ira.

"I was just a dumb kid. No excuse, but that's the way it was."

Ira couldn't look at Fred without thinking about picking up the pencil on the counter and stabbing him in the neck. Hit the carotid artery and he'd bleed to death in under a minute.

"I didn't hurt her none."

"There were bruises on her arm," Ira said.

"They always had bruises, half the time they'd walk into walls and the other half we had to grab'em so they wouldn't."

"Bullshit," Shirley said.

"I never did anything like that before, I swear, and I never did anything like that after."

"Why is that," Shirley said, "because you finally figured out how to do it yourself?"

"Hell, if it wasn't for me, Ira here wouldn't exist."

Shirley grunted, but he had a point.

"It happened a lot back then. I know that don't mean nothing now, but it did to a twenty-six year old kid. I wish I could undo it, but I can't."

That's a nice wish for a father to make, Ira thought, fingering Rhonda's crystal in his pocket, which she had left out for him on the kitchen table. He felt nothing. The powers of the universe must still be trapped inside. Maybe crystals were like disposable lighters, his could have been emptied long ago by some prehistoric hunter in desperate need of better luck. He couldn't believe that he owed his existence to a lobotomy and the once in a lifetime urge of a janitor-turned-orderly.

"Do you have any idea how this feels?" Ira said speaking more to Shirley, as if Fred needed her as a translator. "What do I do now? What do I tell my kids and my wife? What do I tell the rest of my family?"

Fred leaned against the broom. He was old enough to know that there was no point in getting too excited. Most of what was important had already happened to him. There was really only one big thing left.

"I'll tell you what we're havin a little family get together tomorrow. It's our anniversary, Edna and me. I got no secrets from her. She knows I had this thing with a patient before I met her. Told her back then, ya know, just in case anything came out, said it like we had a few dates. Never hurts to make'em a little jealous. She doesn't know about you, but I'll tell her. But I ain't gonna say anything about any rape, so keep your mouth shut about that. It won't hurt the brats to meet a McCaw with some brains and a good job."

"I'm not a McCaw."

Being called a McCaw sounded worse to Ira than being committed.

"Suit yourself, but come if ya wanna."

Ira put Eva's picture back in his wallet.

"I'll think about it."

"Sure, take your time," Fred said taking out a little pad and writing down his address and telephone number. "It's up to you." Fred patted him on the back when he handed him the paper like a football coach with one of his players and smiled at Shirley. She'd have kneed him in the balls if he was closer and she could lift her leg.

Fred looked pleased with himself. The day hadn't been a total loss. A small burden had been lifted from his shoulders, like a confession. Sunday's family gathering would be his penance, removing the last obstacle in his path to heaven, just what Shirley wanted to avoid.

"It's been one helluva day, ain't it?" Fred said disappearing up the stairs with his broom and dustpan.

Orderly even under pressure, Ira thought, he must get that from him. Ira sat down on the stool and felt Fred's warmth on the seat.

"You want my advice," Shirley said, "skip the god-damn family reunion and go back home tonight . . . but don't tell Rhonda I said so."

He nodded, stood up, and headed for the stairs.

"Going home?"

"I don't feel so good."

"Where you going?"

"To Rhonda's."

"You're a jerk."

He couldn't argue with that. By the time Ira got to the car, his head cold was roaring like the blizzard. He could hardly stay awake on the ride to Rhonda's apartment and his eyes were so watery that he could barely see. He headed right to the bedroom. The rest of Rhonda's apartment may look like a Pilgrim State annex, but her bedroom had some character. Most bedrooms do. They possess a certain intimacy, if only because of their histories and dreams. They also contain the single most important piece of furniture in anyone's life. An invitation to relaxing summer mornings and nights wet with anxiety; a witness to couplings and uncouplings, sickness and health and, unlike most spouses, they remain faithful until death.

Of course, there were a few other witnesses in Rhonda's bedroom, although they spent most nights on the floor unable to see what was going on. Ira tossed them all off the bed. He knew she'd be unhappy since her stuffed animals each had their own special place on the floor, but he couldn't be bothered trying to remember where they each belonged. A couple of them, he remembered her saying, didn't get along and had to be kept apart. Rhonda was still a little girl in some ways, which must happen when you have a shit for a father, an alcoholic mother, and no luck finding a man of your own. Ira then climbed under the covers and lay there shivering his loud and labored breathing rocking him into a restless sleep constantly interrupted by one long dream, a variation on a dream he used to have as a teenager.

In the old dream, Ira and his parents, that is his aunt and uncle, were spending a carefree summer in a cottage by a lake. There were bigger cottages all around them, full of kids that he didn't know, but Selma wouldn't let him play with any of them. She was constantly yelling, "don't go near the lake, stay away from those kids, watch out for the poison ivy, don't go into the woods, watch out for bees, try to keep clean." It was as if she was reading from a laundry list of don'ts.

Suddenly, he realized that it was all a dream, and when he told her that she didn't believe him. "You're really crazy," Selma said, a label that fit now more than ever. But Ira was so sure it was a dream he figured he could do anything he wanted without any consequences. He thought about jumping into the lake, which he wasn't allowed to do, or joining the other kids in their kissing games. He knew the names; spin the bottle and seven minutes in heaven, although he didn't have any idea of how to play. Unfortunately, he never did anything, because by the time he decided to try something it was too late and he woke up. In this afternoon's dream, he and Ellen were vacationing in Cape Cod with two couples from home. He was sitting with Jeff and Mitch on the beach while the wives were off shopping.

"I can't believe we're finally on vacation, look at that sunset," Jeff said pointing straight out over the ocean. The sun hadn't moved in an hour. Jeff could look right at it without blinking, but Ira had to shield his eyes.

"And you thought we would never get here," Mitch said to Ira.

Mitch had lost a lot of weight, an incredible amount of weight. He looked like he did twenty years earlier.

"I could stay here forever," he said.

It must have been the middle of the summer, because Ira had never felt a hotter sun. The skin on his forearms was turning bright red right before his eyes. However, instead of a saltwater smell, there was an overpowering fragrance of orchids, his favorite flower. Birds were singing everywhere and boats were crossing soundlessly in all directions. Remarkably, there was no one else on the beach.

"Something's not right," Ira said.

"What?"

"It was just the winter. There was a big snowstorm."

He looked around for snow, like this was Candid Camera and at any moment the curtain would part to reveal a winter wonderland. He stood up and scanned the horizon. It was summer everywhere. No matter which direction he looked, he saw the sun.

"This is a dream," Ira said.

Mitch laughed.

"You're crazy," Jeff said his hair suddenly puffed up and dyed an unnatural reddish brown like his mother's before she let it go gray.

"Where are the girls then?"

"Shopping, where else?"

"But it's too hot. It's unbearably hot."

"Then come over here and sit in the breeze," Mitch and Jeff said neither one of them sweating in the least.

"I know how to make sure," Ira said.

"Make sure of what?"

"That it's a dream."

"You're scaring me," Jeff said.

"Now I'm curious," Mitch said, "how?"

"The same way I used to do it when I was thirteen."

Ira stood very still with his arms out like a cross and concentrated on his stomach. He ignored the soft, moist breezes, which he now felt coming in off the water, because he knew they were just trying to distract him. He had to concentrate.

"It's all a question of density," he said. "If I feel light enough to fly, then it's a dream."

Jeff and Mitch smiled at each other, then Jeff opened a magazine and Mitch started working on a sandcastle.

"It's a dream," Ira said lowering his arms, but they both ignored him. "Don't you realize what this means?"

"No what?" Jeff said his nose still buried in the magazine.

"We can do anything we want. Drive a hundred miles an hour off a cliff . . . rob a bank."

"I don't want to do anything but sit right here and read," Jeff said.

"Go out with girls half our age."

"That part I wouldn't mind."

Ira grabbed Mitch's arm and tried to pull him up, but he couldn't budge him. It was as if he weighed a ton.

"Come on," Ira said, "let's do something crazy."

"But what if you're wrong?"

Ira lost his grip and fell down on the hot sand. He should be screaming in pain, but he didn't feel a thing.

"I can't be wrong. Look at the sun. It's been in the same place all day, like it's caught on the rim of the horizon."

"An optical illusion."

"When's the last time you saw the sun set over the Atlantic Ocean."

Ira tossed a shell into the water. It disappeared without a ripple or a sound.

"And where's the splash? This has to be a dream."

"Well dream or no dream I'm sitting here enjoying the view."

"But I'm burning up," Ira said, "and I can barely breathe."

He lay down in the sand and closed his eyes. When he opened them, Rhonda was standing over the bed feeling his forehead.

"You're burning up," she said.

"It's a dream."

"It's no dream, you've got a fever. It could be the flu."

"This is the way I get a cold."

"I guess you're not up for a movie," she said handing him a fist full of vitamin C tablets, two aspirins, and a glass of water.

"My legs ache."

"Flu symptoms, you might have to stick around for a few more days."

"It's a cold. This'll be the worst of it."

Rhonda shrugged.

"Get some rest, maybe you'll feel up for a matinee tomorrow," Rhonda said walking out of the room.

Ira collapsed back on to the pillow. He couldn't keep his head up. He wanted to be sick at home, where he'd normally get sympathy and soup. The rest of the night Ira drifted in and out of sleep, waking up occasionally to the sounds of the television and Rhonda moving about. He could swear sometimes that he heard Ellen asking if he wanted some more tea.

SUNDAY

Ira's eyes snapped open at 6:20. For a moment, he was back at home wondering what he had to do at American Family Care. Then the room came into focus and he realized that his body was at war. There was a blockade patrolling the nasal passageways allowing everything out, but nothing in. His mouth was dry and lifeless, the victim of some kind of germ warfare. He was being bombarded with sweat, drowning in it, and he had to use his hands like windshield wipers just to see past the tears.

He fought the urge to cough so as not to wake Rhonda and lay very still as he unsuccessfully tried to push his pinkie deep enough into his ear to reach this life-threatening itch. In short, he was the before commercial for Sinoral the "can't have a cold today" medicine. Santa would soon be popping up in every major magazine holding a Sinoral package right below his big, red nose, Rudolph by his side. It was the first cold medicine endorsed by Mr. Claus and his staff. Of course, he came cheap. On the radio, a very solemn voice would soon be announcing that "last year over fifty million work days were lost to the common cold. After years of research and testing, American Family Care is proud to announce the ultimate cold beater--Sinoral, America's back to work medicine. Already the pharmacist's favorite." Of course that was because the drug stores were all getting steep introductory discounts.

Sinoral was virtually identical to every other cold remedy on the market. The only difference being that it was buffered and supposedly easier on the stomach, which was important for someone like Ira, who threw up at the sight of an antihistamine. He tried Sinoral once and didn't get nauseous. Most of American Family's products seemed to work well on him. The fact that they're free probably helped.

Ira got up and dragged himself to the bathroom. There were no cold medicines of any kind in the medicine cabinet. His home was a warehouse of free samples.

"Rhonda," he called out forgetting that she was still asleep.

"What are you yelling about?"

"Where do you keep the cold medicines?"

"I don't."

"You don't?"

"I don't take that crap. Vitamin C is all I ever use."

His eyes were bloodshot. He felt like a drug addict going cold turkey. The last thing he wanted to hear was a lecture from a new age, holistic witch doctor.

"It's all a question of the right vitamins and nutrients," she said. "I can't remember the last time I had a cold."

"Well I have a doozy," he said rummaging through the medicine cabinet for something left over from the previous tenant. "Shit." He'd take anything, even if it had expired. Unfortunately, there was nothing but make-up and a bottle of aspirin.

"You get more colds," he said, "when you get older."

"That's baloney, age has nothing to do with it."

"And they get worse."

He picked up the aspirin bottle and then put it back down. It wouldn't stop the sniffles or the congestion, and it usually gave him a stomachache. He was lucky that it didn't make him throw up last night.

"I can't go to my father's party like this."

"I didn't know you were going."

He must have made the decision in his sleep.

"I've got to take something."

"Try spreading the germs around . . . that's one way to get even."

"Whatever I take will need time to be effective," Ira said.

"Drive in any direction you'll hit a strip mall, every one of them has a drug store."

Rhonda walked passed him to the kitchen.

"What are you so annoyed about?"

"Nothing like being awakened by a screaming druggy searching for a cold capsule fix, especially after spending most of the night listening to him snore."

"I don't snore."

"Yeah, right."

"I hope they have Sinoral."

"I never heard of it."

"You need a new light bulb in the lamp."

"I'll buy one."

"You should buy a couple of extra to keep around the house."

"There's no place to put them."

"Two light bulbs?"

"I like things dim," Rhonda said. "Who wants to see this place anyway?"

He washed his face. He didn't have the energy to shower, but it wouldn't make much of a difference in terms of his appearance. Dark rings had already pushed his eyes so far back in his head that there was room for a couple of candles. All the color in his face had drained into his nose and his hair stood straight up making him look like a human pincushion. He had never been this sick away from home and his muscles ached for his own bed. Homesickness was apparently as much a symptom of the common cold as the runny nose.

Ira got dressed. He wasn't as anxious this morning about Eva and Fred. Things you can't do anything about diminish in importance when the body is focused on its own mortality. Mothers that aren't mothers, fathers with rap sheets and jobs teetering on the brink of extinction are easier to put in perspective when the things we take for granted like breathing and swallowing are threatened. He missed the way Ellen touched the back of her hand to his forehead to check his temperature and the way Jaime and Scott would do anything that he asked without complaint. He missed the kitchen smells and the remote. He even missed the feel of his own toilet seat. He walked into the kitchen. The only thing on the table was a cup of coffee and that was attached to Rhonda's fist. She didn't move, so he poured himself a cup.

"I need something to eat or I'll throw up when I take the medicine."

"There isn't very much."

"Toast?"

"No bread. There's puffed rice."

"What about soup?"

"For breakfast?"

"For my cold."

"There are a few cans of cream of mushroom."

"I hate mushrooms," Ira said pulling out the bag of puffed rice. "Any milk?"

"Soy."

Ira groaned.

"Let me guess, you hate soy. Your experience with food is about as limited as your experience with women."

"Which is just the way I want it."

Rhonda shrugged and watched Ira try to wash the puffed rice down with coffee. She was no longer so irresistible. Her posture was bad. Big breasts could do that to you. Her hair hung limp against her shoulders and there was a hint, just a hint, of dowdiness in her future. Her sour breath reached across the table as they drank in silence. Afterward, they sat in the living room and watched a program about homes for sale. He must have dozed, because they were about to show a house worth three-quarters of a million dollars, but when he opened his eyes it was a small, semi-attached ranch.

"When's the big reunion?" Rhonda said.

"One."

"You should get going if you're gonna find a drug store."

"It's way too early."

"I thought you needed time for it to kick in."

Rhonda walked over to the window. It was absolutely dead outside. All the neighbors were probably sleeping off last night.

"Are you trying to get rid of me?"

"I'm tired and you're going anyway . . . right?"

He nodded.

"I could use the peace and quiet."

"What else is bothering you?"

"Nothing."

"Something's on your mind."

Ira could always tell when he was annoying a woman, that much he was good at.

"You could've asked me to Fred's party."

Imagine the McCaw envy if he showed up with his arm draped around Aphrodite. Roy's keys would start jingling of their own accord. But what if Ellen found out? Did he really want Fred thinking he was a chip off the old block?

"I have to go alone."

"I'm OK to sleep with, but not good enough for your janitor family, is that it?"

"That's not it."

"Then what is it?"

"It's not . . . not . . . appropriate."

"Appropriate?" Rhonda said. "When did you turn into Ann Landers?"

"I didn't ask Shirley either or my wife."

"That's bullshit, at Pilgrim State I am your wife."

"Give me a break," Ira said shading his eyes from the televised sunlight. The tour of the inside of the ranch was over and now they were in someone's backyard. "I feel like shit. There's nothing to eat. I'm going to meet my god-damned family for the first time. You can't expect me to show up with my mistress?"

"I'm not your fucking mistress," Rhonda said stomping off into the bedroom and slamming the door.

"I'm sorry."

He really was. He didn't want to leave like this, but what choice did he have. Maybe it was for the better. It would make it a lot easier a year from now when her picture started burning a hole in his head.

"I'm going."

Rhonda didn't answer.

"Thanks for everything, I mean it, I couldn't have found out anything without you."

No matter what, he was always taught to be polite.

There were tanks rumbling through his head and rounds of artillery pounding in his chest. Only an opening the size of the eye of a needle kept him from suffocating. Yet he put on his coat and left. It was barely past ten. The only way he could think of killing a couple of hours was to head for Shirley's house. Shirley was sitting down to a breakfast of donuts, bran flakes and coffee.

"Need it for the morning sit down," she said pointing at the box of bran flakes. "Want any?"

He felt too nauseated by now from all the mucus he'd been swallowing to eat anything.

The National Inquirer was on the table in front of Shirley. The headline read "Statue of Elvis Sighted on the Moon."

"How do you suppose it got there?" she said.

"Wishful thinking."

Shirley turned the page.

"I like this one better. *Man Lives With Talking Chair that Sounds Like Late Wife.*"

"What if there's a spirit trapped inside that one?" he said pointing to Shirley's chair.

"Then it deserves to be crushed."

Ira's laugh turned into a couple of sneezes.

"You and Rhonda have a fight?"

"I don't know. I guess so. What's the difference?"

"You got that right." Shirley inhaled a donut like a breath of fresh air. "She'll get over it, she always does. Want some coffee?"

"Please."

"Cup's in the sink, just rinse it out."

He got it and Shirley poured.

"She wanted to go to Fred's party."

"His sons would've ripped her clothes off."

"I just want to get this over with. I don't need anymore distractions."

"You hear me arguing?"

"She over-reacted."

"She gets like that at the end. She wants to feel like she's more than just a good lay, like someone actually cares."

"I do care."

"Yeah right, Rhonda's problem is that she still believes in fairy tales. She has this fantasy that there's actually something more between the two of you, something with a future."

"How do you know that?"

"Because she said so."

"But I was clear about it," Ira said.

"She jumps in too fast and hopes for too much. You'd think she'd have figured it out by now."

Ira wiped his nose and eyes on a napkin.

"I know what you're thinking," Shirley said, "because all men are the same. So I'm warning you right now, don't call her in six months to see how she's doing and pretend you wanna take her to a movie, when all you want is a quickie."

"It hasn't crossed my mind."

"Bullshit, because if you do she'll wind up like me."

Ira nodded.

"I mean it, if you come around again I swear you'll think Fred is the good fairy."

"You don't have to worry."

"Good. Then you should skip the fucking family reunion and go home to bed."

Shirley took another donut and turned the page. He could read the headline upside down, "Man Changes Into Ape."

"This one I can believe," Shirley said. She took a spoonful of dry bran and spit some of it back out into a napkin. "Maybe she'll get lucky next time. They can't all be assholes out there. Maybe she can find one like you, her own age, who's not married."

Shirley stopped talking and drank some coffee.

"Well don't cry about it," she said.

"It's the cold. Do you have any cold pills?"

"Check under the bathroom sink, I got everything."

There were dozens of different kinds of medications there, over the counter and prescription for every ailment imaginable from gas to warts, although most had expired. Sinoral was too new to have made the collection, so he had to rely on a competitor. He swallowed two pills without water and walked back into the kitchen.

"Look here," Shirley said pointing to an article with the headline "Mysterious Shadow in the Road Collides with Truck."

"Who writes this stuff?" he said.

"It's funnier than the comics and right at the checkout."

The pills were starting to dry him up, but they were also making him more nauseated. He should have eaten something.

"Listen, Ira, you've had the fling you should have had twenty years ago. You discovered your real parents. There's nothing left for you to do here."

"How about meeting the rest of my family?"

"If you like getting pissed on."

"I have to do it . . . for Eva."

"They put people in jail for things like that."

"That's not what I'm talking about."

"You know," Shirley said with her familiar food filled grin, "the thing that really kept you here this long was your penis . . . not your parents."

He would have smiled if he could, but he was feeling too sick. Besides, Shirley was wrong, at least he hoped so. It wouldn't bode well for the future if she were right.

"You think I would have liked my mother?"

Shirley got up slowly.

"You have more in common with your father. Sex got both of you in trouble. Fred knocked up your mother, got scared, and settled down. You settled down, then screwed around and got scared. Fred's way makes more sense."

Shirley moved to the doorway.

"Time for the morning sit down."

"I suppose I should get going."

"Say hi to Ellen for me," Shirley said with a chuckle. "And tell Fred to go fuck himself, preferably in front of the whole family."

"Thanks for everything."

"The same kiss off you gave Rhonda, I'm honored."

With that Shirley walked into the bathroom and Ira let himself out. Even though it was still early, he decided to head for Fred's house. He couldn't come empty-handed Selma had trained him well about that. He had to clutch something, if only to keep his balance, perhaps a cake or some flowers. A six-pack would be more Fred's style. The only place open was Dunkin Donuts, so he bought some munchkin balls. They were still using the green and red Christmas boxes.

It was better than nothing.

He drove around Fred's neighborhood passing his house half a dozen times. It was a neighborhood of cars on blocks with for sale signs in the windshields and trucks on the lawn. It was full of unfinished projects, garages half-painted, driveways half-shoveled, tarp-covered roofs and plastic blowing loosely off windows. Garbage cans, never brought in from Saturday's pick-up, rolled around the street and Christmas trees in torn plastic bags leaned against the curb. Paint was peeling everywhere and a forest of dead, brown shrubs sat half buried in the snow. The front windows, however, glowed with the excitement of televised Sunday sports. The Pro Bowl from Hawaii, boxing from Atlantic City, bowling from the motor city, and a diving competition from Mexico.

Ira could imagine the summer, legs sticking out from under cars and radios blasting the Mets game. Cans of beer crushed into objects of art. Dogs patrolling the property and barking at anything that moved. Boys without shirts sitting on the front stoops, cigarettes dangling from their lips, watching girls in bikini tops wash cars.

Fred's house was at 108 Kings Lane. It sat on a flat, treeless lot like all the others. It was one of the better cared for homes on the block, green with white trim. The snow had been cleaned off the driveway and walk. Puny evergreens on either side of the front door were still decorated with Christmas lights. There was an old Ford Falcon on the side of the driveway that obviously hadn't been moved in years, probably one of Fred's restoration projects. His green Malibu was parked on the street. Ira was cruising by very slowly for the seventh time when Fred came outside and waved him in.

"Ya keep drivin up and down the street and the neighbors'll think you're casin out the joint."

Fred extended his hand. He was one of those people whose self-image was closely tied to his handshake, as opposed to clothes, vacations or intelligence. His sixty-six year old muscles proclaimed their youth and vigor with each fierce and painful grip. It was an endurance test. Ira didn't pull his hand away, but his eyes did fill up with tears. It was the head cold and the outside cold, although he was sure that in Fred's mind it was a measure of Ira's real worth.

"Remember," Fred said still squeezing his hand, "tell it the way I say it."

Fred released Ira's hand, which he put behind his back to rub.

"What's that?"

Ira handed him the box.

"Donuts are good."

"Not donuts, donut balls."

"Balls?"

"Little round donuts, munchkins."

Fred shook the box like he was checking for something alive and then looked inside.

"Roy could polish these off in two bites."

Ira wondered if the munchkins were his second strike; weak handshake, now little balls – one more strike and he'd plant his foot on his rear end and propel him back Ellen.

"Let me show ya somethin before we go in," Fred said, "so ya know ya not the only one with money. Ya father has done alright for himself."

The words ya father made Ira wince.

Fred opened the garage.

"Get outta the way and I'll back her out."

Fred drove out a classic red and white convertible. The kind you'd see at car rallies and old movies. It was in perfect condition. He turned off the engine and carefully closed the door.

"It's a '57 Chevy Bel Aire convertible."

Fred walked around it admiring the shine.

"It looks nice."

"Nice my ass, it's a classic. Everything's original and in perfect condition. They really knew how to make cars back then, all steel, none of that shitty aluminum. What makes this baby so valuable is the engine. It's the original 283 power pack with power glide. Best engine ever made. Ya not gonna find another one like it anywhere, not like this, not in this condition."

Fred's eyes got misty.

"That's my retirement. Maybe it's worth forty or fifty thousand normally, but with the original engine purrin like a kitten you're talking seventy, maybe eighty grand to one of those fat cat dopes on Wall Street."

Ira really did like the car. It would make a nice inheritance.

"And I'm not just blowin smoke outta my ass, cause I've already turned down sixty from this big shot doctor who saw me drivin it around. Said it was his first lay. He woulda gone a lot higher if I were interested."

Ira nodded and tried to look impressed.

"You should see the heads turn when I take this sucker out for a spin. I could still pick up a babe or two in a car like this." Fred stuck his face in Ira's face. "That's if I had half a mind."

A quarter is more like it, Ira thought.

Fred walked over to the Chevy and stroked the hood. "Who knows, a few years from now maybe a hundred or a hundred and a quarter?" Then he gave it a pat like it was his wife's rump. After a moment more of silent rapture, Fred pointed to the front door.

"I'll leave it out to get some air. Too much dry air ain't good for the paint."

You entered the McCaw house through the den and what hit Ira first was the color. Everything was green. The den was painted the same mossy color as the outside of the house. The carpet was a shade lighter, more the gray-green color of vomit. The two upholstered armchairs and couch were a matching green floral print. No accents of red, blue or brown, just green, as if they were pretending to live in the forest.

There were family pictures all over the wall. Little boys and girls dressed in green. There was a green candy dish on the coffee table and little green plants on the windowsill. The only un-green object in the room was the television, and that had a little green lace doily on top with a green Jets bobble head doll, obviously the work of Fred's Irish wife.

Fred marched Ira up the stairs to the kitchen. His blocked nasal passageways were no match for the smell of sausage that filled the room and he had to fight the urge to gag. He could feel the cold medicine burning through his empty stomach. A small, robust woman, with breasts that wrapped around her stomach along with her apron stopped stirring a pot almost as big as the Chevy.

This was clearly a big eating family.

"This is Edna," Fred said adding "my wife," as if he might not be able to figure it out on his own.

"Edna this is . . . ."

"Ira, I'd know him anywhere. He's the spiting image of you twenty-five years ago."

Ira hated her immediately.

Edna dried her hands on a dishtowel and grabbed his. He tried a strong grip, hoping it was buried somewhere in his genes ready to emerge under the tutelage of his father, but Edna didn't seem to notice. She just smiled and crushed his fingers.

Was there any significance, he wondered, to the fact that "Edna" and "Eva" were so close, or that his wife was named Ellen. Maybe the McCaw men had an affinity for E-women.

"Ira brought some . . . donut balls," Fred said with an emphasis on the word balls.

"Balls?"

"What'dya call'em?"

"Munchkins."

Edna opened the box.

"Aren't they cute, the kids will love'em."

Ira was desperate to eat a few, he needed something to coat his stomach, but Edna closed the box and put it on top of the refrigerator.

"What a surprise this must have been for you," she said.

Ira nodded.

"Imagine finding out you have a whole 'nother family. It's pretty exciting when you think about it. You know what Fred always says."

How could I? Ira thought to himself.

"The more the merrier. He'd have had a dozen kids, if I'd a let him, but I wanted to keep some of my figure."

Fred gave her a pinch on the behind.

She almost looked pregnant to Ira.

"You never knew your mother?" Edna said.

"No."

"What a pity. Fred says she was quiet, but sweet. It's a terrible thing."

"What?"

"You know, her mental problem, and in such a young woman. At least she had some happiness in that god-forsaken place."

"She did?"

"I mean with Fred." She pushed Fred away from the stove as he picked in the pot for a sample. "They were very close for a while."

"A very short while," Ira said.

Fred gave him a fierce look and a nod.

"I hadn't met Fred yet when . . . you know, it happened. But I can't be mad, not after forty years. You do some stupid things when you're young. Who thought about protection back then? You shouldn't blame your mother either . . . Ava."

"Eva."

"Eva."

"I don't blame her."

"Good for you. Why don't you boys watch some television in the den, I've got things to do in the kitchen. We're having Fred's favorite, sweet sausage."

The word sweet didn't suit him. Before Ira could think of something more to say, Fred put his hand on his back and propelled him down the stairs.

"You did good," he said, "but be a little more careful when the kids come, ya hear me?"

Ira nodded. This wasn't turning out the way he fantasized. He felt like kicking himself and running out the door. Instead, he sat down on the couch and Fred put a beer in his hand. It was too early for football, so he and Fred watched an old movie -- "Great Expectations." Fred looked bored, but he paid close attention to avoid talking which was fine with Ira.

After a while Ira picked up the family album from the coffee table. There was a picture of Fred playing baseball in 1951, the year of his conception. This was the Fred he could hate, all muscle, and a large, mean mouth. He looked taller than he was now. Maybe Fred was getting psyched for his turn at bat or maybe Eva was on his mind. He could imagine Fred scooping her out with those dry, thirsty eyes.

Fred and Edna's wedding picture was next. It was dated December 16, 1951. It was the first bride he ever saw wearing green. Ira wondered if he married out of guilt, or whether it was just the need for a full time maid.

Then there was a parade of short, fat kids, Roy, Mike, Phil, Fred Jr., Mary and Alice, no one escaped the mean McCaw mouth. Fred grew softer and rounder over the years. His eyes lost their hardness and his mouth relaxed like it was losing its grip.

Fred watched him out of the corner of his eye, while Pip learned that his real benefactor was a murderer.

"You have any pictures of my mother anywhere?

"Are you crazy?"

"Half."

The front door opened and a legion of Freds poured in. He couldn't remember names, son, son, daughter, son-in-law, daughter-in-law, grandson, granddaughter; it went on and on. All short and fat with the same mean mouths. It looked like a Halloween party. The McCaws all had strong grips, but, pleasantly enough, they were all shorter and stockier. Ira felt like a giant - finally, a contribution from his mother.

Everyone stayed in the den to stare. He was feeling very queasy. The medicine was wearing off and what had been a tolerable stuffed nose for a while was turning back into an open faucet. His stomach was filling up with mucus and beer.

"Didn't surprise me," one of Fred's boys said.

Except for Roy, he couldn't keep them straight.

"That's the asshole that works at Pilgrim," Roy whispered none too softly. "Like I don't have enough idiot brothers."

"He's only a step-brother asshole."

"Half-brother jerk."

"Step."

"Half."

The battle raged, but Ira couldn't follow it, because his ears were stuffed as well. It was like trying to listen underwater.

"Chubby enough to be a McCaw."

"Big mouth," one of the daughters said.

"Tallest."

"Bullshit," Roy said.

Ira was a sideshow attraction. It didn't dawn on them that he could hear every word or whether that might matter. He was about to say something when he had a sneezing fit, two sets of three.

"Ick, he's sick."

One of the wives quickly pulled her son away as if Ira might burst out in flame at any moment.

"Like his mother."

"I've got a cold," Ira said.

"He's taller, I'm telling you."

"Bullshit," Roy said.

"Stand up a minute. What's his name again?"

"Ira."

"Stand up next to Roy."

Ira stood up and Roy waddled over.

"You think I'm an idiot," he whispered as they stood back to back.

"What do you mean?"

"How come ya didn't say nothin in the hall?"

"I didn't know what to say."

"Ya found the fuckin words to tell him."

Roy pointed at Fred with his middle finger.

Ira didn't respond.

"I think you're full of shit. I think ya should have one of those D & A tests."

"DNA."

"Fuck off."

Roy was fighting for his honor. Once the eldest and tallest son, now he was neither. They all gathered around for the pronouncement by father Fred.

"No contest."

Ira could feel the top of Roy's head about midway up on his own.

"A good inch taller."

"Mother must've been a fuckin Amazon," Roy said waddling off without demanding a recount.

"Watch your language," Fred said.

". . . crazy."

"Nympho."

Ira caught bits and pieces of the other conversations.

"Had a different mother for Christ's sake."

"A loon."

"Shut up girls," Fred said, "and go upstairs to help ya mother."

They all obeyed leaving the males to man the den, beers in hand. Ira forced himself to take a sip of the new beer Fred put down in front of him. He was sitting at the end of the couch nearest the television when Roy came over and stood over him.

"Move over, ya in my seat."

He glared down him, his hand in a fist. When he didn't immediately move, Roy turned to sit down anyway and Ira quickly squeezed over to the left. He found himself sandwiched in between three brothers on a couch that was barely big enough for two of them. He'd need a shoehorn just to get up.

"I'll be damned if the AFC doesn't win this one."

"With Marino, forget it. That guy couldn't pass a car."

"You a Jet fan?" one of his half-brothers asked.

"Not really."

"Giant?"

"I don't watch football."

They looked at him like something stuck on the bottom of their shoe.

"Marino's gonna choke, just the way he did against the Bills."

"Five fuckin interceptions."

"No one gives a shit about this game anyway."

"How's Toon's ankle?"

"Do I look like his wife?"

"A little bit."

"Funny asshole."

"Turn off that movie for Christ's sake. See if there's a pre-game. There's gotta be somethin better on than this crap."

"Watch ya language," Fred said.

Pip was in a boat trying to save his benefactor when Fred switched the channel. Pip would never have tried to save Fred, Ira thought. That was another kind of debt and another kind of felony. Fred's accidental gift of life didn't deserve a reward, particularly when it involved no more than a few minutes of effort for a few seconds of pleasure. Eva paid any debt that Ira might owe.

The question was what Fred owed in return, even after all these years.

Fred stopped flipping when he came across Charles Bronson blowing away an entire motorcycle gang. The room erupted with cheers.

"Ira doesn't work at Pilgrim," Fred said to Roy during a commercial, "he was just there tryin to find out about his mother."

"What's he do?"

"He makes coupons."

"Coupons?"

"What kinda wimpshit job is that?"

"I hate coupons. They're always fuckin expired. And who can ever rip'em out of the paper."

"Not in one piece."

"What's he do, draw'em?"

"No," Fred said, "he puts'em in the paper. He pays for'em."

"Big fuckin deal."

"Big fuckin deal," Fred repeated. "I'll say it is . . . . he makes a helluva lot more money than the whole bunchaya."

"How much?"

"Don't know," Fred said, "how much boy?"

They all looked at Ira, who shook his head from side to side instead of answering.

"He don't wanna say," Fred said, "and I don't blame him, but I bet it's more than six figures."

Ira figured that Fred didn't want to push him for an answer, not in front of everyone, because he wanted so save the money question for a more tender moment between the two of them . . . when he could do a little horse trading.

"Good," Mike said, "let's giv'em a list of our birthdays."

That got a good laugh from everyone but Roy. They continued to talk about Ira like he wasn't there watching Charles Bronson step around a half-dozen road kills while calmly reloading his gun. He had this Mona Lisa smile on his face, like he'd just taken care of business after a long bout of constipation.

"What can ya get us for free, I. . . ra?" one of the brothers said turning his name into two words.

"Like what?"

"Coupon shit, I don't know."

"How about some pretzels and chips, we could use that."

"And beer."

"You ever see a coupon for beer asshole?"

"We sell drugs," Ira said.

"What kind?" Fred Jr. said suddenly looking interested.

"Over the counter stuff for colds, headaches and hemorrhoids."

"Butthead here could use a tubathat," Mike said pointing at Roy.

"Up yours."

"Don't you wish."

It wasn't quite the same light-hearted banter that Ira remembered between Wally and the Beaver.

"What do you do?" Ira asked Mike.

"Mike's in auto parts," Fred said.

"Yeah," Roy said, "in the warehouse."

"At least I don't push a broom."

"Watch it," Fred said baring his teeth.

"How about you?"

"Phil's an auto mechanic," Fred said. "Always was pretty good with his hands."

Ira wondered why no one answered for himself.

"Fred Jr.'s between jobs, your place hiring?"

"Oh, yeah, he'd be real good workin with drugs," Roy said, "can you get high snortin Preparation H."

"Shut the fuck up."

"Seriously," Fred said, "you have any jobs?"

"We don't have offices in Long Island."

"I don't want no office job," Fred Jr. said.

"Too bad, with those legs you'd make a great secretary."

"I could drive a truck."

"I don't know."

"Maybe ya can ask?"

Ira nodded. He felt like a coward sitting there answering questions like that, like he was already one of the family. He was letting Shirley and Eva down, not counting himself.

"Turn on four, the game's about to start."

No one moved for the remote except Fred. The announcer ran through the lineups. Toon was not playing.

"Shit, the one fuckin Jet on the team."

"Ira," Fred said, "you own your own house?"

"Yes."

Fred looked over at his four legitimate sons.

"Hear that?"

"How many cars?" Fred asked.

"Two."

"Fuckin A," Fred said with a nod.

Ira wondered if he was about to muscle out Roy and become the favorite son.

"How many kids?" someone asked.

"Two," Fred said, "one boy, one girl."

"They play sports?"

"Scott's in little league," Ira said, "and Jaime's active in the Girl Scout's jamboree."

That last word cracked Roy up. "You know where I'd like to jam my boree."

The brothers cackled like hens.

Ira turned his attention to the TV to take his mind off the nausea that was washing over him like waves at the ocean.

"What was his mother like?" Phil said.

"Stacked, I bet . . . the way dad likes 'em.'"

"I don't remember what she looked like," Fred said, "but she was all over me like a case of hives."

"Hives?" Ira said.

Fred gave him a savage look. He'd be cold-cocked if he so much as opened his mouth.

"A crazy nympho," Roy said with a laugh in Ira's direction.

Ira wished there was a little Charles Bronson in him. He'd smile when he was done and help himself to some sausage on the way out.

"Excuse me," Ira said wiggling his way off the couch with the help of a triple sneeze, "where's the bathroom?"

Roy stared at him like it was the dumbest question he'd ever heard.

"The crapper's behind the stairs," Fred said, "on the way to the kitchen."

Ira ran to the bathroom.

"What a wimp," someone said as he left the room.

"Shut up," Fred said.

There was a trial size package of Sinoral in the medicine cabinet, purchased no doubt with one of his dollar off sample coupons. The ones that went out to certain test areas before the national campaign. The subliminal call of his red-nosed Santa was obviously irresistible to the paternal side of the family. It was probably an inherited weakness. He bet there was a trial size box in every McCaw household.

Ira took two Sinoral capsules, a mega-dose considering everything else he had taken, along with a couple of aspirins. His head was pounding and he couldn't find any Tylenol. He sat down on the toilet to give the pills a quiet moment to work their magic. The bathroom was a few feet from the kitchen and he could hear fragments of conversation through the heating duct.

" . . . don't like him."

" . . . just this once."

" . . . can't leave well enough . . . beyond me."

" . . . mother's fault, Dad . . . ."

" . . . won't see him again," Edna said.

He recognized her voice.

" . . . retarded."

" . . . before dad ever met you . . ."

" . . . felt sorry for her."

"Yes," Edna said moving closer to the heating duct. "Pathetic creature . . . her whole life . . . had a crush on your father . . . something to see in those days."

" . . . raised by his aunt."

" . . . one of those brain operations."

" . . . got money."

"I feel bad for Roy."

Why Roy? Ira wondered. Perhaps because Ira now owned the right of primogeniture and stood to inherit the golden car.

" . . . put out dinner early . . . leave and that'll be it."

Not even a card on his birthday?

" . . . hardly speaks . . . got what his mother had."

"Ssssh."

His stomach was churning. He'd been swallowing mucus all morning. He stood up and flushed the toilet for effect. It silenced the conversation upstairs. Ira went back to the den. There was no longer any room on the couch. In fact, there was no place to sit except the floor. The game had started.

"I don't know why anyone would watch this game. They're only there for the tan."

"The AFC's defense sucks."

"They'll still kick the NFC's butt."

"Both of you shut up," Fred said.

He was looking at the back of five heads bobbing up and down like they were floating in barrels, instead of resting on identical squatty little bodies, each one with a blotchy skull that rose high above a ring of stringy, dirty hair. Shirts were pulled out from pants and the four boys leaned forward exposing cracks like canyons that ran between mammoth mountains of flesh.

"My wife tackles better than that."

"That's about all she does better."

"Fuck off."

"See if there's a fight on another channel."

"Shit, I'd even watch golf."

That got a good laugh.

Two of them had found a place to keep their hands warm in their noses. All Ira could smell was sausage. The Sinoral wasn't working. Mucus was pouring down his throat and into his stomach creating a chemical reaction with the beer and aspirin. He couldn't remember what he took at Shirley's. He needed to burp, but he couldn't. A good burp would probably have broken the ice and elevated his standing among the McCaw men.

Fred turned around. "Sit down, Ira. Boys make room for your brother."

The words were like a punch to the solar plexus. He wanted to be an only child again. The boys glared at him, making splendid use of their natural talent, the mean McCaw mouth. They looked like defensive linemen staring up at the opposing center.

"I said make some room."

Two of the boys shifted their loads away from the center of the couch. That was all that it took. Ira immediately began vomiting on the carpet, retching repeatedly in a brighter shade of green. He couldn't stop. They all ran down from the kitchen. The women were horrified and the boys hysterical with laughter.

"Shit," Fred said.

"He can't hold a fuckin beer."

No one moved. Ira finally finished and wiped his mouth with something that was draped over the chair. It was Roy's shirt.

"Hey!"

With that, Ira bolted for the door and jumped into his car. He was five miles away before he realized that he'd forgotten his coat and pulled over to the side of the road. He wasn't going back for it, but he didn't want to leave like this either. He had to do something more than throw up. He thought about it and the answer appeared like a sign from above. Actually it was a sign from above – it was the sign from the convenience store he had stopped beside. Ira went inside and bought a five-pound bag of sugar. It was the largest one they had. He put it on the front seat. He couldn't drive by the house, because someone could be looking out the window, so he decided to park on an adjacent street and sneak across the lawn.

Could he do it or would he chicken out? What if Roy or Fred caught him and sent him home with a boot in the ass or else the police cruised by and arrested him. He could wind up doing time in jail for malicious mischief, while Fred got away with assault, rape, and unintentional infliction of life.

Ira parked the car around the corner and surveyed the situation. There was very little neighborhood activity. Everyone was glued to the tube. Most of the window shades were down for extra warmth. He was shivering without his coat, his nose was running and his head was pounding, but he didn't care. He just hoped that his chattering teeth wouldn't give him away.

He cut through two back yards, advancing slowly on the enemy, taking cover wherever he could find it, a small bush here, a garbage can there. He reached the side of Fred's garage without incident. Now came the hard part. The Bel Air was still outside, gleaming and alive without any sense of its mortality. Unfortunately, the enemy had a strong defensive position. The gas tank in the old cars was behind the license plate. That meant he'd be visible from the den window. Hopefully, someone would be driving for a touchdown or better yet they'd all be wolfing down sausages, as if it were a Coney Island hot dog eating contest.

Ira's knees hurt from squatting, but he stayed crouched. He made it to the back of the car safely by duck walking there. He could see the light from the television flickering from the window, which had been opened slightly to clear out the smell. He could hear the announcer, but no voices. He'd probably driven them away from the television snack tables and up to the kitchen. Roy had probably claimed his coat by now in payment for his shirt.

He opened the sugar and poured the whole bag into the gas tank. This had to be the sweetest gas in the whole world, even sweeter than the way Ellen made her coffee. He wasn't 100% sure whether it was sugar or salt in a gas tank that destroyed the engine, but he was pretty sure that it was sugar. In any event, it would never be the same.

Why should he be the only one?

Ira closed the tank and crawled off the way he came.

Maybe he had a natural talent for crime, he wondered, as he sat in the car a moment to catch his breath and fantasize. In a little while, Fred would be waving good-bye, Edna standing beside him, when she'll notice that the Bel Air was still outside.

"You didn't put it back."

"I forgot with that jerk around and all that puke. I don't know why I even bothered to show it to him, he don't appreciate cars. Coupons," he'll say with a laugh, "now there's a useless job if I ever heard one."

"Well he won't be back and I say good riddance." With that Edna will go back up to the kitchen, because she has a big, grimy pot to scour.

Fred will take the keys out of his pocket, where he keeps them on weekends, and walk over to the car. He'll pause a moment to caress the hood, more gently than he ever did with a woman. One hundred thousand, he'll mutter to himself, blowing a kiss to the original engine. He'll close his eyes and imagine the little house in Sarasota, Florida, where the winters will be warm and he won't have to push another broom. Then he'll start the car and for a second, just a second, he'll hear the old hum, smooth and valuable. But then it will happen. The engine will open its sleepy thirty-five year old eyes and gasp, as if to say "why me?" Then it will stagger forward like a big man whose ticker has suddenly stopped, but whose brain hasn't yet got the message. It'll try to keep going, to move into the garage, but it won't be able to. The tires will have grown too heavy, like wheels of stone, the fan belt tightening like a noose around its neck. With a loud moan and a quick rattle, the Bel Air will give up the ghost. It'll be a quick, but painful death and Fred will be able to do nothing but watch.

When he opens the hood, the steam will rise like a soul ascending to heaven. Maybe he'll smell something funny, like burnt candy apples, and go back to check the gas tank, where he'll see the traces of sugar Ira left around the gas tank. He might even open the cap and taste the residue . . . like cotton candy. The original engine will be gone forever, along with the Florida plantation.

Fred will shake his fist and start to curse at him and Eva. Maybe he'll grab at his chest and fall to the snow, although Ira realized that was hoping for a little too much. Still, Fred won't be able to speak and his hands, those vices of strength and indifference, will begin to quiver. He'll never have the same grip again.

Ira thought it over some more. It really wasn't too much to imagine Fred staggering a bit and collapsing back against the garage, his shoulders folding into his chest. His future, he will realize, has been violated as surely as if it had been raped. Eva's revenge, she just took her sweet time.

"IRA!" he'll scream with enough emotion for the cry to travel forty years back in time.

Eva will finally be able to rest in peace.

If he didn't think that they'd be eating for another two hours and watching the game, and he didn't feel like shit, Ira would have stuck around to watch. Instead, he drove away, his first crime under his belt, surely a felony like Eva's rape in light of the value of the car and also one not likely to be reported. Fred should be proud. They now had something else in common.

He thought about calling Rhonda to tell her and to make a proper good-bye, but the thought died instantly. In the rearview mirror were a thousand uncertainties while ahead was a world of familiar things. Things he would recognize even if he were deaf and blind. He felt like Jimmy Stewart in "It's a Wonderful Life" crying out for Clarence to let him live again. He wanted to know again what he'd be doing tomorrow, next week, next summer, next year and for the rest of his life. He wanted to come home every night to Ellen and the kids and every weekend to a mountain of bills, an un-mowed lawn and a thousand errands. He wanted to spend the second week of every August at the beach and fight the endless battles against weeds and weight.

He wanted to complain about their spending, about his bonus, and plan coupon campaign after coupon campaign, each one identical to the one before it. He wanted to keep doing that until he was confined to a wheelchair and then he wanted to sit at home with Ellen talking about the grandchildren and watching all the same shows on television every day. He wanted to eat the same meals and have the same conversations. He wanted to be surrounded by the same furniture. He wanted an ordinary, middle class, suburban existence, with its hundreds of little certainties.

Tears ran down Ira's cheeks as he drove home. He sneezed every few miles and he no longer had anything dry to wipe his nose with, but he was looking forward to suffering at home. He drove faster, as if a single minute might make the difference between being too late and being on time. He'd forget Fred soon enough, that wouldn't be too difficult. The monotony of work will reduce him to a dull ache at first, then a curiosity, like the doctor who delivered him or his first teacher. In a few years, he'll have trouble remembering his name.

Dealing with Eva would be much more difficult. He had to find someplace to put her, some compartment in his mind, preferably something with a lid. What if he considered her some kind of surrogate? She didn't want him. She certainly didn't need him. She probably didn't even realize she had given birth. In her mind, he was probably little more than some sharp gas or perhaps a case of food poisoning.

Maybe it was all some kind of cosmic joke. Eva abandoned Ira to her barren sisters who had abandoned her.

Ira exaggerated Eva's illness in his mind in an effort to make her repulsive. He pictured her drooling on the floor, covered with excrement and babbling like an idiot. That didn't work, so he tried killing her off, speeding up the mourning process so that she turned instantly into a faded memory. Unfortunately, that worked no better. It was clear that he was not going to be able to forget Eva. He'd need time and space to reduce her to the size of an old friend, a former classmate or a distant relative. To put her someplace where she wouldn't pop up too often or be jarred loose by a song or smell.

In the end, he'd probably put Eva alongside Paul, a student in his high school class who was killed in a car crash and his old high school biology teacher who jumped off a bridge . . . people who don't belong with anyone else and who don't fit neatly anywhere in time or place. People, whose lives have no explanation and have to be attributed to some greater force and unknown purpose, sometimes requiring the suspension of belief and understanding, sometimes even the acceptance of fate and God. He'll think of her occasionally, as he does them, but after a while she won't enter his idle thoughts, except maybe on Mother's Day and his birthday. That'll be enough. The rest of the year he will forget. He can train himself to do that. It's a family trait.

Ira was on the Tappan Zee Bridge, five miles from home, when he became aware of this sharp object in his pocket digging into his thigh. It was the crystal. He took it out. This time he did feel something, a shudder and chill. Was it the power of the universe or the fever? He had this irrational thought that the crystal was connected to Rhonda's crystal like an open phone line, chips off the same block, Rhonda's tie to the rest of his life. He had to end the connection, so he opened the window and tossed it into the Hudson. He just hoped it wasn't bad luck to drown a crystal, particularly in fresh water.

He knew that Ellen would not forget Rhonda easily, but she would, maybe not completely, but enough over time to bring back some level of trust. As a teacher, she's been trained to forgive errors in judgment, and as a good teacher she refuses to lose a single soul. How does Ellen put it to her students? An error becomes a mistake only if it's not corrected. Well, he was correcting this one now.

It was dark out, just passed six when he got home, but Ellen's car was not in the driveway. As soon as he opened the front door, he knew that no one was home, not even the kids. After fifteen years in the same house, it's a sixth sense. The air was too still, the house was too warm and the door creaked open like in a horror movie. It was better this way, Ira thought. It made his return easier. He could climb into bed without any scrutiny or explanation. He felt a little like a burglar returning to the scene of the crime. Everything looked familiar, but a little different. He didn't remember the couch that close to the television. Maybe he was picturing how far apart they were at Rhonda's apartment.

The firewood box by the fireplace was empty and Ira made a mental note to fill it. Everything else in the den looked fine, except the room looked a little sterile. There were no food crumbs on the coffee table, no open TV Guide, and no crushed pillows spilling on to the floor. It didn't have that lived-in-lately look. There was an enormous pile of unopened mail on the kitchen counter. He didn't know how he resisted going through it, but he did. The cold had robbed Ira of his energy.

Before climbing into bed, he had to check out every room. Get reacquainted. Confirm that there hadn't been any changes. The dining room looked the same, a big empty spot at the center where it waited eagerly for a table, but the living room had a shadow that he'd never noticed before, a sinister shadow that crossed the sofa and came to rest on the family portrait.

Being in the grip of a fever, he figured it was a delusion. When he walked over to the portrait, he caught a glimpse of something behind him in the mirror on the opposite wall. It lunged at him and for an instant everything in the room came alive in the reflection of the nighttime mirror. The pictures and the furniture took a step closer. He spun in a circle, his heart racing around the room. A moment later everything was still. It was his own back that he saw reflected in the mirror. The problem was that one of the spots in the track lighting was out. He got a new one from the pantry and dragged in a kitchen chair to replace it. Once he did, the shadow disappeared.

He tiptoed down the hall. He was still shivering from the fever and a little shaky from the mirror. Scott's room was as neat as always. Jamie's was a mess. It was all very reassuring. Their bedroom door was shut. He was almost afraid to open it. He was startled when he did, this time by the unmade bed. That wasn't

Ellen's style. She believed, as did he, that beds should never be left undone. It was a sign of illness or sudden departure. There was something very unsettling about a pillow bent in half and a blanket lying limp on the floor. It looked like the same sheets were still on from last week. Tiny blue stripes, one hundred percent cotton. They were his favorite, because of the high thread count. They always seemed so soft and warm.

His clothes were neatly folded on the chair by his side of the bed. Some of Ellen's clothes were on the floor. He had to do something to reaffirm his return, so he put her clothes into the washing machine and turned it on. He loved the sound of the drum going round and round. If he had the strength, he would have vacuumed.

The alarm clock was blinking 8:47, the result of a power blackout and he reset it. Their wedding picture was face down on the dresser, which was probably no accident, so he stood it up. His toothbrush was where it belonged, so was his wedding ring. Just standing in the bedroom was as good as a hot bowl of chicken soup. There were closets filled with favorite clothes, drawers with clean, comfortable socks and underwear, bank books that promised financial security and shoe boxes brimming over with sentimental photos and souvenirs. There were familiar bedroom smells everywhere, hair, clothes, powder and perfume, and that beautiful king size bed.

His eyes were closing. It felt as if he hadn't slept in a week. His chest was heavy. He couldn't breathe through his nose. His head throbbed like it was running full steam away from a fire. He was burning up. He collapsed into bed. It was like falling into Ellen's warm and inviting arms. He was asleep before he could turn onto his side and had a wonderful dream. He was riding the train to work, returning from vacation with gifts for everyone at the office. The conductor knew his name and welcomed him back, so did all the regulars. Men and women he'd been riding with for years, people who had never said one word to him before. They all waved and called out that it was nice to see him back.

"It's nice to be back."

He never realized that his absence upset their order and routine as well. They studied him for a moment, looking for a tan or some sign of injury or illness. When they didn't see anything they just assumed it was a business trip.

They were waiting eagerly for him at work. There was a coupon campaign to get out, a top-secret new product. They couldn't go forward without him. It was a new drug called "Gone Tomorrow" that caused selective amnesia. Whatever you thought about the moment before you swallowed it was gone forever. He had to test it. He had something important to forget only he couldn't remember what it was.

"Think," his boss said.

He closed his eyes and tried to remember. It didn't work and when he opened them Ellen was standing at the foot of the bed.

"Where were you?"

It was a question he had no right to ever ask again.

"With Gail."

"And the kids?"

"With your mother. They'll be home soon."

What a nice sound.

Ellen stared at him. His reflection in her eyes was like a portrait in a museum hanging exactly where it belonged. He began to cry, softly almost soundlessly. He hadn't cried for a very long time. He wondered why he had waited so long.

"I'm sorry," he said.

"It's going to take a lot more than that."

"I know."

"It's going to take time."

"We've got time."

Ellen stared out the window. He had all the right answers so far. He was down for a year's worth of detention, but not expulsion.

"You look awful."

"I've got a terrible cold, probably from sleeping on the couch in a drafty living room."

Ellen walked into the bathroom.

It'll be easier, he thought, if he stopped talking about it.

"I can hardly breathe," he said.

Ellen didn't say a word. She gave him a pill and some water and sat cautiously at the edge of the bed. The kids came home and didn't ask any questions. He was in bed. They didn't need to know anything else. Jamie did get a part in the school play, not a big part, but she did have a line.

"Supporting roles are important," Ira said. The world needs good supporting players, he thought, more than it needs stars.

Scott was sullen and quiet. He nodded, but refused to look him in the eye. It would be harder for Scott, everything always was. He'd probably need thousands of dollars in therapy before he reached thirty.

Ellen brought him some soup. She didn't say very much, but that was better. He'd have to carry the ball for a while; he knew that. He'd tell her about the money he'd lost and about Fred. He planned on keeping the murder of the Bel Aire a secret.

She felt his forehead.

"You're burning up."

He felt lousy and wonderful at the same time.

Ellen changed into a nightgown and climbed into bed, staying as far away as she possibly could. They watched television, the Sunday night movie. He had no idea what it was about. He only pretended to watch. Ellen wasn't paying attention either. They both lay apart, very still, immersed in their own thoughts.

He admired every object in the room, the envelopes filled with old photographs piled high on the desk, Ellen's make-up spread out on the dresser and the hand-painted mirror they bought last year at the craft show, even the picture of his parents, his adoptive parents. The basket of single socks by the dresser was out of view, as was the jar of pennies behind the door, but he knew they were there. They were always there. He didn't have to see things anymore to know where they were.

She turned off the set and they tried to sleep, no good nights, no sweet dreams, no evening kiss. This was uncharted territory for both of them. They both knew where they wanted to wind up they were just not sure how to get there. Ellen lay very stiff on the far side of the bed. Her eyes were closed, but he could feel her awake, assessing the damage, reviewing her behavior, and making plans.

He should apologize again, he thought, but he was too tired. He'd rather listen to the kids sleeping in their rooms, the determined sound of the heat rising from the baseboard, the gentle hum of the refrigerator and the stubborn creak of the nails in the beams protecting them against the cold wind outside.

"Did you tell the kids about my father?" he said with barely enough energy to move his lips.

"No."

"Let's leave it that way."

Ellen didn't disagree. That must be the way it started with Eva.

He drifted off to sleep. It was a restful sleep, disturbed only by an occasional cough or sneeze. Ellen hugged the far edge of the bed, keeping her distance, but it was an old bed with an imperceptible sag in the middle, a great conciliator. By the early morning hours, if not tonight then tomorrow night, they'd meet in the middle, unconsciously anyway.

Awake it was going to be a lot harder.

MONDAY

The alarm went off at 6:10 as always. Ellen pressed up against his back. She was still asleep and so completely unaware that he could have easily pretended it was just another day in a long string of other days. He pushed the snooze alarm for an extra nine minutes. The next few minutes would undoubtedly be the best time they spent together for a long while.

He was feeling a little better. He gets severe colds, but they pass quickly. Maybe all he needed was a good night's sleep in his own bed. It was a frigid, black morning, but Ira didn't care. He was actually looking forward to work. The few moments of awkwardness in the beginning would disappear as soon as they started discussing the next coupon campaign. He recalled that a lubricated suppository was up next. Hemorrhoids were one of his specialties.

He looked at the clock and saw that he had another seven minutes in bed. Then he looked at Ellen. The hairs on the back of her neck were almost transparent, like they were made of thin, wispy clouds. Her breathing was shallow and uncertain, but there was a sweet, half-smile on her face. She looked almost like a little girl.

He always loved to watch her sleep.

He figured that there was a chance that they wouldn't make it. Perhaps they'd hang on by a thread until the kids went off to college, which would come sooner than either of them expected. Nothing passed quicker than a life filled with routine. Perhaps they'd go their own way, remaining friends, sending birthday cards and sharing milestones with their grandchildren.

Ellen wouldn't be alone for long, but he would, which is the reverse of the way it usually happens. He couldn't imagine too many Rhonda's out there. Fortunately, he did not believe it would happen that way, not as long as he was prepared to do whatever was necessary in his new role as the repentant student. He'd turn groveling into an art form.

Ira lay on his back and stared up at the ceiling.

What about Eva's hospital records? He still had them. Now she didn't exist for Pilgrim State, as well as his family. She only existed for him. He decided to keep the file in his office. The bottom right hand drawer of his desk was like an old shoebox. Things he couldn't bear to throw away wound up there, like old birthday cards and elaborate doodles that at one time he considered works of art. It was filled with ideas on scraps of paper, matchbooks, office memos that he couldn't recall the reason for saving, and lists, lots of lists of people, expenses and reasons. The drawer was safe. No one ever went into it. He'd put Eva's file at the very bottom.

He looked at the clock. Four minutes until the alarm would ring again and he'd have to get up to shave and get dressed for work. With the throw rug in front of the sink, his feet wouldn't freeze the way they did at Rhonda's.

Eva's picture, he thought, should probably go into the drawer as well, along with Rhonda's nude picture, although he realized that he should probably throw that one away. Ten years from now, he might kick himself if he did. What if Rhonda called him a year from now on the anniversary of the day they first met?

"Come on," she'll whisper, like they're a couple of kids sneaking out behind their parents' back, "take a hotel room for the night. Make up a trip. We'll see a movie and fool around."

She'll anticipate his initial reluctance.

"I'll bring some marijuana."

She'll read too much into his pause.

"Don't say a word to Ellen and I won't say a word to Shirley."

She'll make it sound so easy and so harmless.

"I have a new stuffed animal," she'll tell him, "Ira, the teddy bear. He's the only one that gets to watch at night."

He'll be very tempted. He hasn't had much practice resisting women, but he will. He won't repeat the same mistake, which is probably the big difference between him and his half-brothers. The memory will just have to suffice.

Ellen stirred.

Ira looked at the clock. Another minute until life resumed its steady march through time.

He had to remember to pay the parking ticket that was in his briefcase.

He closed his eyes and visualized the train ride, the rocking motion expanding his consciousness from tomorrow to next month to next year to the next twenty years. He saw countless mornings on the 7:28, cold mornings, warm mornings, wet mornings and dry mornings. Work days that whizzed by and accelerating nights on the 5:56. There were fields of roast chicken and macaroni, rooms piled high with homework, steamy months of reruns and falls filled with new situation comedies. He heard the endless ringing of the telephone, the eternal swish of traffic to the Cape, the ceaseless Circuit City commercials and the infinite, out of tune renditions of Happy Birthday. There was coffee and cake with Selma who would still play the role she knew best. There mountains of bills and long stretches traveled on the couch, quiet dull days with spurts of passion, good movies and bad movies, good restaurants and bad restaurants, perpetual trips to the supermarket and family back-to-school shopping expeditions.

Soon they'd have to start planning for retirement. He'd make sure they stayed far away from Sarasota.

Ira couldn't help smiling. It was funny, but his expectations were higher now than they were a week ago. He could even see the new dining room table . . . country American . . . he loved it.

ABOUT THE AUTHOR

Howard Reiss is a graduate of Dartmouth College and Columbia Law School. He won writing prizes at both institutions, but confined his creative energies for the first 25 years after graduation to designing greeting cards and writing songs for his wife and daughters on the guitar. He also wrote a law book, which sat proudly on his parents' coffee table. Howard helped found a soup kitchen in Nyack, New York where he lives and runs, supports book publishers by buying more books than he can possibly find the time to read, and is somewhere north of 50.

10584014R00201

Made in the USA
Charleston, SC
15 December 2011